Alex Marwood is the pseudonym of a journalist who has worked extensively across the British press. She is the author of the word-of-mouth sensation *The Wicked Girls*, which won a prestigious Edgar Award, *The Killer Next Door*, which won the coveted Macavity Award, *The Darkest Secret* and *The Poison Garden*. She has also been shortlisted for numerous other crime writing awards and her novels have been optioned for the screen. Alex lives in south London.

THE
ISLAND OF
LOST GIRLS

ALEX
MARWOOD

SPHERE

SPHERE

First published in Great Britain in 2022 by Sphere

1 3 5 7 9 10 8 6 4 2

A CIP catalogue record for this book
is available from the British Library.

Hardback ISBN 978-1-4087-2549-8
Trade Paperback ISBN 978-0-7515-6601-7

Typeset in Sabon by M Rules
Printed and bound in Great Britain by
Clays Ltd, Elcograf S.p.A.

Papers used by Sphere are from well-managed forests
and other responsible sources.

MIX
Paper from
responsible sources
FSC® C104740
FSC
www.fsc.org

Sphere
An imprint of
Little, Brown Book Group
Carmelite House
50 Victoria Embankment
London EC4Y 0DZ

An Hachette UK Company
www.hachette.co.uk

www.littlebrown.co.uk

This book was meant to be Jane Meakin's.
So now it's for Freya.
Nothing is more lovely than love, my duck.
May your life be filled with music.

O wonder!
How many goodly creatures are there here!
How beauteous mankind is! O brave new world
That has such people in 't!

WILLIAM SHAKESPEARE,
The Tempest

Prologue

She stares at the cliffs that tower over the Grota de las Sirenas. He can't be serious, she thinks. They're fifty metres high, at the very least, and any fool knows that a sea cliff is always as deep as it's high.

'But Felix, *nobody* fishes here.'

'Well, yes,' he replies, surprised. 'That's sort of the point?'

She gives him her Look, and he laughs out loud. 'That's why it's teeming with lobsters,' he tells her. 'It's liquid gold down there.'

'But there's a reason why ...' she begins, then shuts up when she sees his face.

Felix Marino bursts out laughing. God, he's an annoying boy. He finds everything funny. Everything.

'Oh, my God, Mercedes! Really? You're scared of mermaids?'

She feels a spike of irritation. People have been avoiding the Grota for a thousand years. Who is he to laugh at myths and legends?

'Don't be stupid,' she snaps. But she eyes the deep water with quiet trepidation.

'Come on, Mercedes. You know you're the only one who can get to the lobster pots. Nobody else can get down that deep. Just close your eyes and think twenty American dollars a head.'

'Oh, shut up,' she says. It's a beautiful day, the breeze so gentle that the waves barely make foam as they hit the great golden cliffs. The sun has dropped from its zenith and bathed their side of the island in light. But still. Below that shelf those waters will be dark.

Mercedes feels another twinge of unease. What if the mythical mermaids hear me down there? *Las sirenas?* What if they come out, with their muscled tails and their sea-wrack hair and their thousand silver teeth, and pull me down with them forever?

'How far down?' she asks, doubtfully.

Felix shrugs. 'It can't be more than six or seven metres,' he says. Pauses, just that fraction too long. 'Maybe ten. The pots are caught on something, I can't haul them up and my dad will kill me if he knows I've come here.'

She thinks for a moment. 'Can you drop me an anchor? So I have something to brace on?'

'Sure.' He ambles up to the prow, drops it into the deep. The rope runs beautiful and straight, dropping past the shelf a metre out.

The rush when she hits the water: there is no sensation that compares. The jar of the cold after the heat of the sun. The moment when her head cuts the surface and her body jumps instinctively, as though it has encountered a solid wall. The sudden, glorious transition to weightlessness. This is the closest I will ever come to feeling how it is to fly, she thinks. She kicks with her fins and cuts through the water. Sunlight pours over her shoulder, fading in the depths below until it is swallowed by the black.

2

Beads of phosphorescence spiral up towards her. Mercedes feels the familiar chill. That moment where she hovers on the edge of panic and has to push it back inside. Every time she enters the sea she has this moment, because the water itself is alive.

She kicks on. Tries not to think of sharks.

Mercedes has a secret she's never shared. She wishes, quietly but fervently, that mermaids did exist. That she could one day join their ranks and become something more than a plain little teenager on an isolated island with a talent for holding her breath.

Hand over hand down the anchor rope, legs kicking to take her deeper, dimming sky above. The light comes in layers. Clear violet near the surface. Then the shades of blue that strip the suntan from the surface of her skin. And down below, where the rope vanishes, a deep, soothing green. And then the black of the abyss, where the lobster pots are. She pauses as she reaches the edge of each band, pinches her nose and blows until her ears clear and the pressure resets inside her head. So practised that it only takes a couple of seconds each time.

A school of silver bream, flanks striped yellow, darts past. A hundred. Two hundred. *Sarpa salpa*, the dreamfish. Common, for the fishermen always throw them back. Eating their flesh can produce hallucinations that last for days.

Mercedes barely registers their presence. She is focused.

Her heart beats slow and steady; the blood pumps gently through her system. Eight years' practice – curiosity at first, then determination, then, since Tatiana Meade gave her this mask and fins, absolute awe – have taught her the stasis of profound meditation when she enters the deep. She barely needs oxygen to maintain life, down here. At thirteen, she can hold her breath for over six minutes. She intends to have extended that to nine by the time she's twenty.

I'm so lucky to live now, she thinks, when girls can go into the water without causing a scandal. This is where I belong.

She sees now why Felix can't haul up the lobsters caught in his trap. The rope is tangled in a great mat of urchins, and it's stuck fast. She unhooks her knife from her belt and pokes them, gingerly. The bed ripples like a flag in the breeze as one tells another tells the next that an invader is near and they shrink away. They're so weird, she thinks. Like creatures from another planet. Like so much down here.

A fine red octopus slips from a crevice and creeps away, glaring balefully.

Maybe if I go in from underneath?

The pressure on her ears is intense, but she dives down further, follows the rope all the way to the underside of the shelf. It's cold, away from the sun. And dark. Mercedes feels the chill on her skin, and hurries about her work.

Here's the problem. A big fat knot of spikes, holding fast to the rope. She takes the knife and chips away. Levers beneath, flinches as her hand catches on a spike. You owe me, Felix Marino, she thinks. Dislodges a colony the size of a blanket, lets them fall into the deep and feels the rope come free.

Something moves. Something pale and bloated.

Mercedes jumps. Kicks back violently, jerks on the rope.

No. No. No panic. You can't panic. You die if you panic. Stop, Mercedes. Stop.

It's coming.

The urge to kick away, to race for the surface, grips like a vice. Now she feels her breath begin to burn.

Stay calm. You have to stay calm.

4

A larger wave passes by, stirs the water like a gust of wind. Something separates from the pale and swollen mass, flops down and hangs. A school of tiny fishes, startled by the sudden movement, darts back, mills, then returns to grazing on it.

It takes a moment to realise that she's looking at an arm. White as the snow she's never seen, scraped and dented, swollen with water, the hand pointing down towards the abyss.

Her diaphragm spasms. A bubble of air leaks from between her lips.

The wave comes back and the body moves once more. Rolls over, and shows her the white, staring eyes of her sister Donatella.

Sunday

1 | Mercedes

'Mercy!'

Mercedes feels her shoulders rise. How she hates that nickname. Thirty years she's had to tolerate it, without the power to fight back.

'How are you, Tatiana?' she asks.

'I'm fine, darling. Well, apart from having to make my own bloody phone calls.'

'Oh, dear. Where's Nora?'

She's been expecting Tatiana's personal assistant to call for days. That sinking feeling she's had about the silence looks as though it was justified.

'Oh, gone,' says Tatiana, with that special brightness that means the opposite. 'I got rid of the silly bitch.'

'Oh,' says Mercedes. She liked Nora. Those efficient American tones on the phone always reassured that chaos was not about to break the door down.

'Anyway,' says Tatiana, the employee already consigned to her internal rubbish bin, her non-disclosure agreement an assurance that there will never be any comeback, 'at least I know I can rely on *you*.'

'I'm not sure you should,' replies Mercedes, evenly. 'For all you know, I could be a secret agent.'

Tatiana takes it as a joke. Oh, lord, that laugh. That tinkling socialite laugh that tells you that the laugher has no sense of humour. My greatest power, Mercedes thinks, is my talent for being underestimated. Tatiana would *never* think I had the imagination to betray her.

'Will we see you soon?' she asks. They've been on tenterhooks for days, now, waiting for news.

'Yes!' cries Tatiana. 'That's why I'm calling! We're coming in on Tuesday.'

Her mind starts racing. So much to do. So many people to tell. There's still a fake tan stain that looks horribly like a streak of diarrhoea, left by some oligarch's ex-wife on one of the white sofas, and Ursula's doubtful it will ever come out.

'Great!' she replies, cheerily.

Would Nora Neibergall have booked the house out to a bunch of oligarchs' exes last week if she'd still been in the job? Probably not. Everyone knows oligarchs are bloody animals. She's clearly been gone a while, and nobody has passed the news on.

'How many will you be?' she asks. Tatiana's casual 'we' has filled her with foreboding. 'We' could be anything. It could be two, or fifteen. Oh, God, where is Nora? Why does Tatiana have to fall out with the people who make other people's lives easier? Flowers. Is it too late to order white roses? The urn in the entrance hall requires white roses. No other colour will do. House rule. Even in deepest December.

'Oh, just me and a couple of girlfriends,' says Tatiana.

Mercedes prickles with relief.

'Well, four,' she says. 'But they'll be sharing the back bedrooms.'

All she needs to know is in that sentence. Not really girlfriends, then.

'And Daddy's coming in on the boat on Thursday,' she continues, 'and there's some others. But they'll be coming on the heli, I think.'

Okay, VIPs. The duke only makes his helicopter available to people who matter. The rest have to charter their own.

'Great. Should I book the boat for valeting?'

'No,' says Tatiana. 'Don't bother. He's moved his Stag forward this year. They're going out on Sunday morning, first thing, straight from the *party*. You can book for when they get back. Are you all *terribly* excited? I imagine a party like this is the most exciting thing you've all seen in ages.'

Yeah, that would suggest we were invited.

'Of course,' Mercedes replies, eventually. 'St James's week is always a special week.'

'Yes, but the *party*,' says Tatiana. 'The island's going to be *buzzing* with movie stars!'

Movie stars are the least of her problems.

'How many are we expecting, in total?' she asks. 'So I can make sure we've got the bedrooms right?'

'Not sure,' says Tatiana. And, after a little bit, adds an adolescent, '*Sorree*.'

Mercedes says nothing.

'Three, I think,' she says eventually. 'And Daddy, obviously. But you know what he's like. He never passes on information one might actually *need*.'

Like father, like daughter.

'Maybe four,' she says. 'Better allow for four.'

'I shall have all the bedrooms ready,' she says. 'Any dietary requirements?'

'Oh, yes. Tell – what's his name?'

She waits to hear who 'he' is.

'Chef,' says Tatiana impatiently.

'Roberto,' she says.

'Right. Well, small party Friday night. The usual pre-Stag get-together.'

Ugh. She knows what that means. Still, a night off for all the house staff. So that's ... she can't tot up the numbers in her head. 'How many?' she asks.

'Well, *I* don't know, do I?' snaps Tatiana. Thinks better of it. 'Sorry, darling. I'm under the cosh and it's making me terribly stressed. Trying to get packed to fly to Rome tomorrow, and I've literally no one to help me.'

You're stressed. 'I'm sorry,' Mercedes soothes as she scribbles everything she can recall onto the notepad that lives on her desk. She's fairly confident that her eight-strong New York counterparts will rally round to put Tatiana's clothes in a suitcase. Sometimes her head swims at the thought of all the people on Matthew Meade's payroll. The number of people around the world who worry every day about simply maintaining the supplies of paper in their toilets.

'And of course, we'll all be at Giancarlo's on Saturday.'

Giancarlo. She'll never get used to the casual way the Meades refer to the duke. It's only two generations since the peasants had to turn their faces to the wall when his ancestors passed by.

The island has been in a frenzy of preparation all through July. The duke turns seventy this year, and the castle will host a *bal masqué* that is billed, according to the magazines that drop regularly through the door, as *the party of the year.*

The vineyards look like painted canvas backdrops, the veal calves have been fattened on a diet of milk, the house fronts in Kastellana Town have had new coats of paint. According to *Hello!* magazine, La Kastellana is the chicest of the chic this year. The New Capri at last.

'Yes,' she says.

'Oh, Mercy,' says Tatiana, 'I can't wait to see you. We must have a good old gossip.'

'I'll make sure there's a lovely bath ready for you when you arrive,' she replies, 'and a nice cold drink.' She won't actually keep running baths in anticipation. The staff at the helipad call ahead when VIPs land.

'Oh, God, you're an *angel*,' says Tatiana, and rings off.

2 | Robin

Robin Hanson hurries to the rear of the top deck and hangs over the railing, as nausea makes the world spin. She gulps in salt air with her eyes closed, waits for the internal lurch to subside.

Gemma, says the voice in her head. *Gemma, Gemma, please, please, please be okay. Please be here. Let me find you.*

La Kastellana hovers on the horizon, golden cliffs in a sea of lapis. At any other time this would be a pleasure, being out on the Mediterranean again, in the sunshine, going to a place she's never been before. But without Gemma she can't enjoy anything.

Another wave of the nausea that's assailed her ever since she lost her daughter washes over her. Inactivity makes it worse. While her mind is occupied – when she's persuaded that she's *doing* something – the giddiness fades. But if life makes her stop, if her mind wanders, it bubbles back up. The cold sweeps over her upper arms and grips at her shoulders, and her gorge rises.

The past year has involved a lot of waiting.

*

She had imagined, somehow, that she was going to a place where money bought one beauty. That the celebrated development that's 'transformed' this island into the New Capri would have been done with an eye to the Old Kastellana. But of course she hadn't been allowing for the tastes of the rich. The new marina is crammed. Row upon row of huge white yachts, every one the same. A hundred billion dollars of identical fibreglass real estate, and a city of concrete and glass to service them, sprawled out across the cliffs above.

A crowd has built up by the gate where the gangway will be lowered. Standing in the midday heat carrying the weight of her backpack seems foolish, so she walks on up to the prow to watch them disembark. The tractor tyres dangling from the ferry's sides bump, rebound, bump again. The crowd shifts in anticipation.

'Funny, isn't it?' says a voice. 'The way we rush for exits as though they'll shut us in if we're not fast enough?'

Robin turns and sees that a man has settled against the railing. He smiles, pleasantly. A few years younger than her – mid-thirties, maybe, but an oddly mature mid-thirties in his cream linen suit and Panama hat. The skin of a man who's seen a fair amount of sun. Wispy eyebrows.

Robin nods, all dignity, not sure she really wants a chat.

'Holiday?' he asks.

She nods again. She doesn't want to share her mission with some chancer on a boat. And she doesn't trust her voice. She still can't talk about Gemma without emotion flooding her system.

'First time?' he asks.

'Yes,' she says. Then, because she's British and cannot be rude, she adds an 'And you?' She eyes him doubtfully. He's almost a caricature of the Englishman abroad. Fair hair cut

15

neat but dull, and all that linen. And his accent is pure public school, which has always made her feel a bit squashed and mistrustful. And brogues. Eighty degrees in this sun, and he's wearing *brogues*.

'Oh, no,' he replies. 'I've been here many times.'

'Oh. Friends?'

He shakes his head. 'Business. I'm a wine merchant. Well, obviously the lines blur a bit in my line of business.' He laughs.

Why is she talking to this man? As though she really is on holiday, shooting the breeze?

'I didn't realise there was a market ...'

He throws his head back and laughs again. One of those men who find the world endlessly amusing. 'Oh, good *lord*, no! I'm not *buying*! That muck's poisonous!'

'Oh, really? I'd heard it was good.'

The man laughs again. 'It's fine for the tourists, I guess.'

He's telling me he's a cut above, she thinks. Doesn't want me to think he's *hoi polloi*. I don't know why he's talking to me. I'm practically a walking suburb.

He gesticulates behind them, at the fleet of sleek white yachts, then sweeps his hand up to the villas, the apartment blocks, the hotels. Funny how rich people love white. Must be something to do with showing that you can afford to keep them white. In the end, most of what they do comes down to showing off their money.

'Ah,' she says.

'July's a great month for trade,' he says. 'And of course, this year there's a great big party up at the castle. I've a container coming in tomorrow.'

'How interesting,' she says, politely.

He doesn't really pause to take a breath. 'You've booked somewhere to stay, haven't you? The place is suppurating

16

with social press and the main hotel's been booked out for the duke's guests for three years. Apparently they've gone mad outbidding each other for the B&Bs. You won't stand a chance if you haven't booked already.'

Robin nods. 'I think I got the last room in town,' she says. She's virtually had to take out a second mortgage to secure it, too, and still she doesn't get a private bathroom.

'Good,' he says. 'These pavements weren't really made for sleeping on.'

The engine shudders and dies.

She stares at the boats in the marina. My God, they're huge. The contrast with the fishing boats isn't so much because the fishing boats are small. They're floating mansions. McMansions, with their pointed noses and their three-storey upper decks and not a feature to distinguish one from the other.

'If I had the money for a yacht,' she says, randomly, 'I'd make it look like a pirate ship. They look so ...' she struggles to find the word '... samey.'

He laughs again. 'Oh, my dear, nobody ever got poor by underestimating the conformism of the rich. They don't want *unique* things. They want the things everybody *else* wants. That's why the museums can't afford Old Masters any more.'

'A sort of membership badge.'

'Yes.'

On the dock, two grizzled men in waterproof boots wheel the gangplank into place. The crowd shifts again, jostling as if they're about to board a Ryanair flight. These aren't the rich, though this is no Ayia Napa. These are the Lonely Planet bourgeoisie, tick-boxing their way round the islands to say they've been. Five years ago, they were all about Pantelleria, but the migrant boats have dampened their enthusiasm for

Greece, though they'd never say it out loud at an Islington dinner party. They love a bit of local colour, but turds in plastic bags is a bit more than they can bear.

She picks up her rucksack and attempts to swing it onto her shoulders. It's been a quarter of a century since she last used a backpack, and it's made her aware of the passage of time like nothing before.

'Here, let me,' he says, and hoists the bag up so she can do up the buckles. He continues talking as though he'd never broken off. 'Anyway, it's always worth making the trip in person at this time of year. A lot of people turn up for the duke's birthday, even in a normal year. Handy for Cannes, of course. And then they'll be off to Scotland for the bird murder season. Too hot on the Med in August; they put 'em out to charter for the people who can't buy their own ...'

She realises that he's not going to stop talking, and starts for the exit. He follows, prattling as he walks. All he has with him is a weekend bag and a suit carrier. How fortunate men are. She can't go ten minutes without needing an unguent of some sort.

He pauses as they set foot on land and Robin's legs adjust to the shock of a stable surface. The trip from the mainland has taken eight hours and the sun is conspicuously below zenith. In the dockside cafés, beneath gaudy parasols, people finish lunch while her fellow passengers line up to claim their tables.

He gazes about him, reflectively. 'It's changed a lot, of course,' he says.

He snaps suddenly back into the world. Checks his chunky watch – something she suspects she's meant to recognise and register – and clicks his heels in a weird combination of military and Emerald City. 'Right,' he says. 'Must get on. Full schedule.'

He walks away without another word, and she is alone.

Chatty, she thinks. The archetypal chatty Englishman. Glad I won't be staying in the same place he is.

3 | Mercedes

Mercedes goes down to the village along the tarmac road that was a goat track when she was a child. Back then – though you had to keep your eyes on the ground to avoid breaking your ankle – the views, when you stopped, were breathtaking. To the right, the azure Mediterranean, tiny rainbow boats riding the currents. To the left, across miles of goat-grazed scrubland, the regimented chartreuse of the vineyards that swept up to the castle ramparts.

Now, the road is perfect and her footing is sure, but all there is to look at is the purple bougainvillea, delicate pinky-white of determined caper flowers, spilling over the tops of high white plaster-coated walls. Every hundred metres or so, the black face of a wall-high metal gate, and cameras that swivel as she passes.

There used to be a breeze up here. Now, July sun bounces off dazzling white and the road is like an oven. Doesn't matter to the residents, of course. It's only the servants who have to navigate the route to town without air-con.

Mercedes is never more than fifty metres from a body of cool blue water as she walks. When she was young, they would clamber down the cliffs like little geckos, to bathe off the tiny rock beaches at the bottom. Now, rock-hewn stairs lead down to the sea, but the beaches are only accessible to those who can afford the houses above.

The ferry has docked and the Re del Pesce is thrumming. Over half the tables are filled, and the pastry display case is almost empty. Her mother sees her approach from the cliff road, and nods. Too busy to pause. And Laurence is already here, sitting at the family table, toying with a cappuccino. Mercedes waves, and goes inside. Takes a moment to bask in the flow of the air-con unit above the door, then smiles at the chef as he puts two plates of fried potatoes on the counter.

'*Jolà*,' she says, and picks them up. Checks the order chit. For a pavement table, of course. It's a tourist time of day. All this lovely cool air, and still they sit out on the dockside in the tiny saunas the umbrellas create from sunlight, eating chips.

'*Jolà*,' he replies. 'You're early.'

'Not here to work. Sorry. Family's coming in on Tuesday.'

'Damn,' he says. 'Looks like we're going to be busy tonight.' He tosses his head as though the tourist season has come as a surprise. 'You want anything?'

'*Café con jelo*.' She picks up the plates and heads outside as he turns to the espresso machine.

The chips are for a middle-aged couple in matching straw flowerpot hats and blue chambray shirts that look as though they might have come from the same catalogue. English, she thinks. 'There you go,' she says, as she puts the food down. 'Can I get you anything else?'

They look up from their guidebook, complacent in the assumption that the whole world is Anglophone. 'No, thank you,' says the woman. Another of those northern habits. They're all so confident. Kastellani women still don't speak for their husbands.

She collects her coffee and takes it to the staff table, swaps *jolàs* and air kisses with the wine merchant.

'It's lucky you were coming here today,' she says. 'I know you were meant to be coming up to the house on Tuesday, but I just got a call. She's coming in early. We'll need to be stocked up by then. I'm sorry to be a pain.'

'No problem,' he replies, smoothly. 'The container's not set off from Marseille yet. You've still got a couple of hours. I can get a restock up to you for Tuesday morning.'

'Oh, thank God,' she says.

'Any thoughts on what you need?' he asks.

Mercedes laughs. 'It doesn't matter what *I* think.'

Laurence laughs, too. 'True. We're basically talking whatever *Forbes* has bigged-up this year, aren't we?' He glances at his screen. 'Have you got Bluetooth switched on?' he murmurs.

She checks. 'Sorry,' she says. Turns it on. Nestled up together, the phones give out a tiny vibration. Laurence smiles.

'So what do you need?' he asks.

Mercedes stirs a spoonful of sugar into her espresso. Tastes it, pours it over her glass of ice. Puts it beneath her nose and inhales deeply. There is no coffee more fragrant than this, or more cheering on a hot day.

'I'm not sure. We're low on all the white and we have almost no rosé. We had Russians last week.'

A little raise of the eyebrow. 'So you'll be needing vodka, then, too?'

She nods. 'All the vodka.'

He makes a little note in his tiny notebook, with the tiny

matching pen that's chained to it. 'I've some really delicious Grüner Veltliner at the moment.'

'That doesn't sound French,' she says.

Laurence rolls his eyes. 'That was what your mother said.'

'I think maybe just a reorder of what she knows she likes, eh?'

Laurence rolls his eyes. 'I'll pop a bottle in with the order,' he says. 'Maybe you could try drawing her attention to it?'

Mercedes laughs again. For a Europol agent, he's still very keen on selling wine. 'Sure. But I can guarantee she won't listen.'

The phones emit another little buzz. Their pupils stray down, rise up again to each other's faces.

'I'm sorry,' she says, quietly. 'I never feel as though much of what I give you can be useful.'

'I have no real answer to that,' he replies. 'I'm a minor figure myself. Some of the stuff I pass up the line might well mean something to someone. I'm very unlikely to be told if it has no bearing on *me* directly. But you never know what knowing who was where when might mean to someone, somewhere. That's *why* we pool resources. And with your duke keeping everything private right down to immigration records ...'

He breaks off as Mercedes' mother, tucking her order pad into her apron pocket, comes to the table and kisses her daughter.

'You're early,' says Larissa.

'Yes. I'm sorry, Mama. I came to tell you I can't work tonight. Tatiana called, and she's coming in on Tuesday.'

'Ah,' says Larissa, and sits down.

'Sorry,' Mercedes says.

Larissa gives a shrug of resignation. 'Nothing you can do about it. Did you eat already or do you want something now?'

23

'I wish I could. But I've got to go to the florist and then I've got to get the house ready for the cleaners tomorrow. You should see how those women last week have left the bathrooms. Dark brown rings all round the baths. Like oil slicks.'

'Ugh,' says Larissa.

'And she wants *local* lobster for Friday, of course. So I've got to find Felix, and there's just no—'

'It's okay,' says Larissa. There's an edge of panic in her daughter's voice. 'You're still doing the Saint's day, though? Please say you are.'

Larissa still can't name the Saint. In a way, she blames him for all her sadness.

She looks tired, thinks Mercedes. Sixty-seven's not old, in the modern world, but it's obvious that the work gets heavier each year and the bone spurs in her heels hurt more. I have to confront the Tatiana issue. She can't keep me there forever. I'm forty-three and my mother limps by the end of the evening and I sleep alone in a single bed most nights of the week.

She puts a hand on her mother's. Scars from a lifetime in a kitchen beneath her palm.

'It's not for much longer,' she says, as she's said for the past twenty years. 'I'm done by the end of the summer, I swear.'

Larissa flips the tea towel from over her shoulder and flaps it at her. '*Pfffft*. As long as you're here on Wednesday. Not even a sandwich?'

She looks away as a group of four – so flushed with sun that they can only be German – ducks beneath the umbrellas. Waves to them and starts to get to her feet.

'No,' says Mercedes. 'Thanks.'

'And you?' She nods at Laurence.

'Thank you, Larissa, but no. I've got to eat at my next stop.'

Larissa gives him an arch look. 'Where's that, then?'

'Mediterraneo,' he says, oblivious.

'Oh, well,' says Larissa, sourly. 'Obviously if you get the chance to eat *there* . . . '

He reacts as though it's just a competition issue. 'Oh, come, now, Larissa. You *know* I'd always eat at the Re if I could. But he's a good customer, and there are a lot of—'

'Oh, I *bet* he is,' snaps Larissa, and stalks away.

Laurence looks bemused. 'Sorry,' he says. 'I've obviously said something wrong . . . '

Over his shoulder, Mercedes sees the Marino boat pull up to the dock. Jumps to her feet, relieved to have an excuse to avoid the conversation. She's surprised that Laurence knows so little of her family history. That her father has never been forgiven for deserting the Re for the glamour up the hill. I shouldn't be, she thinks. We're not friends. We've known each other for years, but in the end I'm a contact like any other. And it shows how often Sergio talks about me. We're all ghosts, to each other.

'Never mind,' she says. 'She'll get over it. Anyway, sorry, Felix is back. I'd better get down there and get the lobster order in before he disappears.'

'I dare say you should tell him you're not coming home tonight, too,' Larissa calls over from where she's handing out English-language menus. '*Jala luego*.'

'*Ensha*. Bye, Mama.'

'That man has the patience of a saint.'

'What*ever*.'

Island

April 1982

4

The cobbled road from town to castle is festooned with dusty black crêpe. Two kilometres of cloth, three metres wide, ruched every fifty metres over the top of an upright wooden beam, mark the route the duke's cortège will take when he makes his journey to join his ancestors in the church crypt. On the castle ramparts, the ducal flags – the crimson, gold and blue – have been replaced with satin banners of jet-black parachute silk that stream out in the light spring breeze.

Over Kastellana Town itself hovers an eerie hush. People dressed in black, heads bowed, voices lowered, walk slowly and solemnly from house to house and salute one another with mournful kisses. On an island with fewer than a thousand inhabitants, even a funeral is a red-letter day. A release from the monotony of the everyday. A chance to wear your good clothes, a communal feast, a day of leisure.

The funeral of a duke is a different order of magnitude.

The Delias and the Marinos walk together from Kastellana Town to the castle to pay their respects, Larissa and Paulina and the girls hot in scratchy headscarves, for modesty. And Donatella is grumbling.

'I don't understand,' she declares in that ringing-bell of voice of hers, 'why everyone's so sad. It's not as if he was *here* much.'

Larissa and Paulina leap to quiet her. 'Hush! Oh, hush, Donatella!'

They scan about them for eavesdroppers. The road is filled with straggling parties of mourners, and you never know who's listening, even in normal times. All the tenants – which means, of course, the entire population – are expected to doff their hats to their deceased landlord. The entire population will be passing through the castle gates between now and Saturday morning. Everyone. And twelve years old is quite old enough to be judged.

'He was our *duqa*,' says Paulina Marino. 'His family's loss is all of our loss.'

A crêpe-draped horse and cart rumbles past. They step off the road and wait as it passes. The old. The infirm. And the *solteronas*, the island spinsters. Women whose very virginity makes them creatures of honour. Crones with hunched backs and walking sticks and the ancient framed mantles, the *faldetti*, that ride on their shoulders to catch the breeze and protect their modesty. Then tiny old men, outnumbered five to one, bow-legged and hidden beneath wide-brimmed felt hats.

Mercedes watches beneath her eyelashes. Theatre, she thinks. They're doing mourning as theatre.

'Look at them,' mutters Donatella. 'Like crows on a rooftop.'

Larissa pinches her. *Don't, Donatella. Don't attract their attention.*

Felix Marino, nine years old, smiles his admiration, and

30

Mercedes feels a nip of annoyance. The way the boys all love her twelve-year-old sister is starting to grate.

They walk on.

On a summer day these headscarves, the long-sleeved, high-necked, ankle-brushing dresses, would be unbearable. She still finds it hard to imagine that her grandmother dressed like this all the time, at her age. But on this fine spring morning, with wildflowers bursting through the soil at the roadside and skylarks getting up above the newly sprouted maize fields, it's only a slight distraction. She knows she should be sad, but she's quietly filled with joy. Once they're done at the castle, they're going to the western cliffs. Larissa has packed a picnic of lamb and cumin *pastizzi*, *foqqaxia* filled with goat's cheese from the mountains and last year's dried tomatoes, pastries filled with apricots and prickly pear jam. And a small bottle each of the magical brown Pepsi-Cola that they've recently started stocking for the tourists at the restaurant. It's so rare and so precious that Mercedes has only tasted it twice. Her mouth waters, as she walks, at the prospect of that sweet abrasive mouthfeel.

'And where's the *new* duke, anyway?' asks Donatella. 'If we're so sad, why isn't he here?'

Hector Marino throws a look at Sergio. *Your daughter's out of line. Shut her up before someone hears.*

'Shut up, Donatella,' says Sergio. 'Just be quiet for once in your life.'

'He's in New York,' says Larissa. 'It's on the other side of the world.'

The sound of horses trotting on the cobbles, the grind of wheels, the rattle of harness. They turn to look and see the castle's nineteenth-century *grande diligence*, with its scarlet-padded upholstery and ducal crest, speed smartly up from the

31

town. It's been washed and polished, and the horses look as though they've been lacquered in honour of the dead.

The old duke's friends, from the yachts moored up in the harbour, cramping the fishing boats, come to make their farewells.

Creatures from a different planet.

The family a hundred metres behind them has already stepped into the ditch and lowered their eyes. Sergio and Hector snatch their hats from their heads and clutch them over their stomachs. Larissa pulls a protesting Donatella into the ditch by her arm. Paulina grips a hand to the back of Felix's neck. *Bend your head, boy. Know your place.*

Mercedes can't resist. As the carriage approaches, she peers up through her fringe and takes a look.

Five faces, white as snow, old as the castle itself, disdainful as conquering corsairs, stare only at each other. This beautiful island with its green and gold, its crimson poppies, its azure sky, its mountains topped with clouds, of no interest to their weary eyes.

Vampires, she thinks, and shivers, though the sun is warm. They've lived so long that nothing is new to them.

Hurriedly, she turns her gaze away.

Larissa pokes her in the back as the line shuffles forward. Another couple of steps and the duke's face will be in view. For now, all she can see is a huge oak coffin, cut from trees planted for this very purpose by generations long forgotten. How confident they were, she thinks, that their line would last a thousand years. And the new duke has no heirs. Imagine. In her lifetime, it might all come to an end.

Bored, Mercedes gazes up at great oil portraits of stern men whose features change subtly over the years. Where did they come from? They're aquiline and handsome in a way you rarely see among their tenants. High cheekbones, liquid brown eyes, noble Roman noses. As though they didn't come from La Kastellana at all. How funny.

Sergio pokes her this time, and she springs from her daydream and steps forward.

Donatella starts to shift uneasily as the old man's collapsed and waxy visage enters her sightline. Only life appeals to Donatella. Death disturbs her so much that she's generally excused coffin viewings. But not today. Failing to pay her respects would be a slap in the face to his son. Even though he isn't here.

She turns, abruptly, and buries her face in her mother's bosom. 'Want to go, want to go, want to go,' she mutters.

Larissa freezes. A spectacle. She's making a spectacle of them. Attracting attention. After all they've taught her, the care they've taken, still she's attracting attention.

'Don't be stupid, Donatella,' growls her father.

'Please.' Donatella's voice catches. She's close to tears.

Larissa takes her by the shoulders and pushes her away. 'Stop this. Stop it now. Stop.'

'I CAN'T!'

The low-volume shifting murmur around them stops dead. Women, frowning. Always the women. Larissa and Sergio's heads drop in shame. Mercedes hears the whispers, feels them pass the length of the room. Feels their chill. *Who is that? The Delia girl, of course. What, the restaurant people? They can't control their daughter? Have they no shame?*

Sergio slaps his daughter on the cheek. A performative slap, but heartfelt nonetheless. *See me? Head of my family. Disciplining my women. The way a man should do.* 'Pull yourself together!' he barks.

33

Donatella's voice cuts off with a startled hiccup. A shuffle and a sigh of approval all the way to the double doors. *Girls should never shame their families. Everybody knows that. Good to see a father exert his authority, even if he did leave it a bit long.*

Donatella presses her hand to her face. Walks forward, humbly. The way she's supposed to.

The reception door opens and a castle guard steps forward to block their way. Mercedes hears the brief roar of cocktail party voices, which cut off as it closes.

They're having a party. And here we are, she thinks, with no duke.

Out from the noise step three people. A man, huge and heavy-set; dark grey suit and a thick head of hair as black as his thin black tie. A beautiful, melancholy woman with smooth blonde hair who looks as though her heart is broken. And a girl. Around Mercedes' age; plain and solid, with her father's heavy eyebrows, a skirt so short that Mercedes hears a hiss of indrawn breath among the *solteronas*, and white socks. White socks and black sandals, in a place of grief! And she's skipping. Skipping out ahead as though she owns the castle!

Mercedes prickles with a strange admiration. Imagine! Being so sure of yourself that the rules don't matter! She's seen them down at the harbour. Yacht people. Their boat is the same as the other boats. Big and white and pointy. Always the woman, standing on the deck, gazing down with that tragic face, something the colour of amber in a glass that chinks with ice. There's a woman like that on every boat, like the figureheads they used to have on old sailing ships, only living and breathing. Sort of. The boat – which is it? They're all the same. She tries to remember the name painted on the side. *Princess* something. What is it? *Princess* ...

'Tatiana!' the man's voice rings out. 'Slow down!'

The girl stops and turns round.

'Stay with us,' he says. He holds out a hand. She skips back to take it.

'Good girl,' he says. Soothingly approving, as though talking to a horse. The girl beams up into his face. The melancholy woman watches them and something ugly passes across her features. Envy? wonders Mercedes. Hate? Disgust? She can't tell. Then the expression smooths away, and the woman is only sad again.

She's the only one who cares about the duke, she thinks. The others aren't sad at all.

'Who are *they*?' mutters Donatella from the side of her mouth. She already seems to have forgotten her humiliation. And her fear of the corpse.

'I don't know *everything*,' Sergio mutters back.

Larissa purses her lips, then whispers. 'The new duke's friend,' she says, 'from London. They do business together.'

Sergio looks sceptical. 'But you said the young duke is in New York,' he says.

Larissa tuts. 'London, New York, it's all the same. It's not *here*, is it?'

'But how do you know that?' he asks.

'I listen, Sergio.' She stares ahead. 'I listen.'

They toast the duke with Pepsi-Cola.

Half the population of Kastellana Town has had the same idea, and, despite the sombre occasion, the mood up on Temple Plain is almost festive. And though the throng of friends and neighbours means that she never gets to taste more than a sip of the special drink before it's snatched and passed on, Mercedes doesn't mind that much. Her parents

35

are so caught up in showing off their wealth by offering around this drink all the way from America that it renders them inattentive. And inattentive parents, as far as she's concerned, are the best sort. As far as all the children are concerned.

She sits, knees together, on the ground beneath the stunted sea-cliff olive trees, smiles nicely as her mother and Paulina gather with the same women they gather with every day and pitch into the endless rolling stream of news. Someone is pregnant again. A daughter needs to go to the mainland to get her hare lip corrected and it will cost a thousand dollars. The cloth for their curtains – did you see it? Peacock feathers. You remember the son who went to Australia? He sent it. Isn't it nice that a son will remember his mama from all the way across the world? Aren't peacock feathers bad luck? Yes, but she says she doesn't care!

A hiss of indrawn breath. Only a fool tempts the fates.

She feels drowsy and dull, as she so often feels, listening to the women talk. The tedium of adulthood, the smallness of their worlds. The men have gathered by the cliff. A bottle of grappa has appeared, as it always does at funerals. At weddings. On holidays and holy days. When dinner is finished. When visitors appear. When agreements are struck and disagreements repaired. To celebrate friendship. To fill a lull. It's how it is. It's how it has always been.

She looks around and notices that Donatella is gone, with Felix and most of the other children. Dammit, she thinks. I almost missed my chance. She slowly unwinds her crossed legs and gets to her feet. Brushes old oily leaves from her shins and thighs and backs away while the grown-ups are distracted.

No one glances up as she goes.

*

36

The temple was magnificent once. Traces of the elegant marble frieze that once ran beneath its eaves are still visible on scattered stones. Naked bodies, bearded satyrs, the remains of frolicking legs that would have caused her grandmothers to cross themselves and beg Holy Mary to protect them. Paving cracked and warped and warm beneath her feet, the scent of crushed camomile as she walks. Fallen roof beams. It's taken two thousand years, but it won't be long before all that's left of Heliogabalus's temple is a clutch of jagged hyperstiles, cutting the air like broken teeth.

Sometimes tourists wander around here with their cameras and their self-conscious watercolour sets and their portable canvas chairs, and sigh about the beauty of solitude before ordering chips at the Re del Pesce in the evening. And the Delias smile and smile and bring them *limonxela*, and never say a word about the ghosts on the plateau beyond. You don't want to frighten the milk cows with ghosts. And you don't let your children see them for themselves.

But children have minds of their own.

She hurries through the ruins. Glances at the altar as she passes, checks it for traces of ancient blood. A couple of oleanders have rooted themselves in the cracks at its foundation and have slowly raised it over the years until it stands lopsided among their tangled roots.

The distant sea, a hundred metres down, murmurs as she walks. The adults' voices fade into the blue of the breeze.

Mercedes realises that she is still wearing her mourning scarf. She snatches it from her head, shakes out her curls with pointed fingers, and tucks it into her pocket. She steps out into the sunshine and sighs with pleasure at the feel of the breeze in her hair. Her destination is a few metres away, on the edge of the cliff where the land drops away. She hurries towards it, determined to see the Grota de las Sirenas with her own eyes before her mother realises what she's doing.

All the other kids are there already. When she reaches the false horizon, she sees a whole knot of her peers gathered round the venthole, staring, silently. Felix Marino's little gang. And her sister Donatella, three years older and half a head taller than the tallest of them, but gaping, like the rest, like a child.

'Can you hear them?' she calls.

Felix looks sharply up and presses a finger to his lips. *They'll hear you. Hush.* 'They', the parents. And 'they', the inhabitants of the hole in the ground.

Mercedes slows, walks the rest of the way on the balls of her feet. Tingles with excitement. All their lives they have heard the tale of the *sirenas*. The lost souls of impure girls, flung into the dark and transformed by the ocean. *You can hear them, if you're quiet enough*, said their *abuejas*. *Mourning their fate, pleading for forgiveness. Never go up there by yourself. It's dangerous. All they want is more to join them. They'll draw you in, seduce you. Their song will make you dizzy and you'll fall, be lost forever.*

Donatella glances at her as she comes to stand beside them, and grins. There's a glow about her face. She could be a mermaid herself, thinks Mercedes. Imagines the girls below, their silver scales, their naked breasts, hands stretched up to the patch of blue sky above them. Such wanton display.

She worms her way into the ranks and peers into the dark. The mouth of the sea vent is narrow – no more than a couple of metres round – and she can only see a short distance before the rock walls vanish. So dark, she thinks. What must they have seen as they fell? How did it feel, their broken bodies lying on the broken rocks, washed by the tide, staring up at their tormentors?

She strains to hear voices. Hears only the sound of her companions' breath, the rustle of their clothes as they shift and settle, the groan of the waves inside the cliff face.

Their bones are still there, she thinks. They may have transformed, but I bet if you went down there on a rope you'd find that cave scattered with shattered skeletons.

She listens some more. Nothing. The bleat of sheep in the distance. A lark so high above that he is unseeable, singing a song of pleasure so pure it makes her shiver. But no human voices. Just Felix, breathing through his mouth because he gets congested away from the water. They can't really think I'm going to marry him, she thinks. Imagine. Listening to that noise in the night for the rest of your life. And the smell of fish, on his clothes, under his fingernails. No. The boy I marry will be fragrant. He will shower every day, like my father.

As she concentrates, she slowly becomes aware of a strange throb in the air. For a moment, because it's where she's looking, she thinks it must be coming from the cave. But then she glances at her companions for validation and sees that they have all turned away, hands shading eyes like a military salute, and are gazing out to sea.

Something is approaching in the distance, over the water. A sound they've never heard before. Mysterious. Dynamic. Strangely ominous. Coming closer.

'What is it?' asks Eriq.

'Is it the end of the world?' asks Maria.

'Don't be stupid,' snaps Felix, and Donatella laughs.

They squint to find the source of the sound. It goes from throb to rat-tat-tat. Low over the sea in the northwest, a glittering silver-white thing flies towards them over the fishing boats and the four white yachts that anchored this afternoon outside the harbour walls. A flying beetle. And then, as it gets closer, a dragonfly: wings above the fat little body whirring so fast they blur.

'What is it?' Felix tries to sound bored, but his squeaking voice betrays him. 'An aeroplane?'

'No,' says Maria. 'Aeroplanes look like this.' And she puts her arms out at shoulder level. The remains of a German aeroplane from the war lies abandoned on the hillside above the castle, a play-fort for generations of Kastellani children.

'I know what it is,' says Mercedes, confidently. She's seen a picture in a book. 'It's a helicopter.'

They stare.

'*Jala!*' cries Lisbeta. 'Really? That's a *helicopter*?'

They've never even seen a car.

'Yes! Look! You see?'

From a hundred metres, the rotor is clearly visible. She can see the pilot's dark glasses, and the shadows of the passengers in the back. It is shiny white. Stripes of gold and azure run along the sides from nose to tail, a painted azure shield with a golden coronet and a silhouette of their own castle on the door.

Felix frowns. 'That's our flag!' He has to shout, for the air is throbbing now. 'What the—'

'The duke!' yells Donatella. 'It's *el duqa*!'

The helicopter beats over their heads and continues towards the castle as they turn to stare at each other. *Sirenas* forgotten, they take to their heels and run in the great bird's wake, to see where it lands.

Sunday

5 | Mercedes

Felix is far from pleased. He throws the rope he's been winding down and curses.

'Fucksake, Mercedes.'

Oh, don't. Please don't.

'Seriously. She treats you like a slave.'

She bites her lip.

'Sorry,' he says, and picks up the rope again, fatalistic.

'It's okay,' she says. The Meade family's expectations have cast a shadow over the whole of their marriage. At the very least he deserves to sound off a bit every now and then.

'But you've got to tell her. Even if she kicks off. You don't owe her anything.'

'We *hope*.'

That contract. That bloody contract. *Compound interest*: the gift that keeps on giving.

'You need to face up to her. I can't live like this much longer.'

She looks at him stiffly. 'Is that a threat?'

Felix sighs. 'No. But it's a shitty way to live, Mercedes.'

'I know,' she says. 'I'm sorry.'

Sorry, sorry, sorry. Always apologising. It feels as if her entire life has been an apology.

'There are a lot of jobs where people have to live in,' she says. 'You know that.'

'Yeah, I do,' he says. 'And I still think it's shitty. I just want you to come home.'

'And I want to come home too,' she says. She misses their little bedroom more every day. Misses waking up with him in the dark, the quiet shuffle as they make their coffee and drink it in the garden as the sun colours the horizon.

I miss everything, she thinks. All of it. I miss having children. I miss . . . just the ease of talking through the day, or not. Of being able to ask his opinion without having to make an appointment. The little bits of news we miss because they've been and gone before we see each other. Sex on a whim. Holding hands. Not having to lock the door when I have a shower. Working side-by-side and joking our way through the tiredness. I miss my husband.

He goes back onto the boat and starts hefting the creels. Holds out a basket of shiny sea bass. 'Take these, can you? Dad's coming down in a minute. Might as well have it ready for him.'

She takes the basket, lays it down on the dock, turns back for the next. 'So, she wants lobsters.'

'Of course she does,' he says. 'When for?'

'Friday.'

'Right.'

'We could go out Thursday morning, maybe? Together?'

'Oh, good. So you're still coming down Wednesday night, then?'

She nods. Takes a wide, flat basket of plaice and sole and

44

flounder. The boats are doing well this year, the restaurants up the hill paying top dollar since the Source Local movement caught on. The yacht people have taken to asking, signalling their environmental credentials as they sail their diesel palaces around the world at fifty knots an hour, and what the yacht people want, the yacht people get.

'I've got to go, darling,' she says. 'I need to beg the florist for roses.'

Felix pauses and puts his hands on his hips. 'Okay,' he says. 'You'll be careful, won't you?'

'Always,' she says, and gives him a smile.

He steps over to the edge of the boat, leans down and gives her a kiss on the lips. In public, for all the world to see. Even after twenty years, she can never get over the thrill of that.

6 | Robin

Sinjora Hernandez jingles keys in her hand as Robin turns back from the window to survey her temporary home.

'It's lovely,' she says, eying a garish painting of St James slaying the Moor that would render her London neighbours puce with righteous indignation. The room is hot. She'll be glad of the rickety old standing fan in the corner.

Sinjora Hernandez nods with no great pleasure and jangles her keys again.

'*Bahnjo*,' she says, 'this way.' She points out onto the landing, where Robin can glimpse patterned floor tiles through an open door. She hopes whoever she's sharing it with is as thoughtful as she intends to be.

'Thank you,' she replies, and puts her bag on the bed. Sinjora Hernandez hangs on, like a porter awaiting a tip.

'Thank you,' Robin says again, then tries the local language, to see if it's more effective. '*Mersi*.'

'You holiday?' asks Sinjora Hernandez. A grumpy old bag. The eyebrows of Eleanor Bron with none of the humour.

'Yes – I – no . . .'

You have to start some time. You need to start asking.

'I'm looking for my daughter,' she says.

A frown. These people are fond of frowning.

'Looking?'

She opens her bag, brings out a flyer. Gemma's name, the last photo she ever took – her lovely curly-haired daughter laughing as she teases their idiot spaniel with a tennis ball – Robin's phone number, the British dialling code included. Her email address.

MISSING, it reads across the top.

She offers it to the older woman, who takes it and holds it on the very corner, as though it's contaminated with dog shit.

'Gemma,' she says. 'Hanson.'

'How old she?'

'Seventeen.'

The *sinjora* looks up from the paper. 'You lose you daughter, she only seventeen?'

Robin quails at the judgement in her voice. 'She ran away,' she says. 'Last year.'

The judgement goes on. Robin has never forged armour against it. Everyone, whenever you confess to a runaway child, looks at you as though you've confessed to abuse. *I didn't do anything!* she wants to scream. *I didn't DO anything!*

The woman softens slightly. 'She run here?'

'No,' she says, 'not straight away. I've been looking for her since she left. But I found she was coming here. I saw a ...'

How do you explain encrypted phone apps to someone who looks as though they haven't really grasped the concept of television yet?

'She's been leaving messages. On the internet. With her friends. Only they didn't tell me because, you know ... teenagers. One of them texted me, in the end.'

The woman looks blank as a rock. Too complicated. Robin

47

gives up. She has screenshots, if she ever finds someone to show them to, but this woman – there's no point.

'Anyway, they all knew where she was, her friends, because she was writing to them, but then she stopped . . . '

She should be grateful, she knows, that Naz got in touch with her, but she's not. She's angry. Ten whole months, those dim little bitches denying all knowledge. Teenage girls and their stupid fantasies. Thinking they were closing ranks to stop the Old People spoiling Gemma's break for stardom. Enlivening their dull little journeys through the sixth form with her tales of glamour, giggling behind their hands, while Robin searched and wept and lay awake and felt the dread.

Sinjora Hernandez looks again at the photo. Robin's lovely daughter with her creamy brown skin and her corkscrew curls, the legs that go on forever.

'No,' she says firmly. 'I no see. You go *xandarmerie*?'

It takes Robin a moment. A word familiar and yet not. 'No, I haven't. I'll do that next. Can you tell me where it is?'

'Sure. You go back harbour, is there.'

'Thank you,' she says again, and feels, suddenly, indescribably weary.

Left alone, she sits on the bed. Its headboard is gold, and carved in the shape of a giant swan. But it is dressed with two thin pillows, a white cotton sheet that's been darned at some point and an orange candlewick bedspread, and the mattress is hard, unforgiving.

Just what I deserve, she thinks.

She gives herself a few minutes to rest, then she goes to the bathroom to wash and brush her teeth and make herself look respectable. The pipes are naked all up the plaster walls, but a gold-plated dolphin vomits water into the sink beneath a mirror in a Lewie Kanz gold frame. Appearances clearly matter a lot here.

Gemma

April 2015

7

Hindsight is 20/20, of course. When she looks back, it seems obvious that everything started to fall apart the day she bought a scratchie with her lunch money and won five thousand pounds.

Gemma Hanson stands on the pavement outside Costcutter and stares at the card. And she checks and double-checks, and yes, the three cross-fingers symbols are there, all in a row, and the magic number. Five thousand pounds.

She goes back into the shop. Waits until things quieten down at the till and there's no one lurking by the beer fridge, then goes and presents it to the man behind the counter.

She somehow expects to get the cash there and then, in a plastic bag or something. But he just looks bored. 'Yeah, no,' he says. 'We don't pay out those sorts of prizes. You need to send it and they'll pay it into your bank account.'

Oh.

'I don't have a bank account.'

His eyebrows rise. 'Everybody has a bank account.'

Gemma gives him the not-me hand spread.

'How d'you pay your bills?'

Blank. Bills? Her mum gives her cash on Saturdays – lunch money and allowance to last the week – and pays her phone on her own contract. She says it's easier and cheaper that way, but Gemma knows it's really a form of surveillance.

The man's eyes darken as she thinks.

'How old are you, anyway?' he asks.

'Maybe you should've asked that when you sold it to me,' she snaps. Then she hurries off, because she's only fifteen.

'Ask your mum,' says Harriet. 'She can pay it into hers.'

'Don't be stupid, Hattie. She'll kill me!'

'Why?'

Harriet can be painfully naïve. She doesn't have difficult parents, of course. Naz gets it straight away. She's had a double life for years, with her big bag of clothes she can change into in the bogs so she won't get laughed at.

'Let's see,' she says. 'I'll go with buying an illegal lottery ticket with my lunch money, for starters.'

Harriet does an 'oh' face. 'It's *illegal*?'

Naz does a 'doh' face. 'Yeah. You have to be sixteen. And then, yeah, there'll be "What else have you been doing that I don't know about? I told you those girls were bad news. What do you get up to on those sleepovers, eh? I s'pose you're all *drinking* and getting off with *boys*." That too.'

Harriet giggles, for that is, actually, true. They've been covering for each other since they were fourteen. *No, Mrs Khan, she can't come to the phone. She's in the loo. I think she's having a poo. I'll get her to call you when she comes out. Yeah, no, I think she's a bit bunged up, to be honest.*

Yes, the project's coming on great. We're totally going to ace it.

'I know she'll be pissed off,' says Harriet, 'but five grand's five grand. A lecture's worth *that*, isn't it?'

'You don't know my mum,' says Gemma.

'Oh, come on,' says Harriet. 'She's not that bad. What's she going to do?'

'Call my father,' says Gemma, gloomily.

'That's it,' says Robin. 'I'm going to have to call your father.'

Gemma's in tears already. 'No, Mum! You don't! What's it got to do with him?'

'He's your *father*, Gemma.' And Robin heaves her martyred sigh. The one that's been making Gemma feel like shit for years. *Look at me*, it says, *dumped with you. Look at poor, burdened me. I never get to go out to dinner or take mini-breaks to Amsterdam, because I'm stuck with you. I wish I'd never had kids. I wish I'd never had you.*

All in a single exhalation.

'I know,' Robin says bitterly. 'You don't want anything spoiling your lovely weekends. Everything's lovely at *Dad's*, isn't it?'

Every time. Every time. The slightest infraction and she throws the divorce in my face. Like it was Gemma's fault.

'I didn't ask you to get divorced,' she says. It's true. And of course it's the wrong thing to say. She literally doesn't ever seem to manage to say the right thing. *But Mum, this hurts. You start going on about the burden I am, and my head goes all weird inside and I can't find the right words. All I can think of is this red-hot ... something ... that's eating me up from the inside. It HURTS.*

And of course, her mother loses it. 'You think *I* did? Christ,

53

Gemma. If you want someone to blame for how bloody sorry for yourself you are, why don't you start with *Caroline*?'

She says the name the venomous way her schoolmates talk of girls in the out-groups. That nasal whine, the emphasis on the first syllable, that makes her stepmother sound like milk gone off. All that's missing is the air quotes.

Robin has worked up a head of steam now. I want to get out, thinks Gemma. I *knew* I shouldn't have told her. I want this to stop. Was it too much to ask that she'd just go, *Oh, you bad girl, let's find a practical solution*, just once? Must I always be the devil?

'Oh, no, I forgot,' her mother is continuing. '*Caroline* buys you silver necklaces and cooks you pomegranate chicken from Ottolenghi. Caroline's bloody *perfect*, isn't she? Not like your boring old *mum*.'

'Stop it!' she wails. 'Stop it!'

'Well, let's just see what *Caroline* thinks about this, eh? How about that?'

Gemma storms out of the room and runs up the stairs to her bedroom. Slams the door and wedges the chair under the handle.

On her bed, she stares at the ceiling. She wants to cry, but she won't. Lately she's been wanting to cry all the time, to peel the skin from her face and howl at the moon. Why? she thinks. Why did they have me if they didn't want to love me?

Patrick is annoyed. Not because of the scratchcard *per se*, but because of the inconvenience.

I'd love it, thinks Gemma, if the words 'family conference' didn't always mean 'Gemma's in trouble again'. Have they even noticed that? That the only time they're ever in the same room is when it involves me being shouted at?

'I'm in the middle of a *really important* negotiation,' he says. 'Did you even *think* about that? Have you *ever* thought about other people?'

'Jesus,' she says. 'All I did was buy a scratchcard. I wasn't actually thinking about *anything* much at the time. It's not like I killed anybody.'

A boy at her school *did* kill someone, last year. He stabbed another boy in a stupid fight outside the chicken shop on York Road and the boy bled out before the ambulance even got there. After the trial, the local news was full of the killer's weeping family: the mother and the aunts and the sisters. *He's a good boy really. He's never been in trouble before. We love him.*

Patrick slams a hand down on the kitchen table.

'It's against the *law*, Gemma!' He raises his voice. 'Which bit of "it's illegal" do you not understand?'

Robin is all pursed lips and reproachful silence. Gemma truly hates her right now. I'll never tell you anything again, she thinks. I'll never, ever trust you. Something nice has happened for once, and you've spoiled it. And now *you're* all poor-wounded-me. Fuck you. Fuck both of you.

'And what have you been eating for lunch if you're squandering the money on scratchcards?'

'*A* scratchcard.'

'Oh, sure,' says Patrick. 'We believe *that*. The first time you get caught is always the first time you've done it. Right.'

I didn't get caught. I *told* you. Big difference. Still. I've learned my lesson now.

She gives up. Turns spiteful. 'Well, it's nice to see you two presenting a united front, anyway,' she says. 'Really cheering.'

Patrick pushes his chair back and stamps over to the window.

'Don't be cheeky,' says Robin.

'Well, it's true,' says Gemma. 'The only thing you two ever agree on is that I'm a little shit.'

She hates herself as she says it.

Patrick does a breathing exercise. Finishes. Turns back. He takes his specs off and polishes them on a little cloth from his pocket.

Why do they always cut those with pinking shears? Gemma wonders. That happens a lot. When she's waiting for the axe to fall. Unrelated thoughts just pop into her head as though they're trying to fill the silence. Then she thinks, I wonder if he wears those in bed? And she feels sick because she hates the thought that her parents have sex. Well, her father does. Her mother hasn't been near a man since they split up. She doesn't really know which is worse.

'So,' he says, 'the question is, what do we do?'

I'm sure you'll tell me, she thinks.

'I'm tempted to give the lot to charity,' he says.

Gemma's appalled. 'That's *my money*!'

'Not really, Gemma,' he says, crushingly. 'D'you want me to explain why, again?'

'Patrick, I really don't think—' Robin begins, but he holds a hand up, as if they're underlings in his office.

'I know you're thinking you're going to spend it all on shoes and iPods,' he says.

Yes! she thinks. Yes! I'm fifteen, for God's sake. Everyone I know has three times as many clothes as I do! And they can just buy a cappuccino if they feel like it and not juggle their budget to pay for it! It's embarrassing, having to make excuses because I can't do things my friends think is totally normal.

She twiddles her thumbs.

'Well, that's not happening,' he says. 'I'll tell you what we're going to do. I'll cash the thing and start a savings account. And you can get access when you start university.'

Three years away. A lifetime. She's only doing GCSEs this year. And what if she doesn't go to uni? What then?

'Can't I have *some*?' Her eyes well up. She can't help it. She's seen herself in that black velvet Zara dress, and it's hard to just let go.

'What for?'

Gemma gives up again. Presses her hands into her temples and says nothing. 'Never mind,' she says.

'And don't sulk. You should be glad we're letting you keep it at *all*, frankly. Plenty of other parents wouldn't, believe me.'

A big fat tear plops from the end of her nose onto the table. It's not the money, she thinks. It's the fact that I'm tired to death of you not loving me.

She knows they've both seen the tear, but neither of them comments. She gets that they're cross now, but they never give her a hug even when they aren't.

'You never come here unless I'm in trouble,' she says.

Patrick is silent for a moment. 'Perhaps you should try not getting into trouble,' he replies.

'And then I'd never see you.'

His chair scrapes back. 'Right, that's enough,' he says. 'I'll see you Friday week.'

He doesn't kiss her goodbye.

Monday

8 | Robin

The police station and the customs post share a building. She walks past it three times before she spots it, because the *xandarmerie* sign is half-hidden by one of the many national flags festooning the street for the festival.

She pushes the door open to a high-ceilinged old warehouse, where uniformed staff from the yachts queue at a kiosk on the right and three swarthy men in uniforms of royal blue lounge, playing with their truncheons, behind a reception desk on the left. She goes left. Leans on the desk and waits to be seen.

The three men stare as though she were from outer space. Offended by her intrusion. They mutter among themselves, sweeping her with their eyes. One grunts and leaves his chair, comes forward.

'What you want?' he asks. Defaulting straight to English, because her nationality is that obvious.

Rude.

She takes a breath. Minds her manners.

'Help, please. I'm looking for my daughter.'

He cranes around the office. 'No daughters here.'

He smirks, pleased with himself. I'm not upset enough, she thinks. He's mistaking my British manners for not being upset.

'No, I—'

He picks up a pen and clicks it.

'I'm sorry,' she says, 'I really need your help. My daughter is missing. And I saw something – on the internet – that suggested she might be here.'

He pretends to scan the empty office again. He's still not taking her seriously.

Men.

'No, not *here*. On La Kastellana. She said she was coming to La Kastellana. Something about a birthday party. So I came. To look for her.'

He stares, silently.

'I've been looking for almost a year.' Her eyes fill with tears.

He perks up. 'A birthday party?'

'Yes, she ...'

He puts his elbow on the desk and smiles, suddenly warm.

'All of La Kastellana has birthday party this week. *El duqa* – our duke. His birthday. Official birthday. Like your queen, yes? A celebration. A *festa*.' He studies her a bit more, and his face clouds. 'Your daughter is friend *el duqa*?' he asks, doubtfully.

She tries to find words. She knows so little about her daughter, about the life she's been living. That stuff she's been telling Nasreen and the others could be pure fantasy, for all she knows. Gemma could be staying with one of her friends, or shooting up in a basement in Newham. But some of the stuff semi-checked out, when she Googled. People and places and times.

'I don't know,' she says. 'I think maybe a friend of a friend.'

The man's face darkens some more. 'How old she is?'

'Seventeen. She's just turned seventeen.'

Some reaction she can't pin down. A flickering eyebrow. Something.

He asks her the question Sinjora Hernandez asked. 'You lose your daughter, she only seventeen?'

Robin wants to howl. 'Please,' she says. '*Please* help me. She's just a kid.'

'What you want I do?'

'I – maybe ... they check the passports when the ferry comes in, don't they? Can you check the records? See if she's in there?'

'Is confidential,' he says.

'She's only a *child*!' she wails again.

The *xandarm* abruptly turns his back to her and calls out to his colleagues. Their feet drop to the floor and they listen, and she hears a few words she half-recognises. *Filja. Mama. Perdida. Pasaporte.* The older of the colleagues replies and he nods in response, picks up the phone and dials.

Robin waits, afraid to ask what's happening in case she somehow sabotages the outcome. As the phone is answered, the officer drops into Kastellani and speaks rapidly. *Sinjora. Filja. Perdida. Forse loqo. No sé. Si. Si.*

He hangs up. Looks at her again. Points to a wooden bench that sits against the wall by the door, in the shadows.

'You wait,' he says.

She waits for nearly three hours. The bench is shallow, and she can never find a position to sit in that doesn't make her feel as if she is about to slide off onto the floor. And she quickly regrets not having thought to buy a bottle of water, but she senses that if she deserts her post even for a few minutes, she will find herself back at square one. So she sits on in the afternoon heat, bag in lap, and watches the minute hand crawl across the face of a giant clock looted from some long-gone steamer.

As the hour hand approaches three, the door opens once again, and a man walks in. A sweaty man, balding pate damp and tummy hanging over the belt of his suit trousers. A good suit, though. Not cheap.

Even from her seat, Robin can smell the fumes of alcohol and cigars. But, when he comes in, the one she's started to think of as 'her' policeman jumps to his feet. He points at Robin and the man turns, slightly unsteadily, to look at her.

He shambles over. '*Sinjora?*' he says.

She looks up, hopefully.

'I am Cosmo Albert. Chief of Police, La Kastellana island. If you will follow me, please?'

He leads her into a back room. An old wooden table with five chairs, and on its surface a paper bag, a knife and the remains of a salami, a jar of cornichons sitting open beside it. The room smells savoury and garlicky, and damp from its proximity to the water. An old computer with a boxy monitor, behind which is another picture – an oil painting, this time – of St James slaying the Moor.

She remarks on it as he sweeps up the sausage, re-lids the jar and puts it all away in the fridge. 'I see you have St James here,' she says. 'There's one in my room in my *penzion*, too.'

'Yes,' he replies, his back to her. 'He is our saint, our patron. So he is everywhere. He keep us safe. *Sant'Iago* and our *duqa*, they keep our borders strong. That is why his birthday is the Saint's day. Whatever day the duke is born, his birthday has been same-same for thousand years. Since Duqa Lorenzo, the Relief of La Kastellana. They keep invaders away.'

Except the ones with money, she thinks. Those seem to be conquering this place without any pushback at all. But she keeps her counsel.

He encroaches on her personal space a little as he returns to the table. Smiles close up into her face and breathes his fumes, huffing slightly.

'Some people believe that our duke is descended from St James,' he says, and grins with a set of unnaturally pearly whites. 'But I don't know.' He sits in front of the computer and boots it up. 'Others say they are from the Roman emperor who was here. Heliogabalus. I would think is more likely. Heliogabalus was here for vacations, after all, and you know how the Romans were. *Heliogabalus* wasn't saint.' He snorts with pleasure at his witticism. 'Sit, *sinjora*. Please.'

Robin sits. He pecks at the keyboard, index fingers only, logging in, and she waits. A couple of mouse clicks and he turns back to her.

'So, you lose your daughter?'

'Not lo—' she begins to protest, then, humbly, 'Yes.'

'How you lost her?'

'She ran away ... left home. Last year. We had a disagreement, and she left ...'

'A disagreement?'

'I – yes.'

'What about?'

What's that got to do with you?

'The usual stuff. Teenage stuff. She didn't like my rules, I didn't like her behaviour ...'

She searches in her bag for a flyer, lays it down on the table. He eyes it impassively, then looks up. 'And why you think is here?'

65

'Something one of her friends showed me. On the internet. She's been messaging her friends on an app called PingMe.'

'An app,' he says, pensively, as though she's given him some sort of clue.

'Yes. They all thought it was some hilarious secret, that they were protecting her from me or something, and all this time I could have found her—'

He interrupts. Looks her hard in the eye with something akin to contempt.

'And why, *sinjora*,' he asks, 'do you think she wishes to be found?'

Robin

September 2015

9

She waits with the lights off, reading on her phone in the darkness on her daughter's bed. But the long wait, and her long day at work, get the better of her and she falls asleep. And she's woken by the overhead light coming on, and her daughter's slurred cursing.

She sits up. Gemma stands in the doorway of her bedroom, glaring, make-up awry, dressed like a whore.

'Fuck,' Gemma says.

The alarm clock tells her that it's three a.m. Gemma's dress barely covers her crotch, and it looks as if it's glued to her skin. It actually is, in places, for it's damp with sweat, and sticky. She has scraped her curls up into a topknot, looks a bit like a pineapple. She looks more forty than sixteen. The skin beneath her foundation is pale, and greenish.

Ridiculous, thinks Robin. You look ridiculous.

She's wearing diamond earrings, and smells of Diorissima.

Christ, thinks Robin, where's she getting the money for this stuff? And where's she hiding it? I've not seen anything like this dress in the laundry. Diamonds? At her age? Maybe they're fake and I just don't have the eye. Please, please let them be a guilt gift from her stupid dad. And those ankle-breakers she's wobbling on have scarlet soles, and we all know what that means.

'Where the hell have you been?' she asks. Hears every angry mother in history in her voice.

Gemma suddenly clamps a hand – glittery green fake fingernails – over her mouth and runs from the room. Robin sits on her bed among the K-Pop posters and the rainbow-feather pencil toppers, listening to her retch, and wonders where the hell her little girl went.

When Gemma falls quiet, she gets up and, clutching her old woollen dressing-gown closed, goes through to confront her. Gemma is limp on the lino, hugging the pedestal of the lavatory bowl. Jesus, she's got so thin, thinks Robin. She's been hiding it with extra layers when she's in the house, but I should have noticed.

One of the shoes has fallen off, and a glance at the interior confirms her suspicions. Sixteen-year-olds don't own Louboutins.

'Where've you been?' she asks.

Gemma stirs, then looks up, all defiance. Robin can barely make out her pupils.

'What do you bloody care?'

'Oh God, don't be ridiculous.'

She can't bear the sight of her. The dress has ridden up over her hips, revealing a nasty little black nylon thong that disappears between her buttocks. I suppose I should be glad she's wearing knickers at all, she thinks, and feels sick.

She goes back to the bedroom and fetches Gemma's dressing gown. It's pink and fluffy and has matching slippers, and it actually seems to have got bigger in comparison with her daughter since she got the set as a Christmas present last year.

She takes the robe back to the bathroom and thrusts it at her. Gemma takes it, sulkily. Drapes it over herself as she rests, knees up, against the bath. She glares at the wainscot, pouting. She's been wearing red lipstick. The remains still cling to the edges of her lips.

'Where the hell have you been, Gemma?' Robin repeats. 'It's three in the bloody morning.'

'Oh, fuck off,' says Gemma.

'No, I won't fuck off. And don't talk to me like that.'

'Don't pretend like you fucking care all of a sudden.'

She's pulled up short. Guilt. The howling harpy that stalks all mothers, just waiting for an open window. I bet Patrick doesn't have to feel like this, she thinks resentfully. I bet *he's* not sitting up all night, wondering where he went wrong.

He can't be buying her clothes like this, surely? Even Patrick wouldn't be that stupid?

'Of course I care,' she says. 'I've been out of my mind with worry.'

Gemma sneers. 'Yeah, I *totes* saw you out of your mind with worry on my bed just now. You were so worried, you were *snoring*.'

And the first thought that flashes through her head is God, do I snore now? and then she pulls herself together and makes another attempt at being the adult.

She steps over her daughter's feet and fills the tooth mug with water from the basin. Hands it to her. 'Drink.'

Gemma takes the mug but doesn't drink. Just sits there, a resentful goblin on the lino.

Don't you dare look at me like this is my fault, missy. I've got to be up at seven to trudge round the suburbs selling houses to keep a roof over your head.

'This has to stop,' she says. 'You can't go on like this.'

Gemma sighs.

'Gemma, it's just ... *wrong*. You're not old enough. Don't you understand? You're not old enough to be hanging around in nightclubs. You've got to get a grip.'

'Oh, who cares?'

'*I* care, Gemma!' She realises that she's almost shouting. '*I* care!'

'Minding what the neighbours think isn't *caring*,' says Gemma. 'You don't give a fuck what I want, do you?'

'It sort of doesn't matter what you want. You're underage.'

Gemma does the *blah blah blah* thing with her fingers. '*And while you're in my house you will abide by my rules*,' she mimics.

Robin's temper rises again. 'Yes!' she snaps. 'Yes, that's right! If you want to chuck your life away, you're not doing it on my dime! If you don't get a grip, you'll ...'

'What?' sneers Gemma. 'I'll end up being an estate agent?'

Ouch. That stings.

'Yes, well.' She tries to be dignified. 'People make sacrifices when they have *children*. You might understand that one day.'

Gemma's eyes well up with self-pity. 'So now it's *my* fault you're a miserable old failure, is it?'

The response is out of her mouth before her brain has caught up. 'Oh, shut up, you selfish little cow!'

Gemma's head snaps back as though she's been slapped, and Robin wants to shake her till her teeth rattle. *Just look at you. Look at you! You're in the wrong, and you're behaving like I just drowned your kitten!*

Breathe – one … two … three.

'Drink your water,' she says, sternly, 'and let's get you into bed. We'll talk about it tomorrow.'

Three and a half hours to getting-up time. Three showings to get through before lunch. She'll just have to leave her in bed with a bottle of water and hope for the best. Which will no doubt become another entry on the Shit Mother list.

Moments like this make Robin wonder how her life would have been if she hadn't done the normal thing. If she hadn't got married and had a kid. If she'd Followed Her Dreams like an inspirational meme. She sure as hell wouldn't be in a semi-detached a thirty-minute bus ride from the tube, taking depressed millennials round studio flats where the bed's next to the cooker.

Gemma's defiance seems to have run out of steam. She drains the water and allows herself to be helped to her feet. She leads the way out of the room, supporting herself on her wobbly legs with the flat of her hand on the wall.

Robin can't resist getting the last word in.

'One thing's for sure,' she says. 'You're not seeing that Naz any more. I wonder if her parents know what she's up to?'

Gemma whirls round. 'No!' she yells. 'No! Fuck you! *NO!*'

'I'll give the Khans a ring tomorrow,' she says, and feels childishly triumphant, even though she has no intention of following through.

'Don't you dare! Don't you fucking *dare*! She's my friend!'

'Oh, yes?' She's pleased to get a rise, though she knows it's appealing to her worst self. 'I don't think you even know what a friend is, frankly, you go through them so fast.'

Gemma slaps her.

Robin is stunned for a moment. Her head rings and her heart thuds.

'You didn't,' she says, and Gemma spits in her face.

And then the dam breaks and Robin gives her daughter the shaking she wanted to give her five minutes ago. Grabs her by both shoulders and shakes and shakes, and watches her stupid little adolescent head bounce around on her neck. All the rage, all the worry, all the resentment courses through her shoulders and into her hands. And inside, she's shrieking, *There! There! see what it feels like now, you horrible little*—

She stops, as abruptly as she started. Gemma's mascara is streaked down her cheeks and her mouth hangs open.

Robin's cheek stings where her daughter's hand connected.

'Go to bed,' she says.

Gemma is crying, rubbing the tops of her arms.

'Go to *bed*,' she commands.

'I hate you!' wails Gemma.

Robin stands and glares. She doesn't know, of course she doesn't, that this will be their last exchange.

'Oh, trust me, darling,' she replies, triumphantly, 'I don't like you a whole lot right now, either.'

Monday

10 | Mercedes

The women are cleaning the upper floor. The reception rooms gleam: silver and gold and crystal and marble shining so bright they might have come fresh from the factory. The floor-to-ceiling windows that overlook the pool and the sea have been washed and dried and polished with such care that only the air-conditioning tells you that they are even there. Even the fake-tan stain is gone.

The whole house smells deliciously of bleach. She'll have to cover that up with Jo Malone room spray, of course. If there's one thing Tatiana hates more than a dirty room, it's evidence that it's been cleaned.

Mercedes takes a moment to clear her phone of the photos she transferred to Laurence's yesterday: the passports, the cards, the Bank of Kastellana slips that the wives who filled this house last week left lying about the place. They're as helpless as babies in a lot of ways, especially the wives and children. So dependent on other people to do everything.

She goes into the kitchen, where langoustines are being

counted and counters polished, and collects an orange-pistachio cake, which she takes down to the security quarters for Paulo. She always assumes he must get lonely down there, and, despite his granite muscles and his hidden side-arm and the fact that he's a few years older than she is, she can't help mothering him. It's a funny old place, as he's fond of pointing out, for a man of action to finish up. But, after nine years in the SAS, two thousand pounds a day goes a long way towards alleviating the boredom. His days are mostly spent reading Plato, pumping iron and working on his suntan, and he goes home for one week in every six to south London to spend it all on his wife and daughters, who know him as Paul.

'Ahh,' he says, spying her gift. 'Last one of these I'll be seeing for a bit. Gluten-free from tomorrow, I guess.'

He cuts a large slice and eats it, his arm muscles bulging in his Armani T-shirt. Paulo is amiable if you're a friend. And he could snap your neck in a single movement.

'All ready?' he asks.

She sighs. 'I wish. The cleaners will be leaving in a few minutes. I came to tell you.'

'H'okay,' he says. 'Just let me finish this first. It's going to be quite busy in here once the bodyguards arrive. I'm making the most of the peace and quiet.'

'Bodyguards? You've got a list?'

He looks away from his cake for a moment, surprised. 'Well, *yah*.'

'Oh, God, Paulo, have you got a copy? We're flying blind.'
'Sure.'

He pulls up a file on the computer, presses CTRL-P. Paper spits from the machine under the desk and he fishes it out.

Mercedes starts to read, greedily.

'Pity about that Nora,' he says. 'She'd never have left you hanging.'

She turns the page to see who is coming in with Matthew on Thursday. Blanches. 'Is that the movie star?' she asks, pointing at a name.

Paulo nods.

Jason Pettit. She remembers him from the nineties.

'But no wife? Didn't he get married?'

Paulo makes a *pffft* noise. 'Lord, Mercedes. I know you grew up on an island, but you're not *that* green, are you?'

She blushes, and shrugs. Reads some more. Stops. 'A prince?'

Paulo takes a final bite of cake. Nods as he chews.

'*Oao.*'

'I know, right? They must be beside themselves. They've really hit the big time now. I mean, it'd be better if it was a prince with, you know, an actual country, but still. It'll be all her dreams come true.'

I must look up what princes expect, she thinks, and gulps. Perhaps he'll expect us to turn our faces to the wall when he passes by, as the old dukes did.

'He's come down in the world,' says Paulo, 'if he's slumming it with the Meades. Or else he wants something.'

'Can't think what,' she says, but he blanks her. The way they all blank each other when the below-stairs banter crosses the undrawn line.

'Now, this one . . .' He points at a name. Bruce Fanshawe. 'Film producer. I assume that's why the actor's coming. Probably chasing work. Watch him. Not Safe In Taxis, if you get my drift. He'll hit on anything, apparently, and he's got arms like a gorilla.'

'I heard that about the prince too,' she says.

'Oh, he's a pussycat by comparison.'

'Right.' Her heart sinks.

Paulo puts the computer on snooze. Cuts another slice of cake. Looks at it, puts it back. Sighs.

'What's up?' she asks.

'Oh, nothing,' he replies. Picks up his gun and slips it into his shoulder holster.

She'll never get used to being around guns. The thought that they might be needed.

When he's finished, he looks up. 'Between us, right?'

Mercedes nods.

'I don't know that I'm going to be doing this much longer,' he says.

'Oh,' she says. 'I'm sorry.'

'No, it's not that. They love me. She keeps raising my money.'

She doesn't comment.

Paulo sighs. 'It sort of ... this wasn't what I had in mind, you know? For my life.'

'At least you've never had to wipe their backsides,' she says.

He chuckles. 'Seriously, though. It's getting hard to look my girls in the eye. I mean, we *all* like the money, but I think this is going to be my last year in private security. Frankly, your average mercenary has more reason to respect himself.'

'Yes,' she says. She understands.

'Don't *you* ever think about leaving?' he asks. 'It can't be fun, being away from home so much. Di's been on my arse for months. Doesn't Felix mind?'

Do I tell him? She's strangely ashamed of her situation. Trapped by a contract, by a debt that never decreases.

'Yeah, it gets lonely,' she says, eventually. That little white housekeeper's room often feels like a prison cell. But the thought of telling him why she's there is more than she can bear.

*

There is more to do before she gets to rest, and Mercedes heads to the storage room, a discreet door at the end of the staircase corridor. Once inside, she puts away the abstract oils of tropical flowers that the latest interior designer pronounced *perfect*, and which have been hanging on the walls for the past month. You don't leave the silver out in your Airbnb. It's the same even when your renters are made of money. Then she gets out the paintings the spaces were really designed to house, and props them one by one against the wall.

She remembers the first of these portraits, from when it came off the ferry in 1986. It still jars, as it did even when she first saw it, with her experience of the real man.

Matthew Meade, in his forties, stands with his elbow on a majestic mantelpiece, one hand rakishly pushing his jacket aside by plunging into a trouser pocket. He wears a tweed suit that makes her hot in the summer heat, and brown brogues whose mirror finish reflects the roaring fire by his thigh.

It can't have been painted more than five years before they first met, but the man in the portrait is a creature from another reality. She remembers staring and staring as it sat on the dock, and wondering if he even knew how much the artist had flattered him. Matthew Meade's real face, even back then, had been speckled with raised moles, his eyebrows so bushy they partially obscured his eyes, his jaw soft and doughy and melting into his neck. This man's clear blue eyes shine alert from an intelligent brow; his jaw is strong and shapely, his skin as smooth as the best kid glove. And, where the bulging mammaries and apron groin should be, the neat lines of a man whose days are spent on a rowing machine.

She takes it to the main house and hangs it, and, as she does so, her breast brushes the canvas. Mercedes shudders, as though she's touched the man himself. He will be here soon, she tells herself. You need to find your control. Your family retainer smile and your respectful voice. Felix may think you can just walk away, but it's not as simple as that. He still owns you.

The next portrait is of Tatiana. In the 1950s style, black satin and pearls, perched on an elegant little bench with her skirts spread out, leaning slightly forward to share just a hint of cleavage in her fitted bodice. Pearls on the décolletage, at her ears, on her wrists. Her sallow skin blessed with a glow Mercedes has never seen in real life. As with her father's portrait, her natural jaw, her putty nose, have been replaced by neater, narrower versions. Unlike her father, the artist hasn't needed to tell a lie. Tatiana's nose had entirely changed shape by the time she was fifteen, when they came back for the launch of Mediterraneo. By the time she went to university, she had a jaw like a pixie and a chic little haircut to match.

They are both heiresses, in a way, Mercedes thinks. Matthew's money, Sergio's debts. They've both settled on the next generation.

She hangs Tatiana on the far side of the room, facing her father. And she goes back for the last, the family portrait.

A family reduced. Matthew Meade's family, these days, consists only of Tatiana. Thirty-three years after she mixed her amber-coloured cocktail with sleeping pills and lay down to die in her Berkeley Square bedroom, there is no trace of Tatiana's beautiful mother anywhere in the house. Not a photo, not a knick-knack, not a word of remembrance from one day to the next. She was virtually gone by the time Mercedes first went onto that boat. If you spoke to her daughter, you wouldn't know that she had ever existed. You would think Tatiana had been created by plucking out one of her father's well-covered ribs.

They look so complacent, so certain, the two of them. Painted in this very garden: green lawn and white statuary and the blue, blue Mediterranean. The king on his golden throne, smirking as he fondles a wine glass with a gilded rim. He sports holiday casual: pink polo shirt and madras-check cotton shorts, his hairy – oh, so hairy – legs crossed over at the knee, linen deck shoes on his feet. And his heiress, as Mercedes remembers her so often from their childhood, perches on those knees in a halter sundress, hands folded in her lap. The two of them smiling boldly, directly at the viewer. *Look at us*, say the smiles. *We are one.* And Tatiana's smile says so much more. *I am my daddy's girl*, it says. *Whatever I am, he made me. And all that he has will be mine one day.*

She remembers those summer days on the first boat. Tatiana darting on and off that knee, flirting with her daddy, batting eyelashes at the rich old men who came on board to drink champagne. I knew, she thinks. I think I always knew. But wealth is so seductive. Its glittering beams can blind one to the ugliest realities.

This portrait was painted ten years ago. The Matthew it portrays was in his sixties. And Tatiana was thirty-four years old.

Island

1982–5

11

The New Capri: same-same. But different.

First he builds a helipad. Then he builds a road. It's hard underfoot and the tarmac soaks up the heat and blasts it back up again. But it protects the suspension of the castle limousine, so it is a *good thing*. And then that boat, the *Princess Tatiana*, moors up in the harbour, cramping the fishing fleet, and the duke brings the big man who lives on it to the church on Christmas Day to announce that their island home is to become the New Capri and the big man is going to be its architect.

'What's a capri, anyway?' Mercedes asks as they walk home through the gathering dusk. Candles burn in windows to welcome the infant Jesus, and the scent of spice and roasting meat drifts through the cracks around the windows and doors.

'I've no idea,' says Larissa. 'Some kind of boat?'

'It's an island,' says Donatella. 'Off Italy.'

'Why can't we just be an old Kastellana?' asks Mercedes.

'Because rich people go there,' says Donatella. 'It was all goats and fishing boats, and now it's full of palaces.'

'Oh, really?' says Sergio, perking up. 'Palaces?'

'Well, villas,' says Donatella. 'Big-face rich people's villas.'

'How do you know all this?' asks Larissa.

Donatella shrugs. There's a library at the school, filled with books and magazines discarded by the castle. Donatella has read almost everything in there. She's a great reader. A great dreamer, too. Mercedes worries that she will end up disappointed by life.

And the army of Chinese labour he has imported builds more roads – into the empty wastelands on the cliffs on either side of the town, and from the western road another branches off and runs up to the abandoned quarry that built both the temple and the castle. The islanders are to get a desalination plant. A reverse osmosis. The children, who are learning English for two hours a day in the hope that the skill will pass on to their elders, mishear the phrase, and what they tell their parents is what it becomes: the Rivers of Moses, bringing running water to Kastellana Town for the first time since the Romans.

And still Mercedes gets up at six to prepare the restaurant for breakfast before she climbs the hill to the school.

'But where will they live, the rich people?' asks Mercedes.

'He's going to build houses. Big ones. And a second harbour, so they can even moor up in winter.'

'I see that,' says Sergio. 'We can't have them mooring out in open water any more, if they're going to be coming.' Last January, a big storm had carried a yacht the size of their house up onto the rocks on the edge of Ramla Bay when her owners were staying at the castle. A specialist team was flown in from Monaco to refloat her, but still it took the combined efforts of most of the men on the island to get her back out to sea, a great hole in her hull and pumps running hot to keep the water out.

'But if they've got boats, why do they need houses?' asks Mercedes.

'Oh, good grief,' says Sergio. 'The Marinos have a house, don't they? Are you saying they should live on their boat?'

Men who wear suits below their hi-vis jackets and hard hats walk about busily and stare at their homes and businesses and take notes, or ride the new roads with Matthew Meade in his fat man's golf buggy, and gaze down on their rooftops from the cliffs above.

One day the ferry comes three days in a row, and the Chinese army unloads a bewildering array of heavy goods. Huge petrol-driven machines that need construction once they've been positioned on the shoreline, networks of metal frames rising like arms into the air above. Cranes, says the harbourmaster self-importantly. Forklifts, diggers, pile-drivers ... and then he drops the list, because he doesn't know what the others are, just that they are for the new harbour wall, which will be five times the size of now! And Matthew Meade stands on his deck and smokes his cigar as metal beams and sacks of cable block up the quayside, and the *boom!* of dynamite echoing across the land soon becomes just another part of the daily landscape.

'Maybe we could have a dry dock,' says Larissa. 'That would employ a lot of people.'

'Don't be ridiculous, Larissa,' says Sergio. 'That's not what he's got in mind.'

'Well, I don't know, do I?' snaps Larissa. 'They must need to get their stupid boats serviced *somewhere*. Why not here?'

'Didn't you listen to what he said at *all*? He's got *ambitions*. The sort of people who'll be coming here won't want *cranes* and *welding arcs* disturbing them.'

Even at ten years old, Mercedes knows that the way her parents speak to each other isn't right. That the contempt in Sergio's voice is not how a man should speak to his wife.

And still: same-same, but different. Donatella is taken out of school to help at the restaurant. They'd like to do the same with Mercedes, but the law says she must stay until she is thirteen. And Donatella cries in her bed at night, quietly, because she loved the learning, and now the reality of life as a Kastellani girl is coming home to roost.

The boys are training up in the old-new skills – in plastering and painting and plumbing and glazing – for the town is to be given a facelift to make it look as though it's always been that way. They're learning skills that can keep them earning here or carry them away across the world; their choice. For the girls, same old-old skills: scrubbing floors and washing clothes, hoeing and digging and cooking and chasing children until they're grey. Only now it will be other people's houses they will be cleaning. Other people's children they will be raising with unacknowledged love.

Same-same. But different.

The old Auberge de Castile, the island's only hotel, is so full for so long that they can soon afford to install bathrooms. Two new *bodegas* and a café open on the harbour but don't dent the Re del Pesce's trade one bit, and every house with a spare bedroom becomes a bed-and-breakfast. A real, proper doctor's surgery opens on the square, for all to use, at the duke's expense. The pharmacy attached sells a cornucopia of goods for people to spend their new-found incomes on. Shampoo! Little bandages that stick to your skin! Shoe inserts for flat feet! A whole shelf of pretty colours to paint your eyes, your toenails, even your lips! Disposable sanitary towels! Who knew the world contained such luxury?

One day Mercedes sees Donatella standing by a table whose diners have just left, holding something in her hand and frowning.

'What's up?' she asks, and comes over to look.

It's an American dollar. No, *two* American dollars.

They don't get wages in the restaurant, because, obviously, the restaurant is their whole family's living. So two American dollars is something of an event in their lives.

'It's weird,' says Donatella. 'This is, like, the third time this has happened.'

'Did they just forget it?'

'No,' she replies. 'I caught them as they were leaving this time, and tried to give it back.'

'And they didn't take it?'

'No! It's weird! They just waved me off and said, "No, it's for you!"'

'Like a gift or something?'

Donatella nods. 'Yes.'

'Foreigners are *weird*.'

'They are,' says Donatella. She tucks the money into her bra. 'Don't tell Dad,' she says. 'That's *five* dollars I've got now.'

On her day off, she goes up to the new pharmacy and buys a tube of black stuff with a brush in that you paint all over your eyelashes, and a bottle of Pepsi-Cola for her sister. Mercedes drinks the whole thing all herself, in the garden at her grandmother's house, and nothing has ever tasted so good.

A whole new city rises from the cliffs as the harbour wall rises from the sea. A huge hotel with a fountain in its lobby. Apartment blocks with balconies, one, two, three – then five, then fifteen. A *plasa* that will be surrounded by shops, and a funicular railway that will lead directly to it from the marina, so the rich don't have to use their feet. She's learning new English words, new phrases, that the school has never thought to teach them. *High-end. Six-star. Premium luxe. Bidet.* A huge glittering restaurant is built across the end of the Via del Duqa, cutting it off to pedestrians: glass walls and terrace looking out on marina and ocean. Sergio spends hours each day watching it rise, a gleam in his eye.

'I must talk to *el duqa*,' he says. As though such a thing has ever happened before. 'They'll need someone to run that.'

'We already have a restaurant,' says Larissa. 'You'd still be making food for strangers and cleaning up their shit.'

And then she closes her mouth, for she's seen his eyes turn dark, and she's had enough of his discipline for one lifetime.

On the eastern cliff, a magnificent house begins to form with a commanding view of the whole Mediterranean. Glass doors the size of walls and a tower of its very own. He's going to paint it yellow, says the grapevine. Imagine! A yellow house! But then the apprentices descend on Kastellana Town, and one by one the crumbling façades are stripped and sanded and coated with fresh new stucco, and each one is painted a different colour, and some are yellow, some are turquoise, some are pink like salmon.

It's lovely, say the young ones. Our capital is like a rainbow! And the *solterona*s purse their lips and the old people mutter that they might as well be in Italy.

And Mercedes grows, and Donatella grows, and Larissa gets sadder and angrier, and three St James's days pass them by, and the Yacht People begin to arrive. And with them, the summer holiday when she is twelve, the girl who will change her life.

12

Their grandmother's house was once a Roman sepulchre. Although Heliogabalus's pleasure palace was torn down stone by stone and hurled into the sea when he died, the other villas remained. Those excellent foundations, the mosaic floors, the underfloor hypocausts (excellent storage!), the drainage, the baths, the courtyard gardens, the rainwater cisterns, were too good for practical people to waste, whatever the historical resentments, and became the basis of Kastellana Town.

And, after a couple of hundred years, the Roman graveyard, a small collection of square, domed buildings a short walk along the cliffs with a lovely view of the sea, lost its ghostly mystique, and people added a room here and a subdivision there, and surreptitiously dropped the urns over the cliff edge and made little homes where the bodies used to lie. And this little clutch of hovels up above the town are special in one particular way. Because they were a cemetery long before the dukes came to power, they are the only buildings on the whole island that are freehold. On the rest of the island, the death of a leaseholder will trigger a reversion to the duke, and the family left behind must petition to be allowed to take the lease over. To assume another generation of indebtedness for a house they've paid for over generations. But the cemetery houses simply pass from owner to heir, and though they have no monetary value – you need a population that *has* money for anything to be *worth* money – or running water, or drainage, they carry enormous status.

Larissa's mother left hers directly to her granddaughters. She saw the way the wind was blowing with her son-in-law.

Mercedes finds Donatella in the old kitchen, huddled against the wall, her legs curled beneath her, crying.

'Oh, Donita.' She flings herself down on the ground to hold her. 'Oh, *kerida*.'

Donatella winces as their faces touch. The bruise from their father's fist is swelling, and her eye will soon be black. Donatella is fifteen now, and everyone knows that fifteen-year-old girls need discipline, to save them from hell. It's how it's always been. How it always will be.

Mercedes reaches up and brushes the wound with her fingertips. Donatella hisses. 'Does it hurt?'

Mercedes is only twelve. Her punishments rarely stray above the buttocks. They don't yet need to be performed for the *solteronas* to see. She knows her time will come, but for now she just looks at her sister's pain in fascinated horror.

'Of course it bloody hurts,' snaps Donatella.

'Hold on,' says Mercedes. Pushes herself to her feet, finds their grandmother's blunt old kitchen knife in its place on the ledge above the stone sink, and ducks out into the daylight. A big old aloe grows near the door, pushing up through a battered mosaic pavement. Mercedes saws a few inches from a spike, strips off the leathery skin with its rock-hard thorns until she's got a nice wedge of juicy flesh, then scrambles back indoors and holds it out to her sister. 'Here,' she says.

Donatella takes it and presses it against her cheek. Winces again as it touches, then holds it there.

'I'm so sorry,' says Mercedes, sympathetically. Then, 'What did you do?'

'Nothing,' says Donatella, and sobs again. 'Nothing!'

'You must have done *something*. You don't get punished for nothing.'

'Shut up,' says Donatella. 'Just you wait till it's your turn.'

'If you just did what you're told, you wouldn't make him angry,' she tells her. Island opinions, passed down unthinkingly.

Donatella's lip curls. 'Even when what he says is stupid?'

She feels her head jerk slightly. Their father? Stupid? Of course he's not stupid. He's their father.

'If he told you to put your hand in a pot of boiling water, would you do it?'

'He wouldn't do that, though, would he? Don't be ridiculous.'

Donatella shakes her head, disgusted. 'Oh, God, forget it. You'll learn.'

Donatella frustrates her so much. She has everything before her. She gets more beautiful by the day. She's witty and smart, and their family is blessed in comparison with so many others. If she'd only embrace the womanly virtues, be more modest, not answer back ...

'You really think that's all you need? Just to be obedient and then everything will be all right?' Donatella shifts her aloe to the inner corner of her eye. The bridge of her nose is beginning to swell. Once she's back at the Re del Pesce, serving *frijoles* and rabbit *pasta al'arabais*, the whole island will know that the Delia girl has got above herself again.

Mercedes shrugs. 'Anything for a quiet life,' she says. Their mother's favourite maxim.

Donatella drops her hand, punches her thigh. 'But I don't *want* a quiet life!' she cries. 'Do you really think that this is all there is?'

Mercedes is shocked to the core. 'What do you mean?'

'This! This ... *littleness*! This ... everything the same? This, forever?'

She's puzzled. They have lived like this for a thousand years. Why would they change it? 'But what else is there?'

'*Everything!*' cries Donatella. 'There's a whole world out there!' She hisses with pain and puts the aloe back.

Mercedes is appalled. The world outside is full of danger. Everybody says so. Is there a woman who's left La Kastellana who's ever come back?

'Donita!' she cries. 'You can't!'

Donatella pushes her away and gets to her feet. She paces the limestone floor, looks out at the glimpse of sea through the old arched gateway. Near the horizon, a container ship, all black paint and rust, labours past Algeria on its way to the Malta free port. Closer to land, a white boat speeds across the rolling water towards the harbour, the size of a house but small to her eye, brightly coloured little figures basking like seals on the prow deck. Mercedes has seen passenger ships the size of cities pass by from time to time, the people laid out in row after row like corpses fished from the deep after some terrible disaster. She's glad they never come here; that the harbour is too cramped and the sights not grand enough. She imagines that if all these people were to disembark at once, it would be like encountering a plague of locusts.

'I can't live like this until I die,' says Donatella. 'I just can't. I would be praying for death to take me every day.'

Mercedes is chilled. 'Don't let St James hear you say that!'

'Oh, please!' Her older sister whirls back into the room and glares. 'You don't believe all that, do you?'

'What?'

'That St James will slaughter sinners as he slayed the Moor? Seriously? He's been dead a thousand years!'

'But he came back for the Battle of Clavio ...'

Donatella snorts.

'But all those girls! Marcela Perez! Elena Heroux! Karisa Dracoulis ...'

Donatella rolls her eyes. 'God, Mercedes, you're so naïve.'

'What do you mean?'

'They didn't get taken by St James. They left. They just left.'

Tuesday

13 | Mercedes

The reception room is filled with people. Tall people, tall like gods. And they're having a party.

How did you get in here?

Mercedes rushes from god to god, tugging on sleeves, calling out. *You can't be in here. This is not your home. You need to leave. Leave! The owners will be back soon and they mustn't find you here!*

A crash of glass and a gale of laughter. Someone has overturned a table and the floor is thick with shards. The gods guffaw as her hands fly to the sides of her face. They are drinking Pepsi-Cola from champagne flutes as thin and as tall as they are themselves.

She overflows with panic. *No! No! I've only just cleaned this! Don't you see? Don't you see? She'll walk in and everything will end! If Tatiana sees this, all these breakages, my debt will grow again and I'll never get away.*

Mercedes starts to weep. Feels her shoulders shake, the tears pour down her face. She opens her mouth to howl, but no sound comes.

The gods ignore her.

Through her panic, a single thought: I must clean it up. If I can't make them leave, I must clean it up.

They're getting taller, and louder, and she can never make them leave, but, if she sweeps and sweeps, perhaps the glass will be gone before Tatiana comes.

She weaves her way between the legs. The store cupboard, behind the stairs. There are brooms and mops and portraits. If I can open the door, I can ...

Her sister Donatella stands at the far end of the corridor. Thirty years gone. Soaking wet. Her hair clings to her blue face like seaweed. She holds her hands out. *Help me, Mercedes. Help me.*

Mercedes hears herself call out, and suddenly she knows that she is dreaming. *You're dead, my darling. You're dead and I am lost.*

Donatella raises a hand and points to the blank white wall behind her. *I'm in here, Mercedes. Help me. I'm in here.*

She jerks awake in her white single bed. Dawn light filters between the curtains. The sheets are soaking wet, as though she has been in the sea.

She puts her hands to her face and forces herself to breathe.

The helicopter blats in overhead just after lunch, and three minutes later the phone rings with the courtesy call from the heliport. Tatiana will be here in twenty minutes. Neighbours helping neighbours. Her employers would never think to call ahead. They assume, she sometimes thinks, that house staff are like robots. That they wait on charge until a motion sensor or a call bell trips them into action.

Mercedes' uniform is black. A matronly black shirt dress,

102

white piping at the edges and white cloth-covered buttons from collar to knee. Not a practical garment, for a physical job. It gapes when she has to stretch or bend, so she has to wear a black slip underneath that traps the heat. But the Meades like uniforms, and that is all that matters.

In the Hollywood mirror, bright LEDs encircling the frame to highlight every flaw, she checks herself over. Shadows beneath her eyes from her bad night, though Tatiana will never notice those. A couple of locks have strayed from the chignon she wears at work, though, and she will see that in an instant. She fishes in her pocket for her spare hairgrips and fixes the locks back in. Then she checks her face for smuts and her fingernails for grime, and strides out in her orthopaedic shoes to inspect the troops before the boss does.

Tatiana has lost weight. A perpetual struggle for the daughter of Matthew Meade. She went through her twenties and thirties on a diet of steamed fish, boiled eggs and amphetamines, but every year her will broke and her taste for Pop Tarts reasserted itself. Her poor starved body would put on eight kilos in a fortnight and she'd be off for a month in rehab. In a world where half the women look like tiny dolls made of pipe cleaners, being cursed with a builder's frame that will never go below a size 40 must be torture.

Mercedes steps forward, and puts her best smile on. She's belonged to the smiling classes all her life. Has often envied Felix for a job that lets him frown all he wants.

Gaunt, she thinks. She looks gaunt. She's done it. She's found someone to give her that gastric band.

'Wow,' she says, 'you look fantastic!'

Tatiana is pleased. 'Oh, you flatterer,' she says. She smooths her satin pencil skirt over her thighs and turns back to the car.

There's nothing left of her buttocks. She'll be having implants put in to make up for that.

The house staff are lined up in the shade of the porch. Smiling.

Mike, Tatiana's personal bodyguard, gets out of the front passenger seat and glares up and down the empty road from behind his dark glasses as though he expects Al Qaeda to rise from the tarmac like wraiths. Self-important, Paulo says. But he's employed as much to *look* as though he's doing his job as he is to actually do it. Only A-listers want their bodyguards to look as if they're not there.

Satisfied, he turns and looks at Paulo. Nods. Paulo nods back. The chauffeur starts to unload the boot. And as Tatiana's Vuittons pile up, a thin little leg six feet long in its cheap platform shoe emerges from the darkness, attached to a thin little girl in a bustier top and a pair of denim hot pants.

The gardeners rush forward to collect the bags. Carrying bags is their main chance to spend time in the cool indoors. And sometimes, of course, there are tips. Unlikely today, though. These girls are virtually children, and children don't generally do gratuities.

Another little girl steps from the limo, even thinner than the first: so blonde and pale that she could be albino. She looks about twelve, thinks Mercedes, and swiftly dismisses the thought.

Another girl, another halterneck: a tiny little thing from east Asia, all waist-length hair and amber eyes. And then the last one. Maybe seventeen. Golden-brown skin, a mop of dark brown corkscrew curls highlighted gold blonde, a fat little nose and full, shapely lips. An expression of innocence that must be worth a fortune.

She's brought the full gamut, she thinks, and smiles and

smiles. All the choices. They must really want to butter that prince up. And they may look young, those girls, but they're all old inside.

Only Paulo doesn't smile. He's not paid to smile.

Tatiana turns at last to the rest of her staff. Peers at them all doubtfully, as though she doesn't know them. She really doesn't, of course. Staff come and staff go. Only Mercedes is a permanent fixture.

One of the gardeners comes back and picks up a little pink backpack. Slings it over his shoulder. The pale little girl squeaks and starts to run towards him, hands outstretched.

'*Hanne!*' Tatiana barks. The girl halts in her tracks.

And then the honeyed voice is back. 'No need to worry. That's what he's here for. You're not in Magaluf now.'

The other girls smirk behind her back.

'They'll put your bags in your bedrooms,' explains Mercedes.

The girl stares, big-eyed. Mercedes wonders where she's been recruited from. She always wonders. They can't just find them on the streets, can they?

'And Mercy will unpack for you. Won't you, Mercy?' says Tatiana.

'Of course,' Mercedes says smoothly. 'Now, would you like a drink? Food? You must be thirsty.'

'I think we'd all like a swim,' says Tatiana. 'Would that be good, girls?'

'I'll come out to the pool,' says Ursula.

We're a well-oiled machine, thinks Mercedes. Nobody has any idea the muck sweat we were in yesterday.

She goes upstairs to the sound of splashing and girlish laughter from the garden. Tatiana's luggage is piled up outside her door and she carries it in, puts the big case on the stand, the vanity case in the bathroom, the jewellery box straight

105

into the safe. Tatiana's private portrait stares at her from above the bed, the one that lives in the upstairs store-room. Buck-naked, back arched, a finger pressed to her lower lip, gazing at you wherever you go. She has never been able to bear to look at it for long. I knew her when she was a child, she thinks. And then: But was she ever a child? Really? And she decides to do the girls' rooms first, while everyone is busy.

They are quartered at the back of the house. Two to a bedroom, a view of the top storey of the Casa Azul over the road blocking out the view of the mountains.

Those little girls, she thinks. We all know what they're here for. And none of us will say a word, because what happens to them isn't happening to our sisters and our daughters. The dukes have always kept us safe, and life is better here than it's ever been. Who's going to stir the pot, when there's so much to gain? They didn't exist for us before today, these girls. They won't when they're gone, either.

A bag sits on each bed – convent-like single beds like her own, in rooms of whitewashed plaster. If these girls think they're here as equals, they will be disabused of that notion when they see where they're sleeping. Not that they'll be spending that much time here. Only when they're dismissed.

They're sweet, kiddish bags. Someone's told them to come with hand baggage only, and they've all stuffed them so full she's surprised a seam hasn't split. She unpacks them, gingerly. In one room, the pink backpack, and a hard-shell wheelie bag in silver chrome that the owner must have been immensely proud of when she bought it. In the other, a soft-sided carry-on in a print of tropical flowers, and a black leather thing that proves, when she opens it, to contain a maze of pockets, and half a dozen compression bags which have crumpled the rolled clothes within so badly that Stefanie will be working overtime.

She tries to guess which belongs to whom. She guesses that the black one belongs to the first girl who got out of the car, the one with the legs. She had the look of someone to whom none of this was new. So the hard-shell wheelie is probably the Asian girl's and the flowers belong to the curly girl. She gets the contents out, lays them on the beds, contemplates them. Short, tight, high, low. Not clothes for girls who plan to hide away. Four little jewellery rolls, identical, as though they've been given them, filled with tinny little necklaces, pendants on chains, charm bracelets, earrings. The odd precious stone so small it probably started life as a sweeping on the floor of the Tiffany *atelier*.

She hangs the dresses, folds underwear – tiny, scanty things of lace and satin that are more an idea than a piece of cloth-ing – and separates them by suitcase into the small drawers at the tops of the chests. She unrolls the jewellery and lays it out on surfaces, where they can see it all and know that nothing is missing. She takes the washbags to the marble bathrooms and lays every bottle, every unguent, every battered toothbrush, out on glass shelving, like knick-knacks in a souvenir shop.

And she finds their passports, one by one, tucked into outside pockets, and slips them into the large pocket that is the one redeeming feature of her uniform. And, when she has them all, she goes and sits on a toilet, where even the Meades' cameras don't reach, and photographs them for Laurence.

14 | Robin

She had assumed that an honorary consul would be some sort of diplomat, but it turns out that he's just a drunk who makes himself available in the lobby of the Heliogabalus Hotel during cocktail hour, to tell people like her what can't be done. A prissy little man from another era by the name of Benedict Herbert. Good shoes, though. There's a last in London with his name on.

'You understand,' he tells her, 'this is a very busy week. We've the *festa*, on Wednesday, and then on Saturday the duke is throwing a *bal masqué* for his birthday. He's seventy, you know. We're swarming with VIPs.'

We. Easy to tell where his loyalties lie.

He is drinking a martini. A stemmed glass, condensation on the outside, a single olive on a stick. He turns, turns, turns it on the table-top, coaster discarded, leaving damp trails on the wood for someone else to clean up. As he affects giving her his attention, his eyes wander the crowd, looking for stories more interesting than her own.

'I know,' she says. 'That's why I'm here.'

His attention immediately reverts. 'Oh, really?'

He looks startled. Ha. He thinks he's misread her. He thinks she's a VIP in mufti. Bet he wishes he'd paid more attention to what she was saying now.

'My daughter,' she reminds him. 'She said she was coming for a party.'

The lights switch off again. He looks her up and down, checks her jewellery and calculates her net worth. Places her back in her pigeonhole.

'I don't think so,' he says.

He raises his glass to a passing woman, pantomimes tapping his watch and rolling his eyes. He doesn't even try to conceal the gesture. It must be a real pain to him that consular status comes with the burden of occasionally having to have contact with the British taxpayer.

'Really? Is that all you've got to say?'

He sighs. Fishes out his olive and chews it, slowly. Probably all the solid food he'll be having tonight.

'Mrs . . .'

'Hanson.'

'Hanson. Yes. Oh. You're not . . . ?' Again a flicker of interest.

'No, not one of *those* Hansons.'

'Ah. Okay.'

'We were talking about my daughter.'

'Yes. So look, Mrs Hanson. I hate to break it to you, but it doesn't work that way. The duke's worked like hell over the years to make this tiny country somewhere where the international set want to come, and he didn't do that by inviting random teenagers to parties. Do you think Bernie Ecclestone goes about handing out tickets to the Monaco Grand Prix in Starbucks? I mean, where would she even have *met* him?'

'Are you going?'

A puff of self-importance. 'To the ball?'

'Yes.'

'Of course.'

She looks at him.

'I went to school with the duke,' he says proudly.

Eton, probably. 'That's nice. So you're old friends?'

'Yes. Very.'

'So couldn't you just ... ask him? If she's on the guest list? I mean, it's not *completely* impossible she's got herself an invite, is it?'

'Invitation,' he corrects. 'I don't really—'

'She's a British citizen.'

'I'm afraid,' he says, 'you're rather overestimating what my job entails.'

'Mr Herbert, I'm desperate here,' she says.

'I don't doubt it,' he says, superciliously.

Her jaw clicks shut. 'She's just a kid.'

'Bit of a grey area, that, I'm afraid. As I'm sure you know.'

'Yes, but—'

'Presumably you've spoken to the police? At home?'

'Yes, but—'

'And what did they say?' His tone is ostentatiously patient.

She wells up. Gulps back the tears and stares at him, hope ebbing.

He nods, satisfied. 'Because, as it happens, I made a few calls after the Chief of Police told me you were hanging around.'

Hanging around? Really? That's what she's doing?

'And what I gather,' he continues, 'is that your daughter isn't strictly speaking "missing" as such at all, is she?'

'She's only seventeen, and her father and I have no idea where she is.'

'Yuh, I'm afraid as far as the police are concerned they

can't actually *force* a seventeen-year-old to go back to a home they don't want to be in. Can't be done. It never takes. She's clearly alive and she clearly doesn't have mental health issues and she's clearly not been kidnapped, Mrs Hanson. She's left home at an age one wouldn't think ... ideal ... but she's not *missing*. She just doesn't want you to know where she is. I gather she's been in touch with friends all along.'

'But *I* told you that! And they don't know *where* she is, not really, any more than *we* do. Just because she's been on her stupid ... webchat thing ...'

Another sigh. 'That's how they all communicate these days. One needs to accept the times one lives in. Look. If there were, you know, suspicions that she was being held against her will ... if Interpol had been on to us ... The duke is rigorous in co-operating with the international authorities when it's necessary. But they haven't, have they?'

'I ...'

'Have they?'

'The police are useless,' she says, resentfully. 'Look at all those little girls in Rotherham. They literally did nothing.'

He signals to a waiter. Does the universal air-writing signal. His voice, when he speaks, drips patronage. 'Oh, Mrs Hanson. This is hardly comparable to a mass grooming scandal, is it?' He drains his glass and eyes her, more in sorrow than in anger.

The tears are so close to the surface she can barely speak. Rage tears. No sorrow here. 'So you're not going to help me?'

There's a prissy little man-bag on the floor by his feet. He picks it up. 'Mrs Hanson, do you really believe it's the government's responsibility to resolve family arguments? I'm sorry you fell out with ...' he glances down at his damp notebook '... Gemma, but that's not something I can involve myself in, and nor can the *xandarms*. Citizens' private rights also, I'm afraid, involve private responsibilities. Now, I'm afraid I have another appointment, so I must take my leave.'

'So what should I do?'

'Well, you're welcome to stay around and see if she turns up,' he says, and gets to his feet. Waves at a group who've just come in and are heading for the Seafood Grill. 'It's a free country. As long as you stay within the rules, of course. But just a word in your ear. Don't be bothering the extremely busy police, and don't be pestering private citizens. There's word already getting round that you're throwing around some sorts of ... implications, and people aren't taking it too kindly.'

He tucks the man-bag under his arm and saunters towards the double doors that lead to the street. Robin watches him go, her head a storm of rage and weeping.

A waiter comes over, clears away the glass, wipes down the tabletop.

'Can I get you anything, *sinjora*?' he asks. 'A cocktail?'

She doesn't look at him. Just stares at Benedict Herbert's retreating back. The cocktails here are – she calculates quickly – eighteen pounds each, and she's been made to look like enough of a dick already today. 'No, thanks,' she says. 'I'm off in a second.'

She keeps her emotions under control as she crosses the lobby. The eyes of passing flunkies scan her, find her wanting, turn away. By the time she reaches the revolving door, her cheeks are flaming. She's so flustered that she tries to push it open clockwise, and finds herself struggling, face to face across the glass divide, against that wine merchant from the boat. Laurence somebody. Looking remarkably cool in forty degrees of heat while every inch of her pulses crimson.

He stops. Raises his hands. Grins and steps back. Points a finger at the ground and draws a circle, anticlockwise, in the air.

Robin stops pushing. Turns round. Pushes the other side. The door turns, smooth as silk, a tiny sucking noise as it opens and hot air meets cold. She steps out.

'Sorry about that,' she says.

'That's okay,' says Laurence. 'Happens to everybody at some point. Been for a drink?' he asks.

'Sort of,' she says, and bursts into tears.

Laurence's face drops. 'Oh,' he says. 'Oh, dear.'

Her embarrassment soars. Crying on the doorstep of a hateful hotel, in front of a strange Englishman, while women in dresses that cost her annual mortgage payment stalk past and avert their gaze. 'Sorry,' she mutters. 'Sorry.' Dashes the tears from her cheeks, tries to hide her face.

'You clearly need a drink.'

She shakes her head. 'I'm fine.'

'No, you aren't,' he says. 'Look, come on.'

'Not in there.'

'No? Okay.'

He leads her across the street, away from the hotel, to a bench by the cliff wall. Helps her sit, solicitously, as though she were an old lady with a wheelie bag. Fetches a Kleenex from a little pack in his pocket and offers it to her.

She blows her nose. 'Sorry,' she says again.

'So, can I get you a drink?'

'No. Thank you.'

'Some water, at least?'

'No, I—' But he's gone already, hurrying over to a street vendor who loiters by a chunky, fifties-retro coolbox in the shade of a large red parasol.

Robin sniffs. Blows her nose, tries to compose herself. The view from where she sits is quite spectacular. The geometry of the marina, the funicular crawling through the palm trees on the hillside like a silver millipede, the blue-black Med spreading unbroken to the horizon. Wherever Gemma is, Robin hopes she has a view like this.

He returns with two little bottles of Evian, hands her one and sits down. 'Feeling better?'

She opens the water, takes a sip, realises that she is very thirsty and half-drains the bottle. 'Yes, sorry,' she says. 'Encounter with an arsehole.'

Laurence watches the passengers debark from the funicular. 'Plenty of those around to choose from.'

'You've probably come across him,' she says. 'Chap called Herbert?'

'What, Benedict?'

She nods.

'Oh, now,' he says, 'that really *is* an arsehole,' and she finds herself smiling. 'God only knows how he got that job,' says Laurence.

'He went to school with the duke,' she says.

'Mmm. Honestly, though? All the money washing about here, you'd have thought we would have upgraded to an *actual* diplomat by now. I don't suppose he knows one end of an attaché case from another.'

'Well, he certainly wasn't rushing to help *me*,' she says.

'D'you mind if I ask ... ?'

'No. Sure. I've lost my daughter.'

'What, here? I didn't see you ...'

'No, no,' she says, 'back home. She ran away. Well, left, and I've not seen hide nor hair for nearly a year.'

'And you're looking here because ... ?'

'A message she sent some friends on an app,' she says. 'She said she was coming here for a party.'

'Ah,' he says.

'Of course, *Herbert* didn't seem to think so,' she says.

'Ah, no, he wouldn't,' says Laurence. 'He's rather limited by his raging snobbery, that one. Where's she staying, do you know?'

'If I knew that, I'd have gone there, wouldn't I?'

'Yes, sorry. Stupid.'

'Anyway. Doesn't look like there'll be any help forthcoming from Her Majesty's Civil Service,' she says bitterly.

'I'm sorry,' he says. 'D'you have a picture?'

'Oh, sure,' she says. Digs out a flyer and hands it over.

He's the first person she's given it to who's actually looked properly. 'Gemma Hanson,' he says. 'How old?'

She tears up again. 'Seventeen.'

'Oh, I'm sorry,' he says again. 'I'll certainly keep an eye out.'

Gemma

June 2015

15

Stupid. I'm so stupid. Oh, God, *stupid*. I'm so bloody desperate to have someone love me, anyone, I'll literally fall for anything.

Oh, God, I fucked him in here. Literally on this bed. Now I'm never getting that out of my head. Every time I even look at it, I'll remember him sitting there looking at himself in the mirror while I went down on him. I glanced up and saw us both with his hand on my head, and he was smirking. And I just pushed it out of my head because ... God, I'm so *stupid*.

She feels sick. Sick at her credulity and sick at the fact that she is the kind of girl to whom every rejection feels like a little death. And boys are so ... they'll just use you. And every time. Every time a boy shows even the slightest bit of interest, she rolls over like a puppy. *Love me, love me. Please, just love me.*

She hears her mum come home. Hears her move around downstairs, humming. She goes into the kitchen, then back

119

out into the hall, and a door shuts. A couple of minutes later, the loo flushes and she calls up the stairs.

'Gem? You home?'

Gemma sits up and wipes her face with the sleeve of her uniform jumper. Catches sight of herself in the mirror – the red-raw face, the salt-stiff bird's-nest hair, the general air of woe.

Why would he fancy you anyway? she thinks. You're pathetic.

'In my room,' she calls. Gets up and throws a scarf over the mirror.

'Come down!' calls Robin. 'I closed on two houses today and I've got you a present!'

Oh, God.

Hurriedly, she scrubs her face with a cleansing wipe, rubs in tinted moisturiser with the hand mirror, and trudges downstairs.

Robin is at the sink, washing up the breakfast dishes and singing. 'Dancing in the Moonlight', an ancient song from what she calls her 'clubbing days', that she always seems to sing when she's feeling cheerful.

'Finally managed to get shot of Sternhold Road,' she says. 'A couple looking for a fixer-upper. Honestly, I thought it was going to be on the books till the roof caved in.' She turns round, drying her hands on a tea towel, beaming. 'Treat supper tonight. I got some fillet steak. Hey, what's up with your face?'

She's the last person Gemma is going to tell. As if she'd understand the first thing about it. It would just be yet another opportunity for a lecture, and some excruciating offer to take me to Family Planning.

'Ugh, an allergy,' she says. 'I tried on some perfume in the chemist's and it blew up. It's okay. It's getting better.'

Robin laughs. 'What are you like? Honestly, you're just

like me. Skin like tissue paper. That cheap stuff's horrendous. Anyway – your presents are on the table.'

She points, though Gemma knows perfectly well where the table is. There are two bags, the posh sort: thick paper with string handles.

'Funnily enough,' says Robin, and she's still smiling, pleased with herself, 'turns out one's completely appropriate.'

She picks up one of the bags and hands it over. It contains a bottle of Jo Malone: Lime, Basil and Mandarin. Proper expensive stuff, the sort of thing Gemma's allowance would never buy.

'Probably best to wait till *that's* died down before you try it, mind,' says Robin, nodding at her salty face, and laughs with the sort of unobservant sympathy that makes Gemma cringe. Everything in her mum's world is interpreted through the lens of the mood she's in at the moment. Of course she's never going to notice how miserable her daughter is.

'Thanks,' she says, and puts it back in the bag, and the bag on the table. She just can't work up the enthusiasm. She musters a 'Can't wait to try it', and Robin looks semi-satisfied.

'Aren't you going to open the other one?' She nods encouragingly at the other bag.

I'm being shitty, thinks Gemma. But her heart feels like a lump of lead. Once someone's lost your trust it's hard to get it back, and she's not inclined to confide in her, after the scratchcard fiasco. Gemma's not stupid, nor is she blind. She knows perfectly well that that whole episode was more about getting at Dad, about Letting Him Know the Consequences of his Desertion, than it was about the seriousness of her infraction. And she knows that Patrick's continuing reproaches are about still being annoyed that she'd put him in that position. Whatever, she's learned her lesson.

She picks up the bag. It bears the logo of the boutique on Duke of York Square, where they were a couple of Saturdays ago. Her heart sinks. She has a good idea what it is. A couple of Saturdays ago, she would have given her eye teeth for it.

What a difference a fortnight makes. When she was longingly fingering the jade crêpe cloth, the sequinned shoulder straps, the self-covered waspie belt of this dress, she was thinking about what Nathan would think when he saw her in it. But it's all spoiled now. Everyone is laughing at her. If she ever goes to a party again, which at the moment she doubts she will, and wears it, she'll be right on the 'trying too hard' list.

'Thanks,' she says, dully.

She sees hurt cross her mother's face. Sees the hurt, as it so often does, transform into annoyance.

'Really?' says Robin. 'That's it?'

Gemma doesn't have the energy.

'You were all over it two weeks ago,' says Robin. 'I thought at least you'd manage to be pleased about *this*.'

'It's great,' she says, dully. How did you explain? She feels enough of a fool already.

Robin snatches the dress away and bundles it back into the bag. 'Christ, you're a piece of work,' she says. 'I literally can't do anything to please you, can I?'

Something wells up inside, and Gemma wants to scream out loud. Wants to cut her skin with a knife, just to watch the blood come out and relieve the pressure. *Can't you see? Can't you see me? Help me, Mum! Help me! Just put your arms round me and give me a hug, for God's sake!*

She takes a breath to speak, but her mother has already flounced from the room.

Island

July 1985

16

Something brushes her thigh, then something else her forearm, then she's flailing in the water because, where they've touched it, her skin is burning.

Medusa! Jellyfish!

Mercedes backs up and feels another brush her ankle, and then she's sprinting as fast as she can for shore. Her progress is slow, for the last thing she wants to do is put her face in the water.

'*Puta mjerda!*'

To her right, a snorkeller heads for the rocks, propelled by rubber fins. Mercedes doggy-paddles awkwardly along, hot with envy. The snorkeller reaches land and hauls themselves out. It's a girl. Short dark hair and a turquoise bikini printed with sunflowers.

Ow, ow, ow. But dear God, it burns. The currents around La Kastellana rarely bring jellyfish inland, but she's heard tales of their vicious stings from the fishermen. She'd never really taken in the reality of it.

She reaches the old boat ramp, lets the incoming waves carry her in until her hands and knees touch concrete, then shimmies through the shallows onto solid ground. Stumbles onto the shingle beach and inspects her injuries. They're round, the size of coffee saucers. Little red blisters bulge from her skin, ready to pop.

'*Mjerda! Sangre de Cristo! Porco MADONNA!*'

Suddenly, she doesn't love the sea so much.

The girl, twenty metres away, pulls off her snorkel mask, treads down the backs of her flippers until they suck away from her heels. She looks at Mercedes musingly as she ruffles the water from her short hair, then picks her way barefoot across the shingle until she's standing over her.

'Hard luck,' she says.

Mercedes looks up. They've been learning English at the school for three years now, and she understands.

'How many times did you get stung?' She examines the lesions. 'You're lucky. There's a whole shoal out there.'

She's not a pretty girl. She has rough, dull olive skin and a heavy jaw like a boxer's. Her eyebrows are bushy and meet in the middle, and her nose is like two little spring pota-toes, one on the end of the other. I know who this is, thinks Mercedes. She's Sinjor Meade's daughter. I remember her at the funeral. She looks just like him, poor girl. She's going to need her dowry.

The blisters are beginning to ooze and the patches are throbbing. Despite the high July sun, she feels slightly chilled, slightly dizzy. She drops her head towards her knees, and props herself on rigid arms.

'Oh, shit,' says the girl. 'Are you okay?'

She shakes her head. Speaking feels too much like work.

'Okay, look, hold on.'

126

To Mercedes' astonishment, the girl hooks her thumbs into her bikini briefs and pulls them down. She was already scandalously naked by Kastellani standards, but now the sight of her, of the coat of downy fluff at the tops of her thighs, makes Mercedes gasp in embarrassment. She puts her hands over her face and covers her eyes.

A hand snatches her right arm away and presses the hand on her knee so the blemished wrist is next to the sting on her thigh.

The girl begins to squat. Mercedes realises what she is preparing to do, and leaps back.

'No! No! What you are doing?'

A huff of frustration. 'Oh, for God's sake, I'm *helping*!'

She stands up and takes hold of the arm again. Bends to look into Mercedes's face. Her breath smells fresh, like mint.

'I'm just – *ajudate*! It'll help! It's acid ... *acidio*! *Para el* ...' She's clearly reached the limits of her multilingual knowledge, so she starts to invent. '*El pico. No. La pice.* The sting, for God's sake!'

She speaks too fast for Mercedes to keep up. But she gets the drift.

'*Ajudate*,' the girl repeats, and firmly places Mercedes's hand where it was before.

Mercedes closes her eyes and turns her head away. She is too overwhelmed to resist any more, and the girl seems determined to piss on her, whatever she does. What will be will be, she thinks, as a trickle of warm liquid splashes onto her arm and thigh, then, the girl's hand on her shoulder for balance, moves on down her shin to her ankle. At least it doesn't smell, she thinks, and it won't for a while. I can wash it off when I get to ... oh ...

The stinging is diminishing. My God, she thinks, as the

girl drains her bladder and takes her hand away. It's actually working!

She opens her eyes and looks down at her leg. The girl is already pulling her bikini bottoms back on, and she could swear that the wounds are less livid. She doesn't want to touch them yet, but the angry red is already fading to mauve.

She looks up. The girl is smiling. Suddenly she looks almost pretty. She has bright blue eyes, and her teeth are white. But oh, that jaw.

'Better?' she asks.

Mercedes nods, still astonished. 'Yes. Thank you.'

'Lucky I didn't pee in the sea,' says the girl. 'I was just about to.' And without another word she sets off up the beach to where her little pile of belongings lies.

Mercedes watches as she collects them and comes back. She's about her age, maybe a little older if her pubic hair is anything to go by. She carries some puppy fat, but her body is strong. Not hard-work strong; expensive strong. She's seen similar stomachs on the yacht women. A mysterious flatness – skin sliding loosely across rigid muscle as though they're not actually connected. Mercedes has scars and blemishes – on her knees, on her shins – but this girl's skin is as perfect as the day she emerged from the womb. The bikini fits as though it were made for her, and its print of tropical flowers is gaudy and bright, brand new. But lord, she has a face like a goblin.

Mercedes, in Donatella's faded black hand-me-down swimsuit, with its heavy thigh-length skirt and top that's cut high to the collarbone, feels dowdy and poor. And somehow exposed.

The girl flops down beside her, digs in a cotton beach bag that actually matches her bikini.

'Ah!' she declares, and produces a foil strip of little white pills and a bottle of water. She offers them. 'Take one of these.'

128

Mercedes inspects them. 'What is?'

'Antihistamines.'

Mercedes shakes her head, none the wiser.

'I have allergies,' the girl says, proudly. And when she sees that the word means nothing, she tries again. '*Alergia. Allergie.*'

She wheels through facial expressions as she wheels through the languages. Alert as she speaks Spanish, supercilious when speaking French. When none of them work – allergies don't exist on La Kastellana – she shrugs. 'It'll help,' she says. 'For the—' and she fake-scratches her own arm, showing her teeth like a flea-ridden dog.

Figuring that she's just allowed this girl to piss on her leg, Mercedes takes one. What harm can it do? It's only tiny. She drinks some water. Even rich people's *water* is delicious. It tastes of mountains, and sky.

'You like swimming?' asks the girl. She squeezes a stream of water into her mouth, the bottle never touching her lips. Mercedes looks away, embarrassed once again by her faulty etiquette.

'Yes,' she says, 'I love.'

A poor description of the degree of love she feels. How do I explain it? she wonders. When I feel the sea's caress, it's like being held in the encircling arms of a tiger.

'Yes,' she says again.

The girl holds up her snorkel and mask. 'You should try one of these,' she says. 'It's better. You can see everything.'

To see beneath the surface. What a thing. They have one of these on Felix's father's boat. She's been fantasising that she might get to go out on that boat one day, put on that mask and see how it feels to soar above the ocean depths.

It will never happen, of course. A young girl who went alone on the water with the men would ruin her reputation forever.

129

Maybe when I'm older, she thinks. Maybe one day I'll have a boat of my own. She shakes her head, sadly.

The girl, this stranger, holds it out. 'Take this one,' she says.

Mercedes hesitates. This thing of glass and rubber represents more money than has passed through her hands in her whole life. Then she shakes her head, reluctantly.

'Go on,' says the girl. 'I've got two more on the boat.'

She feels slightly tearful. She longs to say yes, but how will she explain it to her parents? How will they explain it to the village? Girls who come home with mystery gifts are inviting speculation.

'Thank you, no,' she says.

The girl seems annoyed. 'But why not? I *told* you I have more!'

She's embarrassed to say. Suspects the girl won't understand. 'I don't know how.'

The girl beams. 'Oh, that's all right! I'll teach you. The jellyfish will have gone by tomorrow. You come here tomorrow? Same time? *Manjana*? *En la tarde*? Okay?'

Whatever that pill was, it's working. The itching has almost gone. What harm can it do? she thinks. Just to learn? To see beneath the water?

She nods. 'Okay.'

'Good,' says the girl. 'And you can be my friend. I'm stuck on that boat the whole summer and I'm bored shitless.'

She sticks her hand out. The nails are neat and shiny, no dirt beneath, and all the same length. 'I'm Tatiana,' she says. 'Tatiana Meade.'

Mercedes takes the hand and shakes it.

'Mercedes Delia,' she says.

17

'So how old are you?'

Mercedes counts up in her head. She still can't do the English numbers above ten without doing that. Same with the days of the week. 'Twelve,' she replies. 'You?'

'Thirteen,' Tatiana says, proudly. That single year makes all the difference. 'When's your birthday?'

'December.'

'Ah! Sagittarius! I'm a Gemini.'

This information means nothing to Mercedes. She decides she's best just nodding nicely.

'And how many brothers and sisters do you have?'

'One. Donatella. She nearly sixteen.'

'I,' Tatiana declares proudly, 'am an only child. So have you always lived here?'

Mercedes nods.

'And where else have you been?'

The question surprises her. 'Nowhere.'

'Not even Sardinia?'

Why would she go to Sardinia? It's full of monsters. Everybody says so. Fedi Bastiani was stabbed in a dockside bar there three days after he went away to make his fortune. They brought his body back in a coffin and made them all go and look at his bloodless corpse before they buried him.

She shakes her head.

'Oh, my God,' says Tatiana, 'I've been *everywhere*.'

'Everywhere?'

'Well, I've been to thirty-seven countries,' she says, proudly.

Thirty-seven! *Are* there that many countries? Mercedes realises that she knows very little about the world. She's only heard of maybe fifteen countries altogether. She strains to think of more.

Tatiana reels off a list of names that sound impossibly exotic.

'I've been to all the continents,' she finishes, 'except Antarctica. And Daddy says there's nothing to see there anyway.'

Mercedes determines to learn better English. She wants to drink it all in. Tatiana has shown her what the sea looks like beneath the surface, and that is everything.

Tatiana is talking again. Something to do with her school and something called skiing.

Mercedes cuts in. 'But where you *live*?' she asks.

Tatiana stops short, and frowns, as though she's never considered the matter before. 'I – England, I suppose.'

'You suppose?'

She sighs. 'We have houses *everywhere*, and we're hardly ever there. But I go to school there, so ... but I'm half American, of course. Mummy was American.'

Mercedes can't stop herself competing. 'We have two houses. One in the town and one in the country.'

Tatiana blinks like a chameleon on a rock. She doesn't like being interrupted, thinks Mercedes.

'And I suppose I could be Bulgarian if I wanted,' she continues. 'That's where Daddy started out. Though why anyone would *choose* to be Bulgarian is anybody's guess.'

She stops. That was a set speech, thinks Mercedes, and now it's done. Then she responds to Mercedes' remark, as though she's just made it. A funny way to do an interaction. As if it's a list that needs ticking off. '*We* have ten,' she says. 'At *least* ten. I'll have to count. There's London and the Cotswolds, and Daddy's shooting lodge in Scotland, though I've never actually been there because it's for entertaining his business associates. And New York. And the south of France. And he's got a big farm on the South Island of New Zealand for if nuclear war breaks out. And the vineyard. That's in Tuscany ...'

'There are vineyards on La Kastellana,' says Mercedes. She's starting to feel impatient, a bit belittled by all this listing of places she's never been, and mostly never heard of.

Tatiana's chin jerks upwards. 'This is a *proper* vineyard,' she says. '*Our* wines win *prizes*. And LA, of course. Daddy does *lots* of business in LA. And the Caymans. And the ski lodge in Colorado. Ooh, it's the best snow up there. It's like Christmas icing ...'

Mercedes has never seen snow, except in movies. And she has no idea what Christmas icing is.

'And of course now we've got the house here. It'll be finished by the end of the summer. You can come and swim in the pool,' she says grandly.

'And your *mama*?' she asks, to change the subject. 'Where she live?'

Another stiffening. Tatiana's eyes drop to the stony ground.

133

She picks up a pebble and hurls it at the sea. 'Oh, her? Nowhere. She's dead.'

Mercedes feels a chill as she remembers that beautiful, sad lady.

'I so sorry,' she says. 'When she dead?'

Tatiana finds another pebble and throws it after the last. 'Oh, ages ago,' she says, in a voice so full of false indifference that it's evident that the feelings are still strong.

'I so sorry,' Mercedes says again. Her parents have their faults, but she cannot imagine a world without them. The very thought raises a lump in her throat, fills her mouth with salt.

Tatiana doesn't speak for a few seconds, and, when she does, she has reverted to her gay social lilt.

'Oh, God, it was *yonks* ago. And anyway, I've got Daddy, and I always got on better with him, frankly. She was a bit of a third wheel, truth be told.'

The phrase is beyond Mercedes' English. But she gets the gist. Matthew is Tatiana's favourite, and Tatiana is his.

'What . . . kill her?' she asks.

Abruptly, Tatiana leaps to her feet. 'Oh, who cares? She was weak. That's all that matters. She was weak and I don't miss her.' She drops a diaphanous red and orange paisley kaftan over her head and turns on a beaming smile as her face emerges. 'Come on.' She bends to retrieve the mask and fins, pushes them towards Mercedes. 'Let's go back to the boat. It's nearly teatime.'

Mercedes can tell the time, roughly, by the sun. It is still comfortably high in the sky. A good couple of hours before she'll be expected for evening service. And the thought of going on that boat where no one else has gone is thrilling. She gets to her feet and follows in Tatiana's wake.

18

They have to cross the square to get back to the harbour. Mid-afternoon, and half a dozen men are playing checkers at the little tables beneath the tamarisk outside the bar. Another handful lean against it, nursing beers, looking dopily from gloom to sunshine. On the far side, as far as they can get from the den of iniquity without ceding territory, the *solteronas* sit on the edge of the fountain as they have always done, tatting the lace that no one local wears any more and watching with their laser eyes for infractions.

Mercedes' cheeks burn as they walk. Every eye in the square is trained on Tatiana's naked thighs. The kaftan barely comes halfway down them. It's scandalous, really.

Mercedes herself is decently covered in a knee-length dress whose sleeves go to her elbows, but she's suddenly worried that the damp bathing suit beneath is making the cloth cling more closely than Larissa would like. She casually drapes the towel Tatiana brought for her over her shoulder, to break up the detail, and hurries on.

The *solteronas* fall silent. Even the click-click-click of their tools ceases. Tatiana walks on, hips swinging with the effort of keeping on her leather flip-flops, as Mercedes scurries past and burns with shame as she hears someone mutter her name.

But who is that? The one dressed like a puta?

Next year's sirena, *for sure*, says another. *Just look at her!*

Oh no, she's one of Them, says another. *The gypsies on the boats.*

I thought they kept better care of their girls than that, the Delias.

Have you seen the older one? says a third voice. *Are you kidding me? Looks like this one's going the same way as her sister.*

She longs to round on them, to shout in their faces, for she knows her sister. *What do you know?* she screams inside. *Who do you think you are, trashing my sister's reputation? Just because she's pretty. Just because she sometimes laughs too loud. Jealous old bitches who missed your own chance and have no pleasure left but to spread poison about girls who still have youth and beauty on their side.*

She says nothing. The *solteronas* have power, and no girl on La Kastellana wants to attract their attention.

Stepping onto the gangplank of the *Princess Tatiana* feels like the few times she's been allowed into the castle hall. Festive, exciting and terrifying all at once. She holds her breath as they approach the charcoal-suited security guard who stands at the entrance day and night, but he merely unclips the gate and holds it open without a word. Mercedes dashes past him, half-afraid she will be turned back, and drinks in all the detail she can, to tell Donatella. I'm the first island child on board, she thinks, I'm sure of that.

'Welcome aboard,' says Tatiana as she steps off the gang-plank. She turns and executes a sarcastic little curtsey, princess-style, and Mercedes laughs. Then she puts her index and middle fingers to her lips, kisses them and presses the kiss onto a huge, shiny anchor that sits on a stand just beside the entrance.

'What's that?' asks Mercedes.

'That? Oh, that's for good luck. You should do it yourself.'

'Good luck?' She's never heard of such a thing.

'Oh, yes,' she says. 'We do it every time we come aboard.'

She discards her bag and water gear on the deck as Mercedes examines the unlikely amulet. It's big – far too big for a boat like this – and elegant. The sort of anchor you see in history books, with its two curved prongs and their arrow-head points. But the most extraordinary thing about it is that it seems to be made of gold.

'It's Daddy's good-luck charm.' She walks away from her stuff, towards the stern. 'A souvenir.'

'Souvenir?'

'Oh,' she says breezily, 'from his first million.'

'Oao,' says Mercedes. She's not sure a million *what*, but a million is a big number in any currency. She gingerly kisses her fingers and presses them to the talisman – it can't do any harm, after all – and follows behind.

'Yah,' says Tatiana. 'In the Seventies. Honestly, there were so many family companies run by idiots back then. This was a boat-builder that went under while Wedgie Benn was nationalising everything. He picked them up for a song. An absolute *song*.'

Mercedes doesn't really understand what she's on about, but she's intrigued anyway. 'So how he make this million?'

She glances back and sees a door open amidships. A woman

in white trousers and a black polo shirt steps out, sweeps Tatiana's discarded belongings into her arms and vanishes back inside like a weather vane.

'Oh,' says Tatiana, 'honestly. These people, they were so obsessed with building boats and servicing their debts, they totally didn't notice that they were sitting on some of the Isle of Wight's primest real estate. Bloody idiots. You could hardly buy a *house* with what he paid them. It's a marina now. Like this one. And the warehouses – *Georgian* warehouses – are super-prime condos for the regatta crowd. Anyway. The anchor was going to be for the last boat they ever built. Sold *that* for scrap, of course. But he kept the anchor, to remind him.'

'They had a *gold* anchor?'

Tatiana turns and gives her a funny look. 'Doh. No, it's gilded, stupid. Nobody would have an anchor made of gold. It'd be so heavy it would sink the yacht.'

They emerge onto the bow deck and Mercedes is, for a moment, unable to breathe. The deck, concealed from the land by fibreglass walls, is bigger than her family's living room. Bigger than their restaurant. An awning casts shade for four whole metres before giving way to a sundeck with padded loungers. At the very tip, built into the prow, there's a giant bathtub filled with water at what looks like a rolling boil.

And in the tub, bubbles popping around a fleshy chest thickly thatched with curly hair, great tree-trunk arms spread out along the sides, sits Matthew Meade.

Tatiana throws herself down on a white leather sofa in the shade. A huge table is surrounded by twelve – Mercedes counts them, silently – bucket chairs also covered in white leather, and in its centre sits an urn of flowers and a huge bowl filled with fruit.

Her head fills with questions. How do they keep this clean? How are these flowers so fresh and yet so clearly not from here? Why are there no flies on that fruit? Why doesn't it rot, sitting out in this heat? And what do they do in bad weather? That table is bolted down, but nothing else is. What do they do when there's a storm? Where do they *put* it all?

Beyond the table, part of the glass wall slides back, and she glimpses the salon within. A thick patterned carpet, a host of padded seats upholstered in red velvet. A bar behind which a hundred bottles sit, held in by brass rails. A glass-fronted refrigerator that reaches the ceiling, filled with racks of bottles. A TV screen the size of her bedroom wall.

She is hit by a blast of cold, cold air. Then a steward steps into her sightline and the glass slides to, and her view is cut off. The glass is tinted. It hides the interior from eyes like hers.

The steward has dark skin and flat cheekbones and looks as though he too comes from an island – only one far, far away. Tatiana, lying down and gazing up at the canopy, doesn't even look at him. 'Coke,' she says. 'Full fat. None of that diet shit.'

'On its way,' he replies. 'And for you, *madame*?'

Madame. It takes her a moment to realise that he is addressing her. She stutters, then asks for a Pepsi-Cola, trying to sound as though it's something she drinks every day. 'Please,' she mutters, awkwardly. It feels all wrong. A child giving orders to an adult.

'And something to eat?' asks the steward, and she is flailing again. She doesn't know what to ask for.

He sees her discomfort and takes pity.

'There is some very good cheesecake,' he says, 'left over from lunch.'

Feeling like a rabbit in the headlights, she nods. '*Mersi*,' she mutters. She glances over the guard rail and sees her father on the edge of the Re del Pesce terrace, fists on hips, talking to a figure bundled up in black. He is frowning. He looks up, and out over the water, and nods. The grapevine has reached him already, she thinks. He'll have words for me when I get home.

'Pop Tart,' says Tatiana behind her back. 'Strawberry. And some prosciutto. And grapes. Sit down, Mercy, do.'

Mercy? Is this what she thinks my name is?

She's too timid to correct her. Perches nervously on the edge of the sofa nearest hers.

'You don't need the pleases and thank-yous, by the way,' says Tatiana. 'They're *servants*, for God's sake. We literally *pay* them, yuh?'

Movement in the bathtub. Matthew Meade is sitting up. He calls out, and his voice is *basso*, like a funeral bell.

'Hello, darling! Are you back?'

'Yah,' calls Tatiana.

'Good time?'

'Yah,' she replies. 'Snorkelling.'

With a great suck of water he lumbers, dripping, to his feet.

Mercedes is mesmerised. His clothes are so well cut that when she's seen him before he's merely looked imposing. Sometimes fat. But not fat like this. Matthew Meade is fully, morbidly obese. As he manoeuvres himself from the water and gravity takes hold, his chest slides downwards to form two breasts that put her mother's to shame. And though his skin is tanned a solid teak, she sees undulations of cellulite from his shoulders all the way to the waistband of his gigantic shorts. An apron of flesh beneath the cloth plumps the shorts out and drags the waistband down, rests on the tops of incongruously skinny thighs.

He heaves himself over the edge of the tub and bends to

140

retrieve a towel from where it lies on a sun lounger. It's a large towel, large enough to wrap her own body twice, but he strains to tuck it in on itself as he walks towards them. He is looking at her as he comes, and for a moment Mercedes feels an urge to flee back the way she came.

And then he smiles.

'Well, well,' he says. 'And who do we have here, then?'

19

'Her own bathroom? On a *boat*?'

There is nothing more delicious than your sophisticated older sister being impressed by what you've seen. Usually, after a long night's work, the last thing she wants to do is sit up and talk. But Donatella is bolt upright in bed, sheet over her knees, white cotton nightdress, brushing her hair as she pumps her for information.

Mercedes nods. 'But also,' she says, 'she has a wardrobe you can *walk into*.'

'On a *boat*?'

'And it's full. Completely full. She hasn't just brought a suitcase. She says it gets changed out every season.'

'Completely?'

'Completely.'

'*Oao*.' Donatella's mouth hangs open. She tips a drop of olive oil onto her palm from the little decanted bottle that lives by her bedside, runs it over the bristles of the brush, continues to groom. 'And what happens to the old ones?'

She hadn't asked. She'd been too busy gazing at the summer dresses her new friend had carelessly pressed into her hands. Fine, heavy cotton. One white with watermelons. One green, with orchids. And a shift made of some unbelievably soft, light material, in a rich magenta purple. The cotton dresses are cut far too low and the shift is obscenely short, but she's sure her mother will think of some way to adapt them. You never turn down a gift on La Kastellana.

'I don't know,' she says.

'God, you're so *lucky*,' says Donatella. 'I can't believe you got so lucky. And I can't believe she pissed on you.'

'Don't tell Mama.'

'Sure,' says Donatella, 'I'm going to tell Mama you were looking at some girl's minge. So what was he like?'

'Who?'

'The father.'

She's not sure what to answer. She's not sure what she thinks. He was welcoming enough, this man. All smiles and treats. *Go on, Mercedes. The best chocolate in the world. Chef flies them in from London. The filling is made with fresh cream and he has to store them in the fridge. These little macarons? From Paris. Rosewater. What do you think? Good, eh?* And all the time he fed her, she felt as though she was being tested. That there was some agenda she didn't understand. As if he was being watched.

'Friendly,' she says.

'But?'

Oh, how did you get so smart? 'I'm not sure I like him,' she confesses.

'Well, I don't suppose you have to. It's the girl you want to be friends with.'

Mercedes thinks. 'True.'

'So what else did you do?'

'Watched TV,' she replies airily, as though watching TV were an everyday experience.

'TV? On a *boat*?'

Mercedes bounces a little. 'A *huge* TV! Like, the size of the wall! And she has one in her cabin, too! Imagine!'

'But how do they ...?'

There is no TV where they live. No money. No signal.

'That ... you know that thing on the top? The thing that looks like a huge plate?'

Donatella nods.

'It talks to a satellite,' she says. 'It tells them where they are and it gets TV.'

Donatella heaves a huge sigh. '*Oao*. What must it be like to be rich, eh? Imagine!'

'She says the duke has one too. In the battlements.'

'*No!*'

'Yes.'

Mercedes is loving her new-found knowledge. 'It's another world,' she says. 'Out on the deck everything is white, and not a speck of dirt. And at the very back, there's this great big tub of water that *bubbles*!'

'*Jacuzzi!*' cries Donatella. 'They have a *jacuzzi*!'

She's a bit annoyed. 'How do you know that word?'

'A magazine. At school. You should try reading them. Oh, I'd love to try a jacuzzi. They massage you, apparently. You must go in. Mercedes, promise me you'll go in!'

She's not sure she wants to. Matthew Meade has been in there, after all.

'So when are you seeing her again?'

'You make it sound like a date!'

'Whatever. Did she say? Did she ask?'

'Soon.'

'Tomorrow?'

'God, no. Papa will kill me if I miss another shift.'

'No, but,' says Donatella, 'this is different. He'll love it! Imagine! Our family! Hanging out with people like that!'

Gemma

July 2015

20

She's looking at herself in the window of Alexander McQueen when she notices the woman standing behind her. Staring. And she's about to give her the can-I-help-you response when she thinks, Oh, hang on. She's familiar. Wasn't she in Monsoon? And Selfridges?

Oh, God, is she a store detective? Did she see me?

Gemma stops admiring her cheekbones and focuses on the green leather corset belt directly in her eyeline. Her face burns. Self-consciously, she shifts her bag on her shoulder. That MAC colour palette suddenly weighs as much as a baby.

She turns, casual as she can, and starts to walk away up Old Bond Street towards the tube.

'Excuse me?'

Don't look, don't look. If you look, that's as good as saying you feel guilty.

She keeps on walking. Subtly, oh, so subtly, steps up her pace.

'Excuse me!' the woman cries again.

Gemma takes a stick of gum from her pocket, unwraps it, casually throws the wrapper into the gutter and walks on, chewing. Goddammit, she thinks, God*damm*it, I swear I will never shoplift again. It's boredom as much as anything else. And if they'd let me have my winnings I wouldn't have to, would I? With everyone else away on their holidays there's literally nothing to do. But I swear. I'll find a job, like Mum said. God, if you let me get away, I'll work the whole summer in Kentucky Fried—

'Oh, please!' cries the voice. 'Please wait! I just want to talk to you!'

Gemma composes her face so that she looks both unconcerned and a little bit fierce, tosses her curls, and turns to meet her fate.

'Me?' she asks, and the squeak in her voice betrays her nerves.

The woman is rather beautiful, for an old person. She has long hair, striped in all shades of taupe, and her hands and wrists, her neck and ears, drip gold. Her dress is so plain and simple it can only be expensive, and is an unambiguous red that only someone unafraid of standing out would wear. And it's silk, thinks Gemma. Okay, she's no store detective.

'Yes!'

The woman smiles. Dark eyes. Beautifully shaped eyebrows – not too big, not too thin, not too arched; just *perfect* – and skin like marble. Her cheeks dimple, but nothing creases around her eyes. Gemma's seen a lot of Botox in her time, on the TV and on the red-carpet vids on YouTube, and can tell it when she sees it. Her mum's always going on about people's smiles never reaching their eyes, but in Gemma's view that's just a sign of being able to afford a beautician.

150

She decides that saying nothing is probably her best bet. She stands outside Van Cleef & Arpels, and waits for the woman to speak.

'I noticed you in Selfridges,' she says, eventually, then stops and laughs. 'God, that sounds creepy as hell! Sorry. I just wanted to – I'm Julia Beech.'

The name means nothing. Gemma does a little shrug and a shake of the head.

'Sorry. I'm a model agent. I run the Beech Agency.'

Gemma frowns, but a little spark of excitement lights up in her tummy.

'It's a model agency?' Julia adds, unnecessarily.

'Oh, yes?' says Gemma, trying to sound as though this sort of thing happens every day.

'I – listen, I know this sounds like one of those things you read about in *Hello!* ...'

Gemma blinks. *Hello!* Puh-*lease*. What do you think I am, forty?

'... but have you ever thought of modelling?'

What?

Julia laughs, and Gemma realises that her mouth has fallen open.

'I'm not tall enough,' she says, 'surely?'

'Oh, darling, not *runway*. There's a ton of other sorts of work. Have you never thought about it? You're so pretty.'

'I'm still at school,' stutters Gemma.

A confusing little look – what looks for a moment like a micro-gloat – passes across Julia's face, and then she smiles more broadly.

'That's fine,' she says. 'Lots of our girls start when they're still at school. It takes a while to get trained up.'

'I – I'll have to ask my mum,' says Gemma.

As if. She hasn't spoken to her mum in three days. Not since she took her iPhone away. She's not telling her *shit*.

I'll be able to buy my own bloody iPhone if I'm a model, she thinks. And my own clothes. Nobody will be able to tell me what to do if I have my own money.

'Of course. Of *course*. Look, let me give you my card ...' The woman fishes in her pocket, brings out a smart little silver card case and opens it. Gemma stares at her shapely French manicure and the rings on her fingers. 'And you can talk to your mum and give me a call, yes?'

Gemma takes the card and glances at it, trying to look casual. *Beech Models*, it says across the top in bold black letters, then *Julia Beech, partner*, and a phone number.

This sort of thing doesn't happen to people like me, she thinks.

Julia smiles again. 'Don't worry,' she says. 'Look me up on the internet. I'm kosher. You'll see photos.'

'Okay,' says Gemma. She gets her phone back in two days. She can look her up then.

'Anyway, I'll let you get on with your day,' says Julia Beech. 'I just couldn't walk away without at least trying. You've got a special look. I really think you could be special.'

Gemma glows. Being special isn't something that happens to her much. Take that, Naz Khan, she thinks. Swanning about, batting the eyelashes your parents *pay* for every month. Nobody's approached *you* to be a model.

'If you get through to someone else, tell them I gave you my card.'

Julia turns abruptly on her spike heel and starts to walk away towards Piccadilly. Gemma stays rooted to the pavement, looking down and up between card and retreating back. Julia looks back just once.

'And enjoy that MAC palette,' she says, and winks. 'Hopefully you'll be able to *buy* one soon.'

She walks away.

Well, thinks Gemma, that's a Thing.

She puts the card into the pocket of her denim jacket and heads back to Oxford Street. The new season stuff is in in Zara, and she hopes it'll be crowded enough that something for Saturday night could make its way into her bag without anybody noticing.

21

Of course she checks it out. She's not stupid. As soon as she gets her phone back, she does a mad Google and up the agency pops, totally legit. Not just its own website, but, if you hit the images tab, there are thousands and thousands of shots of catwalks and cover pages, of fashion spreads in everything from tabloids to glossies, with agency credits for the models. And when you search Julia Beech, almost as many turn up. Smiling with models and actresses (no 'I'm an ac*tor*' types in these pictures) whom even Gemma has heard of, smiling with CEOs and directors and magazine editors and jewel-encrusted women. Smiling in front of white backdrops covered in names and logos of luxury brands. Smiling on sun-filled terraces overlooking the sea, in banqueting halls where the chandeliers are the size of spaceships.

That's a lot of trouble to go to, to pull off a scam, she thinks. That Julia has a proper glamorous life. And she dials the number on the business card and calls her. The old-fashioned way, like it's still the twentieth century.

*

It's in a mews house in South Kensington. Old stable doors filled in with plate glass, the interior screened off from the outside world by vertical blinds. She walks past a couple of times, uncertain, because she'd never have imagined that a business dedicated to showing people off would itself be so discreet. But, as she comes back up the mews for the third time, the door opens and the longest, thinnest girl she's ever seen comes out. More tribal carving than human being. She carries a gigantic portfolio under a broomstick arm.

Yes, this must be it, thinks Gemma, and feels short and dumpy as she watches the girl walk towards the tube. There must be a mistake, she thinks. Naz is right. I'm not tall enough. Not nearly. And I'm a size ten, for God's sake; I'm *huge*. But she presses the buzzer beneath the discreet chrome plate that reads, in small letters, 'JB Ltd' anyway, because hope outweighs reality, always.

A bored voice answers. 'Julia Beech,' it says.

'I'm Gemma Hanson,' she says. 'I, um, have an appointment?'

A pause. 'Who with?'

'With Julia,' she says proudly. 'Julia Beech.'

Another pause, then something heavy clunks inside the blond wood door. It glides open beneath her touch.

Be cool, Gems. Be cool.

A woman with a black bob and scarlet lipstick looks her up and down from behind a desk. 'What time were you meant to be here?'

'Three. I'm a bit early.'

'Yes, you are.'

She could swear she sees an eye-roll as the woman turns away to look at a printed list on the desk. Isn't that right? Isn't that what you're meant to do? It's pretty much the only advice she's ever had from her school careers counsellor. That, and clean fingernails. And how polished shoes never go unnoticed.

'Never mind,' says the woman, 'you can wait over there,' and she points to a small square of modular sofas gathered around a coffee table. Two girls already sit there, leafing through copies of *Vogue* and *Marie Claire*. The French one. Which she's heard is better than the English.

The office is weirdly quiet, though she can see that all of the half-dozen people manning the desks are on their phones. Clever acoustics. She smiles shyly at the receptionist and receives a blank stare in response.

She feels like a fairground exhibit in her stolen Zara dress. The other girls are studiedly casual. Jeans, trainers, vest tops, little cardigans in jewel hues to warm their fleshless bodies. No make-up, skin smooth as alabaster, glossy hair tied back at their napes. I must look a twat, she thinks. Everything about me screams *first visit*.

She picks up a copy of *Vogue* and, using it for cover, surreptitiously wipes off her lipstick. Not much she can do about the hours of contouring she put in this morning. But at least she can get rid of that gauche little Cupid's bow.

Someone stands up. A man, thirties, wispy chin beard and round hipster glasses. He picks up a folder, stretches and approaches. Gemma tenses. He comes and stands behind her as she feverishly scans a double-page fashion spread, trying to look *blasé*.

'Naomi?' says the man, and one of the girls composes her mouth into a little round O as though she too has only just noticed him. She gets up and there's some stuff with air kisses, and then he leads her away to a panel door hidden behind a potted plant.

156

Gemma smiles timidly at her remaining companion, who glances at her for one moment, tucks her chin in and returns to her magazine.

Well, fuck you too.

A glass staircase leads to the first floor. People go up and down, up and down. And still no Julia. Her snotty companion is led away, and a black girl so shiny she looks as if she's been dipped in quicksilver takes her place, and her magazine.

This is hopeless, Gemma thinks. I'm too ordinary. I'm Clapham-pretty, not International-Goddess-pretty like those girls. I'm average height. I'm thin-for-Clapham, not South Ken thin. That girl's ankles wouldn't support anything heavier than a pussycat. I bet her knees are thicker than her thighs.

'Gemma?'

She jumps. Julia Beech must have come in through the front door. The day is hot, but she looks cool and composed in a mint-green shift dress, bronzed legs finished off with a pair of matching stiletto mules. Diamonds on her earlobes, on her knuckles.

Gemma drops her *Vogue* onto the table and scrambles to her feet. There's a woman with her, an identically cut dress in cowboy gingham and a witty little hoedown handkerchief knotted at the side of her neck. A *real* tan, bright blue eyes, a little chin so neat it has to have been sculpted that way, a pixie haircut. The first short hair Gemma has seen since she came through this door.

'Oh, *yes*,' the woman says, appreciatively, 'I see what you mean.'

'So sorry,' says Julia. 'Lunch went on longer than we meant.'

'Blame me,' says her companion. 'Everybody does.'

157

Gemma wonders if she's going to be expected to do the whole air-kissing thing, but Julia just turns towards the staircase. 'I hope you don't mind,' she calls over her shoulder. 'My business partner's in town for the day. She's going to sit in with us, if that's okay.'

The woman nods to indicate that she is said partner, gives her a reassuring smile and holds out a hand. 'Tatiana Meade,' she says.

'Oh, hi,' says Gemma. 'Gemma Hanson.'

'Hanson? You're not one of . . . ?'

'Those Hansons?' says Gemma. 'I wish.'

The upstairs office is a drawing room. All big sofas and heavy drapes. A crystal chandelier, an ivory backgammon set, a naked marble woman in one corner. A haughty Siamese cat looks up from a cushion, gives Gemma the once-over, finds her wanting and goes back to sleep.

'What a lovely room,' says Gemma. It's a bit old for her tastes, in all honesty, but there's no point being rude. 'I do love a Knole sofa,' she lies.

'You know what a Knole sofa is?' asks Tatiana. She seems amused.

'My stepmother has one,' she says.

'Ah,' says Tatiana. She sits down while Julia picks up a folder from the desk. Gemma hovers for a moment, then decides she's probably meant to sit as well.

'Two, actually,' she blurts, because she has a sudden need to let them know that there are Big Rooms in her life.

Julia opens a desk drawer and brings out a bottle and a tube of cotton wool pads. Picks up a magnifying mirror from the windowsill and brings it all over to where Gemma sits.

'Now, if you don't mind,' she says, 'if you could take that make-up off, so we can see what we're working with?'

Gemma squirms with embarrassment, but obediently picks up the bottle. Smears some of its contents over her face, and starts wiping. The cotton wool comes away khaki and orange and dirty taupe, and she feels embarrassed again at the obviousness of her preparations.

'I look about twelve without it,' she warns them.

Julia picks up a Polaroid instant camera from the desk and walks about, popping off shots from different angles as Gemma wipes.

'We'll be the judge of that,' says Tatiana. 'And besides, young-looking can be very profitable. So tell me, Gemma, how old are you *actually*?'

'Sixteen,' she says.

'Now, you are telling the truth, aren't you?' asks Julia.

'Yes,' she says, a bit offended.

'Only we do need to know. It does make a difference. Legally. If you're below a certain age you need a chaperone.'

'And a tutor if you're going to miss a lot of school,' says Tatiana.

'Nothing we couldn't get around, of course,' says Julia, 'but it's as well to know now, rather than finding ourselves in a bind because you didn't tell us. And, you know – it's good to know you're truthful. From the start.'

'Yes,' she protests. She hates looking this young. 'I'm sixteen! Really!'

Julia waves a photo in the air to develop, then slips it into the Perspex window on the front of the folder. Gets out a pen. 'Date of birth?'

Is that a test? Gemma tells her. She writes it down on the front of the folder, beside where Gemma's name is already printed in thick black marker pen.

'And what stage are you at, at school, Gemma?' asks Tatiana.

'Waiting for my GCSE results.' She finishes with her face, puts the lid back on the bottle. Casts around for a place to put the used pads. She's about to put them into what she guesses is an ashtray when Julia sticks a manicured hand out in front of her, palm up.

'Ooh, exciting,' says Tatiana. 'How many did you do?'

'Eight.'

'Okay, so you're not thick, then.'

Gemma feels a bit mournful. 'Most of my friends did ten. And my friend Hattie did thirteen.'

'Not all at once!'

'No. She did two last year,' she says. 'My mum was pissed off with me that I didn't, too.'

A tiny hiatus. Something about the mention of her mother has caught their interest.

'I only got seven, of course,' says Tatiana, and there's more of a hint of *and now look at me* about the way she says it. 'So ... sixth form?'

Julia starts shooting her again.

'*They* want me to,' she says gloomily.

'But you don't?'

She pulls a face. The prospect of going back to school, back into having her day divided up by the ringing of a bell, makes her glum. She longs for life to start properly. To no longer be stuck doing what her parents say because they're the ones with the money.

'Darling,' Tatiana looks up at Julia, 'I don't suppose there's any chance of a glass of fizz, is there?'

'Darling, of course!'

Julia puts the camera down and opens one of the cupboards that line the wall behind the desk. Inside is a fully stocked bar. A row of the sorts of branded alcohol her dad and Caroline keep at home. A collection of glasses sparkles under the spots inset in the ceiling. A black leather ice bucket, a set of chrome bar-keep's tools. She opens a little fridge and brings out a bottle of Krug. Collects three flutes and brings them over.

'I assume you'll be joining us?' She flashes a charming smile.

'I ... ' Is this another test?

Tatiana laughs. 'Oh, darling. We won't tell if you don't!'

Julia pops the cork and fills the glasses. 'After all, we have something to celebrate. Just chew some gum on your way home.' She hands her a glass. It is full almost to the brim.

'So what are your ambitions, Gemma?' Tatiana holds out her glass to clink and puts it to her mouth. She doesn't purse her lips the way Gemma usually sees women do when drinking from a flute; but nothing escapes as she tips champagne between her lips. If Gemma's mum tried that, it would be all down her front.

Gemma takes a sip. It's unlike anything she's tasted before. Not like the fizz she's drunk at weddings, not like the sour stuff her parents used to open at Christmas. A million miles from that carbonated plonk Naz swears by – prosecco. It's dry, but not the sort of dry that makes you pucker. And the bubbles are tiny. There – definitely there – but not-there. Like a ghostly memory of bubbles on her tongue.

'I don't know,' she says reluctantly. She's so used to her dreams being pooh-poohed, she doesn't really want to expose herself to another round.

'Well, obviously you want to be a model,' says Julia.

'Well, yes,' she says. Braces herself and adds, 'Maybe an actress more, though.'

Both women smile. 'Yes, good,' says Tatiana. 'I can see that.'

161

'To be honest, you're a bit on the short side for modelling,' says Julia. 'Though I'm sure there's work for you. While you establish yourself.'

'Catalogues and that,' says Gemma, and takes another sip of the lovely, lovely wine.

They both laugh. 'Oh, darling! The Beech Agency isn't in the *catalogue* market!' says Tatiana.

'It'll do you no harm, though,' says Julia. 'A bit of modelling. Spot of spokesmodelling. Wearing people's collections at social things. You'd be surprised how much the designers sell that way, rather than at shows. Going to a few parties. A lot of buyers like to see the collections on real people rather than beanpoles. And of course, good clothes show *you* right off. We know lots of people in showbiz, don't we, Tat?'

'Can't get away from them,' says Tatiana.

'Put your face about,' says Julia. 'Meet a few people.'

'The trick is to let them see the clothes on girls they don't realise are prettier than they are,' says Tatiana.

'It's not *what* you know, it's *who* you know,' says Gemma, suddenly, and both women laugh again, as though they find her genuinely amusing. This is fun, she thinks. As the wine warms her inside, she feels her confidence grow.

'So what does your boyfriend think,' Tatiana asks, 'about this actress idea?'

Gemma thinks about Nathan. His hand in her hair, his smirk in the mirror. Not doing that again. 'Haven't got one,' she says. 'I want to concentrate on my career right now.'

The words sound so grand. So much better than the truth.

'Very wise,' says Tatiana.

'Always good to find out what's out there before you settle,' says Julia. 'And your mum? What does she think?'

Gemma puffs out her cheeks, blows a curl off her forehead.

'That good, eh?' asks Julia. 'Does she even know you're here?'

'You. Are. Kidding?' replies Gemma. 'I don't tell her fucking *anything*, man. All she ever wants to do is harsh my buzz.'

Wednesday

22 | Mercedes

'So are you going down to the *festa*?'

She claps her hand to her heart. 'Jesus, Paulo! You have to stop doing that! I swear you'll kill me!'

Paulo grins. 'Not if you're not doing anything wrong.'

For such a solid-set man, he is remarkably light on his feet. A primary qualification for a security specialist, she guesses. To not be noticed until it's too late.

'Yes,' she says. 'I always go down. I'll be working. In the restaurant. It's one of the biggest nights of the year.'

'I can imagine. And your man?'

'Yeah, him too. You're going?'

Paulo shakes his head. 'On duty.'

'Oh, shame.'

She turns back to the heart-leaf philodendron whose leaves she has been wiping over with a mix of water and furniture polish. His reflection in the window shrugs. On the far side, Tatiana's four girls frolic in the pool in little string bikinis while their host rests against the cushioned back of a sun lounger and swipes at the screen of her mobile phone.

'Goes with the territory,' he says. 'Roberto and I are going to watch from the roof terrace.'

'Ah, yes. It's a good view from there.'

'Yeah. He's got a lovely bit of fillet steak and a bottle of some German stuff that wine merchant dropped off. Freebie. Steak sandwiches, on panini. Béarnaise to soften it all up.'

'Superb,' she says.

'I'm surprised you're not going to be at your da's.'

Her turn to shrug. She wouldn't go to Mediterraneo, with its panoramic view of church and marina and harbour wall and its VIP party, even if her father paid her. And he isn't.

'He's got all the staff he needs,' she says. 'My mama's the one who will be overwhelmed.'

'*Mamasita*,' he says, vaguely. 'I'll be dropping Her Royal Highness and her ducklings off at nine and then I'm done till they are.'

'But the Saint will be out by then!' she protests. 'The streets will be closed!'

A cynical laugh. 'As if she'd let that get in her way.'

He comes and stands beside her and watches their guests at play. They've grown companionable over the clutch of years they've known each other. He's easy to be around, with his jaundiced eye and his wry asides. I trust him, she thinks. What an irony, when I can trust no one here at all. What would he think, if he knew that I was doing the very things he's employed to prevent?

'Well, they're certainly more decorative than last week's lot,' he says.

Wei-Cheng. Sara. Gemma. Hanne. All seventeen years old, except for Hanne, whose passport shows that she turned sixteen three months ago. It's so – *calculated*. It would almost be less disturbing if the odd unchecked fifteen-year-old slipped through the net. But every girl who comes here is always legal, even if it's just by a few days.

Paulo watches in his detached way. Mercedes has never really known what he thinks, and has never asked. If she knew the answer, what then? Would she like him more, or less? Trust him more, or less? They are all tainted, in their way. Anyone who works in these houses, on these boats. She knows she is.

'Yes,' she replies. They are lovely, these little girls. Like kittens, or puppies; still filled with that electric aliveness that adulthood drains away. Skin that needs no nurture, muscles that ripple without help from personal trainers. The women they hosted last week were glossy, fragrant, perfected over decades. But no surgeon, however skilled, will ever achieve with art what nature achieves every single day, and that's the thing these old men seek.

She sighs. 'And yet I wouldn't be young again,' she says.

'Oh, I would,' says Paulo. 'Like a shot.'

'We had different youths, I suppose.'

'I guess maybe growing up in a beautiful place like this you feel as though you *got* a youth,' he says.

So funny, the assumptions people make, Mercedes thinks, when all they see is sea and sunshine.

'It must get pretty small, though. Do you never want to see the world?'

Mercedes shrugs. She's not had a holiday in thirty years. 'I see quite a lot of the outside world here,' she says. 'I'm not sure how much more I need to see.'

Paulo laughs. 'They're not all like the people you see here. Not even the rich ones.'

She pulls a doubtful face.

'Truly. Your duke, he's been encouraging a certain type of people. The ones who buy yachts. And the ones who want to be around the ones who buy yachts. And helicopters. And private planes. And private islands. There's plenty of rich people who don't have 'em. Seriously: someone wants these things, they're making a statement.'

'A statement?'

'Sure. They're not just saying they can afford it. They're putting walls around themselves, aren't they?'

She glances at the girls. Nuno has brought out a tray of fruity cocktails – strawberry daiquiris from the slushy, crushed-ice look of them – and they rush gleefully towards him the way the kids in town swarm the *xelado* man when he appears on the beach. Tatiana, elegant with a silk pareo tied around her waist and a huge-brimmed hat preserving her complexion, smiles indulgently and raises her phone up to point at them. Filming. She'll be sending that on to someone, thinks Mercedes. Like a shopping catalogue.

'So people can't see in,' she says.

'Yeah,' says Paulo. Pauses. 'And, once they're in, they can't get out.'

She glances at him sharply. Yes, she thinks, you may be affable, but you're still an essential part of it all. I must never forget that. You're not a helpless serf, devoid of choices.

Tatiana says something to the girls and they all stop drinking. Put their glasses down, half-drunk, and rush together for the door, like a flock of starlings. Ignore her as they go past. Always they ignore her, the guests here. They deal with the discomfort of not really knowing how to speak to her by pretending she's not there at all.

She hears their laughter recede up the back stairs. Feels sad for a second.

'I must get on,' she says.

'Me too,' he replies.

'Mercy!'

Tatiana is still on her sun lounger. She can't avoid her any longer.

'Oh, hi!' she says, all warmth and smiles. 'Are you not getting changed?'

'Oh, God, not for a bit. One of the advantages of ageing is you've got all that stuff down pat. It takes those girls an hour just to do their make-up. And the rest. I swear they're blind, though. That Gemma had actual *pubes* coming round the edge of her bikini bottoms! I had to send her up to sort it out. Can you imagine?'

Mercedes keeps her counsel. She doesn't understand this obsession with body hair. All these grown women stripping every one away to make themselves look like eight-year-olds. Plenty of time to be bald when I'm old, she thinks.

Tatiana has had every hair below her nose killed by laser, to streamline her self-maintenance. 'I'm as bald as an egg,' she said once, proudly. Another intimacy that Mercedes could have done without hearing. And now that they're all bald like porcelain dolls, their men, of course, are bound to develop a taste for hairy women, sooner or later. Just because they *can*. And the women trapped in the hairless generation will be hunting out merkins on the internet.

'Honestly,' says Tatiana, 'I just wanted a few moments to myself. They're exhausting! God, darling, were *we* that bad?'

You were, thinks Mercedes. I was just dumb.

She collects a couple of glasses, puts them on her tray and smiles. Cleaning up after teenagers, cleaning up after the rich: same-same. Rich people are just like children. They drop things when they're done with them and leave them for the magic pixies to pick up.

'I'd kill for a nice clean vodka, lime and soda,' says Tatiana.

Mercedes goes to the bell discreetly attached to the rear of a pillar, presses it, and carries on towards the other glasses. Nuno can take them when he comes.

'Nuno'll come,' she says.

'Oh, and can you tell your underling – what's her name? – to lay out the Versace?' asks Tatiana. 'The one with the snakes?'

'Ursula,' she says. 'Of course.'

Tatiana sits up. 'Darling! Come and *talk* to me! I've not seen you in centuries!'

She may claim to seek peace and quiet, but she always bores quickly without an audience. Mercedes hides a sigh, collects the glasses, puts the tray down on a little table and goes over to perch on the edge of the lounger next to Tatiana's. She smooths her skirt over her thighs, crosses her ankles. Smiles and smiles.

'So tell me all about *you*,' says Tatiana. 'Did I tell you that that bloody Nora Neibergall just walked off the job? Literally left me high and dry in New York. Can you believe it? I bloody nearly didn't make the plane because I had no idea where my passport was!'

'Oh, poor you,' says Mercedes. 'Where was it?'

Tatiana waves a dismissive hand. 'In my bag. But that's not the point. It's bad enough having to fly scheduled without – *people*. They just ... honestly, Mercy, I think you're literally the only person I can trust. Literally everyone else lets me down. You're so ... *reliable*.'

'Your father,' she says.

'Oh, well, Daddy, *obviously*. But all of the rest of them,

172

it's only a matter of time. Literally all of them. I can't rely on *anyone*.'

Yes, she thinks. Everyone tires of being bought and sold. Everyone.

'So what's been going on in Mercedes World? Any love on the horizon?'

'Same as ever—' begins Mercedes, and Tatiana interrupts.

'Well, you're probably very wise.'

Mercedes smiles, and smooths her skirt. You may own my time, she thinks, but you don't get to own my private life.

'I mean, God knows. Men. More trouble than they're worth, honestly. I don't know why I bother. But you don't . . . Mercedes, I wouldn't mind, you know. You don't think I'd mind, do you?'

'Oh, no,' she says.

'Because you mustn't. Of *course* I want you to have a life. It would be totally doable, you know. I suppose you don't meet people much, though. How about the people here? How about that Paulo? He's pretty lush.'

Mercedes laughs. 'He's married.'

'Is he? Oh. Shame.'

'Everyone here is married.'

Tatiana wrinkles her nose, misses what she's just said. 'Well, you're still an attractive woman, you know, Mercedes. Never say never, eh?'

'No,' says Mercedes.

'Whatever happened to that chubby boy who used to follow you around like a sheep? He was okay.'

She smiles inside. He never left, Tatiana. If you ever paid attention, you'd know that. 'Felix Marino?'

'If you say so.'

'He's still around,' she says. 'Still fishing. He's getting the lobsters for your dinner on Friday.'

173

As a diversionary tactic, it's perfect. Tatiana instantly forgets about Mercedes' personal life. Easy. So easy. Just divert the conversation to her personal comforts, and you're done.

'Oh, God, really? Lobster *again*? You need to have a word with the chef.'

'Oh,' says Mercedes.

'Honestly. It's like he's never heard of sashimi.'

'That might be my fault,' says Mercedes. 'I told him your father loved them when he first came here. I remember him saying he never wanted to eat anything else. Maybe I took him too literally?'

'Oh!' Tatiana stops. Changes tack. 'Oh. Well. He is a bit of a dinosaur, Daddy.'

And he who pays the piper ... Tatiana might be princess, but Matthew, in this household, is still king.

Deep in the house, the buzzer sounds. The front gate, from the tone. A few seconds later, the door to Paulo's quarters opens and he heads up the path, pulling on his jacket as he goes.

'Are we expecting someone?' she asks. With no Nora to keep track, there's every chance that there are guests that Tatiana's failed to mention. Please let it not be, she thinks. The bedrooms are all ready, but Tatiana can't be expected to show her guests the way to them herself. I'm already an hour late getting down to town. They're going to be worrying that I'm not coming.

A little shake of the costly head. Tatiana stretches her arms up and poses in the cooling sun like a Fifties mannequin.

'So you haven't asked a thing about *me*,' she says. No interest in the doorbell. Everything someone else's problem. 'Don't you want to know if *I've* got a boyfriend?'

An announcement, not a question. Mercedes leafs through

the guest list in her head. Presumably one of the houseguests. The prince? No. Since his divorce he has never been seen in the company of a woman his own age. The film producer? Could be. She's looked him up on the internet, and he looks as though his ancestors have evolved after spending fifty generations underground. Though a private plane can improve a man's attractiveness a lot. Then she glances at Tatiana and sees that she's batting her eyelashes coquettishly. She's clearly pleased with herself.

The actor. It has to be the superannuated movie star. 'Jason Pettit?'

Tatiana blinks and looks smug.

'*Nooo!*'

She gets the tone right. Just impressed enough, but not so much that it gives the impression she doesn't think Tatiana could pull a film star.

'You're not to say a *thing*,' says Tatiana. 'It's early days, and he's terribly paranoid about the papers.'

'Of course! Of course!' Apart from to Laurence, maybe. And her mother, for she tells Larissa most things. And Felix, of course, because he likes a laugh.

'And for God's sake tell the other maids not to pester him for autographs. He's here on holiday. He doesn't need a load of fangirls fawning over him.'

Mercedes nods solemnly. She remembers Jason Pettit from the 1990s. His stock-in-trade romantic comedies were seen as wholesome enough for the monthly screenings in the market square. But she doubts Ursula and Stefanie will have more than the vaguest notion of who he is. They're only in their thirties, after all, and he's been desperately giving speeches about global warming and social justice in pursuit of profile for a good fifteen years.

'I'll make sure of it,' she assures her, with confidence.

'And the prince, of course. They know to curtsey, don't they?'

'They do. We'll curtsey as though he were the duke,' she says, and Tatiana laughs.

Paulo comes back and stands in the doorway. They look up.

'Sorry, Ms Meade,' he says. 'Wine merchant's here.'

'What?' Tatiana looks at her dainty little gold watch. 'Darling,' she says to Mercedes, 'can you deal with it? I *have* to get into the bath.'

Laurence has a box of Krug in his hands. Grins when she steps onto the road.

'Sorry,' he says. 'This fell out of your consignment.'

Paulo, confident that she can defend herself against a vintner, wanders away.

'Thank you so much!' she says loudly. 'That's so kind. We might not even have noticed, to be honest!'

'Well, that's as may be, but I'd be beating myself up forever anyway,' he says.

As he puts it into her waiting hands, he leans towards her ear and says, quietly, 'And I need to talk to you.'

'Not here,' she says.

'Okay,' he says. 'But soon. Will you be in town tonight?'

'Of course. I'll be at the restaurant. Working.'

'I'll come and find you.'

Please don't, she thinks. 'Okay,' she says.

Island

July 1985

23

She's sweeping the *terasa* when Tatiana turns up, beach bag on her arm and a lovely little sundress covered in toucans.

'Coming?' she asks.

'Sorry,' she replies cheerfully, 'not today. I working.'

Tatiana bursts out laughing.

Stops, abruptly.

'But I want you to show me that cave.' Her tone is incredulous. 'With the mermaids.'

'I sorry,' she says, regretfully. 'I cannot.'

In the bar, Larissa, replacing votive candles in the holders, stops singing and listens. Mercedes, sharply aware that she's under surveillance, starts to sweep again. Her late return yesterday wasn't appreciated. There's no way she's getting away today.

Oh, to spend the summer doing what you like. How blessed they are, these people. Such golden, fortunate lives.

Tatiana sounds annoyed when she speaks again. 'I thought we were friends,' she says.

We've only known each other two days.

'Sure,' she replies. 'But I have to clean the tables.'

'That's ridiculous,' says Tatiana. 'Don't you have *people* to do that stuff?'

Mercedes stops sweeping. 'We *are* the people who do that stuff.'

Tatiana raises her voice, petulantly. 'But it's *your* restaurant!'

'My papa's restaurant,' says Mercedes.

'Well, *exactly*,' says Tatiana.

She starts sweeping again. 'I would like. Sorry.'

She's about to stamp her foot, she thinks. She really is. 'But I *want* you to!' she says.

Mercedes shrugs. I wish I had the English, she thinks. To explain to this girl that other lives are different from hers. But I think maybe even if I did, she wouldn't really understand.

'So you don't want to be my friend?'

She stops sweeping again. 'No! No! I want! I just ... '

The glass door slides back. Larissa stares at them, arms folded. 'Mercedes?'

'Sorry, Mama.' She starts sweeping again.

'When you're done with that, come inside,' says Larissa. 'I want you where I can see you. You can polish the glasses.'

'*Si, jala,*' says Mercedes.

Larissa throws a sweet, chilly smile at the girl in the street and speaks in her faltering English. 'Hello! Today Mercedes working.'

Tatiana looks thunderous. Stands for a moment in the sunshine, glaring as though summoning a thunderbolt to smite Larissa from the clear blue sky. Then she turns on her heel and marches back to the yacht without another word.

Donatella brings the slops reservoir from the Gaggia to

empty into the bar sink. Larissa's attention swings away. '*L'ostia!*' she snaps. 'What's that on your face?'

'Lipstick,' says Donatella, and tips her chin in defiant self-congratulation.

Larissa begs St James to spare her from the *solteronas*. 'Well, wipe it off! The whole town is staring!'

Donatella looks around. The fishing boats went out at dawn and everyone else is indoors, in the shade, as any sane person would be in this heat. 'There's nobody here!'

'Don't answer back,' says Larissa. 'Get inside, for Jesus's sake. You look like a *puta*. I just thank God your father's still sleeping.'

Donatella's face drops and she goes inside.

Matthew Meade wobbles down the gangplank of the *Princess Tatiana* and walks towards the Re del Pesce. Mercedes, sorting receipts, sees him come and blushes. He is so ... *big*. On an island where constant work and limited diet have rendered the population wiry and short, he looks like Goliath striding through the Israelites.

He reaches the edge of the *terasa*. The brief walk has made sweat spring from his brow and he pauses to wipe it off with a handkerchief. He wears a formal shirt the size of a two-man tent, damp patches from pit to navel. He looks around the tables, spots Mercedes and gives her a little finger-waggle. Mercedes glances around to see if her parents are watching and quickly waves back. Then she bends her head to her task again, cheeks burning.

Donatella hasn't missed it, of course. 'I see your boyfriend's here,' she says. Mercedes kicks her ankle.

He ducks his head beneath the canopy and comes in.

Sergio's head snaps up. Meade has been in a few times, of

181

course. But the fact that he is alone suggests that something is afoot beyond griddled halibut and a bucket of fried potatoes. Sergio throws a tea towel over his shoulder – a sure sign that he feels uncertain, that he needs to assert his authority in his own premises – and goes to greet him with his big host's smile.

Matthew Meade offers her father a hand to shake. A new development. They talk in low voices, and the visitor gestures in her direction with his hand. Sergio shakes his head. Meade nods his. Sergio shakes again. Looks over at his daughter and frowns. Donatella develops a sudden interest in a nearby table.

Oh, God, I'm in trouble, Mercedes thinks. What have I done?

Meade says something more, and Sergio throws his hands out in incomprehension. 'No *inglis, sinjor*,' he says. 'No understand.'

Meade's voice is louder, now. Those commanding tones that carry, just like his daughter's. 'Spanish? *Italiano? Français?*'

Sergio shrugs again. She sees Meade mutter a *Chrissake*. 'Okay,' he says. 'I'll be back,' and he turns back to his boat exactly the way his daughter did earlier. *Our business is done for now, you do not matter to me.*

Sergio watches him go, then comes over to where Mercedes sits. 'Well!' he says.

'What?' she asks, nervously, but he seems in a cheerful enough mood.

'Well, he clearly likes *you*.'

Is that good, or bad? 'What did he say?'

'I don't know. I didn't really get what he was on about. If it wasn't crazy, I'd say he'd offered to buy you.'

He sees the astonishment on her face and laughs. Pinches

her cheek like the priest does to the good girls on St James's Day. 'Don't worry!' he says. 'I'll hold out for a good price!'

He goes indoors and Donatella comes over, perches on her table, long legs swinging, mischief in her grin. 'He really does, you know,' she says.

'Does what?'

'He wants to buy you for his daughter. Like a doll. Or a puppy.'

'What—?' she begins, but is interrupted by a louder, angrier '*What*?' from behind them. Larissa strides over, face purple. 'He said *what*?'

'My English isn't that good,' says Donatella, hastily. 'Maybe he was saying something else?'

Larissa's not having any of it. 'And what did your father say?'

'He asked how much,' says Donatella, po-faced. She can never resist an opportunity to wind the adults up.

Larissa gasps. Throws her cloth down and marches indoors. Oh, God, thinks Mercedes, there's going to be a fight, and eventually it'll be my fault and I won't be allowed out with Tatiana *ever*. She wishes, sometimes, that her mother were more docile, more Kastellani. But then, if her mother were more docile, their father's whims would rule them all.

Larissa's voice, raised.

Donatella grimaces. 'Sorry, Mersa,' she says. The pet name that she uses when she's trying to be nice.

'Dammit, Donita. You're *such* an arsehole. What did he *really* say?'

'That man? No, really. He was saying something about paying you to be his daughter's friend.'

Mercedes is stumped. She's never heard of such a thing. Isn't that the literal opposite of what a friend is?

'No, I . . .' she says. 'You're . . .'

Their father's voice, raised too, responds. Already they've started up with the *putas* and the *l'ostias,* and the scattering of customers is raising amused Anglosphere eyebrows. Donatella shrugs. 'Whatever. He said he'd come back later with someone to translate, so I guess we'll find out.'

Meade returns as the first tourists are coming in off the beaches looking for cold drinks and aloe for their sunburns. This time, he has an entourage. He has Tatiana with him, and Luna Micaleff, the duke's personal secretary. Sergio, lurking indoors, comes out the moment he sees them, smoothing his hair surreptitiously.

He avoids looking at his family. And though Mercedes pauses and watches for some greeting, Tatiana doesn't look in her direction at all. She stands close to her father, looking up at him expectantly like a cat craving fish guts. I don't actually matter, Mercedes thinks. Not me, myself, an individual. I could be any island girl she's taken a fancy to, and if it's not me, it'll be someone else.

But still, she feels a prickle of anticipation.

The men shake hands solemnly, and Sergio leads them into the cool dark of the restaurant. He re-emerges, bottle of grappa in hand, and barks a coffee order at Larissa as though she were an employee rather than a wife. Their discussions didn't end well. They've been ignoring each other for hours.

Larissa purses her lips and starts to wrestle with the Gaggia. She hates it. Always acts as though the hissing monolith contains a real live dragon.

'I'll take them in,' offers Mercedes.

'No you won't,' she snaps, and hands the cups one by one to a smirking Donatella.

Mercedes carries on taking orders, one eye on the glass

doors. This is awful. What is she meant to do? They're discussing *her*. Tatiana rambles around the restaurant, fingering things, while the men, heads bowed, conduct their solemn business. And then she clearly feels Mercedes' eyes on her, for she looks up and meets them, and beams a golden smile on her.

She turns her back. It's all too confusing. The *terasa* is calm. Everyone carries on drinking their sundowners as though this is an ordinary day.

After half an hour, the door slides back and her father appears once more. 'Mercedes? Can you come in, please?' he calls.

Sergio never says please or thank you to his family. She takes off her apron and goes in, her mother's eyes boring into her back.

The room smells of grappa and testosterone. The three men sit at the table, smiling smugly. Tatiana dawdles in the back, tapping the lobster tank, feigning indifference.

'Ah, Mercedes,' says Matthew Meade.

''Riggio, Mr Meade,' she says.

'Come and sit down,' says Mr Micaleff.

'I prefer to stand,' she says. She has a feeling that what little volition she has over her life choices is diminishing even further, and this small gesture of independence comforts her.

The men shrug. Whatever. They know where the power resides.

Sergio doesn't speak. He is the junior partner in all of this, but he looks pleased with his bargain.

'So, as you know,' says Mr Micaleff, 'Mr Meade's daughter Tatiana is here for the summer holidays. I believe you've met?'

Mercedes nods. Tatiana gives a casual wave from the back of the room, as though she's only elliptically involved.

185

'And got on,' says Mr Meade. 'Very well, I'd say. Didn't you, Mercedes?'

Mercedes swallows. Her mouth is dry.

'So we've been talking with your father,' continues Mr Micaleff, 'and we think we've come to a happy agreement. Tatiana needs someone to play with. It's awfully dull for her, sitting on the boat all day while her father's working. She needs company. Entertainment. Someone she can talk to. And she'd like that someone to be you.'

I know I'm meant to be flattered, Mercedes thinks. But this is *weird*. As though she's picked me off a shelf. She nods again.

'So Mr Meade has offered to pay for someone to take over your duties in the restaurant. How does that sound?'

She looks at her father. He's not just taken money for my replacement, she thinks. I know him. My father drives a hard bargain. Even when it comes to selling his daughters.

Sergio speaks up. 'The whole summer, just for playing, *kerida*,' he says. 'All the way to September. Imagine, Mercedes! What would I have given for a summer of leisure when I was your age? What a lucky girl you are!'

'What do you think, Mercedes?' asks Mr Meade, in English. 'Are you on board?'

She doesn't really have a choice. Tatiana watches silently through lowered eyelids. It *would* be amazing, she thinks. No hot days carrying plates and washing up till my hands turn red. Getting to use that snorkel every day. We could visit every beach within walking distance, and maybe the duke would lend us his car if we wanted to go to ... I don't know. The mountains? The temple?

But is this how friendship is, for these people? A transaction? Do I really have the option to say no?

'Okay,' she says.

186

The men sigh with satisfaction. Tatiana jumps and claps her hands. Comes running forward and grabs her by the hand.

'We're going to have *so much fun*!' she cries. 'Oh, Mercy, I'm so glad you said yes! We're going to be best, best friends! Can we go out now, Daddy? Please? There's this beach I want to see, and it's not going to get dark for hours!'

'Of course you can, darling,' Mr Meade tells Tatiana.

The men turn back to each other. 'Great,' says Mr Micaleff. 'So I'll have the contract and the non-disclosure agreements ready to sign the day after tomorrow. You'll all need to sign them, of course. Your wife and your other daughter too.'

Mercedes stares as she turns into a commodity.

'Yay!' Tatiana exclaims. Grabs Mercedes' hand again, and starts to lead her from the restaurant. 'Come on, Mercy! You're all mine now!'

Saint James's Day

24 | 1985

'But I don't understand.' Tatiana eyes the shuttered restaurant. 'Surely this would be one of the best nights to make money all year?'

Oh, hush, please hush. People will hear you.

The Saint has reached the top of Harbour Street. Mercedes can see the statue's head bob above the crowd, borne aloft on an olive-wood palanquin by the island's six strongest men. The streets are filled with praying women, with men with their hats clutched to their chests, and Tatiana just burbles as though she is at a cocktail party.

'Is holy day,' she replies. 'We not trade on holy days. You do in England?'

Tatiana shrugs, as though the concept is absurd.

'We also close Sundays. Was why we met.'

'Oh,' says Tatiana. Then, 'That's weird. You'd've thought God would have made an exception for restaurants. I mean, most people would want to go out to dinner if they had the day off.'

Mercedes side-eyes her. You really are an idiot, she thinks. Amazing how a single week can take someone all the way from goddess to full-on *lilu*.

'Is not day off. Is *holy* day. If you go out, you go to church.'

'Are we going to go to church, then?'

'*Si, jala.*'

'Oh.'

'You must to cover ... shoulders,' says Mercedes. And her bosom, but she doesn't know the English word. She hopes that the shoulder-covering will do the job without her needing to mention it. At least the fabric of Tatiana's dress isn't transparent today. And she's wearing a dress, not trousers. Or shorts.

'Why?'

'Is respectful.'

Tatiana goggles.

'We can borrow a shawl from Mama,' she tells her. 'She have many.'

'Better be a natural fabric,' says Tatiana. 'I'm allergic to man-made. I even have to have cotton bras.'

Of course you do. The list of Tatiana's allergies grows by the day. She's allergic to preservatives, tinned foods, most carbohydrates, pleather, root vegetables, offal, plastic toilet seats, frozen peas, non-feather bedding, non-gold jewellery and distant cigarette smoke. It must be very inconvenient, to be allergic to so many cheap things.

'Poor you,' she says, distantly, and turns to watch the Saint approach.

The procession is led by a ragged knot of boys, faces stained with shoe polish, who run backwards and tumble dramatically to the ground, hands before faces, as St James bears down on them. In his wake follows the regimented squadron of *solteronas*, dressed in white on their annual day of glory, wielding farm implements with all the ferocity of the truly irate. And, behind the *solteronas*, the mortal women. *All* the women. Down from the mountains, in from the vineyards, all falling in at the back as the line passes. Sturdy women and fragile women, great-grandmothers and girls barely able to read. All the women. To not attend St James's Day is cowardice. A betrayal.

And maybe, of course, a sign of guilt.

'We'd call that racist at home,' says Tatiana, loudly, looking at the black-faced boys. 'They'd have banned that in the UK by now.'

Mercedes suppresses a sigh.

'He is our patron,' she tells her again, 'because he drive the Moors out of La Kastellana.'

'Makes a change from snakes, I guess,' says Tatiana.

Mercedes doesn't understand what she's on about. She's proud of her heritage, regardless of the fears this day brings with it. That someone in the vanguard of the coming invasion knows nothing of the island's history fills her with a convert's zeal.

'After he drive the Moors from Iberia,' she says, pointedly ignoring the interruption, 'he come here and save us too. Since he come, no more invaders. By his grace, *grazia nobile*.' And she executes a quick sign of the cross to show her gratitude.

'And *look*!' cries Tatiana. 'There's Giancarlo!'

A dozen pairs of eyes snap in their direction. Mercedes cowers. She wants to cover her face with shame, that someone would speak so casually of their duke in public. Especially today, as he walks with the thousand-year-old broadsword with which his ancestor killed a hundred invaders held aloft before his face. *Shush. Please shush. I can't bear it.*

She tries to shuffle away, put some space between herself and her employer, but Tatiana sticks to her like glue.

'I'm thirsty! I still think you could do a *roaring* trade selling snacks and drinks,' she continues, voice so loud it drowns out the praying. 'Street food. It's totally the coming thing, you know. I ate nothing else on Koh Samui.'

Mercedes feels her teeth grind together in the back of her jaw. Perhaps, she thinks, listening to Tatiana's complaints is my own penance. They're incessant. My feet hurt. It's so *hot*. How much longer? How long is the service? God, these *cobbles*. They're *awful* with flip-flops.

They pass the *Princess Tatiana*. Matthew Meade stands on the back deck, watching, cool drink in hand.

'My *mama* has been walking since they left the church,' says Mercedes. 'Is not so bad.'

'Can't I go and grab a bottle from the boat?'

'No,' she says firmly. Once you've joined the procession, you don't leave. It's the rules.

As they pass the harbourmaster's office, her father comes out with the other men, to watch them go by. Slightly unsteady on their feet but trying to hide it. They have sufficient respect for the Saint that they have at least left their glasses indoors, but only a fool would believe that the glasses aren't there.

Were it not for the women, the great traditions of Kastellani life would have died out generations ago. The thought of all the dignified mothers and sisters and daughters, preserving history and passing it down, fills Mercedes with a strange, resentful pride. This is why we mark this day, she thinks: to mark the heroism of women and the fates of those who betray their duty.

Her father waggles his eyebrows at her as she passes, and she raises her chin and ignores him. 'Is like this everywhere?' she asks Tatiana, nodding in their direction.

'What?'

194

'The men drink grappa while the women do everything?'

Tatiana laughs. 'Oh, lord, yes! Well. Obviously girls like *me* have choices, but generally speaking, yes.'

'Choices?'

'Money,' says Tatiana complacently, 'gives you choices. I can basically be anything I want. Live anywhere I want, do anything I want.'

'And you chose La Kastellana!' says Paulina Marino, sarcastically, from behind them. 'Well, isn't that *fine*!'

Mercedes and Paulina's eyes meet over Tatiana's head, just for a fleeting moment, and a conversation takes place. *What are you doing, Mercedes Delia? Don't judge me, don't judge me. You're not going to get too big for your boots, are you? Never, never. I'm Kastellani to the bones. You wouldn't want the* solteronas *to notice you. That sister of yours is already attracting attention. Think of your mother. Think of her shame. Please. Don't say anything. She's not my fault. If you knew, you wouldn't blame me.*

Paulina sucks her teeth and turns away.

In the market square, Donatella slips from an alleyway and drops into step. Giggly and excited; the naughty girl thumbing her nose at the rules.

'Don't tell Mama,' she whispers.

'Where've you *been*?'

'Ana Sofia's house. We've been hiding in her bedroom. Did she notice I wasn't there? You won't tell her, will you?'

Her pupils are large and she smells faintly of alcohol.

'Have you been *drinking*?' Mercedes hisses. Donatella gives her a little Mona Lisa smile. 'I don't believe you,' hisses Mercedes, and Donatella smirks again. She's wearing nail varnish. Just pale pink, almost the colour of her real nails, but Mercedes is appalled. Painting yourself, on a day like this. The *solterona*s will probably leave Tatiana alone, but if they spot this when Donatella comes up the church steps . . .

Tatiana, oblivious, starts up again. 'So why is it all women, anyway?' she asks.

'You don't know?' asks Donatella.

'Oh, hello. Where did you come from?'

'Don't know what you mean. I've been here all along,' says Donatella, and suppresses another giggle. 'You want to know why the women? Because it was women who helped St James. We killed them with pitchforks and ploughshares!'

She thrusts in the air with an imaginary pitchfork.

'But also,' Mercedes tells her – she takes the St James legend very seriously, 'we keep our culture safe.' She looks an appeal at her older sister, whose English is far better than hers – not just from school, but from all those magazines she likes to buy.

'Yes,' says Donatella. 'When the Moors came, they were carrying everything away. The gold and the silver, all the church ornaments. They took it away to Africa. Melted it down to make heathen idols. Even the stained glass in the windows. They raided the castle and took everything the duke owned.'

'But they not take his courage,' says Mercedes, 'or his love for his people.' They are reciting the story every child has learned by rote since the great battle.

'They burned the paintings,' her sister continues. 'The saints and the dukes and their duchesses, all burned, and the ashes thrown into the sea.'

Paulina rejoins, suddenly friendly again.

'Even the Roman gods and emperors,' says Donatella, 'that used to stand in the temple. They say you can still see them on the ocean floor, if you go down deep enough.'

'Is that right?' asks Tatiana. 'And who was *their* God?'

Paulina puts a finger to her lips and hushes her. 'We do not say his name,' she says.

'But what,' she continues in her loud and confident tones, 'about that *jala* thing you all keep saying? Surely that's ...'

An explosion of *l'ostia*s all around them. *Jesu Maria*. All around them, women are crossing themselves, kissing medallions.

'Mercedes Delia,' snaps the woman who does the laundry for the Re del Pesce, 'if you can't keep this girl under control, you should take her away.'

'What's she even doing here anyway?' mutters another. 'This isn't some ... *espetacula turistija*.'

'Sorry, sorry,' says Mercedes.

'I was only—' Tatiana begins. Donatella cuts across, interrupts to shut her up.

'So we were telling you. But they didn't get it all. Not even a half. Because, while the men were talking and drinking grappa and despairing, the women were spiriting away everything they could get. Under their skirts. In handcarts of linens.'

'In the carts taking food for the animals,' adds Mercedes.

'In their babies' cradles,' says Paulina.

'And they hid them so well, the Moors never found them. Buried in the fields, plastered into wall niches, stored in secret compartments beneath the animals' mangers. And every generation, we whispered the secret hiding places into our daughters' ears. Mother to daughter, mother to daughter.'

Larissa has come up behind them, pushed her way between the bodies. She gives Donatella a look. *I know what you've been up to, missy*, it says. *Don't think I didn't see.*

'Because the men could not be trusted,' says Donatella, pretending not to know what the look is about. 'And when the Sant'Iago came and freed us, the daughters' daughters' daughters went to their secret places and brought the icons back to the church.'

'The ancestors back to the castle,' says Paulina.

'The communion chalice back to the altar. The history of La Kastellana was saved from the Moors.'

'And was the women who saved it,' Mercedes concludes proudly. 'This why we have *festa* today.'

Tatiana has shut up at last. She gets it, thinks Mercedes. At last, she gets it. Our noble history. Why we're special.

'But not *all* the women, right, girls?' asks Paulina. She too learned the Kastellana legend at her mother's knee.

'Noo!' they chorus, and, all around them, women mime spitting and wiping their mouths.

'There were women who collaborated,' Donatella recites. 'Women with no shame, no pride. Women who even laid themselves down for these heathen men. *Puta*.'

'*Puta*,' they mutter. '*Puta*.'

'That's a bit rich …' begins Tatiana, then thinks better of carrying on.

'They shamed their fathers. Some of them even shamed husbands. Left their marriage beds and laid themselves down.'

Another round of spitting.

'And you know what they did? Our ancestors?' asks Donatella.

Tatiana shakes her head.

'They kept a list. Of all the women. The ones who betrayed us, who watered down the Kastellani blood. And after the battle, after the Moors fled back across the ocean, after Sant'Iago returned to Andalucía, the people went from house to house and fetched them out. And they brought them to the church that had been made into a mosque and they made them kneel before the altar and confess their sins. They shaved their heads and made them beg forgiveness.'

'*Waah*,' says Tatiana, her hand going to her hair.

'But though God may forgive, the people of La Kastellana could not. So, once their souls had been offered up to God, they led them up the cliffs to the Grota de las Sirenas and one by one, even as they begged for their lives, they threw them in.'

'*What?*' Tatiana finally looks impressed.

Mercedes nods. 'Is true. Legend say they become mermaids when they die. And they keep our seas safe ever since. From invaders.'

'Their penance,' says Paulina.

'If you go up to the cave mouth when the sea is high,' says Donatella, 'you can hear their voices, crying out for forgiveness.'

Tatiana utters her first Kastellani word. '*Oao*,' she says.

As they enter Plasa Iglesia, the mood darkens. The Saint reaches the church steps, the exhausted sacristans staggering beneath their load. In his wake, as he enters the porch, the *solteronas* take their places. Two by two by two, all the way to the great iron doors. Hands buried deep in the front pockets of their white aprons. Vengeful eyes.

They're so powerful, thinks Mercedes. This power only manifests once a year, but this one day holds us all in thrall. They know everything. Those beady eyes, drilling into your core. No wonder we are so nice to them. Bring them baked goods, greet them with subservient smiles, offer discounts in the market. Because you never know, really, do you? Whether a judgement begins because one day you failed to show enough respect? Or what might make someone go to them with a tale. In a way, they keep us all civilised, in this tiny place where a grudge is something you'll never get away from. Best to avoid provoking one in the first place.

They queue up, thirty deep around the perimeter, and wait their turn.

There are never consequences for men. The adulterer responsible for last year's shaming continued to frequent the bar all year as the *sirena* he'd created hid away, her shutters bolted. He wouldn't even, Felix Marino says, leave when the cuckold appeared; just carried on drinking beer at the bar as though he had nothing to hide. Yet, for the women, their entire lives are constrained by the promise of this single day. There isn't a decision you take all year that doesn't involve at least a moment of *what would the* solteronas *think*.

They've all fallen quiet now. Even Tatiana has nothing to say.

In the church tower that was once a minaret, the bell begins to toll.

The crowd hesitates. Then, one by one, old ones to the forefront, they step forward and shuffle up the steps, heads bowed humbly before God and their judges.

'I don't know why *that* lot have to make such a big show of worrying,' Larissa mutters. 'There hasn't been a *sirena* over the age of fifty since the seventeenth century.'

Donatella looks over her shoulder and smiles. 'Or an ugly one.'

Heads turn and hush them. They fall quiet. But Mercedes sees Larissa fight a smile.

'Dear God, how long does this take?' mutters Tatiana. 'My feet are killing me.'

Maybe you should have stayed on your yacht, then, thinks Mercedes, spitefully. You were the one who insisted on coming.

And on, and on. The sun is off the square, at last, but the heat has done its work. Mercedes' mouth is dry, and the anticipation, the knotted tendons in her neck, have brought on a familiar high-pitched headache. Once you're inside the church, you get water. But until then they must all stay pure.

A tiny ripple of movement among the white robes on the steps. Hands that have been buried deep in apron pockets shift, closing around their contents. *It's coming*, she thinks. And from the electric stir in the crowd around her she knows that they have seen it too. She stands on tiptoe to see the front of the queue, but all she can see is the backs of taller heads. I hate being twelve, she thinks. All I ever do is wait.

The *solteronas*' expressions harden. Is it their lives, she wonders, that have made them so bitter? Or did God choose them to be alone because this is who they are?

It must be giddy hell if you're at the front right now. They all see the signs. They'll all know that *la sirena* is queuing beside them. Can anyone really be sure *la sirena* is not herself?

And on they come. The butcher's wife. A teacher from the school. The dairy farmer's wife, whose six daughters often bear bruises for not being sons. Maria who has taken Mercedes' place at the Re del Pesce for the summer. Maria whose family have cleaned the castle for generations. Another Maria, who sells suppositories in the sparkling new pharmacy. So many Marias. As each runs the gauntlet and hurries, unscathed, shoulders dropping, into the cool, dark sanctuary of the church, the crowd shuffles and sighs as tension rises and recedes, rises and recedes like ocean waves.

Tatiana starts to speak and Mercedes turns her head to shush her. And by the time the collective gasp of the crowd, and Larissa's hand flying up to cover her mouth, alert her that the shaming has begun, the seasoned leather lashes that live in those apron pockets are whipping through the air. Beating the sin from the sinner.

'*Who is it? Who is it?*'

The target is buried in a heaving mass of flailing white. The savage slap of lash on flesh.

Thank God it isn't me, she thinks. Please never let it be me. Please give me a life without temptation.

The wall of white opens up, and a woman, face slick with blood, is kicked down the steps to the flagstones.

I hate this, thinks Mercedes. I hate it. That women can do this to women.

'Oh, God,' says someone. 'It's Camila.'

'Garcia?'

'Yes.'

'What did she do? What has she done?'

'I don't know, do I?'

'She must have done something. Isn't she getting married in the autumn?'

'Lucky she'll be wearing a veil, then.'

'Yeah – if he still marries her now.'

Camila Garcia, the dressmaker, collapses at the foot of the steps, excluded from the grace of God and from her neighbours. The *solteronas* tuck away their scourges and accompany each other to the front row seats for Holy Communion. Smiling, satisfied. For this is their day.

All safe now, for another year.

'So what happens now?' asks Tatiana, suddenly.

Mercedes turns and sees that she doesn't look shocked at all, but – excited. Her eyes are bright, and a strange, toothy smile plays across her lips.

'She walks home,' says Paulina.

'Alone,' says Larissa.

'What if she can't?'

'They always can, in the end,' says Paulina. 'They have no choice.'

She steps over the stricken woman's feet, the sooner to reach her destination and the cool draughts of water within.

Mercedes saw a *sirena* make her way home once, when she was six. Feeling her way blindly, along Via del Scirocco, passers-by en route to the *festa* crossing the road at her approach, for a woman disgraced must be shown that she is disgraced. Shoes long lost, hands clutching the torn bodice of her Sunday dress to cover her shame. A face so swollen Mercedes couldn't tell who she was – just that she was black and sticky and stinking with the old eggs and rotten vegetables, chicken feathers and fermented molasses that the more pious like to throw at them as they carry their shame homeward, just to ensure that they know their sin is unforgiven. Because nothing says *festa* like pelting a woman with rotten fish guts.

'Come on,' says Larissa. 'They're going in,' and she starts to usher her charges towards the church.

'And the men . . . ?' asks Tatiana.

'Just stop,' snaps Paulina. 'It's done. She'll stay indoors and heal, and by the time she comes out everyone will have forgotten all about it. By next year *she'll* have forgotten all about it.'

Mercedes very much doubts that. It's a small island, and she's passed former *sirenas* in the street many times. They never look as though they've forgotten it. Not even the old ones. You just have to see their eyes to know that they have been broken forever.

25 | 2016

Robin sees her daughter everywhere. In crowds, in bars, on the harbour wall, at the ends of alleyways. And when she pants up to where she has seen her, she is always gone. Melted away into the heaving mass of humanity. Or, of course, never there in the first place.

She bumps into St James being carried on a palanquin on the way up the Calle de las Conchas towards the market square and hurries ahead. She's been trying to avoid the procession, for the noise and the dancing make it impossible to engage people's attention. But the market square seems to be a focal point, with its little funfair, the stalls that sell pan-Mediterranean 'local crafts', the buzzing food and drink stalls and the stage and speakers for the bands who will entertain the crowds until the midnight fireworks.

A knot of English people stands nearby, studying a guide-book. She approaches and lurks and waits for her moment.

'It all used to be completely segregated, of course,' says one of the men, authoritatively. 'Men down here and women in the church square. The women went to church all day and the men partied.'

'How Islamic,' says a woman, disapprovingly.

'Not sure about that,' he replies. 'They were profoundly Catholic. I mean, look at what the whole event's actually celebrating. I think it was just a Thing.'

'You know how slowly these isolated places change,' says another. 'For all we know, it was a leftover from the Neolithic.'

'Or the Romans,' says another. 'The Romans were pretty funny about women.'

'Well, I'm bloody glad they've stopped *now*,' says the first woman. 'Though this whole Queen of the Mermaids thing is a bit ghastly. I mean, really. Surely there's a happy medium between beating women for being whores and dressing them up in bikinis?'

'Chill yer boots, Germaine,' says another man. 'It's just a local tradition. It's not like they're burning witches or anything.'

'Not any more,' she says darkly. 'Now they're just dressing teenage girls up in Wonderbras. A marvellous example of progress. Talk about objectification ...'

'Shall we get some drinks in before the Saint gets here?' interrupts the other woman, hurriedly. 'I think they have to close up while he's in the square.'

They stop talking as they look around for a beer stall, and Robin pounces.

'Excuse me!' she says.

They swivel. She plasters a smile on her face. *See me smile. I am not a threat.*

'Sorry to interrupt,' she says. 'Can I just – I don't suppose you've seen this girl, have you?'

She holds out a flyer. They look down at it as though she's trying to sell them lucky heather.

'My daughter,' she says. 'She's seventeen now. This picture's from last year.'

Silence.

'She's missing,' she adds. In case they haven't understood.

The woman who was complaining about sexism gingerly takes the paper and studies Gemma's face. Shakes her head. 'Sorry.'

She hands it to her companions. One by one, they also shake their heads. The last of the men tries to hand the flyer back.

'No, no.' Robin shows him the stack in her hand. 'Keep it. Please. In case you see her. It has my mobile number on it, look.'

'Sure,' says the woman who first took it. She takes it from the man's hand and folds it into the front pocket of her urban backpack. 'Sorry,' she adds. 'I hope you find her.'

'Yes, good luck,' says someone else, and they hurry away, their minds already turned to beating the twenty-minute beer drought.

'Poor woman,' she hears as they walk away. 'Imagine.'

'Yes,' says another. 'Pretty girl, too.' And Robin's eyes fill with tears. Every time she's thought she'd shed her last, she finds that she's only scraped the surface.

Please, Gemma. Please. Be here. Don't be gone forever.

'We're going to have to get out and walk,' says Tatiana. 'It'll be midnight before we get there otherwise.'

The crowds on Duke Street are so thick that the Merc is barely moving, and is attracting self-righteous thumps on its roof and bonnet from passers-by. Paulo has had to turn on the wipers a couple of times, to clear off plastic beer cups that have landed on the windscreen.

'We're almost at Harbour Street,' she says. 'It's not far. It's uphill, but it's only a couple of hundred metres.'

Gemma feels a bit worried. She's not practised walking in these shoes. This girly little pink shift dress Tatiana insisted she put on would fly up over her face if she were to go for a burton, and she feels conspicuous enough as it is.

They get out, and the air fills with whistles and cat-calls. Gemma feels awkward, but Sara looks pleased. She laughs and tosses her hair and does a little wiggle in her Versace bodycon.

'Save it,' snaps Tatiana, from inside the car. 'No point wasting yourself on a bunch of car mechanics. Or is that what you *want*, Sara?'

Sara looks chastened. She straightens up and assumes what she imagines to be the haughty demeanour of a supermodel. There will be some real ones there tonight, Tatiana says. For them to look at and learn from.

Ahead, the street rises sharply towards the brightly illuminated restaurant at the top. But someone has made steps in the pavement and they can, at least, keep their soles and heels horizontal.

'Come on,' orders Tatiana, and sets off up the hill.

'See you later,' Wei-Cheng says over her shoulder. Paulo nods and gets back into the car. He's going to have a laugh turning that round, thinks Gemma, and falls into line behind her hostess.

'This is fun,' says Felix, and flips three chicken breasts in one smooth swish of his spatula.

'You've got a funny idea of fun,' Mercedes says. She's never regained her appetite for the *festa*, even though it's barely recognisable as the loaded ceremony of her childhood. But if the sight of St James still chills her, his effect on Larissa is dramatic. She's as strong as a horse, but July makes her weak. The firework frames rising on the marina wall, the flags unfurling across the narrow streets of the Old Town, the plaster popes on their marbled wooden podiums – they all seem to drain the life from her. By *festa* night, the Re's busiest night of the year, she always succumbs to a howling, nauseated headache, and has to retire to bed.

Mercedes' contract stipulates that she must have the *festa* night and the morning after off as holiday, always. It was the one thing she insisted on. Even back then, she knew that her mother would never be right on St James's.

'Well, it's the most time I've spent with *you* all week.'

She bashes his hip with hers. 'I've got the morning off, too. We can go catch those lobsters, hey?'

'*Jesu*,' he says, 'you know how to make a man happy. I'd been hoping for a lie-in.'

'*Shhhhht*,' she replies. 'Do your work.'

Five hundred flatbreads. They should have ordered more. Year on year, the *festa* grows. Since the duke's PR firm placed a clutch of travel features in the international press, the number of people getting off the ferry has doubled. The marina is full, as well. The yacht-owners will all be up at Mediterraneo tonight, guzzling champagne and nibbling tepidly on langoustine canapés with their white, white teeth.

She leans out into Calle del Puerto to see if the queue has shortened. Glimpses Tatiana's car, pulled up at the end, and two of the girls just vanishing up the steps on the Via del Duqa.

She turns back to the next customer in line, gives him her dignified island smile. '*Tarde!*' she says. 'Chicken, or lamb?'

'No more sausages?' he asks.

'Sorry. All gone,' she says.

He rolls his eyes, as though coming to a local restaurant at half-past ten on a *festa* night should still entitle him to the unchanging menu of a McDonald's. 'Chicken, I guess,' he says, grudgingly.

'*Harissa*? Garlic sauce?'

'Both?'

'Sure.'

A woman hovers to her right. Plain khaki slacks and a T-shirt, large bag on her shoulder. Out of place among the tipsy crowds, her brow knitted pensively. Mercedes throws her a smile. She takes it as an invitation, and steps forward.

'Oi!' someone calls from further down the line. 'Queue's this way!'

The woman looks up, rattled. 'No – sorry – I'm not after food,' she calls.

The queue closes ranks and watches her like a hawk. Mercedes scrapes and flips, scrapes and flips, and waits. The bucket by her feet is only a third full. Soon they'll be breaking out the wings and promoting halloumi.

'How can I help you, *sinjora*?' she asks.

The woman is flustered. She has the look of someone who's been flustered all her life.

'I was hoping you could help me,' she says, digging in her bag as she speaks.

Oh, hell, thinks Mercedes, now's not the time to be selling me stuff. Surely you can see that? But she scrapes on and waits for the woman to continue.

'I'm looking for my daughter.'

'And she was here, *sinjora*?'

The woman shakes her head. Finds what she's looking for and draws a piece of paper from her bag. 'No. She's missing. She went missing ten months ago and I just got information she might be on La Kastellana. Come for the party.' She hands her the paper. 'She's seventeen,' she says.

209

'I'm sorry,' says Mercedes, sympathetically, and takes the paper. Pretends to glance at it, while checking that the meat's not catching in the heat. 'That must be hard for you.'

'I was wondering if you could maybe put this up somewhere? It has my number on it. Maybe someone's seen her. Maybe she'll come here at some point ...'

Her customer interrupts. 'Is this going to take much longer?' Rude.

'All our food is cooked from fresh, *sinjor*,' she says smoothly. 'It won't be long.'

She turns back to the woman. 'Of course. Maybe you should try the big restaurant up the hill, too? Mediterraneo? They always have staff from off-island. Waitresses especially. Passing through. This place is more ...' she waves her spatula behind her '... local.'

'Yes,' says the woman. 'I'm going to try there next. Thanks.'

She turns away. Mercedes stuffs the paper in her apron pocket and assembles the impatient man's flatbread. She calls to the next person in line. '*Tarde!* Chicken or lamb? Or halloumi? We have excellent halloumi.'

After the dark and the crowds, Mediterraneo is a paradise of clarity and cool air. It's the sort of place whose discreet, enveloping doors, designed at once to showcase the interior and hide the diners, Gemma has been looking at her whole life. From the outside, longing to go in. The glass wall that holds the door spans the entire end of the street. *There is nowhere to go but here*, it proclaims. *And if we turn you away, there is nowhere to hide your shame.*

Two burly men in dark suits and dark glasses flank the door. Beyond, a lobby: bright white walls and a floor of Moroccan blue tiles, and a small black podium behind which stands a middle-aged man in a dinner jacket. The restaurant is hidden discreetly behind a high, stuccoed wall. All she can see is a glitter of glass and chrome and ceiling fans and, beyond, the velvet mystery of the night sky.

Will she ever get used to this? she wonders, as the doormen, like automata, push open a door each at their approach and they sweep through.

The floor looks rock-hard and slippery, but it has been treated with something that holds and cushions her soles and heels, and she feels stable on her feet for the first time since they left the car. She sees a strange micro-expression flit across the greeter's face – some urgency, some tiny moment of panic – then she sees his hand reach beneath the desk. Pressing a button, she thinks. And then the expression goes away and his face lights up.

'Sinjora Meade!' he cries, all expansive arms. 'Welcome back! How is New York? We've missed you!'

Sinjora, thinks Gemma. That's Mrs, isn't it? Is he saying she's her father's wife?

'New York is awful, Maurizio,' says Tatiana, seeming unfazed by the address. 'So glad to be back. What a crowd, though!'

'Oh, I know,' he replies complacently. 'Every year, worse and worse.'

Someone comes bustling round the screen. An old man, dressed as a comedy gigolo. Jeans with knife-edge creases, an emerald silk shirt unbuttoned to the waist, salt-and-pepper hair moussed stiff to disguise male pattern baldness, a moustache that looks like a piece of carpet.

'*Tatianabela!*' he cries, throws his arms out wide. '*Como estan la bela sinjorina*? How we have missed you! What a joy to have you back! Now the *soirée* can really begin!'

'Sergio,' says Tatiana, and allows herself to be kissed. 'How are you?'

211

'I am well. But never happy when you're not with us,' he cries.

Behind her, Hanne giggles, and Sara pinches her to shut her up.

'Why do you stay away so long?' he continues. 'You know La Kastellana is empty without you! Please.' The arms fling wide again, ushering them towards the inner entrance. 'Go through. So many people have been asking for you.'

As the door opens, a roar of high-toned, confident conversation tumbles out. The soundproofing is astounding. Tatiana glides ahead, Sergio throwing shapes around her like a mime creating a queen, while the greeter smiles, smiles, smiles and bobs his head, dismissed.

Once Tatiana is out of sight, his smile drops away. As the girls follow in her wake, his eyes run up and down each of their bodies, nakedly assessing as they pass. He doesn't even try to hide it.

Robin leaves the restaurant on the harbour front and weaves her way back to Duke Street. There's some sort of snarl-up going on: a shiny black limo slowly edging its way through a multi-point turn while the crowds bang on the roof and curse it for impeding their way. Who would be so stupid? she wonders. To drive all the way into a place like this on a night like this? And then she turns right to go up the hill to the restaurant at the top and sees Gemma again, for the fiftieth time tonight, step through the glass doors at the top, into the light, and vanish.

This is so hard. She hands out her pictures of her lovely daughter as she climbs, sees them drop them in the gutter after a couple of strides. The crowd is quite tipsy now; early ones heading away from the blare of Euro-rock in the market square to secure themselves a good view of the fireworks.

Robin's feet ache, and the hill is a labour. But I must go,

212

she tells herself. If she's really here for the duke's party and not just this street *festa*, it will be the people here, the yacht people, that she's with.

The beacon of light ahead is daunting. *Welcome*, it says, *if you're one of us. If you're wearing trainers, stay away.* I don't want to go up there, she thinks. But still she climbs. For my girl I'd tolerate any humiliation. Just to see her. Just for the chance to say sorry.

They run out of chicken at eleven o'clock and her apron strap is cutting into Mercedes' neck under the weight of all the cash she's taken.

'I'm taking a break for a minute,' she says.

'Yeah, don't mind me,' says Felix.

'I'll bring you a beer,' she says.

'Big of you,' he replies.

'Ah, a comedian,' she says.

'Someone has to be the funny one.' He flashes her a grin.

In the cool interior, her mother sits on a banquette, grey-faced and drinking coffee. She's come down too soon.

'*Jesu, Mama!*' Mercedes rushes over, puts a hand on her forehead, the way Larissa used to do with her when she was a child. 'You're burning up!'

'I'm okay,' says Larissa. 'I just got a bit hot.'

'You've got to slow down,' she tells her.

'Nonsense,' says Larissa. But her eyes squeeze shut.

'Okay,' says Mercedes firmly, 'one minute and I'm taking you upstairs.'

She hurries over to the bar and taps the code into the safe. Fishes in her apron pocket and brings out her bulging money clip. A brief memory of her father, back in the day, doing the same, with dollars.

213

'It's crazy out there,' she calls over her shoulder. Dips into the pocket for the handfuls and handfuls of coins she'll need to sort and take to the bank tomorrow. 'We must have taken a couple of thousand euros just from the grill.'

Larissa's voice is reedy. 'I should be helping.'

'Oh, hush, Mama. Felix is out there, and Maria's got everything under control in here.'

'He's a good man, is Felix,' says Larissa.

'He's a pain in the backside,' she replies. 'But we're your family.'

She pulls out another double handful of coins, and her hand brushes paper. Thinking she must have missed a note, she pulls it out and finds that it's the flyer the sad woman gave her earlier. Oh, God. More stuff. More demands, more things to remember. And she so doesn't want Larissa seeing this, tonight of all nights. A missing girl, almost the same age as Donatella. It will rip her heart clean out.

She doesn't want to look herself, either. The dull ache of her thirty-year-old loss can still break out, knock her to her knees. You go on. Because you have to. But guilt is a dark and savage beast that waits just out of sight for its opportunity to pounce. It's been thirty years since Mercedes saw her sister's despair and mistook it for courage, yet, when she remembers, the pain is as caustic as a lungful of lye.

She crumples the flyer up and throws it in the bin under the bar. Turns back to her mother and forces a smile into her voice.

'Come on,' she says. 'No arguing. I'm taking you up to bed.'

Hanne has snuck off to a corner of the terrace and leans on the parapet, smoking a cigarette over the edge. Gemma is scandalised.

'You'd better not let Tatiana catch you doing that!' she hisses. 'The top of her head'll come off!'

Tatiana hates smoking. She's noticed a lot of rich people do. A control thing. Hanne straightens up and laughs, though she notices that the hand that holds the cigarette remains behind her in the dark.

'Oh, please! What's she going to do? Send me home? Where's she going to get a replacement for *this* at no notice?'

She sweeps her hand down her body. Hanne's body is spectacular. Even more so in the scrap of black Lycra lace Tatiana provided, that clings to every curve. She may be the whitest girl that Gemma has ever seen, but she looks like a Neolithic fertility statue. A stick-thin torso with buttocks and breasts like cantaloupes. And no surgery to get them that way, either, so she claims.

Three men nearby fall silent and stare. One inhales his drink, and has to be slapped about the shoulders. Gemma feels like a little kid beside her. I wish I were more sophisticated, she thinks. I look about twelve in comparison with these girls. People keep asking how old I am. They don't even ask Wei-Cheng that, and she's barely as tall as the car.

'D'you want one?' asks Hanne.

Gemma scans around. Tatiana encircled on all sides by old men. Sparkling. Wei-Cheng at a table, sandwiched between two gruff salt-and-pepper Russians, laughing at their jokes. Sara at another, gazing in naked admiration at the actress they all recognise but have never actually seen in anything. She's a producer now. Whatever that means. Tatiana pointed her out when they first arrived. *That's what you could be, one day,* she said. *By the time she was thirty, she need never have worked again.*

'Oh, go on,' she says, and turns away from the party

into the dark. Hanne pulls a pack of Vogues from her little clutch bag; so long and thin they look like pretend cigarettes. Gemma takes one and lets her light it. Leans on the parapet and enjoys the head-rush.

'This is something, isn't it?' asks Hanne.

'Christ, yes.'

'I don't think I've ever seen so many sapphires in one place.'

Gemma feels inadequate again. These girls are so far ahead of her. Their talent for discerning real from paste, the cut of one designer from another, the gloss of Chanel lipstick from the grease of No.7.

'It's amazing,' she says tentatively. Hopes that one day these people won't intimidate. That they'll stop seeing her as a perk and start seeing her as a prize.

'How many of these have you done?' asks Hanne.

'My first, actually.'

Hanne mimes reeling in shock. 'For real? You serious? *None?*'

'Well, some parties, of *course,*' she says. 'In London. And a weekender to Cannes. But not, you know, a *trip* trip like this.'

'Ooh, Cannes!' Hanne wiggles and stretches her arms, and her stunning breasts move up her ribcage as though they aren't really attached to her body. 'I did Cannes last year. Fabulous villa in the hills with a two-part swimming pool. You literally swim through a tunnel to get from one side to the other. Did you do any events?'

'Not really,' she says. 'We were on a yacht in the harbour. People came to us.'

'*Nice,*' says Hanne. 'I love a boat party. Any film stars?'

A hand whose knuckles were covered in hair. Polished wood and shining brass. Bedsheets that felt like satin in a low-ceilinged cabin that smelled of spunk.

'No,' she says. 'Mostly executives. Couple of investors.'

'Ack,' says Hanne. 'Isn't *that* always the way? Hey, there's a film star coming tomorrow, though, isn't there?'

'Yeah. Jason Pettit. But I think he's Tatiana's.'

A cynical laugh. 'Oh, come on, that's his *job*,' she says. 'We're the *compensation*.'

As the clock runs down to midnight, their energy fades. Long days followed by a long night, and Mercedes' stamina is at full stretch. Felix is feeling it too. No jokes now; no flirting or teasing. The entitlement of the crowd, their sulks, their increasingly bleary demands, have worn them ragged. Maria comes from the dwindling table service to help, and they scrape and flip, scrape and flip in silence.

'I need my bed,' says Felix. He looks every day of his forty-three years. You can see the old man in him now. What he'll look like when he's seventy.

Mercedes grunts in response. Wonders if maybe they can stay upstairs tonight, save them walking up the hill. It's only twenty minutes home, but the prospect of dragging their weary bodies up the cobbles, skirting round the litter and the vomit and the drunken stragglers who want to dance, fills her with low-level dread.

A man comes to the counter. She doesn't look up. She's too tired. If they want her to meet their eye, they can come back tomorrow.

'What can I get you? Only lamb and halloumi left now,' she says mechanically. She's hoarse from talking, same old syllables, over and over.

'I don't – Mercedes? I need to talk to you.'

She looks up. Laurence Viner is standing there, his face solemn and urgent. Oh, hell. She'd forgotten about him.

Felix glances over and she hears him heave the sigh she's suppressing.

'Not right now,' she says.

'Tonight, though?'

She feels unspeakably weary. 'Can it wait till tomorrow?'

He hesitates. 'No. No, I'm sorry, Mercedes. It can't. I need to talk to you tonight.'

'Laurence,' she says, 'we're exhausted.'

'I'm sorry,' he says again. 'But it's urgent. Really urgent.'

She slaps her spatula down by the grill, starts to untie her apron. Felix and Maria side-eye her as they cook. 'Sorry, guys,' she says. 'I'll be as quick as I can.'

'Not here,' he says. 'In private. Can you come to my hotel?'

Really?

Her husband rolls his eyes. He does, Larissa's right: he does have the patience of a saint. 'It's okay, Mersa,' he says. 'We've got this.'

'Thank you, Felix,' says Laurence. 'I wouldn't, you know. If it weren't ...'

'Whatever,' says Felix, grouchily.

As Robin approaches the entrance, a bouncer steps across her path.

'Sorry, madam,' he says, in estuary English. 'Private party.'

'I don't want to go *in*,' she protests. 'I just wanted a word with—'

'Sorry,' he says.

His colleague steps in front of the door. They haven't even asked if she has an invitation. It's that obvious that she doesn't belong.

'No, but look,' she says, 'I just wanted to ask that man—'

'Sorry,' he says again. His tone says he's anything but.

218

She persists. '—if he could maybe help me find my daughter.'

Silence. The man's expression is blank. She knows the exchange is already over, but desperation drives her on.

'She's missing. My daughter. Gemma. She's only seventeen. Look . . .' She gets out a flyer and holds it out.

He doesn't look.

'She's just a kid,' she says. 'I've been beside myself for almost a year, looking for her. Could you at least give this to him? The man at the desk? So he could see?'

No response.

'It has my phone number on,' she says, barely managing to finish the sentence before she gives up. Hopelessly, she drops her hand to her side and turns away.

She cries as she descends the hill. The tears just won't stop coming. In a minute she'll pull herself together, but, right now, all she has is despair. I'm a terrible mother, she thinks for the millionth time, like picking a scab. You could never hate me as much as I hate myself, Gem. Please, please, God, give me a chance to apologise. To see that she's okay. I just want my baby back.

On the waterfront, the *sirena* is finishing her triumphal progress. Same age as her daughter, carried, in some parody of the Saint, on a makeshift float borne on the shoulders of eight young men dressed as *matelots*, a whole crowd of drunks dancing around them, shouting what she can only assume is crudities as she wobbles on their weary shoulders. It really is awful, her costume: her legs hobbled by a silicone tail, a push-up bra shaped like a pair of cockle shells, three-foot hair extensions rat's-tailing down her back and getting in her eyes and mouth so she's constantly forced to brush them away.

She's not enjoying that, thinks Robin. She'll be very relieved once her night of glory is over. Oh, those moments of triumph.

All those things we wished for so fervently when we were young. How many of them has Gemma found? And have they made her happy?

She's glad she doesn't have to be a teenager again. Glad all those disappointments are behind her now. She takes a final glance at the *sirena*'s queasy face and pushes on up the harbour. She'll hand out her flyers until the fireworks start, and, if she has any left, she'll fix them to every vertical surface she can find. It will be good to have something to do while the fireworks are going on. Gemma loves fireworks, and watching them would probably make her cry again.

Gemma

July 2015

26

Tatiana has her own make-up artist. By the time she's finished *proper* contouring, Gemma looks eighteen, easy. And once she's in the dress Julia fetched from the agency wardrobe, she looks twenty-one and change. Still looks twelve, too, though, and she still worries she won't get past the bouncers.

'Don't worry about it,' says Tatiana, in the taxi. 'Loads of people pay good money to look as young as you do. And we're not going to, you know, *Wetherspoons*.'

'So where are we going?' she asks.

'Issima,' says Julia.

'For real?'

Julia looks amused.

'I've been there,' she confides. 'With my friend Naz. At Christmas. It's lush.'

The dress is really tight and she's finding it quite hard to balance on the seat. And it's short, so she has to keep her knees together. Eventually she works out how to brace herself, by spreading her feet out and pressing her knees together and hanging on to the door handle. She looks like Bambi, finding his feet.

'What, upstairs?'

She prickles. There's a proper private club upstairs. Meant to be a big hush-hush secret, but everybody knows it exists. You can't miss the glass-walled lift with the bouncer on the door and the roped-off red carpet that leads to it, for starters.

'No,' she says. 'The club.'

'And you got in?' asks Julia.

Gemma nods, enthusiastically.

'And that, my dear, is why we use the top floor,' says Tatiana.

They inhabit another world. She hears all these words and names fly about the cab – cryotherapy, George and Amal, Denpasar, Giancarlo, Pavel, Upper West Side, Darling – and little of it means anything to her. But it sounds so ... *exclusive*. She looks at Julia and Tatiana and marvels that they have taken her under their wings so readily. I want to be like them, she thinks. They may be old, but they really *live*.

The bouncers' eyes light up as they alight from the taxi. And then they're breezing past the rope, and the VIP greeter has already called the lift and got it open by the time they've passed the empty early evening dance floor. She feels dizzy with the thrill. Sucks in her tummy and follows her hosts, and everyone *smiles*.

And then they're inside the glass box lift and she's gazing down over the banquettes and the bar and the podium-cages where she and Naz had a drunken dance at Christmas, and she's wondering what could possibly better a place like that.

Not the balcony where the lift lets out, for one. Gemma is massively disappointed. It's like opening a Christmas present and finding that it's socks. It has chairs and seating from which

224

one can watch the swarming ants below, but there's hardly anyone here. A bored-looking bartender polishes glasses and a solitary waiter carries cocktails to the only occupied table.

But they don't stop. Tatiana leads the way, and she sees that there's a door at the far end. She sees Tatiana pause and key in a PIN, then she's led up a flight of quiet, very velvety stairs into paradise.

Gemma gasps. I never knew there were so many blues, she thinks. How can there be so many blues?

The domed ceiling is a gigantic reproduction of that Van Gogh painting, *Starry Night*. A wild expanse of whirling comets, a thousand twinkling LED stars; far beyond her reach, yet tantalisingly close. It's the room she always dreamed of. Filled with people she only barely believed existed. Faces she's seen on TV, faces she knows she'll *never* see on TV. Tables and banquettes and cushion-padded day beds. Little Bedouin tents with drop-down curtains, where candles flicker in hurricane lamps. Staff in uniforms so black they eat the light, circulating quietly with their trays.

She glows with wonder as a *maître d'* comes straight to them and leads them towards a great glass wall where, glowing in the last rays of the evening sun, a green, fecund Italian garden, all paths and poplars and sunflowers, beckons tantalisingly. All across the rooftops, hidden from the street. Taking up half the block.

This world, she thinks. *This. World.* I knew it was here somewhere. I knew. This is what I want. This . . .

She stares at her hosts with newly opened eyes. Who are you? she asks silently. How did you get here? Because only gods can live in a world like this.

The gods are welcoming. And some are even her age. A girl, Sara, sits with three men at a long teak table. Only a bit older, but a world away in sophistication. She wears her bandage dress as though it were a second skin and her earlobes glitter.

The men are all older. She recognises one. He's always on the telly: an avuncular sort who's fond of clipboards and the EU. Her mother likes him. He sucks on a vape like a spliff, and stretches an arm along the back of the bench proprietorially as he watches Sara in a manner that's a long way from avuncular.

The men leap to their feet with cries of 'Ahhh!'. Not Sara. Sara stays seated, one hip jutting and a glass of champagne in her hand, though her smile broadens.

Air kisses. I must learn this, she thinks. How to kiss someone enthusiastically without ever touching their skin. They kiss Tatiana and shake hands with Julia, and just like that she realises that Tatiana is queen and that, though Julia talks a good game, she is the junior partner.

I need to hang on to Tatiana, she thinks. Julia may have found me, but Tatiana is my future.

A waiter comes, takes orders. Gemma sinks into a delicious cushion at the end of a long wooden bench overhung by a cloud of sweet-scented jasmine. Tatiana sits to her left, head of the table, and a man, in maybe his forties (she's so bad at old people's ages), hair cropped short to disguise the thinning and a Rolex on his wrist, to her right.

'Jeremy,' says Tatiana, and he shakes Gemma's hand and smiles at her as though she's a small plate of caviar.

'Well, hello,' he says.

More people join. Mostly men. Oleg, Dmitri, Christophe. An ethereal beauty called Hélène who looks as though she might snap if you twisted her. Someone puts a drink in her hand. A cold, chunky glass that feels as though it was made with only her hand in mind. The drink, gelid with crushed ice, is sharp with limes, sweet with brown sugar. It is delicious.

'Are you liking that?' The man called Jeremy eyes her glass and seems amused.

'It's lush,' she says. *Lush* is her latest word. She likes it. It rolls off the tongue and feels pleasingly retro.

'Caipirinha,' he tells her. Then breaks the word down syllable by syllable. Kai-pee-reen-ya. 'They drink them in Brazil,' he says. 'It's their national drink.'

'Have you been?' she asks.

'To Brazil? Many times,' he replies. 'I do quite a lot of business in Rio.'

Rio. The very name sounds like beaches. 'I'd love to go to Rio,' she says.

'Play your cards right and it might happen,' he says, and gives her a smile that makes her feel a bit puzzled and a bit uncomfortable.

'Gemma's only just come on to our books, Jeremy,' says Tatiana. 'Julia found her on Bond Street just last week.'

'Oh,' he says, and this clearly means something, for the arm that had been snaking along the bench behind her drops to his side and he sits up straighter. 'So you want to be a model?' he asks her, and his tone is kinder, less familiar.

'I hope so,' says Gemma. She finishes her lovely drink, and as if by magic another appears by her hand and the old glass is whisked away. 'But really,' she confides, because the drink is making her feel like confiding, 'I'd like to be an actress, eventually.'

'An *act*ress?' he says, and he seems amused again. She doesn't really get why. She's not *trying* to be funny. 'Well, you must meet Maurice. He's a prod*uc*er.'

227

One of the men looming over Sara twists and looks at her over a fleshy shoulder.

'That I am,' he says. 'And who have we here, then?'

'This is *Gemma*, darling,' says Julia. 'She just signed with us a couple of days ago. We're still showing her the ropes.'

Gemma smiles. Encouragingly, she hopes. Maurice is the first film producer she's ever met. She hopes he survives the heart attack his purple face and fat cigar suggest he's overdue. It would be a travesty if she made a contact this easily only for him to die on her.

Maurice's pupils shoot wide as she smiles. 'New, eh?' he says. 'And how old are you, then?'

'Sixteen,' Tatiana answers for her.

'Well, you be sure to come and say hello when you've got a bit more experience,' he tells her.

The caipirinhas have emboldened her. 'I will,' she says. 'But how can I get experience if I don't get any work?'

The age-old question, asked by every generation. It doesn't seem an unreasonable one to her, but for some reason all the men burst out laughing. Unsure how she's meant to respond, Gemma laughs along.

'That's the spirit!' Maurice says, mysteriously, and turns away.

Another girl arrives, escorted by a man whose hair is so heavily gelled it looks like a plastic shower cap. Sara moves to the far end of the table and the gelled man goes and sits next to her. The new girl slips in between Gemma and Jeremy.

She's exquisite. Shiny hair tumbling over her shoulders, golden eyes the shape of perfect almonds, their colour emphasised by shiny lines of sapphire and metallic gold. And she smells gorgeous, too: a lovely clean mix of citrus and mint and some faint long-forgotten garden flower that combines headily with the jasmine above their heads.

Someone pours her a glass of champagne. She turns to Gemma, assesses her. Not in a bitchy way. Neutral but friendly.

'I like your hair,' she says.

'Thanks,' says Gemma. 'My nan's from Barbados. I've always wanted hair like yours, though.' The girl's hair is enviable. So straight and sleek. Just a subtle curl at the end, like a mermaid's.

Sara gets up and walks indoors. Then the man with the shower cap gets up a few seconds later and follows. The party's not breaking up already, is it? But no one else seems to be moving. A couple of the men near where they were sitting share a joke, watching the man's retreating back.

'Oh, no,' says her new friend. 'Yours is really *special*. You should get some gold highlights put in.'

'What a great idea, Melanie,' says Tatiana. 'We should get that sorted. Yes, Julia?'

Julia turns instantly on hearing her name. 'Sorry, what?'

'Gemma's hair. Melanie thinks she'd rock gold highlights.'

'Ooh, yes,' says Julia. 'Grand plan. And actually, if we took the whole colour up a couple of tones, that would be lovely. You'd look great blonde, with your skin. Colour combinations you don't find in nature can really zing.'

'Sort of light chestnut?' asks Tatiana. 'So the gold really stands out?'

'Perfect,' says Julia. 'I'll make an appointment tomorrow.' And she turns away.

Gemma feels a bit embarrassed. She hasn't let her mum make decisions about her appearance without consulting her since she was seven years old. But these women have her career in mind. They're experts. It's different.

229

How she'll *explain* it to her mum is another question. She'll want to know where she got the money from. I'll say Naz did it, she thinks. Mum couldn't tell a professional colour job if it bit her on the arse. Naz never minds. She's brilliant at thinking on the hoof.

Island

August 1985

27

The sound of Tatiana's voice approaching from the interior alerts Mercedes to the fact that she's up. Pestering.

'But Daddy, *why*? It's shitty up at the castle. It's so boring. There's literally nothing to do. Why can't I just stay here? This bloody boat never even goes anywhere and the one time you take it out you kick me off.'

'It's just for the boys, darling. You know that.'

'*Boys*. Boys! Please! They're all *ancient*!'

'All the more reason you don't want to hang about with them,' he says.

'No, but . . . I mean, come on. I'm practically a bloke anyway.'

'Not really,' he replies.

They emerge into the light. The father in madras-check shorts that bag all the way to the knee and a white towelling robe big enough for a winter quilt. The daughter, hanging on to his arm that way she does, pressing her breasts against it, pleading.

She spots Mercedes and breaks off her monologue. 'Oh. When did you get here?'

'Nine o'clock,' says Mercedes.

Same as every morning. That's what her contract says. Nine a.m. until dismissed. She spends the first hour or two of every day in waiting. But she doesn't mind. It's often the best part of her day. The staff are kind, and spoil her as though they think they've something to make up for. Maybe it's because she's carried on saying *please* and *thank you*. She has a high old time, now she's worked out Tatiana's schedule, trying out every sort of fresh-squeezed juice – watermelon today, the best yet – and sampling whatever pastries the chef has made with his cold, floury hands down in the bowels of the boat. She's even met the captain, who introduced himself to her as Philip. As if she wasn't just some local kid, but someone worth talking to.

Tatiana drops her father's arm, comes over to the table and helps herself to a *sfogliatella* from Mercedes' plate. Making a point of some sort. Eyes Mercedes imperiously as she bites through the pastry.

With an exhalation like a hydraulic hinge, Matthew lowers himself onto a wooden steamer chair. It groans as it receives him. 'It's only two nights, darling.'

'Two nights in *hell*,' she replies, dramatically. She drops the half-eaten pastry back on the plate, takes two huge steps and flings herself onto her father's lap. 'Oh, Daddy, *please*!'

She wraps her arms round his neck and nuzzles his dewlaps. Matthew looks pleased with himself, as though he's won a prize. Mercedes feels uncomfortable. She never knows where to look when they act like this. She can barely remember sitting on Sergio's knee, and it had certainly stopped by the time she was seven. The sight of this teenager snuggling Matthew Meade like a greedy puppy makes her tummy go a bit funny. She wouldn't be able to put it into words, but when it starts, she wants to be somewhere else.

234

Matthew unwinds his daughter's arms and pushes her off with a slap on the bum. Puts chunky hands on wide-spread thighs.

'Right,' he says. 'I've got some phone calls to make. No rest for the wicked. Maybe you should be getting on with packing. The car's coming in four hours.'

Another exhalation. He lumbers to his feet. Ambles off into the saloon, purple feet in backless slippers. Tatiana stares at his retreating back, her face filled with naked amazement.

He stops and turns back. 'Packed and ready, are you, Mercy?'

She jumps. Points a finger at her own chest.

'How many Mercys are there on this boat?' he says.

None, she thinks. But anyway. 'To the castle? You want me to go too?'

'Well, *duh*!' says Tatiana.

'I . . .'

Tatiana puffs up. '*What?*'

She doesn't know how to reply.

A tendon works in Tatiana's jaw. 'Oh, *great*. Oh, that's just *great*.'

'No! No, but you didn't tell me, that's all! I didn't think I was invited! I didn't . . . I haven't told my parents! I can't just . . .'

'Oh, if you're worried about *el duqa*,' says Matthew, the title somehow dirtied by his tongue, 'don't be. Giancarlo will allow anything I want.'

Tatiana strides to the table and picks up Mercedes' plate. 'So you don't wanna *come*?'

Her accent has changed.

'No,' Mercedes protests, 'I didn't . . . I just . . . you didn't . . .'

Tatiana hurls the plate onto the floor. Smashes shards and

pastry all across the varnished wood. 'Fuck you, Mercedes Delia!' she shouts. And she runs indoors.

Mercedes sits frozen on the spot. She has no idea what to do.

'*FUCK OFF!*' shouts Tatiana. 'Just *fuck off!*' And she stamps across the saloon and disappears down the staircase to the lower deck.

Now what am I meant to do? thinks Mercedes.

Matthew Meade picks up a folder that lies on the table, slaps it against his thigh. Pokes a fist into a pocket and surveys his twelve-year-old employee.

'Right,' he says. 'I'll get them to send the car for you in the afternoon. You can go home now.'

'I ...' Her head is filled with noise. 'I'm sorry,' she says. 'I just didn't ...'

'And you'd better apologise to my daughter when you get there,' he says. 'For your shitty behaviour.'

28

The helicopter flies in at three o'clock, and the castle limo enters the dock thirty minutes later.

'This is it,' says Donatella. 'Your carriage to the stars.'

'Shut up,' she says. Glares at her sister from the seat where she's been ordered to wait and not get her clothes dirty. Larissa has scrubbed her so clean that her skin feels raw, has ironed until the sweat poured off her face.

'I'm not having you shame me in front of the duke,' she'd snarled.

'Mama, the duke won't be there!'

'Well, you *say* that.'

'It's true! He's going out on the boat!'

'Well,' she said, 'you're still going to the castle. You never know what the staff will tell him.'

She doubts the staff will be seeking the duke out to report that her skirt was wrinkled, but she accepts her fate. Sits in Tatiana's old orchid-print dress, hair scraped off her face and plaited, best winter shoes clinging damply to swelling feet, and awaits her fate.

The car goes to the foot of the *Princess Tatiana*'s gangplank. Again. She's counted eight guests aboard since the duke arrived and Tatiana left, chin in the air, ignoring Mercedes on the *terasa*. Men in rich-man casual: cream-coloured trousers and dark dark-glasses, and primary-coloured cotton jersey tops that emphasise their nipples.

She'd thought the party was complete. Evidently not. She sits forward to watch.

The duke's chauffeur gets out and walks round to open the door nearest the water. A pause. Then, one by one, four young women emerge and hurry up the gangplank. Creatures so exotic – so curvaceous, clad in dresses that look like bandages, in skirts and tops so far apart they will never meet, in boots of shiny white plastic that rise halfway up thighs and shoes so high the soles need platforms to accommodate the heels – that even Mercedes knows what they are there for.

She gasps. Looks around for *solteronas*. For if they see this, surely, they will be able to tell the difference between Camila Garcia and a genuine *puta*. But there are none to be seen. They're up in Plasa Iglesia, tatting and tattling. By the fishing boats, the men's nets hang frozen in their hands, and Hector Marino administers a firm slap to the back of Felix's head.

The girls step onto the polished deck, pass the *No Stilettos* sign and sway along the gangway to where she can see the tops of the men's heads over the gunwales. She could swear she hears a faint cheer go up.

My God, she thinks. So this is what a Stag is. Does Tatiana know? Do the priests who presided over the St James's Day mass know that our duke goes out on boats with girls like this? Do I tell her? Do I tell them? What do I say?

The chauffeur gets back into the driver's seat and the car creeps towards the restaurant. On the boat, music starts up. Some cold, unnatural electric throb that makes the water tremble. Above the gunwales, she sees thin brown arms rise up and wave in the air in time with the beat, as the captain comes down the stairs from the bridge and hauls in the gangplank.

Donatella watches her set sail, fiddles pensively with a curl. 'It's a shame you won't be meeting the duke,' she says.

'Don't you start,' says Mercedes.

'You're so bloody lucky,' says Donatella. 'Yachts and castles and all those new clothes.'

She doesn't feel particularly lucky. The other kids are giving her a wide berth these days. They look at her in her cast-off finery as though she's sprouted horns. 'It's not *that* great,' she says.

'Yeah, well,' says Donatella. 'I suppose I'd better go and clean the toilet, then. Apparently the English don't know how to flush their own shit.'

Her first car ride isn't as thrilling as she had expected. The interior smells strongly of perfume. Not the subtle aromas that surround the Meades, but a mix of chemical scents, pungent enough to kill insects. And the speed that looks so dizzying when the car passes you on the new asphalt road feels quite ordinary from inside. Slow, in fact. But the seats are covered in the softest kid leather, and indentations in the arm rests of the back seats contain ducky little plastic bottles of sparkling water. The chauffeur watches in the mirror as she takes one out and examines it.

'Go ahead,' he says.

239

'Really?'

There's a particular sort of indulgent fatherly nod that men do around young girls. He does it now. 'That's what it's for,' he says.

It's finished in a few little gulps. Fizzy, but not *that* fizzy. She's not sure what to do with the bottle. Casts around and eventually puts it in the laundry bag of clothes Larissa has forced on her. The chauffeur smiles.

'You can take the other one too,' he says. 'For your sister.'

'Oh, no!' She blushes beetroot. 'I wasn't—'

'It's okay,' he says. 'There are a thousand more in the old dungeons. I'll put more in when I bring you back.'

I wasn't taking a souvenir, she shouts inside her head. *I was trying to be tidy!* But outwardly she nods her thanks, and tucks the other one away.

The portcullis is open and the car drives straight into the courtyard. Cobbles. High windows. And – a great surprise, for the outer walls are stark and forbidding – a riot of patterned tiles. Arab, she thinks. There are a few walls like that left down in the Old Town. And the public baths are covered in them. Here, they cover all four internal walls from ground to battlements. The Moors must have made it all the way into this great fortress and stayed for long enough to decorate. A fact so much at odds with the history she's learned at school that it makes her slightly dizzy. She'd thought the dukes had driven the Moors away. So how come it looks as if they decorated their interiors?

She gets out, gaping. It's stunning, she thinks. Imagine it at night, those torches all lit up.

A door opens. Tatiana. She has on a turban, and a pair of huge pearl globes cling to her earlobes.

240

'Right,' she says. 'Well, I suppose you'd better come in, then.'

The sulk isn't over.

'I'm sorry about earlier, Tatiana,' she says humbly. 'I really didn't know I was meant to be coming.'

Tatiana's chin jerks upwards. She looks haughty. 'Is that all you've got to say?' she says.

'I'm sorry. It was a misunderstanding.'

'Well,' says Tatiana.

'Sorry,' she says again.

Tatiana walks away. 'I was up by the pool,' she says. 'I had to come all the way down.'

'There is a pool? Where?'

Tatiana turns back. The savage smile she wears looks more like baring her teeth, and her eyes are glittering. '*Oh.* Suddenly there's a point in being here, is there? It's on the bastions.' She wheels, and clicks on over the thousand-year-old flagstones.

Mercedes has never encountered a sulk like this before. Has no idea what to do when someone refuses to accept an apology. Eventually, she opts for ingratiation. 'I'm really happy to be here,' she says. 'I just thought I wasn't invited.'

'*Hunh.*'

Tatiana carries on walking.

'Don't touch anything unless I say you can,' she says. 'It's all a million years old and very valuable. It's like being in a bloody museum.'

She leads Mercedes silently through the private quarters where the Kastellani never go. And Mercedes is quietly grateful for the chance to simply stare. It's all so . . . tall. The ceilings must be ten metres up in the air, iron chandeliers barely visible, the plaster a faded terracotta, the wood a glorious turquoise. They walk past suits of armour on tiles of black and white, and generations stare down superciliously from oil paintings. Their footsteps echo as they pass through, as in a church.

Mercedes can barely breathe. I must remember every detail, she thinks, to tell Donatella. I wish I had a camera. No one will ever believe I was here, when I'm old.

Tatiana leads her up a staircase as wide as her house. A stained-glass window, two storeys high, depicts Duke Lorenzo, who saved them all, at the Battle of Clavio, slaying the enemy as St James looks on approvingly. Mercedes pauses to drink it in. It's a horrible thing. Glorious and horrible. Her history.

From behind and above, she hears an impatient sigh. Tatiana looks down, arms folded.

'Sorry,' she says. Picks up her bag and hurries after her.

'So Giancarlo said to put you in the room next to mine,' she says as they march down a long wide corridor, Persian rugs on black floorboards, tapestries filling the great slabs of wall between the doorways.

'Great,' she says.

'Whatever.'

Tatiana throws open a door. Another room the size of the Re del Pesce's forty-cover *terasa*. Walls painted eau-de-Nil, an oil painting of a wizened child in a heavy green velvet robe on the wall, a four-poster covered in carved fruit and gargoyles. She looks the portrait over. Huge wounded eyes stare from a face that's ashen-grey.

'She died of plague, that one,' says Tatiana, 'in 1631. That was painted post-mortem. It's a *memento mori*.'

Mercedes shivers.

Tatiana's voice changes. It has a gloat to it that Mercedes doesn't like. 'I hope you're not scared of ghosts,' she says.

242

The hairs prickle on her arms. Ghosts are serious business. Not something to be tossed casually off the tongue like passing gossip. There are places even in the town where no one would go alone at night. And the *sirenas* wailing from their sea cave fill her with dread even though she has never heard them herself.

'What ghosts?' she asks, tremulously.

'Oh, all sorts,' says Tatiana. '*Full* of history, this place. Dead kids, kidnapped heiresses. All the traitors who died in the dungeons ...'

She makes claws of her hands and swipes them through the air at Mercedes' face, and Mercedes, startled, leaps out of the way.

Tatiana looks intrigued. 'Oh, my God! Are you *scared*?' She narrows her eyes. Starts walking slowly towards her, her head on one side. 'My God, you are, aren't you? You're scared! You actually think they're going to come out and go BOO!'

She shouts the last word and leaps, arms flailing. Mercedes screams and drops her bag. Clutches her heart.

Tatiana begins to laugh. Holds her sides as though they're splitting and points a mocking finger. 'OMG,' she cries, 'that's *hilarious*!'

Adrenalin, still pumping through her veins, makes Mercedes forget for a moment who she is. Where she is. She screams into Tatiana's face. 'That's not fucking *funny*! *L'ostia*! *Mjerda con xerda*! You don't *ever, ever* do that again!'

Tatiana's laughter ceases, abruptly. She raises her eyebrows, runs her eyes over Mercedes, top to bottom to top again. 'There's no need to be like *that*,' she says.

And she turns on her heel and leaves the room.

*

Oh, God.

Mercedes scurries in her wake. Angry Tatiana is as venomous as an aspic viper, but she's done apologising.

'Tatiana, that was a horrible thing to do,' she says.

Tatiana turns and gives her a smile so cold she almost jumps back again. God. This is going to be a long forty-eight hours.

She turns back and continues along the corridor, heading for the dead-end wall at its furthest extremity. Mercedes considers going back, for a moment. Collecting her bag and just going.

'You don't want me here,' she says.

Tatiana doesn't respond.

'Where are we going? I thought we were going to the pool?'

'We are.'

The tapestry hangs from a curtain rail. Tatiana pulls it back, and reveals a small, arched door.

'Shortcut,' she says. 'Servants' staircase. It connects to all the floors. Nobody likes seeing their chamber pots once they've used them. I'm surprised you didn't know. Surely someone in your sainted ancestry used to carry the shit in this place?'

I won't, she thinks. I won't. I'm not like her. I won't respond in kind.

'It goes all the way down to the dungeons,' says Tatiana, 'and up to the roof. Only three storeys. Up. And four down. Though I'd advise against going down. Those dungeons are *rank*.' She gives her an eloquent look. 'And full of *ghosts*, of course.'

Mercedes goes into the entrance and looks. Such a tiny little door, such a narrow little flight of steps spiralling down into the darkness, up towards the bastions.

'It's miles, the long way,' says Tatiana.

It smells of staleness and spiders. A hairy old rope fixed with iron pegs to the outer wall leads upwards, out of sight. Something to hold on to, at least.

'Go on,' says Tatiana.

Mercedes steps in. She grips the rope. It's even darker than she had expected. She'd assumed that there would be little apertures – arrow slits – to let in light, but there is nothing to see but rough limestone walls. It's hot and cool at the same time: the outer wall, baked by the summer sun, emanating heat into the constricted space, stale air rising up from the cellars. I don't like it, she thinks.

Gingerly she takes a step upwards to make room for Tatiana, and the world turns black.

29

Mercedes freezes. Clutches the rope as blood rushes to her head. Feels herself lurch in the darkness.

'Tatiana?' she calls.

Her voice is soaked up by the walls, the ancient air. Muffled. Dead.

'Tatiana?'

Silence.

The sound of a bolt being pulled across the door.

She shouts louder. '*Tatiana!*'

Silence.

Oh, God. Oh, God. She sways on the step. It's so dark. She can see nothing at all.

'Tatiana?'

Mercedes feels her way back down to the landing. Finds the door, grips the latch, lifts it. No give. Nothing. It's as solid as a wall. There's not even a crack of light to show that it's there. Tatiana has pulled the tapestry back over. She's alone.

*

Time vanishes. *I have vanished,* she thinks. *If they open the door again, I will have disappeared.*

She takes several breaths. Counts to ten. Feels the blackness swim back into focus.

Something scuttles on the steps below.

Stop it.

I don't know. I don't know what's down there. These stairs go all the way to the cellar. To the dungeons.

I don't know what's below me. I don't know what's coming up.

Stop it. *Stop it.*

Panic chills her despite the heat and her palms are slippery on the rope. She wants to scream.

If I scream, whatever's down there will hear. It will know I'm here.

She mutters a prayer beneath her breath and waits. Fucking *bitch.*

The stairs below her have vanished. They have receded into the wall. All there is below her now is a straight drop to endless black.

A sound breaks from her throat, somewhere between a sob and a wail.

Shut up. *Shut up.*

Movement again. Down there. In the dungeons.

Run. Run.

To where?

There is no reason in the dark.

She runs upwards. The steps are uneven. Worn and slippy. But nonetheless she runs.

Three storeys. Forty steps.

Let the door be open. Let it be open.

The shush of sandals on ancient stone and the thunder of

blood in her ears. She can't hear what's behind her.

Stealthy. It knows I'm trapped. It doesn't . . .

The dark begins to grey. She can see her arm as it reaches for the rope. Then she sees her hand, the curve of the central pillar, the steps high above her head.

The door. She can see the door. She's panting with the strain of her flight. But, up above, she sees cracks of light between the ancient planks.

Be open. Be open. Be open.

Still dark. But she knows the shape of the door. Her hand is reaching for the latch long before it's within her reach.

It touches. Fumbles. Grips. Raises. The door gives under her hand and she tumbles out into the bright sunlight on the roof.

Golden bastions. Crenellated battlements. Striped umbrellas, sun loungers, a stretch of sapphire-blue water, a huge satellite dish, pointed at the sky.

Mercedes looks down and sees that her arms are a gauzy mass of grey cobwebs. She gasps and bats at herself, bounces off the wall, nearly steps back into her prison. The doorway gapes black behind her. She hurries over and closes it. In case. Just in case.

I'm not staying here. I'm not. If she did that, she'll do anything.

Fear gradually gives way to rage as her heartbeat slows. Mercedes grinds her teeth, makes fists of her fingers. Says all the things she wants to say, inside her head. Fuck you, Tatiana Meade. No, *fuck* you. I'm not staying here to be your . . . plaything.

She strides to the battlements, looks over. Down below, the great central plain bakes gold in the sunshine, the temple like jagged teeth on the cliff edge, the sea beyond, no sound but the song of the cicadas. On a sun lounger, Tatiana has left a pile of belongings. A dress. A book whose spine is covered in bright gold letters. A portable cassette player with plug-in headphones and a pile of tapes that are no doubt the absolute latest, biggest, most up-to-the-minute . . .

Fuck you.

She sweeps everything onto a striped cotton towel, makes a bundle and dumps the bundle into the pool. Watches, grimly satisfied, as the towel opens up and the contents sink down to the bottom. There. Hope you're happy now, she thinks. And she spots the grandees' door to the main stairs and starts the long walk home.

30

Even Donatella assumes it must be her fault.

'So what did you do?' she asks when she comes up to bed, smelling of cooking oil and work. She pulls off the little black dress that Sergio has instituted as uniform for the restaurant staff since he noticed the domestics on the yachts.

Mercedes starts up, outraged. '*What?*'

Donatella drops the dress into the laundry basket. 'You must've done something. They didn't even send you in the car.'

I'm too tired, she thinks. She's been alone in their bedroom since she got in from her two-hour walk, thirsty and dusty, the blisters from her stupid formal shoes burst and leaking. Everyone too busy downstairs to pay her much mind. Waiting for Donatella, for she knew that at least Donatella would be on her side.

'So you assume it's something *I* did?' she asks, and before she can stop herself, she starts to cry.

Larissa brings her a bowl of sausages and lentils, her

childhood favourite, and gives her a hug. 'I'm so sorry,' she says. 'I was afraid something like this would happen.'

Well, why didn't you stop it? thinks Mercedes. And cries, and eats. Cries some more and eats some more. She hadn't noticed how hungry she was until the food was in her lap.

'I'm not going back there,' she says.

'No,' says Larissa, and strokes her dusty hair. '*Jala*, Mercedes, you need a shower.'

'It was ... horrible,' she says, and another gust of weeping overwhelms her.

Larissa's dark eyes darken. 'Oh, my baby,' she says, 'My poor baby.'

Sergio hadn't reacted at all when she turned up on the doorstep. For all the acknowledgement he gave her, she might have been invisible. And when she gets up in the morning, puts on the apron that has hung unused from the back of her door since July and goes back to work in the restaurant, he doesn't acknowledge her presence. Just stares balefully from a distance and goes indoors.

'Don't worry about him,' says Donatella. 'He's just worried about the money.'

'Silly sod,' adds Larissa.

'He doesn't believe me,' she says mournfully.

'When's he ever believed anything that didn't suit him?' asks Larissa. 'Don't worry, my baby, we believe you.'

It's not the first time that Mercedes has suspected that Larissa regrets the father she chose for her children.

The dock remains quiet all day. When lunch service is finished, the castle car pulls up outside the restaurant and the chauffeur gets out. Goes to the boot, and brings out Mercedes' laundry bag of belongings. He walks over to the entrance and holds them out, as though they were *actual* laundry, dirty.

No indulgent smiles now. No cute little bottles of water and more-where-that-came-froms.

Larissa accepts them without a word. And Sergio gazes out at the space where the *Princess Tatiana* should be, and blanks his daughter.

Three o'clock, and she's clearing away the last of the lunch service when Felix Marino swaggers onto the square from the Calle Rosita, the quintessential *boulevardier* in khaki shorts and a striped T-shirt. He waves to his father over by the boats and keeps on coming to the Re del Pesce.

Mercedes gets a sinking feeling. The news has got round and he's coming to laugh at her. She knows what he thinks. What they all think, about her. She's seen the look on his face as he watched her follow Tatiana around like a whipped puppy. She's such a fool. *Such* a fool.

She looks to her mother, pleads with her eyes for her to intervene. But Larissa is suddenly fascinated by a customer's account of their visit to the temple and her back remains resolutely turned.

He comes to the edge of the *terasa*.

''*Riggio*,' he says, in his annoying, belligerent-boy voice. He's carrying a rusty old anchor and a length of bright blue mooring rope. She eyes them suspiciously.

Felix kicks at the leg of the planter that stands between her and the street. He looks self-conscious. As if what he's doing is costing him in discomfort.

'*Jolà*,' she says, eventually.

'So I saw your sister.'

'Oh, yes?'

'She said you were back.'

Here it comes. 'Yes,' she says. 'And?'

'So we're down at Ramla,' he says. 'Me and Lisbeta and Maria and Luis.'

'Good for you,' she replies, haughtily.

'Yeah,' he says.

She waits.

'Luis dropped his fishing rod.'

'Well, that was stupid.'

'It's gone really deep,' he says. 'None of us can get it.'

Boo hoo. 'Okay.'

'But I bet *you* could,' he says.

Mercedes' heart jumps. 'Me?'

Felix makes a 'duh' noise. 'Is there anybody else here?'

'Well, no.'

'So?' he asks.

She's uncertain. People turn on you, on La Kastellana. You never know what they really want.

'I'm helping my mother,' she says.

'That's fine,' calls Larissa from over by the coffee machine. 'I've got everything under control.'

'I've got an anchor, look,' says Felix. 'So you should be able to get down there okay. We've been trying all afternoon.'

'Ramla?' she asks.

He nods.

'That's not that deep,' she says, condescendingly. 'I've totally been deeper than that.'

'Well, come on, then, stupid,' says Felix, and starts to walk away. 'We haven't got all day!'

She glances at her mother. Larissa is smiling. You've set this up, she thinks. You and Donatella. And she pushes herself out from behind her table and trots after him.

'So it's good you're back,' he says, casually, as they walk. 'We missed you.'

Mercedes quietly glows.

'I mean,' he says, 'you don't actually *like* that girl, do you?'

She thinks of the contract. Am I allowed to say? She makes a non-committal noise.

'Ana Sofia was saying the other day that she treats you like a servant.'

'I can't talk about it,' she says.

Felix stops on the corner, looks her up and down. 'That's what we thought,' he says. He walks on. 'Your father's a piece of work,' he says. 'I can't believe he'd actually sell his own daughter.'

The *Princess Tatiana* sails back into port at eleven the next morning, and a few minutes later the castle car appears. It idles at the foot of the gangplank as Matthew Meade shambles up the gangway and distributes handshakes and back-slaps. Mercedes hears voices echo over the stones and the water, and feels a sense of dread.

She'll be back soon, she thinks. But I'm not going to hide.

A tender from one of the marina yachts picks up two more guests. They motor away, reclining in their seats and cracking big bottles of water. Laughing, hearty. They've clearly had the best of times while his daughter was torturing Mercedes.

Donatella comes up and stands behind her as she watches.

'D'you want to go indoors?' she asks. 'I bet there's stuff you could be doing in the kitchen.'

'Fuck that,' says Mercedes, and picks up the cutlery basket to start laying the tables. 'It's my town, not hers.'

Donatella offers her a high five, a gesture they've recently picked up from the satellite TV Matthew has had installed in their living room so that Tatiana doesn't have to go without, though the sum total of her visits to the flat above the Re has turned out to be one. Her expression as she perched on their grandmother's cane settee and stared down at the chipped glass in which her Pepsi-Cola had been served made it clear to all of them that the visit wouldn't be repeated. But nobody's come and taken the TV away. Perhaps they never will.

Over by the restaurant door, Sergio frowns.

'Donatella?' he calls. 'Your mother wants you to go to the bakery.'

Donatella huffs. 'Really? Can't Mercedes go?'

Sergio's voice drops. 'Don't be a little *perra*,' he says. 'Do what you're told.'

Donatella sighs and unties her apron. 'Are the others going out today?' she asks. 'You should go out with them.'

'Maybe later,' she says. 'Felix is out with his dad.'

'Oh, *laaaa*,' says Donatella, 'Felix Marino, king of everything. Can't do *anything* without Felix *Marino*'s say-so.'

'Bugger off,' says Mercedes, but she can't help smiling.

The helicopter blats over their heads and wheels off towards the continent. The car comes back. There's no guard of honour for whoever's coming next. No Matthew Meade and his hearty affection.

The door from the staff staircase opens and heads bob along above the gunwales. The girls. Well, three of them. Shorter than when they came on board, for they have shed their heels and donned loose cotton dresses and a tracksuit. No skin-tight Lycra now. No little brown bellies on show. Off duty.

They walk as though they're old. As though their joints hurt. Hang on to the guard rail as though they're afraid they'll fall. They don't look left or right, but straight ahead, at the idling car. And they don't look at each other, either.

Mercedes waits for the fourth. She tries to remember what she looked like before. But they all looked so much the same – all lip gloss and elasticated lace – that she can't recall her face. Wouldn't be able to distinguish one from another. The missing girl is just a vague impression of long blonde hair. Breasts, legs, buttocks. No face.

The chauffeur opens the door and the girls get in. They drive away.

Funny, she thinks.

'What are you looking at?' asks Larissa, coming up beside her.

'I thought there were four,' she says.

'Four what?'

'Girls.'

Larissa's expression sours. Even if she had seen, she wouldn't discuss it. You don't discuss things like that. Not if you're respectable. Girls like that might as well not exist.

'Weren't there four?'

'I have no idea,' says Larissa.

'You didn't see them go on board?'

'I guess I wasn't looking,' she replies dismissively, and goes to fetch table nine's rabbit spaghetti.

Tatiana arrives at nine-thirty the next morning, as though nothing had happened. She walks onto the *terasa* with her beach bag, waves at Sergio, who waves back, and marches past the breakfast tables to Mercedes.

'You're late,' she tells her.

Mercedes draws herself up and regards her distantly. Donatella has coached her in the night. Her cold stare is perfect.

For a second – just a second – Tatiana falters. Then, 'Oh, come on, *what*, Mercy? You're not still on about *that*, are you? It was a *joke*, for God's sake.'

'Mercedes,' she says. 'My name is Mercedes.' Anger has made her bold. *I'm not your property, to name at your will.* She meets Tatiana's eye and holds her gaze. *I won't look down first. I won't. Go to hell.*

'Whatever,' says Tatiana.

Mercedes stands her ground.

The stand-off lasts a full minute. She counts the seconds, to occupy her mind. *I'm not coming with you,* she beams across the ether. *We are not friends.*

Tatiana's gaze drops. She turns on her heel and walks back to her father's yacht.

At half-past eleven, the car reappears. Only this time it doesn't go to the boat. It stops at the Re del Pesce and Luna Micaleff gets out. He ignores the women and walks straight indoors.

'Uh-oh,' says Donatella.

'Don't,' says Mercedes.

'It's okay,' says Larissa. 'I've got your back.'

Five minutes later, Luna Micaleff comes out and gets back into the car. They work on in the afternoon heat. An Aperol spritz. A Campari soda. Three beers. A gin and tonic. Who drinks alcohol in this heat? People with no work to do, of course.

Sergio comes out and calls her. 'Mercedes? A word.'

She goes indoors. Larissa nods at Maria, at Donatella – *take over my tables for me* – and takes off her apron.

Sergio leans on the bar, his back to them. 'Tomorrow,' he says, 'you go back. Nine a.m.'

'No,' says Larissa.

'Yes,' says Sergio.

'I'm not having her near that girl,' says Larissa.

'You don't have a choice,' he replies.

'Yes, I do. And so does she. She can find someone else to bully.'

Sergio turns round. His face is pale beneath his tan. 'She signed a contract.'

Larissa makes a *pfft* sound.

He reaches over and holds up a wedge of paper. 'Here. See?'

Larissa snatches the contract and rips it up. One, two, three, four. '*See?*' she says back, into his face.

Sergio sighs. Bends to collect the shreds. 'Don't be stupid, Larissa. You all signed four copies.'

'Well, what are they going to do? They can't *force* her to go, can they?'

He straightens, his face purple. 'You stupid, *stupid* woman!' he shouts. 'Did you not read what you signed? Did none of you?'

Mercedes watches them both. I know why he's angry really, she thinks. He didn't read it himself.

He rifles through the papers. Finds a section and shoves it at his wife, stabbing at it with a finger. 'We. Will. Have. To. Pay. The. Money. Back.'

Larissa rears back. 'What?'

'All of it.'

'What about the weeks she's already worked?'

'Doesn't matter! He's paying for the whole job, not part of it. Breach of contract.'

Silence. Of course it's a job lot, thinks Mercedes. He knows no one would stay with that *perra* if there weren't a penalty for leaving.

'You get it? All those new fittings. That new kitchen. The new canopy. We'll have nothing to pay with!'

Larissa's jaw clicks shut.

'And that's before the compensation ...' He hunts again, finds another sheet, brandishes it.

'*Compensation?*'

'Yes! Look! Penalty clause.'

Breathless quiet.

Larissa puts her face in her hands. Out on the *terasa*, Donatella pauses as she reaches into her apron for change, and stares.

At eight fifty-nine a.m., Tatiana appears on the gangplank and comes to the Re, all sunny smiles. Triumphant.

'Ready?' she asks.

Mercedes nods.

Tatiana turns and starts to walk away. 'I need to sort out my wardrobe,' she says. 'You can give me a hand.'

She turns, and sees that Mercedes still stands in the restaurant, dreading the day ahead. Hating her. Feeling the burn of Felix's gaze, from where he's taking the dry nets down from the racks and folding them to go back on the boats when they come in.

'Come on, Mercy!' Her blue eyes sparkle in victory. 'We haven't got all day!'

31

Tatiana's cabin is as big as the bedroom she shares with Donatella. And the ceilings are lower, and to Mercedes' eye it's uglier. But still, every time she's led down here, the luxury always makes her heart beat faster. The deep plush carpet, the upholstery that both cradles and supports, the opulent overkill of hanging full-length brocade curtains to cover the porthole. She despises Tatiana Meade, but oh, she would like to be her.

The walls are lined with wood. Wood that looks like leopardskin. Floor to ceiling, corner to corner. Every piece of furniture – desk, dressing table, *chaise longue*, the bucket chairs, the headboard surround – is framed in the same wood. Painted with layer upon layer of varnish until the wood looks as though it's been sealed in amber.

It actually hurts to look at. Mercedes cannot imagine being in here when the boat is actually moving. I would be sick in seconds, she thinks.

'So what do you think?' asks Tatiana.

There's been a new decorative feature put in, since Mercedes was last in here. Above the bed, hanging from the wall, four pictures: framed photographs, each the size of an atlas. All of Tatiana. Tatiana with her chin on her knuckles. Tatiana with her hands either side of her face, the skin pulled back so that her eyes are delightfully almond-shaped and her jaw is raised. Tatiana with long hair, tipping back on a chair with a coquettish smile, gravity doing the rest of the work. Tatiana taken from above: all eyes, no chin.

She smiles gamely and lets out a *oao*. 'Amazing pictures,' she says, honestly. Never having held a camera, she knows nothing about the photographic arts. But she can tell that the people who took them worked hard for their money.

'Aren't they?' replies Tatiana, complacently.

Mercedes reflects once again on the misfortune that led to the girl's inheriting none of her beautiful mother's features. Still: there can never have been any doubt in Matthew Meade's mind as to who her father was.

Tatiana looks pleased at her reaction. 'They *are* rather spesh, aren't they? We're getting a proper portrait painted, for the new house. You'll *oao* your head off when you see that.'

'Yes, I am sure,' says Mercedes drily. I'll be much more careful in the future, she thinks, about who I form my instant friendships with.

Tatiana lays a hand flat against a panel in the wall, and a door springs open. Beyond, a corridor lined with rails and shelves and drawers, the facings all in the leopard wood, and, at the end, a shiny white marble bathroom.

'Ugh, God,' says Tatiana. 'I'm sick of this. It's so hard to keep it organised when it's all so *cramped*. Right, we have to get this lot out. I've got my autumn wardrobe arriving on Thursday.'

She's trying to make it up to me, Mercedes thinks. She can never just say sorry. So she's doing it with *stuff*.

A pile of cloth. A pile of beads. Another of bracelets. Mercedes has never owned such wealth. I can give some to Donatella, she thinks. The clothes won't fit her.

She fingers the fine gauze of the kaftan that caused her such embarrassment in the market square. It's beautiful. A rich, red and orange paisley pattern. And silk, she realises, though she's never touched silk before.

What a world they live in, she thinks. Where girls can walk about in clothes like this and not have their heads shaved for shame.

'And of course . . . ' Tatiana jumps to her feet ' . . . you'll need something for the party.'

'Party?'

Tatiana sighs, rolls her eyes. 'Yuh-*huuh*.'

'What party?'

'The housewarming, stupid! What party did you *think* I meant?'

'Housewarming?'

She stops. Her brows knit.

'You've not had an invitation?'

Mercedes, bewildered, shakes her head.

Tatiana looks thunderous. Oh, God, thinks Mercedes. What have I done now?

But it seems the thunder is not about her, this time. 'Well, we'll see about *that*,' she says, through gritted teeth. 'Hang on. Look—'

She dives into the wardrobe, re-emerges with the loveliest dress Mercedes has ever seen. Pink satin. No – *flamingo*. Like a ballerina dress: a princess neckline and long tight sleeves, and a skirt that flares and flares and ripples like water all the way to the ankle.

'Try that on.' Tatiana tosses it at her as though it were an old rag. 'I'll be back in a minute.'

She marches from the room. Mercedes hears her bellow for her father.

It's made of some cloth she's never seen before. It *stretches*. In every direction. Like stockings, only smooth and soft and slippery and heavy, all at once. She's overwhelmed with lust. Greedy like a child, mad to feel that cloth against her skin. In seconds she's down to her old grey hand-me-down bra and her knickers, and the dress is dropping over her head like a cocoon, and she is in heaven.

She strokes it. She can't stop. Just stands in the middle of the floor and touches herself. Runs her palms up her arms and pinches the folds between her fingers, and shivers with pleasure at the very *feel* of it.

'Right. That's sorted.'

She jumps. She'd almost forgotten Tatiana, for a moment.

Her mood has cleared. She's all smiles again. 'Some idiot mistake,' she says, sweeping in through the door. 'You're all coming. Luna's going to drop the invitation in this afternoon ... oh.'

She stops dead, falls silent. Looks Mercedes up and down. 'Oh, yes,' she says. 'That's perfect.'

'Not too much?' Mercedes asks, timidly.

'Oh, no. It's perfect.' She looks some more. 'It looks much better on you than it does on me,' she adds, generously. Presses on another piece of wall and opens up a cupboard door with a full-length mirror on the back.

Mercedes looks at herself, and inhales. For a moment, she thinks she's looking at someone else. I look like a princess, she thinks. No, I look like a *queen*.

And Tatiana brings her back to earth. 'What are your mother and sister going to wear?'

Reality. It crashes over her head like an ocean wave. Of course I can't wear this. How stupid I am. I'd make my family look like fools.

Tatiana is quiet again. Thinking.

'Of course,' she says.

'What?'

She wheels, and leaves the room again. 'Come on!'

Mercedes scuttles after, follows her down the corridor.

'There's all of Mummy's stuff,' says Tatiana, 'still just sitting there. Even your mother might be able to get into one or two of the looser things.'

Thursday

32 | Mercedes

Laurence, last night. A bottle of whisky from his suitcase and the radio playing scratchy jazz to drown out their voices. They've known each other a long time now. She wouldn't go so far as to think of him as a friend. Knows that theirs is a relationship based on mutual benefits rather than affection. But still: there's a form of trust between them, and, though what drives them might be different, they still share a common objective.

'Mercedes,' he'd said, 'this money we're following. Have you thought about where it comes from?'

Mercedes had shrugged. Of course she has. Fraud. Drugs. Heads of broken states, securing their share of the embezzled tax. Plunderers of natural resources, making sure their owners never see the benefit. Any number of crimes and moral misde-meanours, really; not just tax evasion. The Bank of Kastellana doesn't ask questions. But its fees are astronomical, and the people love their new-found comforts.

'I know it's not good.'

'No,' he said. 'Thing is, we've been aware for a while that the Meades were up to their necks in something much worse than we'd originally thought.'

'Go on?'

'They buy and sell people.'

Mercedes lurched inside. Only showed it with a blink. She's never known if he knows about her own situation. Perhaps he does. Perhaps all the people he's approached over the years are to all intents and purposes indentured servants.

'What do you mean?'

'People-trafficking.'

She thought of the images she'd seen on the news. Those endless rubber boats, floundering in the ocean. The people streaming across borders, marching south to north. The freezer truck pulled up in an English layby, interior stuffed with blue-dead bodies. They've always joked about how lucky they were, that La Kastellana seemed to be the only island in the whole of the Mediterranean that didn't have a holding camp full of shipping-container dormitories. But of course. Not luck. You just don't shit where you sleep.

'Those girls up at the house?' he said. 'They're the tip of the iceberg.'

Mercedes' father thinks Laurence is a bit of a fool. With the clothes and the clipped accent and the stream of gossip, he's put him in the same category as the idiot honorary consul. It's a perfect cover. The dilettante Englishman abroad, selling wines to the dodgy rich, getting access to their houses. Recording all the boasting that rings around the tables at Mediterraneo, the diners convinced that exclusivity is the same as privacy.

'I don't suppose you've heard of Bernard Reichs?' he asked.

She stared at him, blankly.

'No. Well I don't suppose you would have. It's pretty niche

stuff. Got arrested in New York a couple of months ago. Thing called a Ponzi scheme. Investment adviser. Took people's money and pretended to turn it into more money. Staggering returns on investments, all paid out of the money he'd got in from new investors. You'd've thought people would be wise to this sort of thing by now, but ... well, greed. It's like gambling. Makes people take leave of their senses. So the whole thing collapsed eventually, and there's going to be a lot of houses up for sale in Palm Beach shortly. Anyway, he's in custody, and you know what they say about honour among thieves ...'

'No?' said Mercedes.

He had shaken his head. 'Sorry. It means there is none. Anyway. Bernie. He's been singing like a tweety-bird ever since they took him in. Pointing the finger at *everyone*. And one name's been coming up over and over again.'

'Matthew Meade.'

A nod. 'And I'm afraid there's more.'

The *festa* has broken up by the time she walks back to the sepulchre, weary to her very bones and certain she won't see sleep tonight, for her mind feels electrified. Those girls, on the *Princess Tatiana*. Four went on, three came off. She's put it to the back of her mind all these years, but now she knows the truth. She wasn't mistaken. There were four, and then there were three. And what she's doing at the Casa Amarilla is suddenly a matter of life and death.

The path to the cemetery is unmade: dusty earth beneath her feet, loose stones that can catch one unawares. She walks carefully in the dark.

But it's not dark, really, ever, here any more. Even up here on her headland, the streetlights of Castellana Town throw her shadow ahead, and over the bluff the dancing illuminations, the distant throb, of the Temple nightclub, still going strong at two a.m. Too bright to see more than the moon in the sky. It's a long time since I saw full dark, she thinks. They've changed everything, these people. They've turned a temple into a bordello, and they've even stolen the stars.

You could be free, Mercedes. If you succeed at what he's asked you, you could finally be free.

The thought makes her wince, as though she's bitten her tongue. And those girls. What of them? All those nameless, faceless children, and all you can think of is your freedom?

With every silver lining there comes a thick black stormcloud.

He's asleep in the breeze from the fan. Stirs as she tiptoes into bed. 'You came home,' he mumbles. Opens his arms. 'Okay? Are you okay?'

'Shhh,' she whispers. Settles into the familiar smell of him. Leather and soap and rolling tobacco, the salt air over the sea. The smell of Felix Marino is her comfort and her joy. 'Go back to sleep. We can talk in the morning.'

'What time is it?'

'Late,' she soothes. 'Go to sleep.'

He wraps his arms around her and despite the heat she relishes the embrace. When the family aren't in residence, and there are no rental visitors like last week's Russians, they get to spend three, sometimes four nights a week together like this. When they cannot, she aches for him. I want to come home. I want this to be over. Let me come home. They can't keep me now. Not after what I learned tonight.

I won't sleep, she thinks. God knows I need to. But it's too much. It's too much. And she tumbles instantly into unconsciousness without even being really aware.

*

Moments. Only moments since she was last awake. He comes quietly into the room, sits on the bed and hands her a *café con lexe* as she comes awake.

'What time is it?'

'Nearly seven,' he says. 'I let you sleep in.'

She drains half the cup in a single draught. 'Oh, my God,' she says. 'I need to be back at work by noon.'

'Better hurry up, then,' he says, and whistles his way back to the kitchen to throw together some sandwiches so they can breakfast on the water.

He has some pots on the bay below the Casa Amarilla. They can potter about on the water, and then he can come in close to land and she can swim to shore and climb up to work on the staircase carved into the cliff below the garden. It's a convenient way to cut out her commute – and besides, for Mercedes Delia, being on the water with no prospect of being *in* it would be the cruellest of tortures. She loves her husband, but she's been *in* love with the sea her whole life.

He turns on his radar screen as they enter the bay. Guides them to the first pot by the bleeps from the transmitter attached to its marker buoy. She looks at his boy-toy and shakes her head. Almost a thousand American dollars he paid for it, and she still doesn't see the point.

'You used to just go straight to the pots,' she grumbles as they crawl across the water, his eyes on the screen.

'Yeah, I didn't really, though, did I? You're romanticising. Do you really not remember what it used to be like, going back and forth looking for the bloody things?'

'*Pfft*,' she says, because she knows she's wrong. 'I mean. Look. It's right there! What do you need a screen for?'

'Because I *led* us to it *with* the screen, stupid.'

271

He cuts the engine. Picks up the boat hook and pulls in the first buoy and starts to haul the rope in, hand over hand. 'Come on, Mersa, you don't think the fact that we're pulling in twice the catch this last couple of years is a coincidence, do you? It's because we're not spending hours looking for the pots. I've twice as many now. Because of technology.'

'*Hunh*,' she says.

'And besides. I like knowing where you are when you're off swimming.'

'*Hunh?*'

He keeps hauling. Hand over hand.

'Hang on,' she says. She glares at the transmitter he attached to her sea-belt a few months ago. 'You said it was for emergencies. Are you telling me it's on all the time?'

He doesn't reply.

'Oh, fuck you, Felix Marino.'

He looks over at her, and there's a touch of hurt on his face.

'No, don't look at me like that. I'm not a child,' she says.

Felix shakes his head, turns back to his pots. 'Don't care.'

'You *watch* me?'

Felix takes a deep breath. 'Oh, Mercedes.'

She looks at the tag on her belt with distrust. Maybe I could take it off, she thinks. Too many people watching too many others, in this world.

'It's not that I don't trust you,' she tells him, 'it's the principle. How do I turn it off?'

'Really?' He gives her a slow look. 'It's just love, Mercedes,' he says. 'That's all.'

He takes it from her and holds down a button hidden beneath the bright orange waterproof cover.

'Thank you,' she says.

He goes back to pulling in the pot. 'So now I can just go back to worrying.'

'I promise I'll turn it on if I need you,' she says. 'And, that way, you'll *know* I need you, because suddenly you'll see me.'

The pot breaks surface. Two fine red cock lobsters inside, pincers locked in mortal combat.

'I know you're at home in the water,' he says. 'I know. But think what it would do to me if I lost you.'

'And my mother,' she says. And her loss hits her again like a wave breaking over her head. Same feeling, over and over, all her adulthood. I'm stuck, she thinks. I can't get past it. My sister is dead and we will never really recover.

He sees her expression. 'Oh, Mersa. Oh, I'm sorry. I didn't mean to—'

She puts a hand up. 'No. No. You're a good man. I don't know why you put up with me.'

He hooks the rope over a rowlock, covers the length of the boat in four steps, avoiding the nets like a gymnast. Puts a rough fisherman's finger under her chin to lift it and kisses her lips. 'Because I love you,' he says. 'Because I always have.'

Crazy, she knows, but being out on a boat in the middle of the ocean always feels to her like having a cloak of invisibility. It's where they talk, properly. It's illusory, she knows. There's no real privacy anywhere.

Felix fires up the engine to move to the next pot. 'So are you going to tell me, then? What Laurence wanted?' he calls.

The world comes crashing back. 'Yeah,' she says.

He glances at her, sees her change of mood. Cuts the engine and sits down.

'Something's happened,' she tells him. 'In New York.'

*

'It's not just money, Felix,' she says. 'It's not just money stuff they're doing.'

He's quiet now, his cheerful mood gone.

'Casa Amarilla is the centre of operations,' she says.

'How can it be?' he asks. 'They're hardly ever here.'

'Oh, Felix,' she says. 'They're always here, with the internet. You know those cameras? All over the house?'

He nods. 'The security.'

She shakes her head. 'Blackmail. Old-fashioned blackmail. He's got scores of them now, paying him money. All those girls. All those little girls. The worse they are to them, the more money they have to pay him later.'

'Oh,' he says. 'Lord. But how much money does one person need?'

'All the money in the world,' she says. 'And power. Imagine the power. He gets off on power, I think. It's his thrill.'

Felix puffs out his cheeks, releases the air slowly while he takes it in.

'But it's worse,' she says. The weight of her knowledge comes crashing down on her shoulders. I'm tired, she thinks. I'm so tired. I can't do this. I'm just a housekeeper.

'Go on?'

'Those trips. Those "Stags". They're ... God, I knew they were bad people. You have to have something missing, inside you. To get that rich. To trample over other people's lives, to take it all for yourself. But ... they – the richer they get, the more bored they get. They can have *anything*. And then they want more. And when they've had everything, they still want more, and they ...'

Four went on, three came off.

That woman at the funeral. His wife, Tatiana's mother. She wonders if she knew. Was that why she killed herself?

274

'And then he films it all. And they *go along*. He gives them the films as *souvenirs* and they're so ... mad with their own power they never realise what that actually means. That if they have a copy, then he has a copy too, and they're sitting income forever.'

'I don't ...'

'Felix, they kill them,' she says. 'They take girls onto that boat and they kill them.'

32 | Mercedes

'It's an interesting thing, your Narcissistic Personality Disorder,' says Paulo. 'Did you know it's the only one you can develop as an adult?'

Jason Pettit, former Hollywood A-lister, sits on a lounger, looking disagreeable and scrolling through his iPad. Hasn't looked left or right since he arrived. Gave Tatiana the most cursory of kisses, and ignored staff and girls as though they weren't there at all.

The girls have given up trying to attract his attention and have retired to the pool for a last dip before the prince arrives. They swim awkwardly, heads raised high above the water, for they are under strict instructions not to get their hair wet.

'No,' says Mercedes, as they watch him from the shade of a jacaranda, 'I didn't know that.'

'And I think,' he says, 'that if you view the specimen we have to hand, you might be able to guess the circs that produce it.'

She watches. Such a disagreeable face. So changed from

the Adonis that lit up the screens of the 1990s. It must always have been lurking in there somewhere. But now it's out and proud.

'By fifty a man has the face he deserves,' she says. 'And it's fame, isn't it?'

'Right on both counts. That's why after a bit your celebrities are all the same. Because, unless they're extremely strong-minded, they all turn into the same person.'

'Huh,' says Mercedes. He's so right. Hard done by, entitled, petulant. Faces frozen in startled revulsion if staff address them directly. An incessant droning stream of petty betrayals, delivered with the intensity that normal people use to describe an industrial accident.

'I thought maybe it was just the ones who come here,' she says.

He shakes his head. 'No. It's a type, certainly. I think it has to be in you for fame to bring it out. But no, not just here. It's why I didn't last in LA. I couldn't stand the sound of the whining.'

'Like wind in the phone wires,' she says.

'Give me an honest oligarch any day. They may be cunts, but at least they're not pretending to be victims.'

She throws him a smile. I like you, she thinks. But can I trust you? Then Tatiana snaps her fingers – no *Mercy darling* today – and she's back on duty.

He continues to stare at his screen, chin tucked into Adam's apple and mouth turned down at the corners. The blue eyes that broke a million hearts have sprouted lines that crack his cheeks almost to his ears, and nature – *his* nature – has carved an H a centimetre deep above his nose. Such creepy eyebrows, too. Thick where they exist, unnaturally hairless all around them. Electrolysis. They never think, when they have it done, that age will coarsen their remaining hair and their eyebrows will end up looking marooned, like catkins on a frozen lake.

'Mercy,' says Tatiana, 'Mr Pettit could do with something for his digestion.'

Jason Pettit puts the back of his hand against his mouth and does a silent burp.

'Sure,' she says.

'Not Rennies.' He doesn't take his eyes off the screen as he speaks. Addresses the air, not the housekeeper. 'And not Gaviscon. I don't do *chemicals*.'

The Viagra in his sponge bag would want a word about that.

'A *tisane, sinjor*? Ginger? Peppermint?'

'Both,' he says. 'But *fresh*. It needs to be fresh.'

'Of course. A little honey?'

Jason Pettit's head snaps up. But still he doesn't look at Mercedes. He looks at Tatiana.

'Tatiana, didn't you give the staff my dietary list?'

Tatiana looks horrified. 'I ... my PA's left,' she stammers. Like a schoolkid making up a story about why she hasn't done her homework.

'Gaaaad,' he says, and slams the screen down on his knees. Finally looks up at Mercedes. 'I don't do sugar and I don't do lactose,' he says.

Of course.

'And gluten?' she ventures. In her experience, gluten is the gateway drug to food intolerance.

He picks the screen up again. 'Right,' he says, 'so you *did* get it, then.' He starts to swipe again.

The girls have gathered at the far end of the pool and float with their elbows on the retaining wall, buttocks popping out of the water like four little peaches. Mercedes detours up there

278

before she goes to the kitchen. 'Girls? Do you want anything while I'm going?'

Four sunny little smiles. 'No, thanks!' they chorus.

He transforms when the prince arrives. The moment he sees Paulo cross the garden to open the gates, he leaps to his feet and buttons his shirt up.

Tatiana orders the girls out of the pool. 'I'm not having you curtseying in bikinis,' she says. 'Show some respect.'

Mercedes thinks about the respect they're likely to receive in return and feels slightly sick.

'Remind me what country he's from, again?' says Wei-Cheng.

'I don't think it exists any more,' says Sara. 'I think it's part of Russia.'

'But we still have to curtsey?' asks Gemma.

'Well, yes.' Sara tugs down her skirts and steps into her mules. On duty.

'Why, though?' asks Gemma.

'He's still a prince,' says Sara.

'Prince of *what*, though?' asks Hanne.

'He's the Fresh Prince of Fresh Air,' announces Wei-Cheng, and they all laugh and clatter off through the house to stand in the front courtyard.

Mercedes grins. She's glad that these girls are still able to find humour in their lot – to laugh behind the backs of the men they'll be kneeling to later.

Stops grinning. Oh, God. How could I have been so blind? Oh, please don't let it be one of them, on Sunday. Please.

What are you thinking? That it's okay if it's some girl you've never spoken to?

*

279

She's curious to see him. Tatiana seems so excited to have scored a prince, even if he has been long reduced, like all the dethroned monarchs and the younger sons, to professional Eurotrash.

He's a dapper little man, despite the vestigial remains of the incest his more recent forebears have tried to breed out. A jaw like a children's slide and fat wet lips that smack as he speaks. But his eyes are reasonably normal, if slightly protruding, and his body is straight. He wears a blazer with shiny brass buttons, as though he has just come from the marina rather than the heliport, and pale slacks, and a huge signet ring on his right hand. When he smiles, he shows oversized white teeth with big, sharp incisors.

Once he's straightened up from the car, Tatiana starts to step forward, but Jason is there first, striding across her path, hand outstretched.

'Your Royal Highness,' he says, and does a sycophantic little bow. 'Jason Pettit. We've met before. Last time was the Lisbon première of *Give Me Your Money.*'

The royal smile doesn't waver. He has no idea who he is, thinks Mercedes. Whoever's filling Nora's shoes hasn't sent out briefing notes to *anyone.*

'Oh, yes,' he says. His voice is deep and sonorous, like an opera tenor's. She's noticed that this is common among aristocrats. Especially among the women. Tatiana's clipped little-girl tones mark her out as new money as clearly as her cheek implants. 'Your film. I remember it well. I came with my cousins, I think?'

Jason Pettit reaches his outstretched hand and bows like Clark Gable. 'Yes,' he says.

'Cracking film,' he says. 'High-rise heist, as I remember?'

Pettit looks, for one half-second, as though he's been

stabbed in the groin. But he musters his thespian skills and keeps on smiling too. 'Wall Street fraud,' he replies.

'That's right,' says the prince, smoothly. 'Very gripping. Tatiana, my dear!' He turns away. 'How are you?'

Tatiana's not going to be managing a curtsey that low for many more years. 'So happy you're here, Your Royal Highness. How was your trip?'

'Oh, fine,' he says. 'Giancarlo's helicopter's pretty comfortable.'

'Where did you come in from?'

'Zurich.'

'Oh, how lovely,' she says. 'I love the Alps at this time of year.'

The prince turns and scrutinises the girls, who stand in a little huddle under the portico, looking terribly young and uncertain. His incisors gleam in the sunshine.

'Well!' he says. 'And who do we have here, then?'

34 | Robin

'I'm meeting friends.' Robin has learned from last night's failure. She imitates the voices she's heard coming in and out of the marina. A particular tone that expects never to be questioned. Always to be recognised and accommodated.

She moves a little closer.

'I'm very late,' she says, and fans herself with her hand.

She can feel cool air drifting out from the interior of the Temple. There are air-con units suspended from the undersides of the friezes, blasting downwards. There was a time when Gemma would have been incensed at the waste of energy, she thinks, while I'd be reeling at the aesthetic vandalism. If she's in here now, she's changed completely.

Yes, well, she was thirteen when she was an eco-warrior. All you have to do with teenage sanctimony is wait it out. Though you never know where they'll go next.

Attached to the air-con units is a perfect temple. Was. She's never seen one so intact. Row on row of white marble pillars, a frieze of chariots and gods and cornucopia running all the way around the top, unbroken. Where the roof used to be, tenting of thick white canvas protects the revellers below against rare moments of summer rain.

Bright white spots illuminate the columns. But inside is a mysterious haze of blue, punctuated by the glow of fire bowls. A high chain-link fence cuts the plain on which it stands off from the world.

'Berlusconi,' she says. The first name that comes into her head.

The greeter scans her list. 'Not here yet, *sinjora*,' she says.

'Don't tell me they've left already?'

She scans again. 'No, *sinjora*, they've not arrived.'

'Are you *sure*?'

The woman shrugs.

'We're a party, of course,' she says. 'Could they have come in under another name?'

'It's possible, *sinjora*. What was the name?'

She pretends to rack her brains.

'I've no idea. Sylvia and ... Conrad, I think. Can't I just go in and find them?'

The woman's getting tired of her. '*Si, sinjora*. The entrance fee is one hundred euros.'

Robin almost blows her camouflage by squawking the number out loud. Catches herself just in time. Reaches for her debit card and remembers that its dull green livery will be a sure giveaway.

'Cash okay?' she asks. She'll work out how to pay the taxi later.

A how-could-you-question-our-service moue. 'Naturally, *sinjora*.'

She looks in her wallet and is relieved to find a single hundred at the back of the notes compartment. If you're rich enough, or they recognise you, entrance is, she's sure, free. But even the people who pay have probably never done so with a fistful of crumpled fives. I'm getting smarter at this, she thinks.

She doesn't bother with a tip. She won't be coming back.

Oh, the world these people live in. This antiqued-leather, cut-crystal, Balinese-teak, always-cool world where even ancient tesserae have been lifted and relaid so they are even beneath the feet, and no one ever has to lift a bottle for themselves. Where orchids are always in flower and receptacles once used for collecting animal blood are crammed with roses. A sprung dance floor is half-filled with women who dance like houris and men who dance like satyrs. Elegant barmen shake cocktails behind a marble altar, and impossibly perfect people lounge on couches arranged in squares, the better to turn their backs on their fellow revellers.

Always in groups. Never couples. She has no idea how they do dating. And never women alone, as she is. If I were better dressed, she thinks, they would assume I was a prostitute. There are several draped seductively on those sofas. You can tell them because the other women's shoulders are subtly turned to them, and their silver chainmail slip dresses barely conceal what they have for sale.

A waiter pauses, empty tray balanced on his forearm. 'A drink, *sinjora*?'

'Thank you, I—' She's about to refuse, then changes her mind. She's conspicuous enough as it is. 'A gin and tonic,' she says.

'Any preference for gin?'

Whatever's cheapest, please. 'What do you have?'

He reels off a dizzying list and she forgets each word the instant she hears it.

284

'Seagram's?' she says, and hopes that she has actually named a gin. At home, gin comes from the supermarket and is called London Dry.

He does a funny little silent bow. 'Fever tree, or Indian?'

'Indian,' she's getting bored now.

'Lime, lemon or cucumber?'

Jesus. 'Surprise me.' She gives him a smile.

He whisks away. She positions herself by a fluted column and scans for the long-lost face. Don't let Gemma be one of the chainmail girls. Please. If she's here, let her be carrying a tray, or washing up, or checking gauzy cover-ups into that cavernous coat room ... let her 'party' just be a teenage boast to impress her friends. The parties to which these people invite random seventeen-year-olds to are not the sorts of parties Nasreen and Harriet imagine.

The waiter comes back. He's chosen lime, and she is relieved.

'Would you like to start a tab, *sinjora*?' he asks.

That card. No way.

'I'm waiting for people,' she says. 'We'll start one then.'

'That'll be twenty euros, then,' he says. Nicely.

She's ready for that. Throws a twenty on the tray and uses up one of her crumpled fives. Another little bow. He goes away.

She takes a sip. What she'd thought was a plastic straw is made of glass. It conducts the cold, and makes her lips hurt. I should have asked him, she thinks, if he'd seen her. They must all live somewhere, these lovely young things that serve the rich so decoratively. Probably in dormitories, or eight to a two-bed flat.

The music pauses and she hears the roar of the sea. Then Blondie fills the void; another Studio 54 special, 'Atomic'. Half a dozen girls leap from their seats and pull their men by the hand towards the dance floor.

285

I can't be handing out leaflets here. Those bouncers could bring down a bear. And these aren't people you just strike up conversation with. Half of them have bodyguards. You only get to go to those tables if you're invited. And nobody's going to invite a middle-aged Englishwoman in Birkenstocks who ran out of hair conditioner two nights ago.

What was I thinking? What a stupid, stupid waste of money.

A bodyguard behind a banquette nods to his boss and walks past her to approach a young girl who sits alone on a couch, nursing a glass of champagne. She barely looks old enough to drink. Long and thin, a bleached Afro and honey-coloured skin, a Grecian-style dress in white chiffon that barely reaches her thighs, waisted with a gold belt. Like Gemma, she thinks, and her heart pops a string. How did she get here, so young? She's clearly not a local. What happens, that brings these almost-schoolgirls into this game? Where are their parents?

She knows the answer to that. Doesn't like it. Somewhere there's another mother hopelessly scouring the internet, crying herself to sleep. Oh, hell, why did I come here?

This is awful. Robin feels profoundly demoralised. What a place. All the money in the world, and this is what you buy with it. She can see, now, that most of the architecture around her is faked. There probably was a temple here once, she thinks. But most of those pillars are plaster on an extruded base.

I'll go to the loo, she thinks, and then I'll go.

The loo. Of course.

She has Blu Tack in her bag for just this sort of opportunity.

The toilets are in a mini-temple all of their own, on the far side of the bar; a godlike young marble athlete twelve feet tall marking the gents', a sexy nymph with an amphora on her shoulder the ladies'. Inside, the sound cuts off as though someone's pulled the power. Lush pink carpet, a row of pouffes lined up in front of a wall full of mirrors.

She wonders how long they last, these girls. It's not a long career, probably. They don't have the look of mistress about them. Nobody's going to be renting them flats or giving them diamond bracelets. A couple of years, maybe, while they still look as though they don't know what's coming, and then what?

She pushes open the first stall. Marble, though the toilet itself is mercifully white. It smells delicious: like a perfume shop, not a place where people defecate. That little woman outside must spend hours scrubbing to keep it this way. She'll probably notice my flyer in minutes. Oh, well. Might as well try.

She gets one out, Blu Tacks it to the back of the door, where someone sitting on the throne will spot it and hopefully the attendant won't. Looks at her handiwork for a moment and moves on.

In the fifth stall, she finds a girl. White-blonde hair, pixie-cut, silver chainmail dress, silver platform stilettos, ankle bracelet. Passed out, skirt up around her waist, a line of frothy drool adhering her to the floor and a neat little syringe hanging from the crook of her big and second toes. She stands and stares at her for several seconds. This is what happens to them, she thinks. They dull their emotions until they dull them to death.

I can't. I can't. I can't be involved with this. Oh, God, let me find her. Let me find her.

She doesn't put a flyer in that stall. Turns on her heel and walks out.

The attendant is leaning over a woman whose diamond

earrings drop all the way to her shoulders, offering a tin of hairspray. She glances up, sees Robin, goes back to where the money is.

'There's a girl, in one of the stalls,' calls Robin, 'I think she's sick,' and she hurries away, partly to avoid questions, but mostly because the cloying atmosphere and the sight she's just seen have left her gasping for air.

Back out in the club, she hurries past the bar to the terrace overlooking the sea. The moon is up, and she can see a beautiful river of silver. If she can get there in time, she might be able to avoid throwing up.

The terrace is a lawn. The last thing she'd expected in a place where most of the women are in stilettos. But it's rather lovely. It soaks up the bass and leaves only the music behind. She can walk it easily in her Birkenstocks, and the sea is almost within reach.

A false horizon, of course. The land drops where she had thought it ended, and she sees that on the very edge of the cliff is a horseshoe of seating around a half-moon table. And, elegantly concealed from *hoi polloi*, the duke and a handful of companions watch the silver moonlight glitter on the water. She sees only the backs of their heads at first, until he turns to look for their hovering waiter.

She recognises him immediately. She's seen that noble profile in glossy magazines for decades. He is still exceptionally handsome, for a seventy-year-old. A long, angular face that could be frescoed on a wall in ancient Carthage. The Phoenician diaspora writ large.

He concludes his business and the waiter walks away. Someone says something that makes him laugh, and she sees that one of his molars is made from gold. He *looks* like a duke, she thinks. Like a prince in an ancient text, a man you'd abso-lutely believe to be what aristocrats looked like if you hadn't seen the Habsburgs.

She hovers in the shadow of a pillar and watches.

It's a nice face, she thinks. Benign. The sort of face you'd trust in a crisis and fear in battle. No wonder they love him so, here.

She cannot hesitate. If she hesitates, she'll lose her nerve. She steps quickly down the slope and walks boldly to where he sits.

'*Sinjor*,' she says, loudly. Thinks again. How do you address a duke? What's the word?

'*Gracioso*,' she tries. That can't be far off, can it? Your Grace?

The table falls silent. One by one, his companions turn to stare. She realises that that horrible British consul is among them and her heart sinks.

She feels drab and foolish in her travelling clothes.

The duke turns last of all, and his face is blank.

'I need your help,' she tells him. Looks into his shiny dark eyes and feels nothing come back.

'Giancarlo ...' says a woman uneasily. He raises a hand to quiet her.

She can sense movement behind her. Bodies emerging from the shadows. I have to hurry. I have no time to spare,

'*Gracioso*, I'm looking for my daughter. She disappeared in England last year and I got ... information that she was coming to La Kastellana this week. I've tried and tried, but your police won't help me, and this man ...' she points at Benedict Herbert '... doesn't want to know.'

'Mrs Hanson—' Herbert begins, and she holds up her hand, the way her quarry did.

'Please, *gracioso*,' she says. 'I know now's not the time. But I don't know when *would* be the time. Can I come and see you tomorrow, maybe, when you have a moment? Please? I know a word from you will make all the difference ...'

The dark eyes glance over her shoulder. An almost imperceptible nod. She feels hands grip her arms and start to pull her away.

'Please!' She raises her voice to make herself heard. 'Sir! You have to help me! She's only seventeen! I know you can help. If you'd just ...'

The hands feel like pincers as they close around her biceps. Robin starts moving backwards, despite every effort she makes to stay still. She drops her glass and it shatters on the stony ground. Freezing droplets splash her feet.

'Please!' she cries again.

The duke turns back to look at the sea.

'*Graci-OH-so!*' says Benedict Herbert in his tight little voice as the bouncers drag her away, and her head fills with the sound of their mocking laughter.

35 | Mercedes

'Just do as you're told. Go on.'

Mercedes freezes in the stairwell. This job. This life. I can't bear it. I can't bear it.

The sound of palm on skin. Unlikely to be her face, not at that volume. And they don't like leaving marks; it's probably disrespectful to the next taker.

Not much longer, Mercedes. Not much longer. In a few days you will bring them all down.

'Go on, you little bitch. Get down. That's right.'

Why can't he close the window? For God's sake, he must *know* people can hear.

Yes, that's why he doesn't.

An *aaah* of triumphant masculine satisfaction.

These lovely girls. They should be at school. Exploring. Feeling their way to their hearts. Such pain they must have had, that these are their choices. That the shiny baubles Tatiana offers are worth the crushing death of their capacity to love.

'That's it,' booms the voice. Mercedes has never watched pornography, but she is certain the delivery is derived straight from its scripting. 'Ahh, yes, you dirty little ...' the sound of another slap '... yes, all the way. All the fucking ... ahh.'

She closes her ears. She can hear no more. Hurries on down the stairs with the clean towels for the kitchen.

Hanne sits on the prince's knee, playing with his ear. He and the rest of the party carry on drawling round their brandy and cigars, and pay her no heed. Tatiana caresses the back of Jason Pettit's hand with her pale pink fingernails as he laughs obsequiously at the prince's jokes. Wei-Cheng and Sara, unwanted for now, have retired to the edge of the pool and kick the water, skirts pulled up to the tops of their thighs, their faces blank, as though they've powered down.

And there, in his double-wide armchair, sits Matthew Meade, gloating like the toad that got the flies. Age has not wearied him nor reduced his bulk; it has merely made it slide with the pull of gravity. He walks with a stick now, for his weight throws him off balance and he is easily tipped over. Once he's down, he's like a beetle on its back and it takes two strong men to pull him upright. And still, he keeps a silver box filled with blue pills by his bed, for a man of Matthew's appetites will never be deprived.

Mercedes puts her tray down and distributes tiny Turkish coffees one by one. I am invisible, she thinks again. The invisible woman. Even Tatiana doesn't really notice me. It would only be if I went away that she'd remember I was ever here.

All to the good.

'... never have won that Oscar if he hadn't been sucking the committees' cocks,' says Jason Pettit as she lays his coffee

292

down. It hasn't taken him long to revert to sourpuss. No one, she thinks, can keep their true self hidden forever.

'Wasn't Bruce on the committee that year?' asks Tatiana, and they all laugh and glance up at the balcony above.

'Well,' says Matthew, 'I think he'd be the first to agree he doesn't really mind who's sucking his cock as long as they do it enthusiastically,' and they all laugh again.

It's all they talk about, one way or another. Money and sex, sex and money. If the audience for those glossy magazines only knew, she thinks, what these people are like. And she looks through her lashes at the prince and wonders if the long-since ravished royal courts of Europe were the same.

He looks so pleased with himself. As though he deserves this beautiful nymphet on his knee, as though it's his personal magnetism that has drawn her there. It's almost tempting to walk away, to leave them to get on with it, just to feel the satisfaction of letting him fall into the Meades' trap.

But there's a girl here who has no idea how far it will all go. And I can't let that happen. Now I know, it would be no different from killing her myself.

The room upstairs has gone quiet. She collects the prince's used glass, replaces his ashtray and moves on. Matthew Meade turns laboriously in his seat and contemplates the girls in the pool, eyes narrowed. Choosing, she thinks. They must both know that one of them is his tonight. She wonders how they feel inside as they smile so sweetly. Dread? Or dead inside?

The drawing-room door slides back and Bruce Fanshawe emerges, ostentatiously tucking his shirt into his trousers.

'Aha!' says Tatiana. 'The warrior returns!'

He walks across the patio like an ape. He has already made use of the gym building overlooking the ocean, and his over-pumped body – the thighs that strain his trouser legs, the breasts that bulge through his shirt, the baobab neck – suggest that that is a daily occurrence.

'Had fun?' asks Tatiana, as though he's been for a pizza.

He waggles his hand horizontally in the air. 'She's a crier,' he says. 'Get me a whisky, sweetheart. Scotch. Single malt, Plenty of ice.'

'Certainly, sir,' she says. As she goes into the house she hears him from the rattan couch where he's hurled himself. '*Boo hoo!*' he cries. '*Boo hoo!*'

And she hears them all laugh.

Paulo is on guard under the portico, silently watching. Missing nothing.

'Hey,' she says.

'No rest for the wicked,' he says.

'When does your watch change?'

'Not till six.'

'Lord,' she says.

'It's what they pay me for. His bodyguard's a jobsworth, though. Did his twelve hours and not a minute more.'

'Ugh,' she says, sympathetically. 'I'll bring you some coffee before I go off duty.'

'Thanks,' he says.

'Something to eat, too?'

'No, you're busy enough.'

'I'll bring you a sandwich,' she says. 'I'll wrap it so you can eat it whenever.'

Paulo beams. Nothing endears you to him more than food.

*

294

She goes to the roof to get the linens in. Late night is always best: when they're dry, but before there's any danger of dust blowing in from the Sahara. It's a job she generally enjoys. The last duty, usually. Up in the cool, the breeze coming off the sea, the yacht people's voices faded to a murmur.

The sheets are dry. Strung out across the rooftop, three to a line, five lines altogether. She drags the laundry basket over to the first row. Unclips the first of the clothes pegs.

A cough, over by the road parapet.

Mercedes stops, peers into the gloom. There's a person there, curled up in a ball like a baby waiting to be born.

'Hello?' she calls.

No answer.

She puts down the pegs, ducks under the sheet. Goes closer.

It's Gemma, the little curly-top. The one who looks as though she's barely grown breasts. Stick-thin arms wrapped round stick-thin legs, forehead pressed to her knees. She doesn't seem to register Mercedes' presence.

'Hello?' she says again. 'Gemma? Are you okay?'

Slowly-slowly, the head lifts and the girl stares at her. She's been crying. Her eye makeup is streaked and her face looks grey.

'Are you all right?'

The girl coughs again. 'Sorry,' she says. 'I seem to be having a spot of asthma.'

Thoughts rush through her brain. Has she taken something? Been given something? She looks awful.

'I wanted a breather,' says the girl, and manages to laugh round her laboured wheezing, 'and I left my inhaler downstairs. Ironic, eh?'

Mercedes steps closer again. 'I'll get it for you,' she says.

The girls looks so surprised at this kindness that Mercedes

is overwhelmed by sadness. Has nobody been kind to you in your life? Oh, you poor child. Is that what it is? That you've had so little kindness that you think that this ... life you're living ... is normal?

'Would you?'

'Of course. Where is it?'

'In my bag,' she says. 'It's by the pool. On that little blue table. A little one. Like a pyramid. It's got ...' she pauses to suck in more air '... sequins.'

'Okay,' she says, 'wait here.' As if she were going to go anywhere else.

Deep, bellowing laughter in the hall, and a girlish shriek. She hovers at the top of the stairs, wonders if she should make herself scarce. They don't like it if the servants show themselves when they're heading up with their prey. They must see themselves reflected in our eyes, however deadpan our expressions.

'I say,' says the man. The prince. 'You're a lot heavier than you look. Just a minute. Let's get you—'

Another shriek. A real one, this time. A sliding clatter, a dull thud, a female groan. She peeps over the banister. Hanne lies sprawled on the marble floor, the prince standing over her, chortling. He's giggling. High-pitched, schoolboy chortling. Mercedes makes her decision and hurries downstairs.

Paulo comes into the lobby just as she arrives, hurries over.

'Oops!' says the prince. 'Overestimated my own strength.'

Hanne looks really hurt. She's fighting back tears, clutching her arm. Paulo crouches down, holds out his hands to ask to see. He has medical training. Of course he does.

Hanne glares up at the prince, eyes brimming. 'I *told* you not to carry me!' she shouts. 'Now look!'

296

'HANNE!' Tatiana clacks across the marble. '*Don't* talk to our guests like that!' she shouts. 'How *dare* you?'

Oh, God. Mercedes sidles round them all. On the sofas outside, the men drink on, oblivious.

'But he *dropped* me!' wails Hanne. Winces and sucks air through her teeth as Paulo lifts it up. 'Ow! Stupid bloody ...'

Tatiana turns to her guest. 'So sorry,' she says. 'I can't believe ...'

She steps outside. The pool area stinks of cigars and booze and testosterone. Wei-Cheng and Sara still sit with their feet in the pool, gawping. Christ, she thinks. You'd gawp at a stabbing.

The bag is where Gemma said it was, on a little table by a marble nymph. She glides quietly over to it, glad that she's perfected the art of invisibility. Gives the girls a little smile and presses a finger to her lips.

'I don't think it's broken,' says Paulo. 'Just a bit of a sprain. An ice-pack and a sleep and some ibuprofen and she should be fine.'

'Oh,' says the prince. A fat boy who's had his dough-nut snatched.

Paulo glances up sharply. Glances away just as fast.

'She'll be all right tomorrow, though?' asks Tatiana.

He looks up slower, this time. 'I'd hope so. Might need a few painkillers, but she'll be good to go.'

'Well, what am *I* meant to do?' asks the prince.

Tatiana raises her voice. 'Wei-Cheng!' she shouts. 'Get in here!'

Gemma's got worse. She's really gasping, now, like a fish on the boards of a boat, shoulders up by ears and mouth wide open. Mercedes pushes the bag into her hands. She tears it open, brings out her inhaler, pushes it between her lips, presses the canister down. A hiss. A silence. And then her breath whooshes from her lungs and her shoulders drop and she slumps back against the parapet and closes her eyes.

Modern medicine. It really is miraculous. What did they do before?

'Thank you,' she says.

'You're welcome,' she replies. Hands her a little bottle of cold Fuji water from her apron pocket. She sucks it down in three gulps and the colour begins to return to her face.

'How are you doing?' asks Mercedes.

Gemma nods. Uncertainly. 'I'm fine,' she says. 'It's all a bit more full-on than I'd expected.'

'It won't be for long,' she says, soothingly. Though she knows 'not long' is one of those unfathomable lengths of time that can stretch to an eternity. 'You'll be back in London before you know it.'

The girl doesn't respond for a long moment. Then in a small voice she says, 'And then what?'

I don't know, do I? Mercedes thinks irritably. I'm not *God*. But she makes a soothing sound and takes the empty bottle back.

'I miss my mum,' Gemma says.

'I'm sorry,' says Mercedes. She's not sure what to add. For all she knows, the mother could be dead. She can't imagine what sort of person would abandon their daughter so young. Certainly not one who would deserve to get her back.

She finds *foqqaxia* in the bread bin and fills it with *scamorza* and ham, warms it in the oven for a few minutes before she takes it out to Paulo. As she comes into the hall, she hears the shush of footsteps. Retreats into the shadows beneath the

298

stairs, to be out of the way. It's Matthew, purple feet in black rubber flip-flops, a disconsolate Sara trailing in his wake. Sara looks so little beside him. It must be like having a wardrobe tip over onto you, she thinks. I'm surprised they come out of these weekends with their skeletons intact.

Through the open *sala* door, Jason Pettit complains. 'I thought *we* were getting that one,' he whines.

Tatiana, irritable. 'Well, you'll just have to make do with me.'

'What's happened to the other one? D'you think she's had a bath yet? How about her?'

'Oh, shut up, Jason,' snaps Tatiana. Mercedes guesses that her trip isn't panning out the way she'd hoped.

Paulo looks glum in the shadow of the jacaranda. He takes the sandwich and the coffee, breaks into them with ferocity. 'All right?' he asks.

She shrugs. 'Well, you know.'

He chews reflectively. 'My eldest is four years off those girls' age,' he says. 'I keep thinking about that. She's getting into the make-up and the clothes and the boys.'

She waits. He has another bite, heaves a heavy sigh.

'I'm going to have to stop,' he says. 'I can feel myself turning more and more into a dragon dad. I caught myself shouting at her to *wipe that shit off her face* last time I was back. They don't know, do they? They've no idea what men are like.'

'Some men,' she says, surprised to find herself in this position. Roles reversed.

A toss of the head. 'Yeah. You're right. See? This job is skewing my perspective. You can't turn a blind eye forever, though, can you? Not and keep your soul at the same time.'

She looks at him, thoughtfully. 'No,' she says. 'No, you can't.'

299

Island

August 1985

36

'*Mercedes! Jala,* look! That's its name! It's called Mercedes!'

Matthew Meade's new car came off the ferry a week ago, black and sleek with tinted windows so you can't see in. And now it's here to take them to the housewarming. All the Delia women in a row in their cast-off finery. Mercedes hasn't told them that they're in a dead woman's clothes, and they haven't asked, but they look beautiful. Larissa in a burgundy wrap dress in silk jersey (a slip underneath to protect her modesty and prevent unintentional mishaps, but still, she looks curvy and elegant) and Donatella like an angel in white. In a dress that would be too short for the *solteronas*, its bodice fitted and a skirt that flips around her thighs as though she were skating on ice. Mercedes wears her pink dress, and Donatella has painted some smears of brown on her lids and mascara on her lashes and little streaks of pink on the tops of her cheek-bones, and she feels, for the first time in her life, like an adult.

'You don't think he named it after our girl, do you?' asks Larissa.

Her parents are like children. Childlike in the things they don't know. They're peasants, thinks Mercedes from the lofty heights of her summer serfdom. And then she is filled with shame, for, though it feels like years, she herself only had her first ride in a car a couple of weeks ago. But she can't keep the superior drawl from her voice. Thank God Tatiana returns to England and her boarding school in three more days. Mercedes knows full well that she's getting corrupted.

'It's a brand name,' she says. 'That's all. Like Gaggia. Or ...' she searches her brain, remembers the new TV in their *sala* '... Samsung. You don't name cars the way you do boats. They don't have names, just labels.'

'Ah, I suppose that's right,' says Donatella, 'or it would be the *Princess* Mercedes.'

They bellow with laughter.

They're all in high spirits. Sergio because he is on a guest list among the island's most powerful men. Larissa, because she has watched the fittings and the furniture for the Casa Amarilla come off the ferry week by week and is wild with curiosity. Donatella, because there will be drinks, and a pool and, she hears, a swing that goes right out over the cliff, and because at last, at *last*, she has somewhere to wear this dress where she won't draw tuts of outrage. And Mercedes because her servitude is almost at an end, and the summer isn't finished yet, and there will be hours after school to run across the fields with her old friends and throw themselves into the ocean, and she cannot *wait*.

Matthew Meade's driver opens the door. Smiles and smiles as he beckons them inside.

They get in, one by one. The interior smells deliciously of polish and leather.

304

'Ooh!' says Larissa. 'Oooooh!' and sinks into her seat with eyes like a moo-cow's. Sergio settles beside her, and they spread out like pashas, hands running over the seats as though they were stroking a pussycat.

'It's so soft!' Larissa exclaims. 'Oh, my lord. Like velvet!'

The girls sit facing them, backs to the brand new tarmac road that leads up the hill to the east. Donatella gazes about her as though she were in a museum. Larissa discovers the tiny water bottles and Sergio goes to twist off a cap.

'*No!*' she snatches it from his hands. 'Sergio! No!'

'It's okay, Mama. It's why they're *there*,' says Mercedes, all insouciance. 'There's a whole *case* in the castle dungeons.'

Just to show that she knows *everything* about cars, she presses the catch on the arm rest and the top glides smoothly open to show the box of Kleenex hidden inside.

'*Ay, madre de dio!*' cries Larissa. 'Oh, *l'ostia*, they think of everything.'

The door closes and the air-con cranks up. Larissa lets out a little shriek as the driver cranks off the handbrake and revs the engine. Grips hard on to the hand rests as they move off.

Sergio casually presses the window button and lets it roll all the way down. He pretends he's doing it out of curiosity, but of course it's so that all the neighbours can see who's in the limousine gliding out of town.

The car drops them on the road by the new enclosing wall with its wrought-iron sign, as though anyone would mistake the only house on these cliffs for anywhere else. The Delias stand in a row again while Larissa fusses: straightens Sergio's tie and tugs down the hem of Donatella's dress and drags a comb through Mercedes' hair. Once she's satisfied that none of them will bring shame on her, she takes her husband's hand and they walk in.

'*Oao*,' says Sergio.

Fifty people drink and shout in the grand reception, but still the room feels airy and spacious. Even the roar of their talk doesn't overwhelm, for it rises up and loses itself on a ceiling higher than Mercedes' whole home.

Chandeliers. A marble staircase that spirals skywards from a slippery floor of white hardened glass. Fluted columns holding up the roof. Semi-naked marble women, two metres high, that Tatiana says are the Muses but just look a bit mucky to Mercedes, line the walls. A gigantic portrait of their host in a heavy gold frame. A courtyard fountain centred round a glittering cornucopia of exotic fruit, all carved, according to Tatiana, from a single crystal rock. A black marble nymph in a gold bikini who drapes herself over the pool edge, forever handwashing.

'My lord,' says Larissa, though she looks quite intimidated, 'it's more wonderful than the *castillo* itself!'

'Nonsense,' says Sergio. 'There are things in the *castillo* that are a thousand years old.'

'Yes, but,' says Larissa, 'everything here is *new*.'

Sergio rolls his eyes. Then he spots the harbourmaster by a laden buffet table and strides away, holding out his hand in delighted greeting, for all the world as though they're long-lost friends rather than two people who three hours ago were squabbling over waste disposal. His family huddle by the door, small and inadequate. Oh, to be a man. To know that you have a place in the world. That even among strangers you are *enough*.

Mercedes feels Larissa's hand sneak into hers and knows that the gesture is not intended to give comfort, but to receive it. She squeezes back and feels her mother's shoulders relax. It's worst of all for her, she thinks. Donatella's beautiful, Papa's a man of status, and I've spent all summer play-acting rich. She's never been anywhere like this in her life. She's more aware of being no one, right now, than she's ever been.

One of the women from the boat staff approaches, carrying a little tray laden with drinks. Smiling. The new staff are Filipinas. Tatiana says they make popular staff, because they're *always* smiling.

'Champagne?' she offers. 'Campari? Oran*choos*?'

Larissa helps herself to a flute of champagne, pulls the I-shouldn't-really face and almost giggles at her daring. Slaps Donatella's hand away as she reaches for the same. Donatella tosses her hair and glares. Larissa, wordless, gives her the matriarch stare.

That won't work for much longer, thinks Mercedes. Donatella's right on the edge. Something's changed over this summer, and I think it has something to do with me. She despises our father because he's a lackey, and she despises our mother because in the end she always gives in to him.

Donatella snatches a juice from the tray. Drinks it down in a single draught, staring her mother in the eye, and replaces it before the waitress can move on. Silently, she turns away and walks boldly through the crowd towards the garden.

Larissa watches her go for a moment, then her eye is caught by something more pressing. '*L'ostia*,' she murmurs. 'The duke is here.'

Donatella steps into the evening breeze and inhales in delight, for the air is full of scents and the spectacle is marvellous. She knows this piece of land. Used to know it. Knew it as rough terrain whose thin topsoil made it only fit for prickly pear and goats. Beyond the high yellow wall that encloses this garden, the land remains the same. Just golden stone and scrubby oleander, and the ever-changing sea.

But within, they have built an Eden. A pool runs from by her feet to the very edge of the cliff itself, where it seems to tip over like a waterfall. And it's green. Green everywhere. Not the sparse, far-apart greens she's grown up with – the near-black of the cypress, the yellowing rows of grape vines, the leathery creep of the caper bush, the hard, spiked leaves of the citrus groves, the melancholy silver of the olive – but green that looks like a great swath of cloth thrown across a marriage bed.

A lawn, she thinks. They have a *lawn*.

The lawn is surrounded by trees. Young, but fully grown. No saplings waiting to attain maturity. She saw them come in, wrapped in sackcloth, roots bound in protective plastic, on the ferry, but they look now as though they have always been here, their roots embedded in newly dug craters in the solid rock. Palms and oranges, plums and apples. A walnut, an almond, a quince. A colonnade of weathered golden stone, bougainvillea tumbling over its cross-stones, leads down to where an ancient carob hovers on the very edge of space.

The lawn calls out to her. She's only ever seen them in the movies. Has often wondered how one would feel to walk on.

Donatella slips off her sandals and steps off the flagstones. The ground is springy and gives as she walks, and the grass is cool, and rough, and damp between her toes. Her dress floats about her as she walks, light as a whisper, light as gossamer. She feels like a fairy queen, ready for anything. But first, she's going to find the fabled clifftop swing.

'Mercy! *There* you are! What do you think of my house?'

Mercedes is caught off guard. She doesn't have the words to hand. Or not the ones Tatiana would like to hear. *Big and cold and self-regarding. Boastful. It's ugly. Thank God hopefully this will be the first and last time I set foot in it.*

308

'Amazing,' she says.

Tatiana smirks. She eyes Mercedes, calculatingly. 'You've not seen the best bit,' she says. 'Come on.'

Mercedes hears her mother gasp. So eloquent, that sound. *Don't leave me alone. Your father's gone already, and your sister. I don't know anybody here. You can't!* On a normal day, she would find refuge with the wives, but this is not a normal day.

'My mother,' she protests.

Tatiana stops and looks puzzled. 'What?'

Mercedes lowers her voice. She doesn't want to humiliate Larissa in front of all these strangers. Mercedes feels protective towards her mother. She is such an innocent in this brave new world. 'She doesn't know anybody,' she says.

'Nonsense!' cries Tatiana. 'Of *course* she does!' She takes two steps and plucks at the sleeve of the priest, who is drinking champagne and eating a canapé, talking to a woman in polished black just as though he were a real person. '*Monsinjor!*'

Mercedes is awestruck by her boldness, her confidence among the grandees, as though she were an adult herself.

'You know Sinjora Delia, don't you?'

The priest turns and eyes his parishioner. He doesn't know her from Eve, really. The whole island, after all, is his parish, and Larissa is just one of a thousand mouths that open obediently to take the host from his lofty hands. But he puts on his pastoral smile and greets her. 'Why, yes!' he says. 'And how are you, *sinjora*?'

'Right,' says Tatiana, and leads Mercedes away.

She's so intent on finding the swing that she doesn't notice them until she's right on top of them and it's too late to back out. There's an area of sunken seating by the carob, and the low wall behind hides their heads until she literally steps in front of them. Ten of them, a dozen: young people. Her own age, some a bit older, all dressed as she is, in summer finery. All glossy and gorgeous and drinking champagne and laughing and joking like it's a *real* party, and she recognises immediately that they are from the yachts. And she skids to a halt, but it's too late. They've seen her, and they've all turned to look.

'Hello!' a beautiful blond man, maybe twenty. Dinner jacket, no tie, top button undone. 'A new face! Who are you?'

Donatella feels herself redden, but she's not going to show her embarrassment. She's been longing for adventure for years now. For something different. She screws her courage to the sticking post and gives a confident smile. 'I'm Donatella Delia,' she says, as though everyone should know her name.

The corridor ends in a blank wall, but Tatiana keeps walking towards it after she's passed the last door. And just before they get there, something beeps and the wall slides back, and a great dark space opens up in front of them. Tatiana grins, and waggles some small electronic gadget in the air.

'There are only three of these,' she says. 'Mine, Daddy's and the security dude's. If we all go down on the same plane, it'll stay sealed until some archaeologist teleports inside in the year 5000.'

Mercedes peers into the interior. Wonders if she's being tricked, if she's about to find herself locked up alone again in the dark. But Tatiana presses another button on her gadget and dimmer lights dial up to reveal a room so different from the rest of the house that they might as well be in New York. It's long and surprisingly narrow, a feast of cherrywood veneer and green leather armchairs. One entire wall seems to be made of televisions. A huge one, like the one on the yacht, protrudes a full metre out from the baby screens that surround it, its innards the size of the masculine desk that faces them all. At first, she thinks that there's another on the desk's surface, and then she realises what it is.

'Is that a *computer*?'

'Yah,' says Tatiana.

Mercedes goes over to look at it. 'I've heard about these,' she says. It doesn't look the way she'd expected it to. A series of boxes made of creamy plastic, a clunky keyboard that looks like a kid's toy and a TV that even to her eye is way out of date.

'They're the wave of the future,' says Tatiana. 'They're working on making one you can carry in a suitcase, you know. Daddy's thinking about buying one.'

'What is this place?' She looks around again. With all its technology, it's like being on a spaceship.

'It's a safe room.'

'Safe room?'

Tatiana rolls her eyes. 'In case of home invasion.'

'Of what?'

Another eye-roll. 'Oh, Mercedes. You're such an innocent. It's where you lock down if you get invaded.'

'But who by?'

'Robbers,' says Tatiana, and she seems almost blasé about the words. 'Terrorists. Political activists.'

'I ... on La Kastellana?'

'Oh, Mercedes. *Everywhere.*'

Tatiana slides the door shut. 'Three-inch-thick steel walls,' she boasts. 'And the door's the same. And, if we press this button, security forces will be here literally days before anyone could cut through and get us.'

'Security forces? Does the duke know?'

Tatiana laughs. '*Duh*. He has one of his own!'

311

A safe room. In a medieval fortification. It must be the safest place in the world. In the old days, the whole population would run for the castle at the first sign of a Moorish sail on the horizon. She wonders vaguely when it was that the dukes first started to shut them out.

She wanders the room, running her fingers over the smooth wood. 'But how do you know who's outside?' she asks. 'How do you know when it's safe?'

'Ahh,' says Tatiana, 'I thought you'd never ask.'

She bends over the computer keyboard and starts rattling the keys, and the screens spring to life. Eight different views of Casa Amarilla. The party roaring on, the frenetic bustle in the kitchens and the staff quarters, the empty courtyard with its glistening fountain. Tatiana hits a key and the images change: her father, jiggling the change in his trouser pocket and talking to the duke; her mother, clinging to the wall, alone and awkward; her sister sitting on a banquette in the dark with a group of younger people, laughing as though she belongs there. And Sinjora Bocelli, the notary's wife, in a bathroom, slipping a silver dish complete with bar of soap into her capacious handbag.

On the dining-room table stands an architect's model of card and balsa nearly three metres long. The dining chairs – thrones in gold and Perspex – have been pushed back to line the walls, and people mill about, surveying it.

It takes Sergio several moments to recognise Kastellana Town. But there it is: the harbour front dwarfed by the spread of buildings either side. He recognises their soaring cliffs, built roughly from *papier mâché*. The new marina, its water a startling artificial blue, is filled with rows and rows of identical boats the size of his restaurant.

He comes in closer to study the detail. Here is the church,

312

its dome and tower higher than the buildings on the square around it, as a church should be. But, on the market square, the ramshackle seventeenth-century houses on the sides closest to the sea have been replaced by apartment blocks six storeys high. The square itself is filled with tiny plastic tables and tiny paper parasols and people the size of ants. And the people who sell the spare produce from their land, piled up on old blankets on the pavement, are gone.

Along the new road they came up this evening, the land has been fenced off, subdivided and filled with houses like this one. To the west, the Via del Duqa is cut off at the end by the huge single-storey structure, the restaurant he's been watching take shape all summer. Beyond that, the Via de las Sirenas has been extended all the way along the cliffs, almost to the old Roman cemetery where Larissa's mother's house stands, and lined with more apartment blocks and a huge hotel that looks as if it should be in Paris.

'*Oao!*' he says, out loud.

'What do you think?'

He looks up to see who's speaking, and a frisson chills his skin. He is being addressed by the duke.

Sergio bows. It's one thing serving him in his restaurant. Something quite else to have him engage you in conversation.

'Phase Two,' replies the duke.

Sergio has a tiny moment of panic and looks again. But no – the Re del Pesce is still there on the harbour front, its canopy painstakingly reproduced by some unknown hand. And once he's assured himself that life as he knows it is still included in the grand scheme, the panic is replaced by a surge of excitement. My God! he thinks. The opportunities!

'I am lost for words,' he says. On the far side of the table, the harbourmaster watches enviously.

313

The duke laughs. 'Well, I hope the words will be good when they come,' he says. 'I'm hoping that this is the start of a whole new era of prosperity for us all.'

Too many names, too much champagne. She struggles to remember them – Hugo-Sveta-Christophe-Alexa-Kristina-Sebastian-Dmitri-Serena-Caspar-Jamaldarling-Harry-Conrad – and the face attached to each, when all the girls are blonde apart from Sveta who is from somewhere south of the equator. Eventually, she gives up and just calls everybody *kara*, which they seem to like. And as the bottles empty and someone passes round a cannabis cigarette – the first she's ever seen, let alone tasted – her confidence grows and the fact that they all know each other (school – in England – or their parents being 'old business partners' or just 'I don't know, from around and about the place') matters less and less and the fun she's having matters more and more. Squeezed onto the curved leather sofa between two boys, she listens to their jokes and their references and their in-talk, and she understands not a word of it.

But she doesn't care. Welcome to the world, little girl. Welcome to the great big out-there, expansive, exciting, not-Kastellana world. She feels as though life might finally be starting.

There's mysterious music playing from somewhere, and it takes her ages to realise that it's coming from the big black boulders that form the ends of the sofas and that they are actually speakers, and they laugh at her amazement. *How sweet*, says someone. *Where've you been?* says someone else. *On La Kastellana*, she says. *All my life. An island girl! How intriguing! And who's your father, that you're at this party? A restaurateur*, she says, grandly. *A restauraTEUR! How marvellous! Not really*, she says. *It gets quite boring. Oh,* says Sebastian-Conrad-Jamaldarling, *we can't have you being bored*, and he turns up the music. It's disco from America, stuff she's really only encountered on Tatiana's television, and they all jump to their feet and start to dance. And somebody's hand brushes her buttock, but it's just carelessness, and anyway, the *solteronas* aren't looking, and for the first time ever she's having *fun*.

Tatiana roars with laughter. Mercedes wrings her hands.

'Oh, my God, oh, my God!' she cries. And silently thanks St James that it's not a member of her own family.

And they film in the bathrooms, another part of her brain is thinking. They actually film people in the bathrooms.

The horror of Sinjora Bocelli's predicament drives that from her mind. 'What are you going to do?' she asks. 'My God, what are you going to do?' Her skin crawls at the shaming ahead. The Meades confronting her in front of the yacht people. The constable having to put her in handcuffs. She covers her face with her hands.

Tatiana clicks the remote and the screen fills with a bedroom. Napoleonic sleigh bed, net curtains billowing in the evening breeze by an open window. Through a door to the side of the bed, she sees a shadowy Sinjora Bocelli inspecting her lipstick in the bathroom mirror.

'Oh, nothing,' she says, breezily. 'For now, anyway. Oh, this is priceless, though! We've got them now, don't you see? If that little lawyer man tries to cause problems – *boom*! The solution's all backed up in here for whenever we need it! I can't wait to tell Daddy!'

She rattles the keyboard again, hits enter. Something whirs in one of the boxes and a videotape pops out. 'There, I'll just pop that in here.' She opens a drawer in the panel below the screens. It's full of tapes. Full of them. And she adds her new one to it. Opens another drawer, and gets out a fresh one. Offers it to the slot in the box, which grabs hold and swallows it as though it were alive.

Mercedes is panicking. Did I ever do anything? This summer? If they're filming here, they'll have been filming on the *Princess Tatiana* too. All that stuff she gave me ... is that all on film? Those dresses. I mean, it wasn't just her own, was it? And those dresses of her mother's that she gave me for my family. How do I know you can see in each recording that she's giving them? That I'm not just helping myself?

'Oh, my giddy aunt, lighten up, Mercedes,' says Tatiana. 'It's hilarious. Now, look, sit down. I want to show you ...'

Mercedes lowers herself suspiciously into a chair. 'Show me what?'

Sergio is high on life and possibility. Accosting his fellow guests, he passes out the business cards he had printed especially for the occasion, a rush job from the mainland. He's rather pleased with the little picture of a fish with a tray and a waiter's apron in the top right-hand corner.

'With this card,' he tells them, full of bonhomie and champagne, 'is ten per cent off. A gift from me to you!'

The yacht people thank him politely and tuck the cards into the pockets of their handmade suits.

He's been working his way back towards the duke. He could barely believe their friendly exchange earlier, the way the duke had spoken to him as though he were a neighbour rather than a tenant. But a couple more glasses of champagne and he's beginning to see it as a sign from God. This was meant to be. The duke wants prosperity for all of them. Of course he'll want Sergio's aid in that.

A little Arab man chews on a cigar and points at the restaurant building. 'And this?'

The duke pours out a stream of English. For Sergio, only the odd word – seafood, high-end, function – means anything much. But he sees his chance. Takes a breath and waits for his moment.

'*Sinjor!*' he calls across the table.

The duke looks up.

'If I may be so bold,' he says, 'I have been running the best restaurant on the island for twenty years.'

'There's more than one?' someone mutters, and a little wave of laughter passes behind him.

The duke stares at him long and hard. I've made a terrible mistake, Sergio thinks. He doesn't like being interrupted. But the mistake is made now, so he holds his ground.

'You've eaten my food many times,' he reminds him.

Someone behind him mutters *spaghetti vongole* and he hears another responding titter. It takes all the self-control he has not to turn and glare.

He holds the duke's eye for as long as he can bear. But eventually the silence between them is too heavy, and he drops his gaze.

Tatiana scrolls through the remote and the screens flip and flip and show ever-changing perspectives on the party outside. She points out the guests and tells her terrible truths.

'Right, well. He got rid of wife number one a few years ago, and he's been roaring through the catalogues for number two ever since.'

'Catalogues?'

Tatiana shakes her head. 'Escorts.'

317

'Huh?'

'Call girls?'

Mercedes shakes her head, none the wiser.

'Oh, for God's sake, Mercy. Prostitutes! First wife's for form, second wife's for sex, third wife's for status. Look! Look at them all! That room is heaving with whores! *Putas!*'

Mercedes has never heard anyone use the word in such a concrete way before. All the *putas* the *solteronas* punish are, as far as she knows, metaphorical. She stares at the screens. And she starts to see that the yacht people – the women, at least – clump together in groups.

Tatiana points at a group of women who look not dissimilar to more expensive versions of Mercedes' own mother and her friends. Uneasy in their finery, their eyes following their men about the room.

'First wives,' she says. 'Married when young, or when the men didn't have the cash to get ambitious, looks-wise. Nothing wrong with them, of course. Most of them are probably the *nicest* women they will ever marry. But *nice* doesn't have much currency, in the real world.'

Mercedes is beginning to feel depressed.

'You see that look? That hunted look? That's the face of a woman who knows she's going to be traded in. Silly bitches are usually too honourable to put up a fight for a decent settlement, too.'

Mercedes has turned away from the screen and is staring at Tatiana in amazement. How did you get so cold? she wonders. And which kind of wife was your mother?

Eventually they're all too breathless to dance any more, and they fall back onto the sofas, laughing. Sveta and Sebastian seem to be holding hands now. She feels a bit disappointed.

While they were dancing and he was following her hips with his own, she'd sort of felt they had a connection. But never mind. It's all just a game, isn't it? Flirtation. They don't take things seriously the way the Kastellani do. Good lord, if two young Kastellani people were seen brazenly hand-holding like that, the clock would start ticking on betrothal.

No wonder so many married people are unhappy, she thinks – like my parents. The *pressure*. No chance to flirt or play or identify your options. I don't suppose my mother held hands with literally *anybody* before my father. I want more than that. I want to see the world.

'So what do we do now?' asks maybe-Caspar. Maybe-Christophe – all those C names, no wonder she can't remember! – lopes over to the icy little plunge pool by the carob and comes back with two more bottles of champagne. There seems to be an endless supply.

'Truth or dare!' cries maybe-Kristina.

'Oh, God, you *always* want to play that!' groans maybe-Dmitri.

'Oh, no, I love it,' says someone.

'Go on, then,' says someone else, and a hand takes her glass and fills it up. She's a bit giddy now. She must have had four or five already. But it's such *fun*.

'Okay, you suggested it, so you can go first. Truth or dare?'

'Truth,' says maybe-Kristina.

'Yay! Okay ... who do you fancy here?'

'*You*, of course, *dah*ling.'

'You're meant to tell the truth,' says maybe-Sveta, and they all laugh.

'I *am*, darling!'

A chorus of denial. 'Tell the truth, Kristina, or we're not playing.'

Kristina's face goes a bit serious. 'Okay, then. Jamal. I fancy Jamal.'

Another chorus. Whoops this time. Jamal twiddles his tie ostentatiously. 'I'm totally going dare when it's my turn,' he says, and gives her a great big wink. 'Okay. New girl. Truth or dare?'

She's taken off guard. She hadn't expected that. *I can't do truth. I literally have nothing to tell. They're all so* sophisticated. *If they find out how dull my life really is ...* 'Dare,' she says.

'Second wife,' says Mercedes. Now the shock has worn off, she's warming to the game.

'Cor*rect*,' says Tatiana. She points to a woman whose face is frozen by heavy-handed plastic surgery, her skin pulled so tight she can barely open her eyes.

'Ohhh. I don't know.' Some of the third wives show obvious signs of 'work' but this one is in a league of her own. Her mouth looks as if she's been punched, and her hair is dry like year-old hay.

'Now that,' Tatiana swings back and forth in her chair, 'is a particularly tragic subset of first-wifery. That's your first wife who won't give in without a fight. Either that, or it's revenge surgery. I'm pretty sure it's the first, though.'

'But why? Why would you do that to yourself?'

'Ugh, God,' she says. 'Some of these guys love it when their wives look as if they've been in a house fire. It makes them feel important.'

'So your father,' she asks, 'he is looking?'

Tatiana's face freezes. Unblinking, she presses the remote to move the screens on. 'Over my dead body,' she says. 'Oh, now look, here's a good one.'

A voice bellows suddenly from the doorway.

'TATIANA!'

The girls jump in their seats. Tatiana drops the remote. Matthew Meade stands in the doorway, puffed up like an ogre.

'What the hell are you doing in here?' he shouts.

'I was just ...'

'CHRIST. Are you completely fucking stupid?'

'Sorry, Daddy.' She sounds unusually humble. Curls into her chair like a whipped puppy.

Matthew stamps into the room. Looms over his daughter.

'Never, *ever* do this again!' he shouts. 'Get it? No one comes in here. No one!' He turns on Mercedes. 'Get out. Jesus. Get the hell out of here, you stupid little bitch! Forget you ever saw this place. *Capisce?*'

Mercedes is terrified. She's never seen him like this. Certainly never seen him shout at Tatiana, who seems genuinely shaken. His teeth are bared and his eyes are slits. Like a snake about to strike. She nods, and starts to scramble from her seat.

A hand like a ham claps down on her shoulder. She collapses back.

'You didn't see this place,' he tells her. 'You don't know it's here.'

Mercedes nods vigorously.

'I mean it, Mercedes Delia,' he says. 'If I ever hear this place mentioned, I'll know exactly what the source was.'

Tatiana is frozen in place. She stares at her father and swallows.

'I can destroy you,' Matthew tells her. 'Just remember that. I can destroy you and your whole family just like ...'

He snaps his fingers in the air.

'... *that.*'

*

321

Larissa's not having a good time. She lasted five minutes with the priest, the awkwardness excruciating, and almost wept with relief when he made his excuses. And, since he left, she's just eaten a load of weird canapés and smiled till her cheeks hurt.

There is some etiquette she has yet to learn, for smiling at strangers, it turns out, causes them to look shocked and turn hurriedly away. She feels a fool in her wrap dress and her crucifix, her feet aching in unaccustomed heels. She longs to be back in her restaurant, where she is boss. Where she can talk to anyone and one smile is met with another.

I hate this, she thinks. The whole town's going to want to know all about it tomorrow, and what do I tell them? My entire family's deserted me. Shows how much I matter.

She swears internally. It will be hours before the car comes back to pick them up. If I weren't wearing these stupid shoes, she thinks, I'd just walk home. But I'm stuck here now. She shovels two crab profiteroles into her mouth and washes them down with champagne. And I don't even like champagne, she thinks. I'm going to be up all night with trapped wind.

She wanders over to the glass doors that overlook the garden. It looks so lush and green out there. It must be lovely and cool, now. A different kind of cool from this dry mechanical air. If only I could . . . ah, hang it.

Larissa slides the door back and steps out into the night. Heaves a sigh of relief as she slides the door closed again and the roar of privileged conversation is cut abruptly off.

A shriek, from the dark. She tenses, squints to see where it came from. And then she sees a small crowd, running towards her at high speed, chasing a slender figure in a white dress. A dozen of them, pointing and laughing and baying. And then she sees that the person they're pursuing is Donatella, and she

322

braces to hurl herself into the fray. To fight these attackers off, to protect her child like a mountain lion.

And then she sees that Donatella is laughing. And then she has to cover her face for shame as her daughter barrels past her and flings herself, fully clothed, into the swimming pool.

Gemma

September 2015

37

She's retouching her lipstick in the bathroom when Sara comes in and stands beside her. Gets out her mascara and starts painting her lashes.

Gemma smiles. Sara grimaces back, her eye on her make-up. 'How you getting on?' she asks.

'Okay,' says Gemma. 'You?'

'Good,' says Sara.

'I had to come in here to get away from that Maurice,' she says. 'He's kind of ... handsy, isn't he?'

Sara looks surprised. 'He likes you,' she says.

'Yeah, but ...'

Sara puts the mascara brush back in the bottle. Props her bum against the sink and looks Gemma up and down.

'He's really powerful,' she says. 'He's a proper mogul.'

'Yeah, but that doesn't give him the right to ...'

Sara blinks. Folds her arms.

'You know we're not just here for decoration, right?' she asks.

Gemma frowns. As it goes, that was *exactly* what she'd thought they were there for.

Sara heaves an impatient sigh. 'Gem, just a heads-up. You're going to have to start putting out at some point.'

'Putting ...'

Sara blinks again and clicks Gemma's jaw closed with a manicured finger.

Gemma feels a little twinge of panic.

'He ...?'

She can't be serious. Maurice is huge, and ancient. And sweaty. His jowls hang down so far they vanish into his collar. She can't imagine he's seen his cock in decades.

Sara nods.

'I ...'

She turns back to the mirror. Gets a Chanel lipstick in deep mulberry from her little jewelled clutch and starts painting herself.

We're not real models, thinks Gemma. How on earth did I not work that out?

She stares at Sara. Creamy, medieval skin and a shiny tumble of auburn hair falling across the décolletage of her copper lace mini-dress. A Botticelli Venus, freed from the half-shell. A fantasy girl. My God, she thinks, as she casts her mind's eye over the other Julia Beech models. There's one of each of us, isn't there? They've done us up so the men have a full range to pick from. How did I not realise?

'I'm just saying,' she says. 'I mean, nobody's forcing anyone. This isn't *slavery*. But they've put a lot of money into you and they're going to want to see a return at some point or you'll get dropped. How long's she been bringing you along to things? Like, a month? Are you seriously going to just milk it and not put out?'

328

Gemma realises that her mouth is open again. She swallows. Sara straightens up and laughs at her. 'Oh, honey,' she says. 'You didn't really think all these billionaires wanted you around for your sparkling wit, did you?'

Gemma gulps.

'They've got wives for that. If you want to be a *wife*, go train to be a lawyer or a banker or an art historian. Go to *finishing school*. That's the sort who goes to the banquets and gets presented to the queen. You've got, what – four GCSEs, did I hear that right?'

Gemma blushes. She still hasn't got used to her failure, neither the result nor the rows that followed. Her mother is, like, 'You've let *yourself* down, Gemma,' and Patrick did what he always does and *wrote her a letter*. Didn't give her a hug and a never mind. He *wrote her a letter*. Her friends are back at school and she's all alone now. If it weren't for this – for this secret world she clutches close to herself, soothing and consoling her with its promise as her parents communicate her worthlessness – her life would be unbearable.

'Yes,' she says.

'Oh, honey,' says Sara. 'They don't want us for our brains. They've got all the PhDs in the world back at their mansions.' She rattles her gold bracelets. 'They want us because we suck their cocks,' she says. 'Get used to it.'

She realises that she is trembling. 'I get it,' she says. 'I do. But . . .'

'Oh, look,' says Sara, 'how many boys' cocks have you been on for free? And talk me through the respect you got for that?'

Gemma thinks about Nathan. The boys before Nathan. All soaked in the shit they watch on the internet and convinced that that's what girls are up for. For free. And not so reliable with the hygiene, either. She gives Sara a cynical laugh.

329

Wonders if the note of despair in it is as obvious to Sara as it is to her.

'Ha – yah,' she says.

Sara fiddles with her diamond earrings.

'I know it takes a bit,' she says. 'But once you're done, you're done. God, men. It's so easy to have power over them.'

'*Power?*'

'Oh, just look at them,' she says. 'There's literally nothing else they think about. It's pathetic.'

She opens her clutch and brings out a tiny enamel box the size of her thumbnail. 'How about a nice little pill to put you in the mood?'

'Oooh!' says Gemma. She never has the coin for Es. Then she laughs out loud.

'What?'

'Last E I had,' she says, 'I gave the guy a blowjob in exchange.'

'*Right?*' says Sara, and grins. She pops the lid on the tiny box and taps out a couple of tiny pills.

'Thanks,' says Gemma.

'Tell you what. I'm gonna do one too. Keep you company.' She winks.

They go back out together and wait for the pills to kick in.

'God, it's such a laugh, is this fucking place,' says Sara. 'I thought I'd seen some shit, but ...'

They're standing in front of a giant brown bear. A real one. Taxidermied onto his hind legs, mouth open in a snarl, his three-inch claws sharpened and gilded, a pair of pirate earrings dangling from his ears. He stands at the foot of the staircase and greets guests as they come in through the double doors from the courtyard.

'Who is this guy, anyway?'

'Fuck knows,' says Sara. 'Russian, innit.'

'What's it about London?' she asks. 'I mean, don't they have mansions in Moscow?'

'Ah, sure they do. And Chernobyl and Putin. Now, *there's* a guy who can bear a grudge.'

'Well, I suppose *you'd* be pissed off if someone'd nicked all your country's natural resources,' says Melanie, coming up behind them. 'Oooh, wow, Sara! Are you two on something?'

'Shhh!' Sara presses a finger to her lips. Gemma bursts out laughing, she looks so absurd.

'I fucking love you,' she says.

'That's the spirit!' says Sara. 'Now, go do your thang.'

He's powerful. He's really powerful. Just remember that. There are women with Oscars because of him, and so what if he's sixty if he's a day and can't get out of a chair without farting?

The house is thronged. More have arrived since she went into the bathroom, and the string of reception rooms is hard to navigate. She can't see him for Armani. She squeezes behind a trio of thick-set men who growl at each other in Russian, feels a hand grab her buttock and squeeze it so hard she's afraid for a moment that it'll pop.

Ow!

Gemma whirls round, enraged. Then she remembers where she is, and who she is. *This is your life now, girl. You're a fucking body. Get used to it.*

In the third reception room, Tatiana stands with Julia and a huge man, much older. The women wear their perpetual smiles. But now she knows, Gemma sees also that their eyes are darting around the room. They're supervising, she thinks. There are a dozen of us here tonight. We may have arrived in little knots, but I see us now. Me and Sara, and Melanie, and that girl from Singapore, Wei-Cheng. And three girls I've seen at the agency, though they've probably never seen me. And that woman who looks like a wraith, who was there at Issima that first night.

Tatiana swivels to look at her. The huge man looks her up and down, head to toe, and frowns. Says something to Tatiana, who nods. Julia doesn't speak, but Gemma sees her listen, and press her lips together. They're discussing me, she thinks. They're not happy with their investment. And then a man comes up to them and their smiles switch back on as if someone turned up the headlight beam. Tatiana and Julia kiss the air around his face and the big man's face wrinkles up and he pumps his hand as though he's trying to extract water, and Gemma moves on in search of Maurice Eindorff.

She finds him on a high-backed antique sofa upholstered in gold brocade, his knees spread wide to accommodate his gut, talking intensely to a woman who has her hand on his knee. She hesitates for a moment. Maybe I'm too late. Maybe that's it. I've blown it. They'll let me go tomorrow and I'll have to go to the losers' college on the Wandsworth Road and work in Greggs at the weekends. And then the woman's shiny curtain of hair flips back and she sees that she must be forty if she's a day and Maurice is looking at her the way Naz looks at her mother, and she knows she'll be all right.

She walks over to the sofa, takes him by the hand and leads him away. Past the bear, up the sweeping marble staircase.

She leaves him beached on the bed like a well-fed walrus. Sara is waiting at the bottom of the stairs when she comes back down and pushes a slightly warm glass of champagne into her hand. 'Mouthwash,' she says.

Gemma take the glass and drains it. 'Ta.' Pulls a face as she finishes, because she doesn't really like champagne.

'All right?'

'Sure,' she says. She doesn't really fancy talking about it much, though. She decides to joke her way out of it. Puts on a comedy Cockney accent. ''E's a proppah genkleman and no mistykin,' she says.

Thing she's learned tonight: a cock's a cock's a cock, and a belly gets smaller when the owner is lying down. Another thing she's learned: you can do quite a lot of stuff if you keep your eyes shut.

'Hey, this is a Russian's house, yeah?' she asks. Sara nods. 'Well, there must be some bloody vodka around here some-where,' she says.

Julia comes up to her, beaming. 'I gather you've made Maurice a very happy boy,' she says. 'That's one fan you've got your-self there.'

'Always a pleasure, never a chore,' says Gemma. She's three vodkas in, and that E was quite strong.

'Well, I'd say you had a bright future ahead of you,' she says.

Gemma laughs. 'That's not what my school said.'

Julia laughs too, and gives her a friendly pat. 'Ah, schools. They don't know everything.'

'Is there any more vodka?' says Gemma.

'Maybe slow down on the vodka?' says Julia.

'Mmmmkay,' says Gemma. Waits until Julia's gone back into the crowd and helps herself to another.

*

At two a.m., she falls off her heels and plummets into the bear.

'Oops!' she says. Gives him a friendly pat on the chest, and then a hug. 'Awww, Maurice, you saved me!' she says, and laughs out loud. And then Julia's at her side again, and one of the big men in the grey suits they've got standing about the place, and they're supporting her off into an anteroom and propping her up in a chair. 'Time for a taxi for Gemma, I think,' says Julia.

'I don't have the cash,' she mumbles.

'That's okay,' says Julia, 'it's on my account.'

She doesn't remember the journey. Just a lot of passing lights and increasing nausea.

'I hope you're not going to throw up in my cab,' says the driver. 'That'd be two hundred extra for cleaning.

Her entire night's pay. 'Nah, you're all right, mate,' she replies. 'I can hold it in.'

'Well, you let me know if you need me to pull over,' he says. But instead she falls asleep, and doesn't wake up until he wakes her.

'Where am I?' she feels drugged and drowsy. Probably because that's what she is.

'Top of Thornbury Road,' he says. 'You said to drop you here?'

She peers out through the window. Once her eyes focus, she sees that she is indeed at the top of her road. Her shoes are scattered across the floor. She fishes for them with her hands, but keeps missing. Eventually the driver grabs them for her and presses them on her. Helps her out onto the kerb and waits while she balances against the door to put them on. 'Are you going to be okay getting home?' he asks.

'Sure,' she says. 'It's just a few doors down.' And, once he's gone, she takes a couple of steps forward, then three sideways, and wakes up, cold and a bit sore, in the hedge at No.17.

'Fuck,' she says. 'Fuckitty fuck.' But her shoes are still on, so that's something.

Her nap has done her some good. She covers the fifteen doors to home in less than five minutes, fumbles the lock open and tiptoes in. The house is dark and silent, and she thinks she's got away with it until she pushes open the door of her bedroom and finds her mum asleep in her bed, her phone dropped onto the carpet, snoring.

38

Sara has a whole basket of make-up. And not the cheap stuff. Shiseido. MAC. Urban Decay. Chanel. Dior. None of your Superdrug generics in *her* basket.

'It's sooo much better,' she says, spraying on some Thierry Mugler. 'Seriously. You totes need to throw away all that shit you've got and start again.'

Gemma feels reluctant to do that. It's funny the stuff you choose to take when you leave in a hurry. Her life and the things she values boiled down into a single suitcase. She's been a bit surprised by what she threw in in the ten-minute pack after her mum went off to work.

Things she's forgotten: Knickers. Toothbrush. The sort of loungewear the other girls hang about in when they're not working (this place isn't the paradise of babydolls men fantasise about).

Things she left out deliberately: family photos. Her iPhone (she'll get a burner when she gets a chance to go out). Her house keys.

She eyes Sara's make-up and wonders how she's ever going to catch up. Most of that stuff costs twenty quid a pop, at *least*. Anything of that sort that's in her own collection came into it via birthdays, or slipping it into pockets as she walked through department stores. 'That's pretty spenny,' she says, doubtfully.

'Oh, lord,' says Sara, 'What *else* is there to spend it on?'

Yes, but. She has the £200 from the party the other night – doesn't seem so much after what she ended up doing for it – in her purse and that's it. Julia is going to get her set up with a bank account, but it'll be empty when she gets it.

'I'm going to have to do a lot more parties,' she says.

Sara laughs. 'Yeah, don't think that'll be a problem,' she says. 'Oh, and now you've stopped being such a bloody priss, you'll find the money goes up, proper.'

'Really?' Her heart does a little thud.

'God, yeah,' says Sara. 'I clear a grand a party easy, even with deductions.'

'Deductions?'

'Yeah. You know. Agency fees and tax and National Insurance and that.'

'Tax and . . . ?'

'It's okay,' says Sara. 'They keep on top of all that for you. Nobody *ever* asks what you're up to, as long as your tax is paid and you're up to date with your NI.'

Tax and National Insurance. It all feels so grown-up. She only got a *number* a few months ago.

Sara drops her merino leggings and steps into a little black thong. A dinky little pink pom-pom decorates the junction of the hip strap and the bit that snakes between her buttocks. Rabbit fur. It's good because it squashes flat under your dress but springs straight back into shape when you take it off. She's going out to dinner tonight. City bankers, entertaining their Chicago counterparts. Gemma won't be getting those sorts of gigs until she's passed her table-manners tests and been judged elegant.

'You are going to have such a good time, once you're up and running,' says Sara. 'You'll be able to buy *literally* anything you want. Once, you know, you move on from just the parties. I mean they're good for practice, but they're really just auditions, those. It's the weekenders where the money really gets going. And the weeks are unbelievable. Oh, my *God*. You know there's Saudis who think fifty grand is chump change? I'm going to be able to buy a flat cash-down by this time next year.'

'Really?' Gemma feels weirdly small, bewildered. She's twenty-four hours out from home and the world is big and scary. And full of promise. Oh, lord, the promise. They've never lived, she thinks. My mum and dad. They have *literally* no idea.

'I was thinking Vauxhall,' says Sara breezily. 'One of those blocks going up by the Thames. Oh, my God, the views.'

Island

May 1986

39

When the *Princess Tatiana* returns from following the summer round the world in May, she docks once again in the main harbour, cramping the fishing boats, though the marina is fully completed and the tops of a billion dollars of floating real estate can be seen swaying above the old wall.

Mercedes wakes one morning to find that she's there, and her stomach sinks. Even though Tatiana never came to say goodbye when she returned to school, a tiny devil inside makes her afraid that her contract is still running. That Sergio's failure to read it in the first place has indentured her for life.

The limo pulls in from the heliport and Tatiana gets out. She mounts the gangplank and doesn't look back. Mercedes, placing plates of grilled octopus on a table, pauses and watches her go, and the knot in her stomach gets tighter.

'They're back,' says Donatella.

'You're observant,' she says. 'You should get a job as an international woman of mystery.' And Donatella flicks her with the edge of a tea towel. But still, she feels so nervous that she doesn't notice when Donatella disappears inside and returns with her hair brushed and oiled to a mirror shine and her new dress with the sunflowers and the fitted bodice on under her apron, her only jewellery – her confirmation crucifix and her silver hoop earrings – glittering against her olive skin.

After lunch, Tatiana appears on the gangplank, and Mercedes' shoulders rise up to touch her ears. But she doesn't even glance at the Re del Pesce. Just turns to the right and heads for the marina gate. Punches the PIN into the keypad and lets herself into the tunnel in the old harbour wall. And Mercedes feels such a surge of relief it almost turns into tears. She looks over to where Felix is mending nets in the spring sunshine and sees him looking too, and he feels her gaze and turns and gives her a big smile. It's okay, it says. You're safe. We're safe. She has no power over you now.

40

'What can I get you?'

Tatiana doesn't look at her. Didn't look at her when she came in and sat down at her choice of table without asking, hasn't looked at her since.

'Coke,' she says. 'Not Diet.'

Mercedes hesitates. Waits for an acknowledgement, for any sign that they are more than strangers, but none comes.

She turns to her companions. The new girlfriends. Not paid, presumably, for their clothes fit and they don't turn to her for affirmation. 'And for you?'

'Cappuccino, yah,' says the little blonde one. Mercedes doesn't know her name. She doesn't know any of Tatiana's friends' names. Why would she? None of them was here last year.

'I'll have a *citron pressé*,' says the other little blonde. They're all blonde. Even Tatiana now. It looks terrible with her sallow skin, but it seems it's this year's hair colour. Bouffant, with silk scarves designed to look like old rags tied round the head

343

and jewellery layered upon layer. Donatella has taken to wearing her hair like this too. Her wrap has been fashioned from the see-through kaftan. Everything comes in useful in the end.

'I'm sorry,' says Mercedes, 'I don't know what that is.'

'Yah, Cressy,' says Tatiana, 'we're not in France now. You'll need to go a bit more basic.'

Mercedes feels herself bridle. *Fuck you, Tatiana.* Doesn't show it on her face. A customer's a customer, and, ever since the big hotel opened up on the cliffs, they haven't been seeing as many of these.

'Oh,' says Cressy. Looks at Mercedes as though she's probably a *lilu*. 'Lemonade?' she speaks very, very slowly, enunciating every word. 'You make lemonade? Fresh?'

She pauses. Goggles at Mercedes, unsure whether she's been understood.

'*Limonade?*' she translates, and Mercedes realises that she is ferociously stupid. But amiable, she thinks. No need to be irritated.

The girl searches her inner resources. '*Fresca?*' she comes up with.

Mercedes mines sudden comprehension. 'Ahh! *Limonada! Si! No fresco. Pero Fanta!*' she replies. Sees a twitch of annoyance on Tatiana's face so small that only someone as finely trained as she is would see it. She grins. *See? Now I'm free of you, I can take the piss all I want.*

Cressy looks blank, like Princess Diana. She casts about the table for help.

'They haven't got fresh,' says Tatiana. 'They've got cans.'

'Oh. Okay. Oh, *Fanta*! Yes! Thank you!' says Cressy, and beams. '*Merci!*'

Mercedes beams back. 'You speak Kastellani!' she congratulates. 'Very good!'

Again the look of confusion. Potty-training that one must have taken a while. 'Oh, no, that was French,' she says. 'It means thank you.'

Mercedes smiles and drops her empty order pad into her apron pocket. '*De nada*,' she says.

'You don't need the whole please-and-thank-you thing,' Tatiana says in her ringing voice as she walks away from the table. 'We literally pay them, yuh?'

Donatella sees the rage on her face as she comes indoors.

'Jesus! What did she say?'

'Nothing,' replies Mercedes. 'Literally nothing.'

There is a Kastellani phrase for that moment when a girl turns woman, when she blooms in the light of day: *jimán de xabuesos*. Hound-magnet.

There is a fleeting moment when a girl starts to glow. It heats her up inside and makes her give off a scent that attracts the dogs for miles around. Dogs literal – a girl who shows any affinity for dogs will always raise an eyebrow – and, of course, metaphorical. When the boys start hanging about in the hope of seeing her, a girl is deemed ripe. The women pursue her with shawls and rosaries and cautionary tales, and the race is on to get her married off before disaster strikes.

A boy in the same phase is called a *kabalero de vaqas*. He is allowed to go to the bar in the market square without his father, and is given a hunting knife of his very own. But that's another story.

This year, Donatella is attracting the hounds the way a windfall fig attracts flies. She is no longer a teenage waitress in a two-bit island café: she's Sophia Loren. She's the Queen of the Sea.

And every day, because the boys are there, the girls come

too. The Re del Pesce is quite the place with the teens of yacht world. All the little butterflies. The pretty things. Pretty daughters of beautiful mothers, all looking less like their fathers as their surgeons create the daughters they always wanted. Tatiana's nose has halved in size over the winter. Mercedes wonders if they'll ever be able to do the same for her jaw.

But whatever they can do to change the outside, the personality will always be there.

She comes every afternoon, little bag dangling from her crooked arm as she descends the gangplank from the *Princess Tatiana*. Sometimes she will be followed by a gaggle of blondes, but most of the time she comes by herself. Always looking for boys, the way the boys are looking for Donatella. And, when she sees people she knows, she simply sits down without asking. And the boys generally ignore her, but they don't send her away. They've all known each other for always, the yacht people.

Mercedes wonders if Tatiana would be so tolerated if she had a father who didn't have control of the marina berths.

One day, Mercedes tries an experiment. When she approaches the table to take Hugo-Sveta-Christophe-Alexa-Kristina-Sebastian's orders, she puts on a wide smile and greets her.

'Hello, Tatiana! How are you?'

Tatiana, halfway through an anecdote, stops for a second. Gives her a 'you're interrupting me' look. 'Fine,' she says. 'I'll have a Coke. None of that Diet stuff.' And she turns back and resumes her anecdote with the very word at which she broke off. And Hugo-Sveta-Christophe-Alexa-Kristina-Sebastian look Mercedes up and down with a glance and she knows her place. She slinks away, tail between her legs.

Donatella comes out of the kitchen and her face falls.

'What's up with you?'

'Oh, nothing,' says Mercedes. She doesn't really understand, herself. Why does it matter? I longed to be free of the cow. So why am I upset?

'Oh. Princess Nut-Nut's in, is she?'

Mercedes rolls her eyes.

'Right,' says Donatella. 'We'll see about that.'

'No, don't,' says Mercedes. 'Please.'

'Bullshit,' says Donatella.

Mercedes hovers on the edge of earshot. Please don't, Donatella. You don't know what she's like when she thinks she's been slighted.

But Donatella is a bit drunk on her own power lately. She's forgotten who she is.

'Good afternoon, ladies and gentlemen,' she says.

The table looks up. The girls chorus a hello and the boys mumble, unable, when the Goddess is actually present, to meet her eye. They're younger, this crowd, than the teens she met at the party, and easier to subjugate. Another couple of years and their bumptiousness will dominate, but by then they'll be up at the Heliogabalus, and they won't be Donatella's problem.

'So what's everybody having?' she asks, cheerfully. Gets out her notepad and waits.

'We've ordered,' says Tatiana.

'Have you? What did you want?'

'Coke.'

'Sorry?'

'*Coke*,' says Tatiana, and adds a 'you moron' with her eyes.

Donatella shakes her head. 'No, I'm sorry. I don't understand.'

Tatiana sighs. 'I said I wanted a *Coke*. Coca-Cola? *Capisce*?'

347

A hush has descended over the table. The boys gaze in awe at Donatella's magnificent *balcon*, and the look in the girls' eyes is another level of awe altogether. Nobody's ever stood up to Tatiana before, thinks Mercedes. It wasn't just us. Even the yacht people are scared of her.

'Ohhhh!' says Donatella. 'You wanted to order a Coke! You know there's a word that goes with that, right?'

'What?' Tatiana sounds appalled, as though someone's asked her to wipe their arse.

'Perhaps you'll remember what it is by the time I come back?' says Donatella. Turns on her heel and swanks away.

'What was that all about?' asks a Hugo.

'Oh, God,' says Tatiana. 'We gave the sister a job last summer and they've totally got above themselves now.'

'Really?' asks an Alexa.

'Yah,' she says. 'She was crap, too. We only put up with her out of the kindness of our hearts.'

Donatella stops dead. Fury flashes across her face. *I remember how you were*, says her expression. *You're not doing that to us.*

Mercedes signals wildly from the door, tries to catch her eye. *No. No, Donita, leave it. It's not worth it, my rash and reckless sister.*

But Donatella marches back to the table. 'You can leave now,' she says.

They all recoil. Look at each other, confused.

'What ... all of us?' asks a Hugo, humbly.

'No,' says Donatella, and points at Tatiana. 'Just that one. She can go until she's learned some manners.'

Tatiana swells, visibly. A fighting cock, ready for the fray. '*What?*'

'You heard me,' says Donatella. 'Out!' She points at the exit, just to make things clear.

348

'You can't do that!'

'Oh, believe me, I can,' says Donatella. 'Off you pop!'

Her English has got *so* much better.

Tatiana gets to her feet. 'I'm a *paying customer*!'

'There's no rudeness margin in the profits from a glass of Coke,' says Donatella.

'Well!' snaps Tatiana. 'That's your customer base gone, then.'

She looks triumphantly round the table. Clearly expects her companions to start collecting their bags too.

'A tragedy,' says Donatella.

'There's plenty of other places will want our custom,' she says. And she looks around the table and sees that nobody's moving. They're all staring at the cloth, as though their minds are elsewhere.

She turns back. 'Who the hell do you think you are?' she bawls.

Donatella draws herself up. 'I am Donatella Delia,' she says, 'and I'm telling you to get out of my restaurant.'

41

'I just hope,' Mercedes says, 'that she leaves it at that.'

Donatella sits up in bed. 'What do you mean?'

'Donita, she's a nasty piece of work. You *know* that.'

'I know,' says Donatella. 'But what's she going to do? She's a *kid*.'

Not so much. She's a kid with lawyers. A kid with a father who's friends with the duke.

Maybe it'll be okay. Maybe she'll leave it alone.

'She could take our custom away,' she says.

'Oh, balls,' says Donatella. 'She didn't exactly manage it this afternoon, did she?'

'Yes, but . . . '

'She's just a rude brat,' says Donatella.

Oh, lord. 'But she . . . '

'Mersa, you're such a worrier.'

Because I know. I know better than any of you what she's like.

'Seriously,' says Donatella, 'it'll be fine. I'd have thought you'd be pleased I stood up for you.'

'But the others ...'

'The others nothing,' says Donatella. 'Sebastian asked me to a party on Saturday. Down in the marina. They're going nowhere.'

Friday

42 | Gemma

They've sent the staff away and locked the front gate. Even Paulo the security guy has been sent into town, despite his objections. In the end he's made them sign a piece of paper absolving him of responsibility if anything goes wrong, and gone down to Mediterraneo with the chef to take up Tatiana's permanent booking. The doors and windows are closed. No sound in, and no sound out.

Gemma is filled with foreboding.

'There's so many,' she says to Wei-Cheng.

'Ten,' says Wei-Cheng. 'It's not so many.'

On the yacht in Cannes there were many more. But they were coming and going and there were a lot more girls, too, and they mingled with the rolling party on the foredeck in between punters, just as though they belonged there. Apart from the constant fucking, it was almost like being on holiday.

These men, though. The actor's not met her eye once since he arrived, and now the others, now that company is here, have taken to addressing the air a few inches to the side of her ears. They look directly, all right. Just not at their faces.

The table is laid for the Meades and their guests and, with no servants in the house, Tatiana has ordered them into weird little black-and-white maids' outfits. Boning in the bodices that crush their breasts upwards, net petticoats scratching their naked buttocks. And the men have stared and stared from their low-built bucket chairs on the pool terrace as they bent to serve their cocktails. And Tatiana, the only woman among them, sits regal and complacent in an embroidered gold kaftan, her rings glittering as she name-drops and rough hands thrust suddenly up their skirts while they endeavour not to respond with cries of shock.

This is awful, she thinks. The men get worse and worse. It's as though she started us off gradually, to soften us up. All the way through, bit by bit, I've gone, *Well, I did that, this isn't that much more, is it?* And now I've got bite marks, and my scalp still burns from what that man did last night. And tonight there are ten of them – eleven with the fat old father.

The men eye them like livestock, discuss them nakedly without ever addressing them. Last night there was a pretence; the men asked you questions and twinkled at you as though you might have a choice when they picked you. Tonight? Meat. They're picking which fillet steak they want to share, and the doors are locked.

If I screamed, she wonders, would anybody hear me? And if they heard me, would they come to help?

Tatiana claps her hands as they clear away the remains of the lobsters.

'I think it's time for a party game!' she announces, in her happy-happy hostess voice.

356

The men's voices lull and they look up the table at her, expectantly.

'Who's played Distraction?' she asks.

Behind her, Sara does a little air clap and an, 'Ooh!'

The eyes swivel in her direction.

'I always win this!' she says.

'You do,' says Tatiana, fondly. The eyes swivel back.

Gemma waits. Something's coming, but she doesn't know what.

'Girls,' says Tatiana, 'you go and get the cheese and Sara will fill you in. I'll tell the gents while you're gone.'

They file out. In the pantry, the chef has left two porcelain platters, wrapped in clingfilm, and all they have to do is unclothe them without disturbing the arrangement of cheese, grapes and large ripe figs that have been quartered and splayed like vulvas on beds of white and gold. Two filigree baskets, wrapped, carry crackers, thin as paper. Little crystal dishes glisten with sharp fruit jellies.

'Isn't there pudding?' asks Hanne. She's been enjoying little pots of ganache, elegant *réligieuses*, silky *panacottas*.

Sara left half a dozen lines of cocaine ready chopped out on the marble kitchen surface before they took the main course in. She hoovers one up each nostril with a rolled-up banknote, offers it to Gemma. Might as well, thinks Gemma. She likes cocaine. Likes the way it makes her feel sharp, alert and yet pleasingly numb. She takes it and bends to take her turn.

'They're men,' says Sara. 'They don't do dessert.'

'So what's this game, then?' Gemma straightens up, savours the lovely coldness as it spreads down her throat, holds the note out to Hanne. For a moment she forgets that she's only seventeen. Feels as if she can take on the world.

'A competition,' says Sara. 'Get ready to get your game on.'

'What?' asks Wei-Cheng.

'So they keep talking, and we take it in turns to go under the table,' says Sara. 'Five minutes each, I should think. That's what you usually get.'

'Oh,' says Gemma.

'And if anyone guesses who's getting the blowie,' says Sara, 'they have to put a grand in the middle of the table.'

'Ahh,' says Hanne, 'I love the way they just throw cash around like that. It's kind of ... sexy-sad, isn't it?'

'Well, that should be a nice quick bonus,' says Wei-Cheng. 'Pay for this lot, anyway.' And she takes the straw from Hanne and bends to the counter.

'Not for *you*,' says Sara. 'It's a winner-takes-all scenario. And that winner is always me. Trust me on this.' She smirks, and licks her lips.

'Oh!' says Hanne.

'Well, we'll see about *that*,' says Wei-Cheng.

'You don't stand a fucking chance,' says Sara. Licks her finger and wipes the marble countertop. Sticks it in her mouth, all the way to the third knuckle.

'Honestly, I thought tonight was going to be much harder work,' she says, when she pulls the finger out again.

43 | Robin

Robin is lying on her bed, trying to summon the energy to go back out onto those hot, crowded streets and start again, when she hears footsteps coming up the stairs. Multiple footsteps. And then a rap on the door.

She sits up.

'*Sinjora?*' Sinjora Hernandez's voice. 'You have visitors.'

Her heart leaps. News? Has someone found her? Have they come to tell me? Is it over?

Gemma.

'One moment,' she calls. Hurriedly pulls on a pair of jeans beneath her cotton nightie. Pulls a cardigan over the top and opens the door.

Sinjora Hernandez glares at her as though she suspects her of shitting in the bathroom basin. To her right is the uniformed *xandarm* who was so unhelpful behind the station desk the other day. To her left, sweating and panting from the steep stairwell, the Chief of Police.

She's dead, she thinks, and feels her knees start to give way.

The police chief breaks the silence.

'A word, *sinjora*,' he says, and walks into her bedroom without awaiting permission.

Robin grips the door to steady herself as they push past. The wave of dizziness that hit her when she first saw them is dissipating more slowly than it's taken for reality to kick in. I'm in trouble, she thinks.

She can't decide whether to close the door. She leaves it open.

The police chief drops his meaty thighs down on the mattress. The uniform goes over to the window, looks out at the street, then opens the wardrobe and starts raking methodically through her clothes.

'Now, hang on a sec—'

The police chief raises a hand, commanding silence. Sinjora Hernandez folds her arms and watches, her mouth a straight line.

'Mrs Hanson,' says the COP, 'we need to clarify your position, I think.'

Robin feels chilled inside. She waits, silently,

'Last night,' he says, 'you went to the Temple, no? The nightclub?'

Robin nods. 'I was—'

'Our *duqa*'s representative has been in touch,' he interrupts. 'He is very angry. He doesn't expect to be . . . ' he thinks for a moment ' . . . *accosted* on his own property. Or have his toilets vandalised.'

'I—' she begins. The hand goes up again.

'*Sinjora*, you need to understand. You are not in your own country now.'

I do. I so do.

'Our *duqa* is a very important man,' he says.

360

'I know! That's why I—'

The hand again.

The uniformed cop finds what he's looking for. Pulls her remaining flyers from the chest of drawers and waves them at his boss.

'*Moy bjen!*' exclaims the boss. Rattles off a burst of Kastellani. His subordinate nods, solemnly, and starts to rip them up.

'Hey!'

A booming basso roar in response. '*SINJORA!*'

Robin jumps, tenses.

The chief lumbers to his feet and comes so close that their noses almost touch. Grappa, cigars, garlic. She's interrupted his evening meal.

'We've had complaints,' he bellows, 'about litter. Everywhere, these ... papers ... fixed to everything. Did you ask permission to vandalise our town like this? Did you? Who give you this permission?'

She pulls back. He doesn't follow. Albert, she thinks Cosmo Albert, that's his name. A ridiculous name for such a pompous little man.

'No one,' she says.

'*Alora! Bjen!*'

'I'm sorry,' she says.

He does a strangely wet, chomping *tut*. 'Is too late for *sorry*,' he says. 'If it was just the litter, the bad manners ... but is not, is it? Our *duqa* was *appalled* at what you did last night. Appalled. You cannot disrupt the lives of strangers like this, *sinjora*. People come to La Kastellana for peace. For privacy. They don't expect to be ... assaulted on their own property.'

'*Assaulted?*' She reels.

'A figure of speech, *sinjora*.'

361

'O-*kay* ...'

The hand. 'But, correctly, he says if you can do something like this, you cannot be trusted not to do more.'

'I promise,' says Robin. 'I'll write to him. Tonight. To apologise.'

'Too late,' he says. Pulls a comedy grin. 'Sorreee!' he says.

Island

Summer 1986

44

They will turn their backs on us all. See? They already are. They will shun us all year for this, but I don't care. I don't care ...

They kneel at the bottom of the steps. Feet step over her sister's legs as though they're flotsam on the beach. Faces turn away, skirts are pulled aside. Larissa and Mercedes don't look up. Block out their neighbours' contempt. All they see is their lovely Donatella. Broken.

'Oh, my lord, oh, my lord. Oh, my darling, my darling,' Larissa moans. And Donatella lies still, curled in on herself, and tears wash dirt and blood back into her wounds.

The square clears. The bell stops tolling. The great arched door slams closed and they are alone. Mercedes tugs on Donatella's filthy white hem to pull it down to cover her thighs. Slaps her own tears from her eyes with the back of her hand.

I hate them, she thinks. I hate them, But she doesn't really know who she hates, for there are so many.

*

A sound from above: the door opening. Just a little, just a crack. Just enough to release the priest's voice, droning, the sheepish ululation of response. And then it cuts off again as the door closes and all there is is the shouting from the *festa* in the market square. And then she hears footsteps.

Mercedes looks up. Paulina Marino descends the steps. Carefully, to avoid slipping on the blood in her Sunday shoes.

She reaches them and kneels beside them.

'I'm sorry,' she says, 'I don't know what I was thinking.'

Larissa's tears explode. A loud, unfettered howl. Donatella opens her swollen eyes, looks up at her grieving mother, silently. Her nose is broken and her wrist, blackened with bruising, is bloating in the July sun.

They wait until the howl has passed. Then between them they help their sister-daughter-godchild to her feet and half-carry her through the unforgiving streets.

45

Larissa stays upstairs, bathing her daughter's wounds. She won't be down until the child sleeps, and even then there will be no communication with her self-seeking husband. Or with the women who hedged their bets by going to mass before they showed their faces.

Donatella lies on her side and stares at the air, inert. No recoil when Larissa touches her cuts, her bruises, with the salt-water cloth and the aloe cut from the cemetery garden. Remains passive as her mother unfurls her limbs, one by one, and rubs a flannel along them to wipe away the dirt.

And, down in the street, the party goes on for all the world as though the world is still intact.

Mercedes, standing in the window as her mother does what she can, watches and hates. From here she can see the deck of the *Princess Tatiana*. The evening meal laid out on the table, a great sweating jug of something cold covered by a cloth. A glass lying on its side, broken.

Matthew and Tatiana, standing by the gunwale, watching the same scene play out from the other side.

Laughing, and chatting like spectators at a cockfight.

It was you, she thinks. I know it was.

Donatella lies on the side of her that is less bruised, and stares at the air. And at night, in the enfolding dark, Mercedes crawls into her bed and wraps her arms about her. Breathes the feral scent of her despair.

August comes, and the wind drops. Sailboats lie becalmed and the yacht people bask on their deck-top loungers. Donatella's bruises turn purple, then brown, then yellow, then fade away, and the breaks in her skin turn to scars. Her wrist, bound tightly by Larissa the night they brought her back, was badly sprained, not broken – no thanks to St James. And her nose – well, now the swelling has gone, if you glimpsed her without knowing her history you would just assume she had inherited Phoenician blood.

But something has broken inside her. She no longer sings about the house, no longer teases Mercedes. That ready smile has disappeared. She is forbidden, of course, from serving in the restaurant. Her father will not even look her in the eye if he passes her in the family quarters. And she sits on a hard chair in the *sala* and watches the world pass by, and utters not a word.

And, two weeks past St James's Day, she stands up, puts a shawl over her tangled hair and goes out, her head held high, to face the world.

Friday

46 | Gemma

Sara is triumphant. She waves her winnings, spread out like a fan, in the air, and tucks them into her bosom with a flourish. She sashays off to the kitchen. Some mouthwash and another line, no doubt.

'Someone's pleased with herself,' says the prince.

'One could say cock-a-hoop,' replies one of the new men, and they laugh.

We don't exist, to them, thinks Gemma. Beyond how they can use us as pleasure accessories. The only difference between us and rubber dolls is that rich men can afford us.

She's finding it hard to keep her back straight. Her arms keep drifting up to cross themselves across her body as though they have a life of their own, and it takes some force of will to drop them back to her side. As she stands there, smiling, smiling, smiling, she feels gravity drag at her shoulders, press on her spine, willing it to bend.

I was meant to feel better than this, she thinks. I've swapped one kind of dependence for another, and Sara doesn't look magnificent to me any more. Slipping out every twenty minutes to sneak another line. That smile's not a smile at all. It's the rictus of a skull in a still-life painting.

She feels her shoulders slump again. Forces them back. I want to go home. But I don't have a home to go to now. I don't know what to do. I don't know how to get away.

Matthew Meade pushes his chair back. 'Well, gentlemen,' he announces. 'Brandy and cigars and final auditions, I think.'

Auditions?

Meade hauls himself to his feet and collects his stick. 'If you'd like to follow me?'

'Let the games begin,' says Bruce Fanshawe, and there's another rumble of amusement.

Oh, shit, she thinks. I knew this wasn't going to be all there was. Four of us, ten of them. We're going to be working all night.

She feels weary to her bones. Let me go home, she thinks. None of this is worth any amount of money. Just let me go home. There has to be some other way than ... this ...

The men walk up the corridor that leads away from the stairs, and she hears a grinding noise, like a heavy door sliding back.

'I say!' says a voice.

'Oh, well played!' The prince. 'I'd never have known this was here.'

'Darling,' Tatiana's voice drifts back towards them. The prince has already gone from Your Royal Highness to darling, in the course of a little over twenty-four hours. 'The *architect* barely knew it was here!'

'Very Onassis,' says someone.

'Yes, we were going for a Seventies vibe,' she replies.

'Ah, the glory days,' says someone else. 'What a time.'

Matthew Meade's voice. 'Wasn't it, though?'

'Oh, don't,' says another voice. 'It'll be years before opportunities like that show up again.'

'Oh, I don't know,' says Matthew Meade. 'Plenty of opportunities in global warming before that whole circus winds down . . .'

The voices fade, as though they're entering a space where echoes are forbidden.

Click click click, comes Tatiana up the hall. She has some objects in her hand, some more draped over her wrist.

'Put these on,' she orders, and her hostess voice is gone. Empress now. The cold tones of owner to slave.

Tatiana's accessories turn out to be eye masks. And little rubber wristbands like the ones that let you into clubs, each one a different colour. Red, green, yellow, blue. They don't get a choice. She is handed green and slides it obediently over her hand.

'And these,' says Tatiana. She holds out a bunch of cable ties. To hold, she realises, their wrists together. 'Help each other,' says Tatiana. 'Get them good and tight.'

Her stomach ties itself in knots. *I don't want to. I don't want to.*

And yet they all stand together, and she can see the whites of her companions' eyes, and they pull on the ends of the straps until the plastic cuts into their skin.

And they wait.

47 | Mercedes

'But why does it have to be you, *kerida*?'

'Because there's no one else,' she says. 'You know it's true, Mama.'

It feels like the dinner before an execution. A dinner of lifetime favourites, arranged together on their one big platter: little goat's cheeses from the mountains, fine prosciutto, bottled artichoke hearts charred on the grill in their oil, garlic olives, a head of grilled romaine. A little bowl of anchovies. A bowl of tomatoes from the garden, sliced and dressed with the zest and juice of an orange from their tree. They eat as their ancestors have eaten for a thousand years.

But nobody has much appetite.

'The New Capri,' says Larissa. 'Do you think this was what he had in mind?'

'I suppose it's possible,' says Felix. 'History's full of aristocrats gone bad. Imagine having a whole country to do what you want with.'

Larissa toys with a scrap of bread. Rolls it between her

fingers until it goes back to dough. She's grey with worry, deep lines etched in her forehead. 'That man. Everything went bad when he came here.'

Mercedes isn't sure who she's talking about: the duke, or Matthew Meade.

'Everything went bad when the old duke died,' she continues. 'When *he* came here. He didn't grow up here, you see. He has no attachment to the land. And now he's brought those people here, and everything is spoiled.'

It wasn't that good when the old duke was alive, thinks Mercedes. You're letting nostalgia make you forget. There was no Europol here then, either. You'd just vanish if you were troublesome, and everyone would pretend you had never existed.

'Maybe he doesn't know?' says Larissa. 'Tell me he doesn't know?'

Four girls on, three girls off. I have no cosy palliatives to offer you, Mama.

'I don't know,' she lies. So many lies, so many years. 'But what we need now is for him to no longer turn his face away.'

'But why *you*?'

'Because I'm the only one who can,' she replies. 'I can't let them carry on. All those girls. Think about all those girls.'

Her lost sister hangs between them. A victim of La Kastellana and the duke and, in their way, the Meades, as much as anyone.

'And Mama,' she adds, 'if I succeed, I'll be free. There won't be any contracts in prison. They'll be gone, and I'll be free.'

'I should come with you,' says Felix. 'I hate thinking about you doing this alone.'

She shakes her head. 'It'll never work. Paulo won't let you anywhere near that room. I'm the only person he won't suspect. If I make it look like an accident, like a domestic crisis, he'll let me in.'

'And once you're in there? What then? He's not going to just let you go through their belongings, is he?'

'Oh,' she says, 'he's easily distracted. And he's lovely, but I don't think it's ever occurred to him that someone like me could be a problem. I'll tell him there's pâtisserie in the kitchen and the clean-up's going to take hours, and I'll have all the time in the world. And I know where everything is. There are a thousand DVDs in those drawers. He had the videos transferred across when they upgraded the tech and turned it all to flatscreen. It's all there. I just need a few minutes to work out what's what and slip a few into my apron.'

'He keeps it all on *DVD*?'

'Oh, yes,' she says. 'Of course he does. Imagine getting your cloud hacked and all that being there. Same reason they all keep their secret stuff in the vaults at the bank.'

'Ah,' says Felix.

'Only people with nothing worth keeping keep stuff on the internet. She told me that once.'

Mercedes tears a fig open with her fingers, wraps a scrap of prosciutto around it and pops it in her mouth. This could be her last meal with her family. When she leaves here tomorrow, she might never come back.

'The biggest irony of all,' she says, 'is that it's the one room in the house where they don't have cameras.'

Island

Summer 1986

48

Hindsight is 20/20. How do you know, at thirteen years old, that a farewell to you is a farewell to life?

'Mercedes?'

She's so close to sleep, she barely hears her the first time.

'Mercedes?'

Mercedes rolls over, peers through the darkness at where her sister sits, knees drawn up in her white nightdress.

'What is it?'

'I need to tell you something.'

'What?'

'You need to promise not to tell.'

'Tell what?'

'Promise.'

Foggy with sleep, she pushes herself up against the pillows. 'Okay. I promise. What is it?'

'I can't carry on like this,' says Donatella. In the half-light, with the shadows on her face, she looks like a ghost already.

'Donita,' she says, 'it won't always be like this. It'll pass. Everything passes eventually.'

'Not this,' says Donatella. 'You know that. I'm marked for life. There's nothing here for me now.'

'There's me, *kerida*. You know that. There will always be me. And Mama.'

She doesn't mention their father. She knows as well as her sister does that he won't be there for anyone.

Donatella raises a weary hand and rubs it on her face. 'I'm sorry,' she says. 'I have to go.'

Mercedes jumps.

'No! No, Donita, *please*!'

'Mersa,' says Donatella, 'I don't have a choice. You know that. It's all over. I have no future, now.'

Mercedes starts to cry. 'But what will I do without you?' she says. 'Donita, what will I do?'

That big, cold, empty world. She thinks of her beautiful sister, stepping off the ferry in some unknown place. No one who knows her. No one who loves her, forever and ever. I can't, she thinks. I can't bear this. They've destroyed us.

'I can't live here without you,' she says. 'What will I do?'

Donatella gets off her bed and crawls in beside her.

'You're my brave sister,' she says. 'You'll be fine, in the end. You'll be sad for a while, but you'll forget about me. You will. I'll be gone, and life will go on, and one day you'll be happy, I promise.'

'I won't. I *won't*. How can I be, when you're not here?'

Donatella is quiet. Holds her close and lets her breathe.

'I'll miss you,' she says. 'I will always miss you. You've been a good sister, Mersa. The best. Maybe we'll see each other again some day. But I have to go. You must know that. I have to.'

49

On an island with fewer than a thousand inhabitants, even a funeral is a red-letter day. On the day of Donatella's funeral, the whole of Kastellana Town turns out. Nothing says 'break out your best black dress' like the death of someone young and beautiful. Even if it is a suicide. Even if less than a week ago you were shunning her for her sins.

They are a small party when they set off. Sergio and Larissa, Hector and Paulina Marino, Felix and Mercedes. The fishermen who hauled Donatella from the water wait at a respectful distance by the boats, hats pressed to their chests, then fall into step behind.

'Are you sure you don't want a veil?' asks Paulina.

Larissa walks on, head held high, face pale, tears long dried. Something's happened in the night. Yesterday she was almost comatose in her bed, face to the wall, a creature made of tears. Today, she is angry.

'No,' she snaps. 'I want them to see my face. I want them

all to see my face. I want them to know what they've done. I want them to know I'm not ashamed.'

Larissa walks at the head of the progress to the church. Mercedes feels a perverse rush of pride at the sight of her. She's so strong, she thinks. She won't let them break her. Her father catches the eyes of friends, throws them nods and watery smiles, but Larissa is having none of it. She hates her neighbours now.

You killed her, thinks Mercedes as she looks around her. All you weeping women. You're weeping because you *know* you killed my sister. Where were you? Where have you been? We saw you cross the road. Talk behind your hands. Shun her. We saw you. What are your tears worth now? You drove her to her death.

And I could have saved her. I didn't tell, because she asked me not to, and now she's dead and I will never be the same.

I hate you, she thinks, as Beata Vinci joins the walkers. As Ximena Vigonier tries to give her a sympathetic smile, she answers with a glare. I saw you, she thinks. While she was crawling on the flagstones. I saw you turn your face away. As sure as she is dead, I know who killed her, and every one of you has played your part.

And she thinks of Donatella, and wants to howl at the sky. The guilt will consume her forever. I should have known. I should have told. I should have stopped her, by whatever means I could. I killed her, too. Me, as much as anyone.

On Calle Iglesia, Larissa runs her eyes over the throng, and Mercedes sees the same thoughts run through her head.

'Larissa,' says Sergio, and attempts to put a hand on her

arm. She bats him off like an annoying insect. Turns back and leads them forward to the church.

'Are you okay?' Felix asks, in a voice so low that no one around them hears.

Mercedes nods, and swallows her tears. I will never be okay, she thinks. But still she is glad that he has asked.

It's always been this way, though, she thinks. Less obvious when the restaurant is open and the place is full of sound, but inescapable now. Donatella kept me distracted, kept my eyes turned away, but I know now that my parents hate each other.

She glances at Felix under her wet lashes. He can't be okay himself, she thinks. He saw her too, beneath the water. He went out with the boats that brought her back.

'I don't know what I'll do,' she whispers to the air. And feels him hear her.

'Larissa,' says Paulina, 'we're all with you.'

Larissa tosses her head. 'It would have been better if you'd been with my daughter,' she says, loudly.

A murmur of discomfort. Mercedes eyes her neighbours sharply. You know. You know it's true. I hope you wear your shame forever.

They reach Plasa Iglesia, and Larissa sees what waits. She stops, stock-still, and her shoulders stiffen.

'No!' she says.

The stiff shoulders go back as she sucks in a breath. '*NO!*' she roars, and she starts to run.

They've formed a reception party. The priest and the duke side by side in the doorway. And either side of them, spilling down the steps, all wrapped in their vicious white, the *solter-onas*. His virginal attack dogs. Retained to keep his dominion quaking in fear.

'Larissa!' Sergio is caught on the back foot. Has to run as his wife charges towards the church.

'No!' she thunders. 'No! I won't have them here! No!' Larissa's hand cleaves the air, shooing them like birds from the grain fields.

'Larissa, *please*!' Sergio cries. He tries again to get hold of her arm. But Larissa's rage is superhuman. She throws him off as though he were made of paper.

The *solteronas*' faces drop. Their mouths fall open.

'Go!' howls Larissa. 'Get out of here! Go!'

They shuffle uneasily like cattle ready to stampede, look to their duke for leadership. And the duke gives nothing in return. As he always has, thinks Mercedes. As he always has.

Larissa mounts the steps, full charge. Grabs the arm of the nearest *solterona*, whirls her like a hammer and sends her tumbling to the ground below. The women shriek. Crowd backwards like the cowards they are.

'Get out! Get out! Go!'

She cuts through them like a tornado. A body flies down the stone steps, and another, and another. They hit the ground with dull thuds and the crunching of bones. One struggles to sit up. Blood streams from her nose and stains her starched white bodice.

And Mercedes sees fear on their faces and it is glorious. Oh, my mother, my mother. You are magnificent.

Larissa gets her hands on Madilena Harouj. Both arms. She must be seventy if she's a day. I don't care, thinks Mercedes. The older they are, the longer they have spent torturing us. She hauls her to the top of the steps and pushes her full in the back. The old woman stumbles, staggers down a couple of steps, teeters but stays somehow on her feet, her mouth gaping.

Larissa turns back while Mercedes' father bleats from the square below. 'Larissa! Stop it! Stop! What are you doing?'

The duke looks on. The colour has drained from his face, but he shows no emotion.

Half a dozen men break away from the crowd and throw themselves on her mother. Always the men, thinks Mercedes. Always the men. We'll never be free of them.

Larissa bucks and flails and roars out her rage as they haul her backwards, and still she manages to land a couple of hard kicks on her quailing targets.

'Get off!' she shouts. 'Get off me!'

They drag her down to the square. Hold her still among the fallen bodies as she pants out her defiance. 'You!' she shouts. 'You fucking … killers! You killed my fucking daughter and now you want to come to her funeral? Get out! Get away! I don't want you here!' With a mighty lurch, she pulls away from her captors. Whirls round to face the crowd. 'None of you! Do you hear? You all killed her. Hypocrites! Fucking hypocrites! Every single one of you! I don't want you here!'

Her chest heaves. The men drop back, suddenly respectful. They know, thinks Mercedes. They know she's right.

And Sergio wrings his hands and does nothing.

When Larissa speaks again, her voice is calmer. But no less certain. She glares about her, and her neighbours avert their gaze. 'Are you proud of yourselves?' she asks. 'Driving a sixteen-year-old girl to her death? Is this what makes you proud?'

A collective gasp. A murmur.

Larissa turns back to the church. Fixes her eye on the duke. Raises a hand and points a finger, so he cannot be under the illusion that she is addressing anybody else.

385

'And you. You're no better than they are. You could have put a stop to all this years ago. But no. You love it, don't you? Walking at the head of the parade, leading us all to the slaughter. And bringing *those people* here. All your yacht people with their money and their disdain. You're one of them. Corruptor. You're one of them!'

She spits on the ground.

'You're supposed to be noble,' she says. 'And look at you. Killer. Just like your friends. You may keep your hands clean, but you killed her just as surely as they did.'

Paulina Marino pushes her way into the space beside her and crosses her arms. Turns back to the other women. 'Those were our sisters,' she says. 'Those were our daughters.'

'Paulina!' cries Hector.

'No!' she snaps. 'It has to stop.' She turns back to the church. 'Go!' she shouts. 'Just go!'

Beata Vinci steps forward. Comes to stand beside them. Raises a fist and shakes it at the tyrants. Then Ximena Vigonier squeezes Mercedes' shoulder, throws her a smile so sweet Mercedes thinks her heart will snap, and goes to join them.

And, one by one, the women find their voices. They push forward, shrug off their men and march to the foot of the steps.

'Go!' they shout. From nowhere, a stone flies and catches a tormentor on the cheek, and Mercedes knows that life has changed forever.

The duke has the grace, for one split second, to look ashamed. Then the priest takes his arm and pulls him towards the great carved doorway, towards sanctuary. And a handful of men – the ones who know on what side their bread is buttered – Cosmo Albert, Bocelli the notary and, to her eternal shame, her own father – jog up the steps to form a phalanx and shield him from the crowd.

A hand slips into hers. She looks down, then up, and sees that it belongs to Felix Marino. He stands beside her quietly as the church door slams, and the women shout, and she grieves for her sister.

50

Sergio takes two days to come home. And, when he does, he doesn't speak. They've had no confirmation of where he's been. He's not been in the bars or in the neighbours' homes. The last they saw of him, he was running up the church steps as the duke and the priest retreated inside. Last they saw, he had slipped inside as they closed the door.

Confirmation comes with his arrival. The castle limo enters the docks and he steps out with a huge suitcase to drag behind him, and then they know where he's been. Traitor. Filthy traitor. They kill his daughter and he throws his lot in with them.

He comes home through the restaurant. The women, at the family table in the shade on the *terasa*, watch him pass, and no one speaks. And he vanishes into the interior and Paulina puts a hand over Larissa's and presses down, and they wait.

Twenty minutes later, he emerges, suitcase dragging over the tiles and a duffel thrown over his shoulder. He looks sulky. Adolescent. And yet so full of his own pomp that they already know what's coming.

'I've been given the restaurant on the hill,' he announces.

Silence. Blood money. He's taken blood money.

'It's a fine restaurant,' he says. And the women watch him like a bug.

'You can come, if you like,' he says, and to Mercedes' surprise she realises that he actually thinks they might agree.

They watch him standing there and no one speaks. He shrugs.

'Or stay here. Whatever. Stay small. If that's all you think you're worth.'

Larissa speaks at last. 'And what was your daughter worth, Sergio? What was *she* worth?'

For a second – for a split second – he looks ashamed. *We know what you did,* say the women, though they do not speak. *We know who you are, Sergio Delia.* And then the shame is wiped from his face and he puffs his chest out and walks on. Loads his luggage into the waiting limousine and drives away.

Larissa gazes down at her hands for a long time. Takes hold of her wedding ring and twists it off. She's lost so much weight since her daughter died that it's loose, and comes easily. She drops it into an unemptied ashtray, among the stubs. Then she gets to her feet and picks up her apron. 'Right,' she says. Ties the apron on and goes out to serve the tables.

51

He waits until the day after the official mourning period is done before he releases the hounds. His lust for payback must corrode his very soul, but even the duke knows how it would look to send in the attack dogs while the women are still in black.

And it gives him a month in which to plan.

When Luna Micaleff arrives in the castle limousine, you can feel the fear. Everyone feels it. Nothing good ever comes of a visit from Luna Micaleff. People are used to seeing the car by the *Princess Tatiana*, but, when it enters the dock and draws up outside the Re del Pesce, a strange silence falls over the area. The clatter of the men unloading the boats, the rattle of goods carts crossing the cobbles, the bangs and thunder from the old warehouse that's converting to a new customs outpost/ police station combined, the to-and-fro of shouted greeting and response: everything stops. It's so quiet, they can hear the buildings rise up along the cliffs.

Mercedes grinds to a halt halfway across the *terasa*, plates in hand, as the duke's secretary gets out of the limo, briefcase in hand, spectacles already on the bridge of his nose to show his serious intent. The women who have gathered every day at the family table, offering hands when hands are needed, fall quiet as well. And Larissa, halfway through her three o'clock lunch, stands up, takes off her apron and walks, stroking her hair as if to tidy it, to the entrance to greet him.

'Do you need me to come in with you?' calls Paulina Marino.

Larissa shakes her head and they go up the street, to the house entrance.

Paulina picks up the apron and takes Larissa's place on the floor. Rubs a hand between Mercedes' shoulderblades as she passes her. 'Don't worry,' she says. 'You mother's a strong woman. Whatever it is, she'll handle it.'

Mercedes doesn't reply. She feels as though the earth is about to swallow them up.

There can't be worse, she thinks. It's not possible. I've lost a sister and a father.

'We just keep our heads down and we carry on,' says Paulina. 'There are going to be changes, Mercedes. Trust me, it will get better.'

It doesn't. It gets worse.

Everyone knows what happens when a leaseholder dies. But there hasn't been a divorce on La Kastellana in anyone's memory. Wives disappear. They don't just hang about. Wives disappear and the husbands keep their leases, and the grandparents take the children and life carries on. A divorce? Nobody knows. And in the end the duke decides.

Best not to humiliate a landowner in a public place. It will never end well.

'He can only keep one lease,' says Larissa. 'This one's reverting in a month.'

They gasp.

'Can't you take it over?' asks Paulina.

'Sure,' she says.

'Well, that's okay, then, no?'

'It's a hundred thousand American dollars,' she says.

Shawls tighten round shoulders, lips clamp.

'In a month?'

Larissa nods.

'But how will you make a living?'

'I don't know,' she says. 'Restaurant is all I know.'

'What about Sergio?'

Larissa pulls a face. 'What about him?'

Mercedes' head buzzes. The cemetery? Could we build a café there? But where would we live? And nobody just *passes through* the cemetery. There's no natural footfall. We will die. There is no way out of this.

Sergio appears in the evening. Stands in the entrance, looking smug. He's had his hair cut at the new salon in the Heliogabalus Hotel, and he's grown a moustache that looks just perfect with the turquoise satin shirt he's bought.

'You can still come to Mediterraneo,' he says. 'I haven't closed the door.'

Larissa keeps her shoulder turned as she speaks. 'Mediterraneo? That's what you've called it?'

'Yes,' he says. 'It's going to be beautiful. Far better than this place will ever be.'

'I'm glad for you,' she replies. 'Shame you had to sell your family to get it. By the way, you've forgotten to button your shirt. You'll get a chill.'

'Larissa—'

'What?'

'You're still my wife.'

'In name.'

'You could still be – I'd be ready to forgive you.'

Larissa picks up a plate and hurls it at his head.

'But what will we do?' asks Mercedes. 'Mama, we can't *live*.'

'You want to go with him? *Do you?*'

Thirteen years old. Old enough to leave school, but it's a lot of life she's learning. 'Mama …'

Larissa won't look at anyone. She just works and works, an automaton. Chopping and cooking and serving, her table smile switched off the second she comes indoors. 'Go on, then,' she says, 'if that's what you want. Just go. I won't stop you.'

'Mama, I don't … why are you angry with *me*? What did I do?'

'Why would you stay with me anyway?' she replies. 'There's nothing, with me. Nothing.'

'We can go up the hill,' says Mercedes. 'At least they can't kick us out of *there*. We'll work it out. We will.'

'This is it,' she says. Despair makes people dramatic. 'I have literally nothing. Without this place, I have no purpose.'

'You have me,' Mercedes says, and her voice sounds very small, in her ears. As if she's pleading from miles away. *I know I'm a poor substitute. How can I replace the beautiful one? How can I ever fill the hole where the shining star once shone?* 'Mama,' she says, and bursts into tears. I'm only a kid, she thinks. I'm only a kid.

As if a switch is thrown, Larissa snaps awake. Sees her daughter, goes to her, wraps her in her arms. 'I'm sorry. I'm

393

sorry. Don't listen to me. You're everything, Mercedes. You're everything. We'll find a way.'

But her arms around her feel wrong. Everything feels wrong. Mercedes doesn't want to be held any more.

Sleep is something she remembers. A distant memory. There is no sleep, alone in this room, Donatella's things still all around her. When she gets into her sister's bed, she can still smell her. Find hairs on the pillows, feel the dent in the old mattress where she used to lie.

I want to die, she thinks. I cannot live like this.

Guilt eats her, from the inside out. How did I not know? How did I think she meant she was just leaving? I could have stopped her. I could have saved her. She'd have hated me, for a while. But she would still be here. It's all spoiled, now. It will never be better.

I have to save my mother. This house is all she's ever known, since she was Donatella's age. This house, the restaurant, these people. How can he own us like this? How did it happen? We're just slaves, really, from the day we're born. All the trappings of freedom, but none at all, in reality. Our lives are his, to dispose of as he wants, and she'll never be forgiven for showing him who he really is.

What do I do? What do I do? I can't let them take it away, I can't. But a hundred thousand American dollars? It might as well be a billion. It might as well be the whole of the ocean. I'd give anything. Anything to save her. Anything. I would give up my *life*. But who has a hundred thousand American dollars?

And she sits up in her sister's bed and takes a breath. Because she knows who has the money. And how she will persuade him to loan it.

Friday

52 | Gemma

She's a mess of snot and tears. She's been sobbing out loud, the past half-hour, unable to keep it in any longer. Stands stock-still and trembling. Unable to be certain that they are done, afraid that there will be more to come. And when she hears their footsteps shuffle out, hears the voices rise once more in manly hilarity, her strength gives way and she drops to her knees on the carpet.

Someone cuts the cable ties. When they grab her wrist, she cringes and tries to pull back because she thinks it's starting again. But Tatiana's voice, by her ear, tells her not to be stupid, tells her to sit still, and she's so well trained by now that she does as she's told.

But even when her hands are free, she doesn't touch the mask until she's told she can. They didn't want us to see who was doing what, she thinks. Even *they* have some degree of shame.

'Okay,' says Tatiana, 'you can ditch the masks. Well done, girls. You've done splendidly!'

Gemma peels the mask off and looks around. They're in a room she's never seen before, hidden at the end of the corridor. A *manly* room; all leather and corduroy and polished reddish-brown wood. On a cinema-style screen, a blurred image in black and white that she can't make out, as though someone's paused a film mid-action. A coffee table is scattered with ash-trays and glasses and in the middle there are four Japanese ceramic bowls where someone's been throwing coins. All different colours. Red, green, yellow, blue. Green is fullest by far. Whoever's been aiming at it, they've an eagle eye.

Her hand strays to her wristband, and she wonders if she can take it off yet. Same colour. Creepy.

Sara and Wei-Cheng are still on their feet, but Hanne too has dropped to her hands and knees at some point. They all look drained of blood, pale as though they're in shock. It wasn't just me, then, thinks Gemma. That was too much. But nobody else is tearstained. Only I've been crying. Only me.

'Sorry, darlings.' Tatiana's voice is back to what it was when they arrived. Indulgent, as if she's treating them to ice-cream. 'They got a bit over-excited there. Men!' And she rolls her eyes as though she's talking about someone breaking a window with a football, not ... *that*. 'I should think you could all do with a nice stiff drink.'

Sara staggers slightly as she walks to an armchair. 'Yes,' she says, and even she sounds shaken.

The indulgent voice again. 'You just get cosy,' she says, 'and I'll bring you all a brandy.'

They stumble their way into armchairs. Which are still warm from their previous occupants.

Gemma feels bruised inside. As though she's actually injured.

'Fuck me,' says Sara. 'I dunno if *that* was worth twenty grand.'

'Bloody hope that's really it,' says Wei-Cheng. 'I don't think I can take much more partying.'

Hanne is rocking slightly in her chair. There's blood on her thighs. Gemma hazily puts a hand between her own to check herself. The fingers come up slimed and sticky, but there's no blood. A bit of her is surprised.

'Yes, darling,' says Tatiana, bustling back in. Four huge brandy snifters on a butler's tray, the best part of a quarter-bottle in each. 'That's it. It's all just fun fun fun from now on! A lovely long lie-in and some swims in the pool, and it's fancy dress and champagne all the way! Here! Drink up!' She presses the glasses into their hands.

'I want to go home,' says Hanne.

'Don't be silly,' says Tatiana. 'A good long sleep and a bath and you'll be right as rain.'

Gemma's hand shakes as she puts the glass to her lips and takes a large slug. The brandy's warm, and mellow. I won't do this again, she thinks. They like hurting people. Really hurting them. I thought I was going to *break*.

She wipes her face with her wrist.

Tatiana picks up a remote and kills the picture on the big screen. Gemma's a bit relieved she has, because, although the image was fuzzy and hard to make out, something in her had been finding it disturbing.

'Tatiana?' asks Sara. 'Have you got any painkillers?'

'Really?' asks Tatiana, and looks surprised, as though the things these men have done should not have hurt. 'Sure. What do you want?'

'What have you got?'

'Most things,' she says, casually. 'Ibuprofen? Trammies? Zomorph?'

Saturday

53 | Mercedes

Seven a.m., and Paulo is back on duty at the gate. Staff are clattering in the kitchen while more go into the house with bin liners to survey the damage.

The *sala* stinks of party.

Mercedes looks around. There's a bottle-sized red wine stain; a pool of the stuff on the floor leaking from a bottle that has rolled beneath the sofa has steadily wicked its way into the fibres.

'Oh, Jesus.'

She thinks through the contents of the store cupboard. There's a spare.

The scatter cushions are scattered again, of course. Horrible, useless things, nine of them, covered in pastel marabou feathers.

Mercedes hates these cushions with every grain of her being. She's plumped them every day for two years. Spent more hours than she can bear to think of slowly, slowly unpicking tangles. This is the last time I shall have to do this, she thinks. No more portraits. No more viscous bedsheets, no more suntan lotion greasing the sandstone paving round the pool. I've got so numbed over the years that I've lost sight of how much I hate this life. Hate these things. Hate their owners who've kept me trapped here through all my best years.

Something, caught in feathers and released by movement, clatters to the floor. She looks down, sees Gemma's little bag, with its rattling sequins and the tiny diamante cat on a keychain.

Funny, she thinks, as she picks it up. You'd have thought after yesterday she'd be more careful. She checks inside. Same contents: passport, Ventolin inhaler, pearly brown lipstick, a couple of gold-wrapped condoms.

She'll be wanting this, she thinks. But time is racing and they have a job ahead of them before the house wakes up.

She puts it in an obvious place, on a little mirrored table that hugs the bottom of the stairs, and goes back to rescuing the sofa.

They drift down late morning, one by one. Tatiana in a floor-length robe, the men rusty and stubbled and ill-kempt. All but the prince, who sports his blazer-and-trews uniform as though he's simply put himself away in a box overnight. Having unpacked for him, Mercedes knows that he has eight identical outfits hanging in his wardrobe, and sixteen perfectly ironed shirts wrapped in tissue paper. But he's only changed his underpants once since he arrived. A walking metaphor: shiny on the surface, filthy beneath.

Matthew lumbers to the table by the pool and kisses his daughter on the temple. He's in boxer shorts and a towelling dressing gown, his stomach hanging round and hairy over his waistband.

'Eggs,' he says, 'and toast. And coffee.'

'How do you want your eggs, sir?' asks Mercedes.

'Christ, I don't know,' he says. 'Surprise me. Aren't you eating?' he asks Tatiana.

'Have you seen my dress?' she replies.

'She's put on a bit of weight since the fitting,' says Jason Pettit, and smirks.

'Oh, piss off, Jason,' she snaps.

He smirks again. His eye bags are like ball sacks this morning. He'll be needing that haemorrhoid cream he's got lying by the bathroom basin before he meets the photographers from *Hello!* magazine.

'All okay?' asks Matthew.

'Yes, fine. All loaded and on board,' replies Tatiana.

'Would you like anything to eat, Mr Pettit?' asks Mercedes.

'Black coffee,' says Jason Pettit. 'Egg-white omelette, gluten-free toast.'

He throws Tatiana a *you see?* look that clearly infuriates her. 'I'll have toast,' she says. 'With gluten in. And butter. And some prosciutto, and a fig.'

Jason Pettit raises his eyebrows. He picks up his ever-present iPhone and starts scrolling.

'What time's kick-off tonight?' asks the prince.

'Which cabin?' asks Matthew Meade.

'Mine,' says Tatiana, and turns to her royal guest. 'Ten. We've got a nice big terrace table at Mediterraneo at eight.'

'Girls coming?'

'Of course.'

'If they can walk,' says Jason Pettit, and sniggers. Stops and frowns. 'Oh, God *damn* the *Daily Mail.*'

'What?' asks the prince.

'The usual dirty-minded tittle-tattle. Jesus.'

'Ha,' says Tatiana, 'if only they knew,' and all the men's heads snick round to look at her.

'Oh, by the way, Mercy darling, the safe room needs a clean. We ended up in there for a bit last night.'

A rush of relief. No need for subterfuge. Tatiana has just made her life a whole world easier.

'Let me know when you're ready and I'll let you in,' Tatiana says.

'Of course,' she replies, smiling.

It's lunchtime by the time the girls appear. Hanne, Wei-Cheng, Sara: floral cotton play-suits and shortie kimonos. Hair tousled, sleep still in the corners of their eyes. Walking like old people. She hears them on the stairs and they're not happy.

'. . . didn't sign up for that . . .' says Wei-Cheng.

'Oh, for God's sake,' says Sara, 'What did you think you were getting twenty grand for? Backgammon and a quick nosh? They're not a bloody charity.'

'Yeah, but—' begins Hanne.

'Give it a rest. Nobody kidnapped you. Besides, that was the main event. I think. All downhill from here.'

'Christ, I hope so.'

'They're all off on the Old Man's boat at dawn tomorrow,' says Sara. 'So, you know . . .'

'Christ, I feel like shit, though,' says Wei-Cheng. 'I don't feel as if I've had any sleep at all. D'you remember going to bed? I don't even remember going to bed.'

'Yeah,' says Sara, 'it does take it out of you.'

They round the spiral, catch sight of Mercedes at the bottom and put on their game faces. 'Morning!' they cry.

'Good morning,' she says. 'The others are out by the pool.'

406

'Whoop,' mutters Hanne. Then she smiles brightly. Automatically.

'Can I get you anything?' asks Mercedes.

'I'd kill for a coffee,' says Hanne.

'Daiquiri,' say Wei-Cheng and Sara, together.

'Gemma still in bed?'

Little frowns of surprise cross their faces.

'Oh. No,' says Hanne. 'I'd assumed she'd got up already. Isn't she downstairs?'

'Maybe I didn't see her,' says Mercedes, and looks for the little bag she left out for her on the table.

It's not there any more.

'I say,' says Matthew. 'I fancy some pistachios.'

Mercedes nods. Of course we have pistachios, just lying about in case you want them.

'What a good idea,' says the prince. 'I'll have some too.'

'Certainly, sir,' she says.

'Yeah, and me,' says the hairy film producer. She nods politely. 'Feeling a bit protein-depleted,' he says, and the men laugh uproariously.

Three little dishes, and three empty ones for shells, or they'll be turning up in the gaps between the paving stones for months. Not my problem any more. She loads them onto a tray, then adds more, because it's all monkey-see, monkey-do with these people. She feels strangely light, almost high. Can feel the future coming up towards her.

The girls sit in a row with their feet in the pool. Wei-Cheng has a big purple bruise on her thigh and Hanne keeps reaching round to the back of her neck and straining, as though she's trying to clunk something out.

The actor looks at his little dish as though she's just farted on it.

'Oh, for God's sake!' he says.

Tatiana looks up indifferently, looks away again without asking what's wrong. Jason Pettit glares at her.

'Take them away,' he says. 'Did I ask for them? No. Well, take them away. Are you trying to kill me?'

Mercedes puts the dish back on the tray and gives him her sweetest smile. 'I wouldn't mind, sir,' she says.

Wei-Cheng shouts with laughter. Shuts herself up when she realises that she is the only one. Mercedes throws her a conspiratorial smile. She takes the rejected nuts over to them and gets sunny smiles of thanks, while the actor goggles as though he's been slapped.

Hanne has a pattern of small bruises across her neck and shoulders. As though someone's gripped her there, roughly. She turns to look at her hostess, and the movement is cramped, careful. 'Hey, Tatiana?' she calls. 'Where's Gemma?'

Tatiana doesn't look up. 'Gone,' she says.

'Gone?'

'That's what I said.'

'Gone where?'

'My dear,' says Tatiana, 'I have no idea and I care even less.'

But she's left her *passport*, thinks Mercedes. Where can she have gone without her passport? Her light mood vanishes.

'She got a better offer,' says Matthew Meade.

'Better offer?' Sara looks appalled.

'I know, right?' says Tatiana.

The girls exchange glances.

'Well, to be fair,' says Bruce Fanshawe, 'there was serious money here last night. I guess she got an offer even you couldn't match.'

'Well, she's not getting any of mine, that's for sure,' says Tatiana.

'Oh, God,' says Wei-Cheng, 'why does that sort of thing never happen to me?'

You don't want it to, thinks Mercedes. You don't. I've a good idea where she's gone to and you don't want to follow.

'And after all that blubbing,' says Sara. 'Who'd go with *that*, for God's sake?'

'Oh, I don't know,' says the actor. 'That sort of thing can have its appeal.'

Tatiana throws him a look of pure malevolence.

'Must've been a hell of an offer,' says Sara. 'She's left all her stuff.'

'Probably didn't want to wake you up,' says Tatiana.

'I don't think *anything* would have woken me up last night,' says Wei-Cheng. 'I don't think I even finished my nightcap.'

'She's left literally *everything*,' says Hanne. 'Her clothes. Underwear. Even her earrings.'

'Ooh!' says Wei-Cheng, perking up. 'The diamond ones?'

'Yes!'

'You might as well go and divide it all up,' says Tatiana. 'She won't be back.'

'What, even the jewellery?'

Tatiana sighs. 'If she wants a sugar daddy,' she says, 'he can bloody well buy her kit himself. Besides, I gave her those earrings. I guess I can take them away again.'

'Ooh!' says Wei-Cheng again, and suddenly there's a flurry of getting up and running, droplets sparkling in the air as their feet flip from the pool. The teenage capacity for recovery. Hanne, nearest to the shallow end, is out first, and has a good three-metre lead on the others, despite her limp and her gammy hand. She lopes into the house, cackling in triumph.

And that's how it goes, thinks Mercedes. Show people the shiny things and they'll forget the questions they should have asked. Just like my father. One glimpse of Mediterraneo, and he might as well have never had an older daughter. I hope that girl's okay. That she's still alive. That something didn't happen already, in the night.

Her smile is beginning to hurt. There's nothing she can do right now. She just has to keep her game face on, and hope.

The adults watch the girls' retreating backs with amused smiles on their faces.

'And that,' says Matthew Meade, 'is why I will never be poor. People will do anything for money.'

Bruce Fanshawe's eyes narrow, like a basking lizard's. 'It's the things they *don't* know they're going to do for money that really interest me these days,' he says.

They all laugh.

The actor finds his querulous voice. 'Are you really going to let her speak to your guests like that?' he asks.

'What?'

'Your maid.'

'Oh, shush,' says Tatiana. The honeymoon is definitely over. 'She's devoted to us. I've known her since she was twelve years old.'

Mercedes retreats to prepare for the clean.

Tatiana's voice follows her through the house. 'Mercy will do anything I say. Did I ever tell you about the time I pissed on her?'

She follows her employer down the corridor. Stands politely with her back turned while she keys in the code, picks up her bucket and her bleach when she hears the door slide back.

410

When she turns, she is hit by a gust of old smells. They've left the room closed with the air-con off all night and it's matured. Abandoned alcohol, cigar smoke. Something salty. Something faintly faecal. It smells of death, she thinks, and pulls on her rubber gloves. Even the air feels dead.

Tatiana doesn't comment. Not on the smell, not on the mess. She can't imagine ever reaching such a state of entitlement that she wouldn't apologise for leaving someone else to deal with a room like this.

But of course, they literally pay us, yuh?

'Let me know when you're done,' she says, 'and I'll lock up.'

'I may be a while,' Mercedes says. Under the ceiling spotlights, she sees sticky patches on pretty much every surface. Stains. On the carpet, on the seats of the chairs. She long since passed the point where anything she has to clean in this house brings on nausea. She has heard that there are specialist firms on the mainland that clean up after murders, or when some lonely individual dies and nobody notices until their viscosities start leaking through the ceiling into the floor below. I'd be good at that, she thinks, stepping over the threshold. Only, on La Kastellana, we don't leave people to die alone.

'Whatever,' says Tatiana, and goes back to her party.

On the table, among the bottles and the ashtrays, lies a little pile of cable ties, closed and then cut open. She knows what they will have been binding. I hate them, she thinks, as she crosses the tacky carpet to fill her bucket at the kitchenette sink. They're disgusting. Wicked, and disgusting. They deserve everything that will happen to them. Everything.

This job will take at least two hours. When she's finished, she'll put the plug into the sink, turn the tap on and close the door.

Island

September 1986

54

He grants her an audience as he sits in his hot tub. No freshly squeezed juices now, no toothsome pastries. He's just taken delivery of his second new crew of staff since the ones who used to spoil her as she waited for Tatiana to get up in the morning, and she's as much of a stranger to them as any other teenage girl passing by on the harbour. The only person she recognises now is Philip, the captain.

It took some persuading to get the new security guard on the gangplank even to take him her note, and he kept her waiting so long for a reply that she was beginning to believe that it had never got through.

The emperor lounges in his bubbling water as she stands before him in the blazing sun, his arms spread wide along the rim of the tub. I should have brought a hat with me, she thinks. So I could wring it between my hands as I beg.

The tub is designed to seat four, but Matthew Meade fills it so thoroughly that she pities anyone who might attempt to share it with him. And a memory of those girls who came to the Stag last summer flashes through her head and she wishes it hadn't.

'So!' he says, 'our money's good enough for you *now*, is it?'

'It was never ...' she begins. Realises she's leading herself down a blind alley and changes tack. 'I'm sorry,' she says. 'It was ... when Tatiana got new friends, when she started coming into our restaurant with them, I guess I was ...'

She casts about for the right word, the one that will unlock his triumph. Not relieved, then. Not glad. Not liberated.

He smiles slightly as he waits. He's loving this. Loving it. He takes real pleasure in other people's misery. It's not, for him, just that he should win, but that other people should lose, and know they've lost, and feel the burn of their defeat. He's an awful, awful man. But he's the only man she knows to whom a hundred thousand American dollars is pocket change.

'Jealous,' she tells him, because it's what he wants to hear. 'And my sister, I know she was disrespectful. But she is ... was ...'

The still-unfamiliar change of tense stops her in her tracks. She flounders, bites back her tears.

Matthew Meade's right arm, creased and folded flesh dangling from the underside, lifts up and drops itself into the water. 'Ah, yes,' he says. 'Your sister. A pity about her. Pretty girl.'

She doesn't reply. Stares down at the deck and tries to get hold of her emotions. I can't lose my mother, she thinks. If we don't manage to keep the Re, it will kill her.

She hears the suck and slosh as he shifts in the water. 'So how do you propose,' he asks, 'repaying this money? If I agree to lend it to you.'

Mercedes looks up. The hand is still under the water. She tries not to think about where it might be.

'We'll pay you back from what we earn,' she says.

A hiss of contemptuous mirth. 'Well, *that's* going to take a while. I'm not sure I'll live long enough.'

'We'll give you ten per cent of what we earn, every year,' she says.

She hasn't discussed this with Larissa. But desperation makes her bold. They'll have two fewer mouths to feed now, after all.

A smirk. 'A tithe, is it? The same way you pay the *duqa*?'

She nods.

'That wouldn't even cover the interest, my dear. How about the rest of it? It's not as if you're borrowing money to expand. How are you intending to repay the principal?'

Mercedes stares at him, lost. She doesn't know these words. Doesn't know the language of commerce, the language of debt. Just knows that he's telling her that she's putting herself for years – decades – in his power.

I can't lose my mother, she thinks blindly. I can't! This island has killed my sister. If it takes my mother too, there will be nothing left for me.

'I'll do anything,' she says. 'Anything you suggest.'

Matthew Meade studies her with a look of amusement. 'Anything?'

She swallows.

He lifts the hand out of the water, sniffs his fingertips. 'Well, I don't suppose we have to go *that* far,' he says. 'Pity, really, you're not pretty like your sister.'

He picks a cigar from the humidor behind him with his dry hand. Takes his time preparing it, lighting it. The lighter is chunky. Made of gold, and monogrammed with his initials.

'Well, I'm sure I can think of something,' he says eventually. 'Give me a day or two. Perhaps we might make Tatiana feel better at the same time. You and your sister, you really upset her, you know. It will take a *very long time* to make up for that.'

She is flooded with relief. 'Thank you,' she says. Meets his eye as calmly as she can. 'Thank you so much.'

She understands what she is agreeing to. A lifetime's abasement stretches out ahead. But there is no other option. This is her only hope.

He flicks his finger, dismisses her. She turns and starts to walk back towards the gangplank gate. As she reaches it, he calls after her.

'There'll be a contract, of course.'

Saturday

55 | Gemma

She has a series of nightmares, but she cannot seem to wake up. She is riding the dodgems at the fair on Clapham Common, but the controls won't work. She twists the wheel and stamps on the pedal, and the car does exactly what it chooses, flings her about, head jouncing on her neck as though it's barely attached. Then she's in a coffin, padded satin beneath her skin, and she's being walked towards the church hoist high on strangers' shoulders. But someone has sewn her lips closed and however hard she tries she cannot move her limbs. She tries to scream for help, to let them know she is alive, but no sound comes out. And then she's deep underground, in a cave, in the dark, and she's wedged in a tube of rock and her arms are trapped by her sides and the ground above is pressing down and she's screaming.

Her eyes open to darkness. There's something clinging to her face. Her lashes brush fabric. And something's in her mouth, holding it open but blocking it, and she cannot shift it.

Still dreaming, she thinks. It's that paralysis you get when you've come awake too fast. I need to get this off my face. I've got tangled up in the bedclothes.

And she tries to move her arms and discovers that they are bound together at the wrists, behind her back. And then she is sharply, fully awake.

Blind. The *something* on her face is wrapped tightly around her head, enveloping it. And the something in her mouth is strapped there so she cannot spit it out.

A couple of inches below her eyes, a tiny patch of light. Breathing holes, she thinks. There are breathing holes. It's a mask. But it is tight and compresses her nose, and she's not getting enough air for someone whose body is pulsing with fear.

No, she thinks. *No, no, no, no, no*, this can't be. And the earth lurches as hypoxia takes her and she plummets once again into the dark.

The object in her mouth tastes of chemicals. It gives a little when she presses down with her teeth. She knows what it is. It's a ball gag. She's seen them in films. Never ones with happy endings.

The brain adjusts. The fourth or fifth time she regains consciousness, she knows already what she will find, and blind panic no longer takes her mind away.

It's almost worse than when it does.

She's on her side. Hands behind her back and legs tied together at knees and ankles. The bed – she assumes it's a bed – on which she lies is soft and forgiving, but the surface beneath her skin is plastic and she is sweating where her naked body touches it.

Somewhere nearby, the boom of water shifting against

a hollow wall. She remembers the sound from her cabin in Cannes.

I'm on a boat, she thinks. They've taken me and put me on a boat.

Panic is bad, but despair is a good deal worse.

56 | Robin

Robin feels a hundred years old. Worn out by sleeplessness, pressed down by gravity until the strength has left her body. I want to die, she thinks. I do. At least if I were a hundred years old, I would know that death was coming soon.

I'll never find her. This was my last chance, and I'll never find her now. My little girl. Wherever she is, she is gone from me. I've got what I deserved.

It's worse than a death, she thinks, this not-knowing. A life sentence. No more than I deserve. No more than we deserve. Me and Patrick, tied together forever by a child we didn't love enough. I shall go back to London and tell him that we've lost her, and he'll look at me as though he doesn't understand. But I do. I understand. We were so bound up in ourselves and our petty resentments that we forgot all about her. And now she's gone, and I will never be able to say how sorry I am.

The crowds are thick coming off the ferry, but the queue to board is short. Not many people wanting to leave the island today, with the ducal celebrations spreading all the way down to the town tonight. Another set of firework frames, larger even than the ones for St James's Day, have risen in record time on the top of the harbour wall, and the dock is lined with trestle tables so the peasants can feast.

Robin shows her ticket and her passport at the kiosk and gets in line to board. Another glorious day. Sea smooth as satin, sky high and blue and free of blemish. She looks back at Kastellana Town. I think you were probably a nice place once, she thinks. Somewhere where life was simple and people looked after each other. A community. I think I'd have been happy if Gemma had come here then.

They shuffle forward. She bends to pick up her bag, turns round to look back one more time and finds herself face to face with Laurence Viner. He recognises her, and his usually bland expression changes. Shock, she thinks. He wasn't expecting to see me.

'You're not *leaving*?' he asks. 'Surely?'

Robin nods. 'Sort of have to,' she says.

'No!' He seems genuinely upset. 'No! Robin, you *can't*!'

Why's he so bothered? she wonders. I've not seen him since that day at the Heliogabalus Hotel. He can't be *that* bothered.

'I don't really have a choice,' she tells him. 'The police have basically told me to fuck off.'

He frowns. Steps out of the queue and beckons her to follow. She hesitates. The prospect of having to start again right from the back is unappealing. But she follows anyway. He looks so concerned that she can't resist. He knows something. She can't let her daughter down for the sake of a queue.

'Robin ...' He speaks urgently. But quietly, as though he's afraid of being overheard. 'You can't leave. I can't tell you any

425

detail. I shouldn't be telling you anything at all. But you need to trust me on this.'

Robin's brain whirls. 'But *you're* leaving?'

'Yes,' he says. 'I need to be as far away as possible tonight. I'm sorry. I can't ... look ... '

He reaches into an inside pocket and produces a business card. Thick, stiff cardboard, discreet lettering that declares only the name of his company, his name, his telephone and email. The luxurious simplicity of the very expensive. He pulls a small retractable pencil from the same pocket and starts to scribble on the back. Robin waits. The queue shortens.

He looks up and hands her the card. She looks at the scribble, but it's in Kastellani. But she sees the words *Sra Hanson* and *filja perdida* and understands that it's about her.

'You see that restaurant, over there?' he says.

'The Re del Pesce?'

He nods. 'Yes. Take this to the lady there. Larissa Delia.' He registers her doubt, pushes on. 'She's a good egg,' he says. 'Her English is pretty pants, but she'll understand well enough. Just ... trust me on this, Mrs Hanson. There will be news. Soon. She'll give you somewhere to stay. Just wait.'

She searches his face for more, but there is none. The earnest expression drops away, the bland comes back. 'You'll have a *mar*vellous time.' He raises his voice so that it rings out across the queue. For the benefit of someone, though she's not sure who. 'You won't regret it. *So* worth waiting for. I only wish I could stay myself.'

And he walks back to the last stub of the queue and boards the boat without a backward glance.

She fugues for a few moments, in the blazing sun with her bags around her feet. Then she sees the ticket collector gesticulating, eyebrows raised, and realises that the queue has gone.

426

She throws him an apologetic smile and a shake of the head, picks up her bags and marches smartly across the dock before a member of the duke's constabulary turns up and asks why she's still there.

Her funds have been too short for eating out, so she's not been into the Re del Pesce, but she noticed when she handed her flyer in on the *festa* night that it looked sweet. Far more welcoming than the big-face eateries on the hill. Staff, all women, bustle between tables in the shade and the food smells good enough that her mouth waters. She waits politely by the PLEASE WAIT TO BE SEATED sign, and a woman, hair streaked with grey and an air of melancholy that makes Robin want to hug her, approaches with a pleasant smile.

'For how many, *sinjora*?' she asks.

'I ... I was looking for Larissa Delia?' she says.

The woman nods, gravely. 'This is me.'

'Ah. Ah, good. I was talking to Laurence,' she says. 'Laurence Viner?'

Larissa smiles politely. 'Ah, Mr Viner. A true friend of the Re del Pesce.'

'He gave me this,' Robin says, and hands her the card.

Larissa's face drops. She reads the handwriting slowly. Not particularly literate, thinks Robin. They weren't educating girls much here when she was school age. Then the smile returns. Inscrutable. 'Come with me, *sinjora*.'

She snatches up Robin's backpack as though it were made of feathers and walks off into the street, fishing a set of keys from her apron.

The entrance is perfunctory. A narrow corridor built to carve out a route to the stairs that doesn't involve crossing the restaurant. A door leads through it to the left. Their footsteps echo off concrete walls and concrete stairs. It's all very backstage.

'Please,' she says as she follows her host, 'do you know what's going on?'

Larissa doesn't turn or pause. Just keeps walking. 'I don't know much. But you wait here. I think you will be glad. He send you to me because is safe.'

She stops, suddenly. Looks down at the keys in her hand. 'Everybody knows I will keep them safe,' she says. 'If they come to me.'

So much unspoken. This woman is sad. She's unbearably, unspeakably sad.

They climb on.

The upper storey is windowless and dark, a fan whirring on the landing ceiling. An oil painting of the Virgin Mary on one wall and, on the ledge over the stairs, a statue of the Botticelli Venus rising from a jungle of greenery that, given the lack of light, can only be artificial.

'You stay in my daughter's room,' she says. 'I bring you food, in a little while. Is comfortable there. Maybe you sleep some. I think maybe you not been sleeping?'

'No,' says Robin. 'No, I haven't.'

'You rest now,' says the woman kindly. 'We keep you safe here. And when there is news, you will know straight away. I promise.'

She smiles once again, and for a moment her eyes fill with tears. Then she pulls her shawl tighter – some ancient self-comforting, inherited through generations – and goes to a closed door of heavy mahogany. Incongruous in this world of stippled concrete and plastic ferns, it looks as though it's come from another house altogether.

She gives Robin a watery smile and opens the door.

The light is dim. The room is identical in size and layout to the one she's been in all week, but this one has single beds, either side of the window. Unnecessary pink curtains inside the shutters, for decoration rather than function. Candlewick bedspreads in matching pink. A mirrored dressing table, an open cupboard in which hangs a waterfall of brightly coloured cloth. Five pairs of spike-heeled shoes that only someone young could wear on these cobbles. A mug tree from which dangles a small but gaudy collection of cheap jewellery.

Two framed photos: a pair of girls, photographed some years apart but each time enveloped in a hug, arms round necks, smiling broadly at the camera. The elder is one of those shining beauties you see from time to time in these Latin streets: all black hair and almond eyes and lips with a touch of attitude. The sort of girl who turns your head, just with astonishment that such beauty can exist. The younger is more ordinary. Her black hair lacks that mysterious gloss, her bone structure is less well defined. But she glows in her sister's company. There is love there. So much love.

Daughters, she thinks. She meant daughters' room, plural. Where are they now? She's too old to still have teens. I think the younger one was the one I spoke to on St James's night. She must be in her forties now. But I've not seen the beauty anywhere. Probably gone to richer pastures, the way beauties so often do.

'Thank you,' she says. She still doesn't understand what's going on, but she trusts this woman. No one this sad can carry ill intent. 'You're very kind.'

Larissa nods. Steps out onto the landing and pulls the door to behind her.

57 | Mercedes

As she's taking the newest round of smeary glasses to the kitchen, she notices that water is beginning to seep from under the safe room door. Not much yet. Only a little puddle; could still just be the product of careless floor-washing. But it's coming now, creeping outwards a millimetre at a time. Not long until there's enough drama to involve Paulo.

Roberto is in a bad mood, banging bread dough out on the marble rolling board, knocking it down for its second proving. Twelve loaves, part baked and sealed in plastic, are to go down to the *Princess Tatiana*, along with the feast of pies and cheeses, hams and pastries that Matthew has ordered to sustain the Stag.

'They never damn well think, do they?' He slams the dough down again, punches it as though it were his boss's face. 'I had it all under control and he adds an extra day, just like that.'

'Honey,' she says, 'Stefanie and I spent twenty minutes getting Tatiana into her stays tonight. Count yourself lucky.'

Nuno is rolling pastry for croissants. 'Has it shrunk, maybe?'

'Yes,' she says, 'that'll be it.'

'I saw her,' says Roberto. 'Good lord. Still. It made me think: I might make *crème caramel* tomorrow.'

They all snigger. 'What was she meant to be, anyway?' asks Roberto.

'Milady de Winter,' she says. 'In *The Three Musketeers*.'

'Interesting. Doesn't she get beheaded?'

'We can but hope,' she says drily.

They laugh. This week has tested all of them.

'I think it's more likely she'll just cut off her circulation,' she says. 'Can I get to the dishwasher? I'll get the *sala* squared away.'

'Sure,' he says.

Someone's dropped cigar ash on the arm of the white sofa and she has a moment of wild rage. These people, these people. They have no respect. None. And then she remembers that she will never have to clean their shit again, and she calms down. Especially as she sees the opportunity it offers. She presses the intercom button and calls Ursula down from her room. Better, really, if she raises the alarm rather than Mercedes. Better to put as many layers of deniability between herself and the Meades as she can.

Ursula bends over the stain. 'Oh, for fucksake,' she says.

'I know,' says Mercedes. 'I'm sorry.'

The tension is making her itch, inside. She wants to run about the room, screaming.

Ursula rubs the mark with her fingers and tuts. 'The other covers are still in the laundry,' she says.

'Hell. Do you think you can get it out?'

'I don't know. Maybe. Bleach, maybe?'

'Really? Can't we try some of those stain things in the store cupboard?'

'Sure,' says Ursula. 'We can try. But I think it's going to come down to bleach in the end.'

Mercedes hands her the keys. 'Can you have a look? See if you can find anything?'

'Sure.' She sighs and soft-shoes up the corridor. Mercedes waits. Grinds her teeth and waits. This is almost beyond bearing. So much could go wrong. So much.

And Ursula's voice echoes down the hall, calling her name, and the beginning of the end begins.

'Oh, God,' she says.

'Where's it coming from?' asks Ursula.

'The safe room.'

'There's a room behind there?'

'Yes.'

'I *knew* it! I *knew* this house was an odd shape. I *knew* there was some space missing! How did I not *know*?'

'They sort of keep it a secret,' she says, 'for obvious reasons.'

'But you knew?'

'Someone has to keep it clean.' Mercedes pauses, for effect. 'Oh, shit,' she says. 'I was cleaning in there today. Don't say I left the tap running?'

It's not hard to sound panicky. She *feels* panicky.

'Oh, God, she'll kill me! Oh, God!'

'Well, open it,' says Ursula.

'I can't! I don't know the code!'

Ursula can be slow on the uptake. 'Really?'

'Of course not!'

'Why not?'

Because they don't want me getting in there. 'Because if I don't know the code, I can't tell, can I?' she snaps. 'Sorry. I'm a bit stressed. Oh, God. I'm going to have to tell Paulo. Christ,

432

and he'll tell her, and they'll take the damage off my wages, and there's *hundreds of thousands* of dollars' worth of stuff in there. Oh, God . . .'

She stops. Feels the tears well up for real. Just the mention of all that money produces a reflex response. All those times, all those times when she's thought she might be approaching freedom, only to find that her debt has spiralled through the sorcery of accounting. I will die, she thinks, if I can't get away. This *has* to work. If I'm trapped here for one more day, it will kill me.

Ursula pats her shoulder. 'I'm sure it'll be okay,' she says. 'If it's that secure, they'll have everything protected inside, too.'

She goes off to the intercom to call Paulo.

He's been napping. His hair is mussed at the back and the area around his eyes is a bit red.

'Looks like you've got a flood on your hands,' he says, quite calmly.

'Please,' she says. 'Let me get in there, Paulo. Please.'

'I should call Miss Meade,' he says, 'strictly speaking. I'm not supposed to access it without her say-so.'

'She's at the *ball*, Paulo!'

He scratches the back of his head and thinks. 'Yeah,' he says.

'And it's just going to get worse . . .'

'Yeah,' he says again. 'Okay. Can you guys go into the living room? I'll call you when it's open.'

'Thank you,' she says. 'Thank you, thank you, thank you. You've saved my life, I swear.'

'Not guaranteeing anything,' he says. 'If it's all carked, I'm not going to be able to cover up for us, you know.'

'No,' she says. 'I get that.'

'Go on,' he says. 'Scram.'

She doesn't answer. Waits while Paulo pops open the door panel and keys in the code. She's always wondered how one would access the room fast enough in a home invasion, but then, she knows that that's not really what it's there for. She hears the door grind back, and the sound of water, gushing out, and Paulo swears as it floods his boots.

'Okay,' he calls. 'She's all yours. You're not going to be happy, though.'

The water is ankle-deep, all the way up the hall. The seal on the door is clearly effective. They slosh through it and stand on the threshold, looking in.

'Oh, my word,' says Ursula.

The room is drenched. Soggy carpet, soggy chairs, a film of water on the surface of the coffee table, slowly dripping off. Paulo is at the sink, turning off the tap.

'Yep,' he says. 'Jesus, Mercedes, you've done a pretty thorough job here. You left the plug in, did you know that?'

'*Oao*,' says Ursula. 'My God.'

Mercedes squelches in and surveys the damage. 'Oh, God,' she says, 'she's going to kill me.'

'Yeah, I'm afraid there's no way we're covering this up,' he says. 'I'm sorry, Mercedes.'

She sits down, hard, in an armchair. It's wet under her bottom, soaks through her layers of uniform. Surreptitiously looks at the drawers where the DVDs live. No locks. Of course not. This entire room is a strongbox.

'We'll do what we can,' says Paulo comfortingly. 'I'm sure we can get this a lot better before she gets home. Arturo's got that pumping thing in the garden store, for the pool.'

'I had no idea this was here,' says Ursula again. 'What are all the screens for? Are they *recording* us?'

Mercedes shakes her head, despairingly. 'I just ... oh, God. All these electronics ... I can't even ...'

'I suppose,' says Paulo, and picks up the remote control from where it sits on a shelf beneath the giant screen, 'we might as well find out the worst.'

'No! Oh, my God, what if you short it?'

She leaps to her feet. Tries to snatch the remote from his hand. Paulo laughs and holds it out of reach. He's enjoying this, she thinks. The bastard. Most fun he's had all month.

'If I short it now, it's already shorted. Look. It doesn't look like the water got above the arms of the chairs, and the sockets are way above that level. And the screens. Server looks pretty fucked, but you can't have everything.'

'But . . .' she begins.

'We may as well find out,' he says, and presses the On button on the remote. 'Might as well know what you're . . .'

The screen springs to life.

A video. A woman's face, close up, blown up to the size of a pony. A pulp of cuts and bruises. The expression dulled, hopeless, unmoving. Tears long dried on broken skin. The face moves jerkily back and forth, back and forth across the screen. Slides across some shiny surface, wet with blood.

Mercedes feels her legs give way beneath her.

It's Donatella.

58 | Mercedes

Even Paulo, veteran of sieges and reliefs, of wars and hijacks, is frozen.

Ursula feels for a chair, unable to take her eyes from the screen. Collapses into it. She was barely walking when Donatella died. To her, this is a stranger.

'No,' she says. 'No.'

The video plays on.

Mercedes' head swims where she slumps, weak as a kitten, on the soggy carpet.

'Is that real?' asks Ursula. 'It can't be. Tell me it isn't real.'

I cannot watch this. I must not watch this. I will never forget, as long as I live.

One huge tear rolls from Donatella's glazed eye. Runs across the bridge of her nose and into the other. She doesn't blink.

The camera starts to pan back.

'Oh, no,' says Mercedes. She wants desperately to look away, to cover her eyes, but she is paralysed. 'Oh, please no.'

The cameraman raises his lens and briefly films himself

in a mirror. Grinning broadly. In the background, a circular porthole window, useless brocade curtains to either side, a wall panelled in shiny leopardskin walnut, four photos the size of an atlas fixed to the wall above the bed. Two men, watching. One looks serious, storing his memories forever. The other is laughing.

The man grinning behind the chunky handheld camera is Matthew Meade.

Paulo unfreezes. Points the remote. The screen goes black. They are silent for a long time. Mercedes wonders if she is going to vomit. But the nausea is full-body, not focused on her gorge. She leans forward and rests her forearms on the coffee table. Tries to breathe. Fails. Tries again.

She didn't kill herself, she thinks. But this is so much worse. Oh, no. No, no, no, no. Oh, no. Oh, Donatella.

'Where was that?' asks Paulo. His voice is hard and cold.
She can't speak.
'Mercedes, where was that? Do you recognise it?'
'Yes,' she says.
'Where?' he asks.
'It's on the boat. On the old boat. It's Tatiana's cabin,' she says, dully.
Paulo turns on his heel and strides from the room.

59 | Gemma

Time passes. She has little idea how much. It's marked only by the filling of her bladder and the increasing pain in her tethered limbs. She tries to move around, relieve the pressure, but there's little room for manoeuvre. They have tied her very tightly.

Sometimes footsteps pass beyond the door. But they never pause. Just pass on by and vanish into the ambient sound of moving water.

She strains and strains in a futile effort to stretch her bonds. But they're hard, unforgiving, and all she does is break her skin. After a few hours, the tensing sends her back into spasm, then her intercostal muscles, so that even breathing is exquisite torture, something that has to be done in tiny increments, in, in, in, in, out, in, in, in, for a deep lungful makes her feel as though she is being stabbed.

Already being stabbed.

Time passes.

I am, she thinks. And soon will not be. I know that. At

some point I'll hear the rumble as they raise the anchor, and, once there is no one to hear me scream, they will come for me.

Her bladder gives way, eventually. And, as hot liquid seeps out and cools beneath her on the plastic sheet, she feels a strange satisfaction. This is what they get, then, she thinks. A girl who stinks of piss. I hope they like that.

The satisfaction is short-lived. It's probably what they want. They want me reduced to this.

She doesn't cry any more. The congestion on her constricted airways fills her with a terrible fear of suffocation.

Perhaps I should, she thinks. Perhaps I should weep until I can no longer breathe. Literally cry myself to death. Cheat them with the only power I have left.

But still, she doesn't.

In the dark, a sound. More footsteps. And suddenly her eyes are wide inside her snot-slimed mask. She hears the doors along the corridor open. Quietly, one by one. And equally quietly, they close. Approaching. Coming to where she lies.

They're here, she thinks. They've come for me.

The door opens.

Silence. The visitor draws a heavy breath and steps inside. The latch clicks to. She hears him cross the carpet, feels him stand over her.

Please. Please. If you're going to start, start now. I can't bear it. Can't bear it. I know where this leads and I want it over.

A voice says her name. So quietly she's almost unsure that he's spoken. Familiar. A London accent, a voice she's sure she's heard before.

'I've come to get you out of here, love.'

*

439

Gemma starts to struggle like a rabbit in a snare.

He waits until she exhausts herself. And when she is lying still, panting and giddy, he speaks again.

'I need you to do exactly what I tell you,' he says. 'Exactly. Do you understand? I'm here to help you, but if you don't do exactly as I say, we'll fuck this up. There's still crew on this boat, and they're not on your side. Nod if you understand.'

He's torturing me. He's not here to help. He's here to raise my hopes. She struggles again. He waits.

'*Do you understand?*'

Gemma nods.

'Okay,' he says. 'I need absolute quiet from you. You can make all the noise you want when we're out of here, but, if anyone hears us now, we're done. All right?'

She nods again.

'Good,' he says. 'Right, I'm going to take this thing off your head. That means I'm going to have to touch you. Understand?'

Gemma nods. Lets go her last strands of hope.

She feels him lean over her. A little pool of tight light punctures the holes by her nostrils. She tenses as his arms brush her shoulders, his hand strokes up the back of her neck.

She closes her eyes. Sends her love out into the universe. *Mum, Mummy. I love you. I'm sorry. I love you.*

The grinding metal teeth of a zip, and the mask loosens. She feels his fingers work beneath and peel it off. And her face is out in blessed air and all she can see is bright, bright light, so bright she has to squeeze her eyes closed.

'Oh, Jesus,' he says. 'Right, I'm going to take that off you. Remember, Gemma, no noise. It's very important – not a sound, okay?'

She nods again.

'Shit,' he says, 'you don't know who I am, do you?' and the light moves. Gemma opens her eyes. It's Paulo. The big security guy from the house. Grinning at her as if he's just won a game of hide and seek.

The relief is so great that she starts to cry.

The smile falls away. 'Oookay,' he says, the tones of a groom calming a skittish racehorse. 'Okay. Just breathe. Breathe ...' And he leans forward and reaches behind her head again.

60 | Mercedes

I hate you.

Rage is a white light. It eradicates colour, obliterates shade. I hate you.

Her palms itch. She wishes she were holding a carving knife.

She leaves the Casa Amarilla for the last time and strides the silent cliff road. Blank black windows gaze balefully, lights extinguished, as though the world has ended. As though there were no one left but her. The residents are up at the castle, preening. Swanking through the Great Hall, kissing the air around each other's ears.

Damn them. Damn them all to hell: the duke, his syco-phants. If there were justice, it would burn to the ground with them all inside.

I hate you, barks her heart, in time with the rhythm of her steps. I hate you, I hate you, I hate you.

I hate you, Matthew Meade. Three decades I've carried my grief and my guilt in equal measure. Blaming my neighbours, blaming myself, blaming my mother and father. And now

I would give anything to have that guilt back, if it meant I would never know what you did to her. What sort of world allows a man like you to live? What sort of God?

A big black car crawls towards her up the hill, and she steps off the road to let it pass just as the first firework, crimson and gold and blue, bursts into the air above the castle battlements. Her brain hangs for a moment. Beautiful, beautiful, beautiful. And then she comes back to herself and strides on towards the lights of Kastellana Town.

The Re del Pesce is still open. Late diners, nursing coffee and *limonxela* as the staff set up for morning service. Larissa comes to greet her.

The world tilts.

I cannot tell my mother, she thinks. It will kill her.

'It's done,' she says. 'I'm going to the boat. To wait for him.'

Larissa searches her face. 'Something's happened,' she says, and Mercedes feels her face twist with rage. She turns it away.

'He'll go,' she says. 'The minute he realises he's been uncovered, he'll be on that boat and out of here, and I can't let that happen.'

Larissa speaks slowly. 'Mercedes,' she says, 'be careful.'

For a moment – just a moment – she wonders if she has the strength. If this rage of hers is just driving her to her own doom. And then she remembers her sister's face, on that screen, and she is filled with white heat.

He cannot leave tonight.

She hands her mother her phone. 'Can you look after this?'

Larissa looks doubtful.

'They can track where I am,' she tells her. 'By its signal. Call Felix.'

'And tell him what?'

'He'll know. Tell him I'm on the boat. Tell him I've got my beacon with me,' she says. 'He'll know.'

She has no plan. Just an intention. The plan will come.

She punches the code into the pad and walks through the tunnel in the harbour wall. Deep dark and damp inside, yellow sulphur lights at the far end. She's always hated it in here. The sense of going from one world to another, the fear of what might be waiting.

Someone steps into the far end and she freezes. It's someone huge, and weirdly bulky. They fill the opening, block the dim light from the marina, and they're advancing at alarming speed. An ogre, striding towards her in a place with no escape. And then he gets closer and she see that it's Paulo, huge Paulo, with the girl Gemma in his arms.

'Get the gate,' he calls.

She jogs the way she's come.

Paulo strides past. Bursts the gate open with a kick.

She waits quietly for a few minutes as shouts of surprise rise up from the crowds on the quayside. And then she walks on.

I hate you.

I hate you. You belong in the blackened fires of hell. I hate you, Matthew Meade. I have always hated you, but now I know why.

The *Princess Tatiana* has a premium mooring, close to the foot of the funicular and tucked away for privacy. She hates this place. These boats. All the same, lined up in their rows, the way she imagines cities to be.

I hate them. I hate them all. They have destroyed my home. We fought off invaders for a thousand years. These people are

444

no less invaders because they come with diamonds and pearls and cleaning jobs for all.

A light burns in the bridge and another in a porthole, but she sees no other signs of life.

Mercedes shifts her chiller bag – her cover story if she encounters Philip on board – onto her left arm, and unlocks the gangway gate. Steps softly on to the gangplank, freezes as it takes her weight. To her heightened senses the shift as her weight lands feels extreme, a lurch rather than the small list it really is.

No one comes and no new lights come on, and she walks on up to the deck.

All so familiar. The third *Princess Tatiana* of her lifetime, ever same-same. In all the detail – the layout, the furniture, the furbelows that make his pleasures easier – everything remains unchanged. The same, upgraded. His youthful fantasy of a rich man's life, frozen in time like a fly in amber. Even the gilded anchor is still here, by the gangplank gate, taken from boat to boat like a shiny brass figurehead. To remind him of where he began. To remind him of the lives he has stolen.

I hate you, Matthew Meade.

She slips onto the staff staircase and descends to the bowels of the boat. If she waits in a stuffy little maid's cabin, traces of Blu Tack on the walls above the beds where photos of love and family have sustained its occupants through lonely nights, she can be certain that no one will find her.

61 | Robin

The Re del Pesce is almost two hundred metres from the marina gate, but Robin sees him the moment he appears from her bedroom lookout. He's a big man. She only realises how big when she sees that the burden he's carrying is another human being.

The crowd parts like the Red Sea as he strides towards the restaurant, and for a moment she thinks he's carrying some oversized doll. A naked marionette. But then she sees that the puppet is clinging to him like a drowning man to rocks, that her face is pressed into his chest like a frightened infant. And then she sees the mop of crushed curls that bounces as he strides, and the long, skinny limbs, and something – the umbilical connection that has never really broken – tells her that what she is seeing is her daughter.

She only vaguely hears herself shout out her name.

He carries her daughter like a sack of flour, his forearms hooked under her knees and armpits. She's only marginally conscious. Her head lolls on her neck as though it has come loose. And she is crying.

Larissa has the street door open by the time Robin hits the bottom of the stairs. Gestures her to stand back. And, though every nerve in her body screams to throw herself upon her baby, she forces herself to press herself against the restaurant wall and let them pass.

In the *sala*, Larissa snatches up a shawl to throw over the couch. Gemma is a mess of sweat and snot and tears and blood, and the smell of aged ammonia hangs in the air around her. Something has chafed her ankles and wrists badly enough to draw blood, and her lips are cracked and swollen.

Paulo lays her down, as gently as if she were fragile glass, and she curls into herself, draws her knees up, tucks in her elbows. A baby, trying to get back to the womb. Naked and bruised and dirty. Robin wrings her hands and waits her turn.

The man steps back.

Oh, my girl. My darling, my baby, what have they done to you?

'I've got to go,' he says. 'Got to get back. It's not over yet. You can take her from here, yes?'

'Mercedes ...' says Larissa.

'There's no one at the house,' he says. 'I need to get back.'

'Thank you,' says Larissa. 'Thank you, Paulo. *Mersi milli.* You will find your reward in heaven.'

He looks startled. Then doubtful. 'She'll be okay,' he tells them. 'She's tougher than she looks.'

Robin can't tell from his words whose daughter he's talking about.

She finds her voice. 'Thank you.'

He nods, curtly. Somewhere else in his head already. 'I'll come back when I can,' he says. 'Check up on her.'

447

'I'll let you know. Thank you. Thank you for everything. I don't know you, but you are a good man. We will owe you forever.'

Paulo goes scarlet. Looks for a moment as though his next words will be a struggle. These tough guys. It must take a toll on them.

'Right, well,' he says, and leaves.

Larissa nods at her. 'Go on,' she says. 'She needs you.'

Suddenly, she is reluctant. A little frightened. Of how they will even begin. She looks at the huddled figure doubtfully. She hasn't needed me for a year, she thinks. Maybe I'm the last thing she needs. This skinny young woman, face rubbed and raw, blackened eyes, lips so swollen they have cracked and shed blood: I don't know her. She's a stranger. With a familiar face, but a stranger.

But when did that happen? How long ago? I was assuming I knew her, but I didn't. It's our fault. Mine and Patrick's. So caught up in knowing best that we lost sight of knowing *her* at all.

She steps forward, lowers herself to her knees by the side of the bed. A whole world of unshed tears waiting to fall.

'Gemma? Sweetheart?'

Gemma lies there. Staring at the air. Then something – something in the tone of her mother's voice – brings her back to the world and she looks up.

'I suppose you're going to say you told me so.'

62 | Tatiana

Tatiana's dress is magnificent, but it's so tight it's giving her a headache. The stays dig into her ribs, cut off her breath, and it's giddy torture. The night started in a spirit of *il faut souffrir pour être belle*, but as midnight approaches she realises that nothing, *nothing* is worth this level of pain.

Jason, when she came downstairs, had stared at her breasts for a moment, swallowing as though he were trying not to throw up. A couple of times at dinner, she saw him glance at her from the other end of the table, his head bent attentively to hear the thirty-year-old trophy wife of a German press baron (he's not so implacably anti-media when it suits him). And when they got to the castle, he had vanished into the *bal masqué* without a backward look by the time she'd left the limo.

I must get my breasts done, she thinks. Something more to add to the list. She resents the relentless self-maintenance that comes with ageing. The awful knowledge that it is a battle that will inevitably be lost. But what can you do? Men despise women who let themselves go, and she's not yet ready for a life of Palm Beach sundowners.

When the revellers stream out onto the plain below the castle to watch the fireworks – she's heard that they alone have left Giancarlo little change from a quarter of a million – she slips out and finds her driver to take her home. A quick change into something more forgiving and a couple of tramadol, and she will be all charm again. Ready to dance until dawn.

She closes her eyes.

The roads are pleasantly empty, for anyone who matters is at the castle and the locals are gathered on their rooftops, like peasants watching an eclipse.

This dress is torture. Literal torture. She hasn't taken a full breath since half-past six, and her ribs feel as though they're going to snap under the pressure. I swear, she thinks, those women laced me in this tight out of spite.

The gate is locked from the inside. Its sensors register the car's presence, and she can see them move slightly in their sockets, straining and failing, straining and failing to open.

'What's going on?' she asks.

'I don't know, madam,' he says.

'Well, maybe get out and ring the bell, then?' she says irritably.

She sees his eyes in the rear-view mirror for a moment, looking at her, and then he undoes his seatbelt and gets out of the car. Rings the bell and stands in the road, rising up and down on the balls of his feet as he waits.

Nobody comes.

He comes back, resumes his seat. 'Nobody's answering, madam,' he says.

'Thank you for that,' she says sarcastically, 'I'd never have worked that out.' And again that little flash of eye in the mirror.

She gets her phone from her tiny bag, to call security. Realises she doesn't know his name.

'What's the security guy's name?' she asks.

'Paulo, madam.'

She looks through her contacts. Over five thousand, but not a single Paulo. Damn you, Nora Neibergall, she thinks. Can't you do *anything* right?

'Give me a hand,' she says, 'I'll let myself in.'

It takes a full minute of heaving to get her out onto the road, and, by the time she's free, she's furious. She calls Mercedes to give her a mouthful, because she can't think of anyone else to call. The phone rings out and Mercedes' voice says something in Kastellani.

'What the hell, Mercedes?' she says. 'I'm at the front gate, and there's literally nobody here. Where is everybody? Where are *you*? You can't just go swanning off. You *know* you need permission. And where the hell is Paulo? There's literally nobody monitoring the gate? What if I was a kidnap gang or something? What the hell do we keep you here *for*?'

She hangs up, drops the phone back in the bag. And, rehearsing the more-in-sorrow-than-in-anger speech with which she's going to be dismissing the security man tomorrow, she punches in the code that opens the door in the gate and steps through.

Lights blazing, dead silence. Tatiana lifts her skirts and sweeps across the courtyard, goes into the house. Shouts.

'Hello? Hello? Where the hell is everybody?'

No response.

What the hell? What the *hell*?

She glances up the corridor *en route* to the drawing room, and sees that the door to the safe room is wide open, its lights blazing. And she starts to feel uneasy, because there's only one person who has the code, and he's clearly not here.

Tatiana gets her phone from her bag and holds it in her hand, ready to dial. Steps cautiously into the *sala*, on her guard and ready to run.

They're all there. The cook. The laundress. The under-housekeeper. The sous-chef. Even the gardeners. Sitting on the sofas, a bottle of grappa open on the table between them. Out of uniform, too. Stefanie is actually in pyjamas and a dressing-gown.

'What the hell?' she asks. 'Seriously? What is this? A *party*?'

They all turn at once, and it's only then that she realises that they've been sitting in silence. That they're looking at her as though her hands are dripping blood.

Tatiana almost stumbles. But she's well trained in not showing surprise. Her game face is legendary, at least in her own head.

'Hello,' she says. And she speed-dials her father with a single swipe of her thumb. Waits until she's sure it will have gone to voicemail – he never answers the phone when he's at a party; answering the phone is for staff, he says – before she puts it to her ear.

'Daddy?' she says. 'There's something going on at the house. Don't come back here.'

From behind her, a hand snakes over her shoulder and snatches the phone. She turns to see Paulo, his face black like thunder.

'I'll take that, thanks,' he says.

63 | Mercedes

It's hot in the guts of the boat. Mercedes curls up on a cot-bed
in the maid's cabin and waits. A few doors down, someone
hammers, metal on metal. A radio, playing disco and a deep
male voice singing along. The engineer, making good before
he disembarks at dawn. Matthew only takes Philip when he
goes on the Stag.

He knows. He must know. That's why he's stayed, all
these years, taking his triple wages and his generous holiday
allowance. All these men. Lining their nests and sending their
daughters to private school and turning a blind eye because in
the end what does it matter if there's one less breeder in the
world, from a place where life is cheap?

She wakes before she realises that she has fallen asleep.
Someone has started the engine, and her hot little sanctuary
shudders as they manoeuvre from their mooring.

He's here. We're leaving. Felix, please have got my message.
She thinks for a moment about activating the beacon. And

then she thinks: no. If Felix's little working boat has radar, there's no question that the *Princess Tatiana* has radar ten times better. A tracking beacon igniting in her very bowels would be bound to raise an alert.

I trust him. He's not stupid. He'll know where I am.

She waits in the dark until the shudder turns to a throb and the gentle roll of the cot beneath her tells her that they are speeding over open water, then she lets herself back out into Matthew Meade's territory.

She hears his voice, and freezes. Has to fight the urge to creep back to her hiding place. But Matthew never comes down the second flight of stairs. Not ever. Never goes to staff quarters, here or anywhere else. He's on the cabin deck, and he's on the phone. Bellowing, because he's drunk and there's no one to hear him.

'Yes, gone!' he shouts. 'Not a bloody sign of her. Fucking Philip didn't notice a fucking thing!'

He's been down to Tatiana's cabin. Her stomach lurches as she remembers. He's sick. He must be. Torturing a teenager to her death surrounded by his middle-aged daughter's furbelows. An animal, watching himself in the mirror as he films his 'friends'.

Some sick animals cannot be cured. Sometimes it's better for the whole world if they are destroyed.

Oh, lord, how blind I was. The way she climbed all over him like a little monkey, the way she perched in his lap while he sniffed her hair. But you don't know, do you? When you're a child. You only know the things you know about. Strange behaviour among your peers is just bad personality. It never occurs to you that there's more to it. And the Meades were so strange anyway, to my island eyes. Everything about them was

454

different. I had never seen such a world before. How would you know, when you're twelve years old, where one sort of different ends and another begins?

She's too old for him now, that's for sure. Is that it? That everything she does is done to keep his favour? That the only way to keep him is to enable him? Him, and his friends, and in time the friends' children. The sons invited, the girls with their faces turned blithely away for the sake of a dowry and the promise of a house like the one they grew up in. Raised to marry Men Like Daddy and pass the corruption down through the generations.

The *sirenas* were the Gemmas of the old world. She sees it now. Cut from the herd as their beauty flowered. Pressganged playthings for the dukes, hurled to their deaths with our willing co-operation before they could speak out and make trouble. I see it all now. I see it, and we are all guilty. Every one of us. We carry those sins in our DNA.

At least we never had children.

'I don't know, do I?' he is bellowing. 'Someone. I told her! Over and over. You turn staff *over*. You don't give them time to develop petty resentments. This is where that leads, Jesus. She's had that housekeeper for bloody *ever*. Literally got her when she was a teenager. Yes. No, well, she's gone now. That's all I know. If fucking Tatiana's let the Greeks in through the gate, then serve her bloody right ...'

The voice drifts away towards the back of the boat, mounting the saloon stairs. She catches a glimpse of a hairy ankle as he goes.

'Ugh. Tripoli, of all bloody places. I know. Well, yes. But frankly they're so chaotic there that the extradition treaty's not worth the paper it's written on. I'll be on the plane before they've even got the papers. Yeah, I'm sorry, Geoff. Nothing I can do. The money'll be back in your account next week. Christ, of *course* it won't be traceable. You think I'm a bloody idiot. Yeah, the Al Mahary. I know, right? But I suppose at least I'll be able to get a drink ...'

He stumbles on a step. Swears. He's really, really drunk, she thinks. Good.

She slips quietly up the servants' stairs.

A perfect nautical night. Lights burn on the rear deck, but from her place in the shadows she can see a million stars. The moon has gone and the sea is oily black, white foam breaking over the hull as it speeds its way to Libya.

In the distance, far behind, a single light. Something small, something patient. Lacking the power to keep up, but dogging their wake nonetheless.

Felix. Let it be Felix. There is no way off this boat but over the side, and this water will be very, very lonely.

She hears him again. He's on the rear deck, still bellowing into the phone. Through the porthole she glimpses a whisky bottle, half-empty, sitting on the bar. Good. He may be old and he may be morbidly obese, but sober she would stand no chance with him, *mano a mano*. He's a big man, in every way. Not merely the giant of her childhood memories, but in real life, too. A hundred and forty kilos of thug, all the weight on his side and no conscience to hamper him.

She glances up and down the gangway to ensure that she is alone. Treads quietly from servants' doorway to gangplank gate. Its lock is simple: a metal pin that slides into a socket and a hinge that swings outwards. Greased against rusting, the pin slides out with the gentlest of pressure. She digs in her pocket, finds one of her father's Mediterraneo branded matchbooks and wedges it between gate and guard rail. It may *be* open, but it needs to *look* closed. She pushes it in firmly and it holds. A casual glance would reveal nothing out of place about the guard rail at all.

Matthew appears at the head of the gangway, white towelling robe and slippers, his onboard uniform, black hair shining with oil beneath the swaying light.

No, no. Not yet. I'm not ready.

She freezes. The slap, slap, slap of slowly rolling waves against the hull, the whoosh of blood in her temples. Too late to duck. The movement would be more likely to catch his eye than no movement at all.

Matthew doesn't glance up the gangway. He just gazes out over the sea. Puts his glass to his face and turns away. Starts talking again. He's still on the phone. Words drift down to her from metres away. Slurred, booming. *Giancarlo . . . of course he will, the cunt . . . fucking Tatiana.*

Mercedes scuttles back to the safety of the lobby. Leans against the wall and breathes until her pulse steadies. Her heart bang, bang, bangs beneath her breastbone. She is as afraid as she is angry now. If this goes wrong, it will be the end of her.

She checks her watch. Four a.m. Come *on*, Mercedes. Even a man as drunk and angry as he is will go to bed soon.

Her preparations aren't over. He's too big. She needs ballast. Fat people float.

She looks back out. The deck is empty. Peeking through the saloon door porthole, she sees him by the bar, hand on whisky bottle, in a fugue state. His mouth moves, but the phone lies by his hand, unused. She goes back out.

She kneels beside his boastful, gilded anchor and checks the fixings. Same as it ever was. Everything the same. Two bolts, held on by butterfly nuts. No rope, of course. It's not actually meant to be used. But on the other side of the gate hangs a rubber-covered lifebuoy, and to that is attached a good twenty metres of nylon cord. Fourteen hundred metres shy of the deep seabed, but plenty long enough for her purposes.

She's glad, now, that she actually paid attention to some of Felix's demonstrations of nautical knots, even though she mostly did it to indulge him. It only takes a minute to detach the rope from the lifebuoy and tie a solid three-turn hitch to the anchor.

She ties a quick-release knot on the railing, a body-length from the anchor, and a loop for her hand for when the time comes. Then she heaves the anchor – feels her muscles wrench, knows she will hurt come daylight – over the side. It hangs nicely, backwards from the hook, just above the water. All she'll need to do to let it go is pull on the right point, and it will drop, drop, drop until it can drop no more.

She goes back into her hiding place and waits.

64 | Mercedes

He takes so long to come, she begins to think he must have passed out. There's been no sign of him in the bar for an hour, and the bottle is gone as well. It's almost dawn. He must sleep soon.

Maybe he's just passed out. Maybe he's lying there, snoring, face up to the awning, throat exposed.

I could go to the galley and find a carving knife. Finish him off with a stab to the throat, plunge it into that great fatty heart. If he's that drunk, he won't fight back. If he's that drunk, he'll just bleed out over his white leather, gaping in astonishment like a landed fish.

She is so tense her muscles hurt. Yes, she thinks, I'll do it. And after, I'll ...

A cough. A loud, phlegmy cough only a few metres away. He's bumbling down the gangway to bed.

Mercedes tenses. Edges into the doorway. Waits, hidden by deep shadow, and musters her might. One chance. You have just one chance at this.

His shadow falls across the doorway. She waits.

A foot.

One more pace.

The great bulk of him waddles into the doorway, glass in hand.

Mercedes charges.

It's like running into a brick wall. The impact is so violent she thinks for a moment that she's snapped her collarbone. But she keeps pushing forward, like a bull at full charge. And Matthew Meade, taken by surprise, falls back against the gate, and the gate gives way and carries him over the edge.

He makes a good effort to save himself. Manages to hook one arm over the swinging barrier, feet paddling the empty air beneath, mouthing bleary shock as he stares up at her. She stands over him, slips her arm through the loop at the end of the rope, and watches. Enjoys the watching. The pleasure of his fear is intense.

And then his weight is too much for his ham-hock arms, and he starts to slide. Slowly. Then faster. And with the splash of a whale breaking surface, he is gone.

Mercedes opens the slip knot and dives. Dives out like a swooping gull and swims for her life, for when the rope reaches its limit it will drag her beneath, and the boat is carrying him into their wake.

She sees his white face momentarily illuminated by the deck lights, and then she plunges her face into the water and swims like an Olympian.

Suddenly sober, Matthew is raging.

'What the fuck?' he yells. 'What the fuck do you think you're doing?'

Mercedes doesn't respond. No time. No need. She throws

her arms around his thick bull neck. Lifts her legs and wraps them round his torso, and his torso is so huge her heels barely reach his back. Her skin crawls as she touches him. But still she clings on.

'What the fuck are you—' he begins. And then the weight of the anchor catches the end of the rope. Mercedes sucks in one gigantic breath, and they are dragged beneath the surface.

Face to face in the dark. Matthew Meade struggles as they drop, and Mercedes grips him with every strand of her rage. She feels his fear pulse through her and feels wonderfully, blissfully calm. Gazes into his eyes lovingly, wrapped around him like a netsuke geisha. I am a mermaid. I've been a mermaid since I was a child. This is my habitat, Matthew Meade.

She looks up at the receding moon, at the bubbles that rise above their heads, and looks back into his face.

Smiles.

You're in my world now, Matthew Meade. And you will never leave.

Nine minutes. Nine minutes, I can hold my breath. How long can you?

He starts trying to swim upwards, carrying her with him, fighting against the dead weight below. His huge hands clutch at the moon. Claw to reach the air. And Mercedes rides him like a bronco, and waits as they fall towards the deep.

I can wait as long as I need, Matthew Meade. You don't know what you can do till you don't care any more. I've waited thirty years already. What's a few more minutes, between friends?

His attention turns back to her. Confusion. Fear. Death coming at him from a cloudless sky. He looks her in the eyes. For the first time since she met him.

461

She smiles and nods.

Oh, yes, you see me now.

Her lungs are beginning to burn. They must be deeper now than she has ever been. Her inner ears scream and the fillings in her teeth writhe inside the enamel.

Calm, Mercedes. Calm, my love. You love the water. For him, it is fear.

How deep are we now? she wonders idly. She can barely see the light above at all.

Matthew jerks convulsively and a huge bubble bursts from his mouth.

I could probably let go now.

No. I'll wait. To be sure.

She feels deliciously serene. While she waits, she takes her arm from around his neck and slips it from the anchor loop. They drift in the current, suspended, no longer going down.

He jerks again. More bubbles explode on her face: one, two. One from each lung, she thinks. He's reached the bottom. All gone. Nothing there now but ocean brine.

He is limp as a rag doll in her grip.

Mercedes lets go. Kicks him away in a last gesture of contempt. And then she reaches up and swims, steadily, for the surface.

65 | Felix

The beacon starts to transmit as the moon begins its second circuit. Right on the edge of his equipment's reach, for the *Princess Tatiana* is a Maserati to his little skiff's Fiat. He lost sight of it some time ago, but stuck doggedly to its bearing, assuming that it will have kept to its course, hoping for the best.

When the beacon springs to life, a bright little blinking dot on the outer lines of his radar, he floods with relief. He has loved Mercedes Delia, in his quiet way, since he was nine years old. To lose her to the water would end him.

He has never been this far from land before. Kastellani aren't trawlermen, and the rich waters around their home provide more than plenty without ever losing sight of the western cliffs. The vastness of the world fills Felix with fear. But still he goes forward, grateful that he thought to load a few containers of diesel while he waited for the *Princess Tatiana* to put out. His fuel gauge is almost at the halfway point and soon, without them, there would be no turning back.

So lonely out here, on the endless water, in the dark. So beautiful. He watches the dot slowly move across the screen, and follows the path laid out by the moon to where she is.

He finds her as the sun is rising. She lies on her back, gazing up at the sky. So easy in the water, my Mercedes. So unafraid. She must be cold, but she doesn't show it. Her black hair spreads out around her head like a reaper's halo, and there's a look on her face that he's never seen before. Like the martyred saints depicted in the windows of the church. A glow of happiness. A serenity.

Peace, he thinks. She's found peace.

He kills the engine and coasts the last few metres to where she floats. She flips over and swims to him with her strong, easy stroke. Treads water and looks up.

'Is it done?' he asks.

'It's done,' she says. 'Let's go home.'

Epilogue

'*Pasaporte?*'

Donatella stops dead. Passport. He wants a passport. My God. Oh, my God.

She stares at the ferryman. He's not from here. The ferry is from the mainland, the sailors from everywhere. He doesn't know her. Something she's been relying on, for anyone who knew her would try to prevent her escape. She's waited until the last possible moment, has run across the harbour with her little duffel bag of clothes. To get on board before La Kastellana wakes up to her plans.

'I . . .' she stutters. Her father in her mind, she harnesses him to be her lie. 'My father has it. He took it on board with him. He's waiting for me. In a cabin.'

The man looks her up and down. *Leers* her up and down. I can't, she thinks. I can't bear it. All these men, staring at me as though I only exist for their pleasure. Or their contempt.

'I'll go and look for him,' she says in her best confident tone, 'and come back.'

There must be places to hide. A mass of cabins and a cargo hold full of goods.

She attempts to dodge past the ferryman. He blocks her path.

'*Lo siento*,' he says.

'But he's *waiting*!' she wails.

The man wags his head and snatches a glance at her breasts.

I have to get away from here. I *have* to. This place will *kill* me.

'Please,' she pleads. 'Please.'

He shakes his head. He's pleased with his little moment of power. People like to demonstrate their power over pretty girls.

'No passport,' he says, 'no entry.' He looks her up and down again. '*Sinjorina*,' he adds pointedly.

She stands on the dock and weeps as the boat sets off. People pass by, but nobody stops. She's the *sirena*. Deserving only of indifference.

I am trapped. There is no way off this island. Without a passport I can't leave, and if I apply for one, the news will be with my father before I've even filled out the paperwork. There is no way out of here.

Donatella lifts her face to the morning sun and wails.

Someone says her name. A girl's voice. Speaking English.

'Donatella? What happened? Did you miss the ferry?' Tatiana stands on the dock, looking down on her distress. Curiosity beaming from her. Her face clouds. 'My God, you look awful,' she says. 'Are you ill?'

Donatella bursts into tears. Tatiana squats down beside her and looks up into her face, her brow knotted. 'Oh, no,' she says, 'it's not that bad, surely? You can just catch the next one?'

'How can I?' she wails. 'I have no documents.'

'I . . .'

Tatiana lays a tentative hand on her arm. It feels wrong. Awkward. As though giving comfort is something she's never done before.

'I'm so sorry,' she says. 'Oh, lord, you poor girl.'

People walk past. Pretending not to look; looking. Tatiana glares at the chandler's wife, who stands a little too close. Not looking.

'We should get you off this dockside,' she says, holding out a hand. 'Come on.'

Donatella looks at her, astonished. She's longed for sympathy, but its source has come out of the blue.

'I bet we can find a solution to this,' she says. 'My father's Giancarlo's greatest friend. If anyone can get you documents, he can.' Tatiana may only be fourteen, but she sounds much, much older. 'And he'll be *delighted* to see you.'

The engines of the *Princess Tatiana* are running, but the gangplank is still down.

'They're waiting,' says Tatiana, conversationally. 'Lucky for you, really, or they'd be long gone. There were a couple of ... guests due, and they've got stuck in customs at Nice, and now they're short their star turn.'

'Oh,' she says. She's not all that interested in Tatiana's father's friends. But she's glad to get off the dockside, away from her neighbours' scrutiny. Away from the Re del Pesce, where it's only a matter of time before someone spots her.

They step onto the deck and walk towards the bows. She's weary. Ragged inside. Donatella is so adrift, so uncertain after all her certainty, that she has lost the power of choice. She's barely seventeen and she's afraid, and she wants someone – anyone – to tell her what to do.

*

467

On the banquettes, the Stag guests are assembled. Drinking champagne. Laughing in that rich-man tenor.

Someone catches sight of them, elbows another. The laughter stops. They eye her. Up and down. Up and down.

She feels naked beneath their scrutiny. Silly little girl in her summer frock, all dressed up for an adventure.

'Wait here,' says Tatiana, and leaves her standing at the end of the gangway. Matthew Meade's friends watch her. She tries a watery smile.

'Well,' says someone, 'this is a turn-up for the books,' and his companions laugh. Turn away from her and drink their champagne.

Matthew Meade bustles from the saloon, his face full of concern, his colour high. 'Donatella!' he says. 'My dear!'

She bursts into tears. She wants her mother, but her mother will never understand.

Matthew Meade stands there and looks at her, all sympathy. He lays one of his great big hands on her shoulder and squeezes.

Down the gangway, she vaguely registers Tatiana exit the servants' entrance. She's put on the gigantic sunglasses that make her look like a beetle, and carries her overnight bag, the one with the flowers on. She walks down the gangplank into the sunshine and heads off towards the marina without a backward glance.

Matthew Meade guides her round so that her back is to the dock.

'I can understand,' he tells her, 'why you want to leave. There can't be much here for you now.'

She wells up at his concern. 'I don't know what to do,' she blurts. 'I can't go home.'

'No,' says Matthew Meade, and smiles an indulgent smile.

'Don't worry. We won't make you go home. You can come with us. We'll take you to the mainland.'

She gasps. Looks up into his face and sees that he's still smiling. 'You'd do that? For me?'

For a fleeting moment, the smile's less nice. And then it's back.

'We're all very fond of you,' he says. 'It was a disgrace, what they did to you.'

She nods, quickly.

His smile spreads.

'That's the spirit,' he says. 'We'll fix you up, you'll see. Come inside. We'll pop you into a cabin. If we set off now, we could have you at the mainland by Saturday. And you never know,' he says, leading her towards the saloon door, 'we might even manage to have a bit of fun on the way.'

Acknowledgements

This book was written in lockdown, though I cut and ran for Mqabba, Malta, the very day we were allowed to fly again, and finished it there, surrounded by people I'd not hugged in eighteen months. Boy, I missed the Mediterranean, and in many ways this book was my way of dealing with that.

As always, I've had amazing help and support from Team Marwood, who deal with my chaotic, eccentric working habits like swans gliding serenely on the maelstrom. Ten years I've been with Sphere now, and it's been an absolute blast. Everyone should be so lucky. My heartfelt thanks go to:

Laetitia Rutherford, my wonderful agent, who is the calm spot at the centre of the storm and the sort of friend a writer really needs.

Cath Burke, who gives me far more attention than I deserve despite being Queen.

Cal Kenny, who brought just the perfect combination of robustness and tenderness to the hideous job of hacking my darlings to death.

Linda McQueen, a goddess among copy-editors, who came up with a brilliant last-minute linguistic solution, and who never fails to make me laugh while she's working her magic.

Hannah Wood, whose covers make me bill and coo.

Gemma Shelley and Stephanie Melrose, the wily Svengalis who never cease to amaze me with their ingenuity.

In the world away from books, I owe, as always, huge debts to my friends and family, but particularly to my neighbours, this time, who kept me fed, watered and cheerful when locked away on the 'vulnerable' list. Malou Casimiro, Ariel Lagunas, Luke O'Hea and Claudia Pinheiro, thank you all so much for your kindness and your friendship; you're properly special people.

Jismaelli Norberto too, who keeps my life and my home

liveable with amazing grace, and who is one of the world's great empaths.

Chris Manby and Lisa Jewell, for those lovely, lovely nights drinking ourselves silly WITHOUT MASKS. I got my first hugs in five months from those two, and that's *special*.

Andrew Repasky McElhinney, my new BFF, whom I've never actually met in the flesh. But Friday nights on Skype, drinking cocktails and working our way through our huge project, were a complete lifeline. Who knew you could carry on making real, proper friends without ever leaving the house?

Baloo, who bites my ankles and slaps my face if I fail to follow instructions.

And all my usual suspects, who have been such an important part of my life for so long. Will, Ali, Archie, Geordie, Cathy, David, Elinor, Tora, Antonia, BriBri, Charlie, Gavin, Joce, Nickie, Nik, Bottomley, Venice, Jo, Dougal, Neil, Julia, Jayne, Rose . . . if I've forgotten you, I'm sorry, and know that I love you.

And finally, the ones we lost, here in Sniper's Alley:

Kevin Jackson, who was everyone's favourite colleague back at the *Independent*, a big lolloping moose of a man with the world's most retentive brain.

Darling Robert Phillips, a man of inspiring energy and inventiveness and inspiration, who gave me the best of godsons in Gabriel and has left a huge gaping hole behind him for so many of us.

And Jane Meakin. Lovely Jane, who used to give my books first read and had the greatest of talents for friendship. Oh, how we sang in your garden, darling girl. This book is for her and her beautiful granddaughter, Freya, who entered the world shortly after she left it, in the hope that she'll see it one day and know how much her grandmother loved her, though they never met. Life's a funny old thing. But love makes it all worthwhile.